THE ETERNAL HIGHLANDER

Cathal was so beautiful, he made her heart ache. His touch set her blood afire. He was a wealthy laird, something which would greatly please her kinsmen. Unfortunately, this particular matrimonial prize came with a few less than acceptable characteristics. He couldnae abide the sun, had fangs, was a little too fond of undercooked meat, and it appeared that most of his kinsmen lived in caves beneath the keep. All of that worried her, but not enough to make her walk away from him.

She softly cursed as she walked toward him. She loved him. It was that simple and that complicated. Bridget was not sure when she had lost her heart to him, but suspected it explained why she had not fled Cambrun screaming in terror when she had first begun to suspect what the MacNachtons were. She had made only one rather weak attempt to escape. She stopped by his chair and placed her hand over his heart.

"Ye *are* alive," she murmured.

She did not resist when he tugged her down onto his lap and kissed her . . .

Books by Hannah Howell

THE MURRAYS

Highland Destiny
Highland Honor
Highland Promise
Highland Vow
Highland Knight
Highland Bride
Highland Angel
Highland Groom
Highland Warrior
Highland Conqueror
Highland Champion
Highland Lover
Highland Barbarian
Highland Savage
Highland Wolf
Highland Sinner
Highland Protector
Highland Avenger
Highland Master
Highland Guard
Highland Chieftain
Highland Devil

THE WHERLOCKES

If He's Wicked
If He's Sinful
If He's Wild
If He's Dangerous
If He's Tempted
If He's Daring
If He's Noble

VAMPIRE ROMANCE

Highland Vampire
The Eternal Highlander
My Immortal Highlander
Highland Thirst
Nature of the Beast
Yours for Eternity
Highland Hunger
Born to Bite

SEVEN BRIDES for SEVEN SCOTSMEN

The Scotsman Who Saved Me
When You Love a Scotsman
The Scotsman Who Swept Me Away

STAND-ALONE NOVELS

Only for You
My Valiant Knight
Unconquered
Wild Roses
A Taste of Fire
A Stockingful of Joy
Highland Hearts
Reckless
Conqueror's Kiss
Beauty and the Beast
Highland Wedding

Silver Flame
Highland Fire
Highland Captive
My Lady Captor
Wild Conquest
Kentucky Bride
Compromised Hearts
Stolen Ecstasy
Highland Hero
His Bonnie Bride

Published by Kensington Publishing Corp.

The Eternal Highlander

LYNSAY SANDS

HANNAH HOWELL

ZEBRA BOOKS

KENSINGTON PUBLISHING CORP.

http://www.kensingtonbooks.com

ZEBRA BOOKS are published by

Kensington Publishing Corp.
119 West 40th Street
New York, NY 10018

All Kensington titles, imprints, and distributed lines are available at
special quantity discounts for bulk purchases for sales promotion, pre-
miums, fund-raising, educational, or institutional use.

Special book excerpts or customized printings can also be created to
fit specific needs. For details, write or phone the office of the
Kensington Sales Manager: Attn.: Sales Department. Kensington
Publishing Corp., 119 West 40th Street, New York, NY 10018. Phone:
1-800-221-2647.

Zebra and the Z logo Reg. U.S. Pat. & TM Off.

First Kensington Books Trade Paperback Printing: September 2004
First Zebra Books Mass-Market Paperback Printing: September 2005

ISBN-13: 978-1-4201-5332-3
ISBN-10: 1-4201-5332-3

ISBN-13: 978-1-4201-3396-7 (eBook)
ISBN-10: 1-4201-3396-9 (eBook)

10 9 8 7

Printed in the United States of America

CONTENTS

NIGHTRIDERS
by Hannah Howell
7

THE HIGHLAND BRIDE
by Lynsay Sands
151

NIGHTRIDERS

Hannah Howell

Prologue

Scotland—Winter 1474

Untroubled by the cold, Cathal MacNachton watched the shadowy figures emerge from the depths of his keep and disappear into the thick, mist-shrouded forest surrounding Cambrun, hiding it from prying eyes. Their wild cries were a seductive music, but he resisted the urge to join them. He caught the scent of their prey upon the breeze and felt his blood stir with an old hunger. His brethren would feast tonight and he was pleased for their sake. Soon they would have to accept what else he scented upon the winds that swept around their mountain stronghold—change.

"Ye didnae join the hunt?"

Cathal waited until his cousin stood beside him before replying, "Nay. Not this time."

"Do ye e'er join them now?"

"Nay. I havenae been on a hunt for years. I can still feel the call, but I willnae answer it. Do ye feel the call?"

"Aye, but, like ye, I fight its allure. It has been two years now since I last succumbed to the urge. I am nay as isolated as ye are. Too many eyes to catch a glimpse, too great a chance of discovery."

"That chance is edging e'er closer to us. Tis why I wished to speak with ye." Cathal turned to face his cousin. "The fears of the Outsiders were once our shield, but those fears could now bring about our destruction, Connall. The Outsiders are no longer content to ignore us, to hide in their homes at night and hang charms upon their doors to keep us away. The old ways, the ancient beliefs, are little more than clouded memories, tales whispered by the fire on stormy nights."

"Demons and the stuff of nightmares meant to be endured?"

"Exactly. Now the church has fully captured the hearts and minds of the Outsiders and the church doesnae tolerate such as we. Aye, it has been a threat for hundreds of years, but ne'er so much as now, now that e'en the common folk can be stirred to fight the devil and nay just pray for safety and guidance. Loudan, a Pureblood, was caught by the Outsiders last month. He had succumbed to a need to wander."

Connall cursed. "He is dead?"

"Aye. Dragged before a priest eager to prove his worth, Loudan was quickly condemned as one of the devil's minions. His death was hard. Tortured, garroted, then burned and his bones scattered upon the moors. That is the fate which awaits us all if we dinnae change. Ye and I are proof that we *can* change. We are from both worlds. That was a choice made by our parents, but now it is a necessity if the MacNachton bloodline is to continue."

"What are ye saying, Cathal?"

"Tis time to breed out what makes us different, what keeps us isolated and feared."

"Ye and I arenae so verra different from the Purebloods."

"Different enough. I can e'en tolerate some sunlight. It may take many generations and all that our ancestors bequeathed us may ne'er fully disappear, but it must be done if we are to survive. Tis harder to find Outsiders we can trust to do what we cannae. We need some of our own blood to assume those chores. As lairds, ye and I must lead the others. We must find ourselves brides from amongst the Outsiders."

"Some of our people willnae understand, willnae accept such change. Ye could face a challenge."

Cathal nodded. "I ken it. I will meet it when it comes. There isnae any other choice, Connall. They ken we are here. How long ere they are nay longer satisfied with the occasional fool like Loudan who wanders into their grasp? How long before we are no longer the hunters, but the hunted? Loudan died but a day's ride away from here."

"Too close," Connall whispered.

"Much too close."

Connall sighed and dragged his fingers through his hair. "I understand your concern, can see the sense of your plan, yet, to change what we are? To change all that makes us MacNachtons?"

"Many of us have already begun that change. There are others like us, though nay as many as I would like. It was inevitable. Breeding amongst our own for so many years brings its own troubles. 'S truth, it grows dangerously incestuous. There isnae a lass within these walls that I am nay related to in some way. I believe 'tis why so few bairns are born here. Tis true that we dinnae need the constant renewal of life the Outsiders do, but we cannae continue to have loss without gain. One of our brethren is gone and, as matters stand now, there is little chance that he will be replaced. Bringing in new blood could be our salvation in more than one way."

"Finding Outsider mates who will accept us, ones we can trust, willnae be easy."

"We are proof that it can be done. Are ye with me?"

"Aye and nay. Aye, I see the wisdom of all ye say, but I find it difficult to embrace it with a whole heart."

"I understand. I am nay too pleased myself. There will be no way to hide our secrets from a wife. When she discovers the truth, will I still have a mate, or will I face an enemy?"

"Something to consider."

"Aye, and I ken that is why ye hesitate. Fair enough. Take time to think on it. All I ask now is—do ye stand behind me in this?"

"Aye, always, and in all things."

"Thank ye. I may have need of a strong ally."

"Are ye sure ye shouldnae think this o'er a wee bit more?"

"Nay. I am firm in my decision. Change is our only hope. Without it, 'twill nay be just the whispered tales about the MacNachtons which become lost in the mists of time, but the MacNachtons themselves."

One

Scotland—Spring 1475

Bridget winced as the carriage she rode in hit a particularly deep rut causing her already tender backside to hit the thinly padded seat hard. She was going to be covered in bruises by the time she reached her cousin's home. She pulled aside the oiled cloth that covered the small barred opening in the door of the carriage, coughed as the dust from the road blew in, and glanced up at the sky. They would not reach the next inn today, she mused, and sighed with disappointment. The sun was setting and they would soon be forced to stop for the night.

"I dinnae think we will get round those great hills today," said Nan after peeking out the window.

"Was that the plan?" asked Bridget as she let the cloth fall back over the window and looked at the older woman seated across from her.

"I believe so. The men spoke of it last eve. They seemed most eager to put those heights behind us ere we stopped for the night."

"Did they say why?"

"Nay, not truly. Just muttered some nonsense about spirits and demons."

"I suppose those mist-shrouded mountains could easily stir the imagination," she murmured, but felt the rousing of a keen curiosity she had never been able to conquer.

"Tis certain that many people fear such places, fear what might lurk in such a dark forest or in those clouded hills. But, this time, 'twas some foolish tale they heard in that village we stopped at for the night."

"Ye heard it, too?"

"Nay. The men told it to me. Some tale about a creature from those hills, one who disguised himself as a mon. A mon who ne'er showed himself when the sun rose, only ventured out at night. A mon with eyes like a wolf and teeth like one, as weel. A mon so strong it took near a dozen villagers to subdue him, many of them suffering grievous injuries. A mon who could bewitch any lass into offering him her chastity."

The scorn in Nan's voice made it very clear that she did not believe the tale at all. Bridget was pleased that that scorn did not stop the woman from repeating the tale, however. "Why did they feel the need to attack him, to subdue him? And, what did they do with him after they captured him?"

"They caught him sinfully fornicating with another mon's wife. They dragged him before the priest. Tis then that they realized what they had—a devil, a demon, one of Hell's foul creatures. The priest had the mon tortured, but that mon didnae confess his sins or repent them. They said his wounds healed as if by magic. The priest then declared him a demon, or a witch. I am nay quite sure. They garroted him, burned him, and scattered his bones far and wide o'er the moors so that he couldnae come back to life."

"How cruel. He may have been innocent."

"I certainly doubt he was all they claim he was, but he wasnae innocent. If there was a mon executed, it was probably for the sins of fornication and adultery. He showed the villagers that their women lacked morals."

Bridget inwardly sighed and dutifully nodded her agreement with Nan's harsh judgment. Nan's extremely pious, self-righteous nature was the reason why the woman had been chosen to be her companion on this journey. Her brother Duncan had made it painfully clear that there would be a tight rein kept upon her at all times. Bridget was still not entirely sure where her brother had found the woman. He claimed Nan was a relation, but Bridget had never known a single Callan to be so thoroughly pious or so concerned with morality and correct behavior.

When her brother had allowed her to accept her cousin's invitation, Bridget had been excited. She had never been away from her home, never left Dunsmuir lands. Her cousin Barbara had married a man of means and influence, one who spent time at court. This visit meant the chance to see all the things Bridget had only heard of in the gossip and tales brought by the rare visitors to Dunsmuir. She should have suspected that her dour, overprotective brother would find a way to curtail her chance of thoroughly enjoying such a journey. A woman like Nan was as good as a shackle. It began to look as if all those new clothes and dancing lessons would go to waste.

Despite Nan's smothering presence, Bridget still felt a tickle of anticipation. That made no sense as Nan was the sort of woman who would feel it her duty to fiercely curtail all excitement, pleasure, and gaiety. Yet, within her lurked the feeling that she was about to embark upon some great adventure, that her life would soon change. Bridget inwardly grimaced. It was probably just the result of all her fanciful dreams about a tall, dark, handsome man sweeping her off her feet. All maidens had such dreams. She should not cling to hers so assiduously, as if they were some prophecy. Tall, dark, handsome men had better things to do than to carry on about small, too-thin lasses. Bridget doubted such men would fall to their knees to declare their undying love for her, either. If she continued to anticipate that sort of thing, she would soon suffer a keen disappointment.

The carriage suddenly took a sharp turn. Bridget cursed as she was slammed up against the side, adding more bruises to the ones she was certain she already had. As she straightened herself, she felt a twinge of irritation when she saw that Nan had barely moved.

"Such coarse language should ne'er pass a young lass' lips," scolded Nan.

"Of course," Bridget murmured. "My apologies if I have shocked ye."

"Och, ye didnae shock me, lass. I but remind ye of your manners. Men dinnae like to hear such language upon a woman's lips."

With Nan planted firmly at her side, Bridget doubted any man would dare approach her. If one did prove brave enough, or fool enough, to do so, she doubted he would linger long enough to catch her cursing. Since her brother had strongly hinted that it was time for her to find a husband, Bridget was a little surprised that he would give her a companion who could scare away a suitor with just one look.

The carriage stopped and, a moment later, the door was opened. Bridget smiled faintly at the man who helped her out. Although three days of travel had passed, she still felt a little uneasy around the six men her brother had hired to take her to her cousin's. They were a rough, dour group of men who sold their swords and hoped to find profitable work at the end of the journey. Duncan had seen them as the perfect solution to the problem of needing to provide her with protection during the journey yet not deplete his supply of men during this crucial planting time. Bridget knew he had the right idea, but she would have preferred at least one man she knew, someone whose loyalty she could depend upon.

Once the men had made a fire and tended to the horses, Bridget found herself and Nan left with the rest of the work. The men quickly provided some meat to cook, but Bridget wished they had thought to prepare it for the spit as well. To her relief, Nan took over that chore while she prepared them a place to sleep. It took a great effort to control her rising temper when the men pointed to the places where she could prepare their beds. Biting back curses, she did so, telling herself over and over again that it was not worth an argument.

"Your brother shouldnae have paid them at the start of this journey," Nan muttered when Bridget joined her by the fire, "but at the end. We would have been treated like pampered royalty if these fools had to worry about getting their coin."

It was somewhat comforting to discover that Nan was not pleased by the work allotted to them, either. "Weel, they probably see such things as women's work demeaning to a mon."

"Demeaning or nay, *they* are the ones paid to care for *us,* nay t'other way round. If I wasnae a good, God-fearing woman, I would tell ye to slip some nettles into their beds."

Bridget grinned, thinking that Nan might not be all piety and scoldings after all. "I did consider it, but decided I couldnae be sure how they would react." She frowned slightly. "I am nay sure I fully understand why Duncan hired complete strangers to take us to Barbara's."

"He needed his own men at Dunsmuir. These are unsettled times and the season itself requires many hands, and strong backs, to do the work. Work undone in the spring can mean hunger haunts the winter."

"Of course. I ken it. I just wish he had sent *one* of our own to watch o'er this lot and us."

"Have these men been insolent or ungallant?"

The way Nan stiffened and glared at the men almost

made Bridget smile. "Nay. I am just nay verra comfortable depending upon men I dinnae ken at all. I have ne'er been away from Dunsmuir so have ne'er been without someone I ken weel near to hand."

Nan nodded. "There is a comfort in that. Ye will soon be amongst kin again."

Murmuring her agreement, Bridget stared into the fire. She would have to work harder to overcome her unease around strangers. Nan would restrict any possible adventures quite well as it was. She did not need to add her own nervousness to that, restricting her possible enjoyment of this visit even more. Her sister Efrica would not be afraid. Effie would march boldly into the unknown. Blindfolded. Bridget smiled faintly at the thought of her somewhat untamed younger sister. She had little of that boldness which made Effie such a trial to Duncan. It was time to bring it forth, nurture it until her occasional bouts of unease were smothered. Touching the delicate medallion her grandmother had given her, Bridget told herself she would never forget that she came from a long line of brave, bold women.

She also had to decide exactly what she wished to gain from this journey. Duncan hoped she would find a husband, make a match which would benefit the clan in some way. She had no objections to that, but she would not allow herself to be pulled into a marriage simply because it might benefit her clan and please Duncan. Despite all her dreams and imaginings, Bridget was not foolish enough to think she would soon find the great love of her life. She did want some affection in her marriage, however, some passion and mutual respect. Duncan did not understand, but she would rather remain alone than find herself tied to a faithless man who saw her as no more than a dowry and a womb for his heir.

Nan drew her attention with a sharp nudge in her side. The food was ready and Bridget followed Nan's silent urgings to take her share. Once she and Nan had their food, they moved away from the fire and told the men that the food was ready. The way the men devoured the food made Bridget heartily glad of Nan's foresight.

It did not surprise Bridget when she and Nan had to clean up after the meal, but she felt as annoyed as Nan looked. Bridget had no objection to hard work, but, Nan was right. These men had been paid to care for her, not the other way around. By the time the moon was high in the sky, Bridget was feeling too irritated to sleep.

"I am going into the wood, Nan," she told her companion.

"I dinnae think that would be wise, or safe," Nan said, frowning toward the thick, shadowed forest.

"Weel, I cannae relieve myself here. Nor do I wish to have a wash where these men could see me."

"Ah, nay, that wouldnae be wise. Such things could rouse their base, monly lusts."

Bridget had to bite back a giggle. She doubted exposing any part of her too-slim body would rouse any man into a dangerous state of lust. While she had told Nan the truth about her need to slip into the shelter of the wood, she had not told the whole truth. For just a few moments she wanted to be alone. After three days of close confinement with Nan and the men, Bridget desperately needed some time to stand alone, to breathe the night air, and hear the sounds of the night and her own heart.

"I best go with ye," Nan said.

"Nay, I will be fine. I willnae wander too deep into the wood, just far enough to be private."

After staring at Bridget for a moment, Nan nodded. "I will give ye some time alone, then, but nay too long."

"Thank ye, Nan."

Bridget quickly gathered a full skin of water, clean clothes, and a cloth for washing. She hurried into the trees even as Nan sharply informed the men that she did not need one of them trailing after her. When Bridget reached a place where the trees thinned out a little to allow the light of the moon to shine through, she set down her things and shed her clothes. After a quick visit to the bushes, she stood beneath the moon and washed away the dust of a day's travel. She undid her hair and used the last of the water to rinse away the dust that clung to it.

Once dry, she quickly donned her clean shift, suddenly a little too aware of her nudity. Bridget stared up at the bright moon as she used the shift she had changed out of to rub her hair dry. She had always loved the night, especially when the moon shone full. She loved the smell of the night air, the feel of it, and the sounds that whispered on the air, even the ones that were occasionally loud and sharp enough to shatter that soft peace. Spreading her arms wide, she sang an old song in a quiet voice and danced in the moonlight, giggling now and again at her own foolishness. The freedom of dancing nearly naked in the moonlight, of being a part of the night, would be brief, but she would savor it to its fullness while she could. It was a pleasure she tried to steal for herself as often as possible.

Suddenly she stopped and crouched slightly. It felt as if every hair on her body stood on end. Bridget quickly dressed, straining to listen for some noise, some hint of what had so abruptly stolen her peace. She used her cloak to wrap her possessions up into a rough sack and tied it around her waist. After tying her hair back, she drew her dagger from the sheath at her waist and cautiously started back toward the camp.

After only a few feet she stopped and shivered. There was the scent of blood in the air. Bridget took a deep, slow breath to both calm herself and confirm her suspicion. Silently, she made her way through the trees, halting just inside the shadows edging the camp.

They were all dead. The bodies of her guards were sprawled upon the ground, their killers busily stripping them of clothes and weapons. Bridget could not see Nan, however. Even as she continued to search for some sign of Nan, alive or dead, Bridget silently drew up her skirts, tucking them firmly into the rough belt made by the cloak tied around her waist. It all made for an odd lump at her waist and hips, but it freed her legs for running, and she knew she would soon be running for her life.

Even as she sheathed her knife and took a step back, one of the thieves saw her and cried out. There was nothing she could do for Nan now. It was time to save her own life. Hissing in fury, she turned and bolted back into the depths of the woods. One thing she could do well was run. Bridget prayed she could run fast enough and far enough to escape the men now thrashing through the forest behind her.

Curses and shouts from the men pursuing her cut through the quiet of the night she had savored only moments ago. The moonlight she loved helped her find her way, but it also helped the men chasing her. Bridget wished it was a dark night now, one filled with deep shadows, for she would have had some advantage then. Few could find their way in the dark like a Callan.

A pain was beginning to grow in her side by the time Bridget realized the trees were thinning out. The ground she ran over was becoming thick with stones and slowly rising. She had no idea how long or how far she had run, only that the men chasing her must be blindly tenacious to still be at her heels. The only reason she could think of for their unexpected determination to catch her was a fear that she could find someone to hunt them as they now hunted her. It was a sweet thought, but she began to fear such justice would elude her. As trees gave way to shrubs, heather, gorse, and rocks, she knew she was reaching the end of her race.

When she reached a place that was flat and clear, Bridget stopped to study what lay ahead of her. It was all uphill from this point and she cursed. Most of it looked like an easy climb, but she already shook with exhaustion. From the time of her first bleeding, she had been increasingly restricted in her activities, pulled into training to make some man a proper wife. Such training did not prepare a woman for a lengthy fight to stay alive. Her body could take no more without a rest and there was no time for one.

Bridget turned to face the way she had come. She could hear the men and knew they would soon draw near. She hastily collected up a pile of rocks. It was a pitiful collection of weapons she drew around her, but she had very good aim and might get lucky. If nothing else, she could make the men suffer a little before they got her.

"There she be!" cried one of the men as he stumbled to a halt only a few yards away, panting loudly.

"Aye, here I be." Bridget threw a rock, catching the man in the chest and knocking him onto his backside. "Stay back," she warned, picking up another rock as the man's companions stumbled up to him.

"Now, lass, we mean ye no harm," said the largest of the men.

"Just how dull-witted do ye think I am?" She got ready to throw another rock. "Ye didnae chase me all this way just to introduce yourselves, I vow. Aye, and your blades still stink of the blood of my people." She threw her rock, catching another of the thieves on the side of his head, sending him to his knees. "Leave me be. Fly away like the thieving carrion ye are." She picked up another rock, never taking her gaze from the men.

If the way the men were glaring at her was any indication, her defiance infuriated them. She had not routed her attackers, only made them more dangerous. Inwardly, she shrugged. Dead was dead and she had no doubt in her mind that they intended to kill her. Quick or slow, now or later. They had to kill her because, left alive, she was a noose about their murdering necks. She was cornered. They knew it and she knew it. The only thing in doubt was whether or not she could take some of them down with her. Bridget intended to do her best to make her death cost them dearly.

"Now, lass," said the big man, "we intend only to hold ye for ransom, aye? Where is the harm in that?"

"If ye were as poor a thief as ye are a liar, ye would have been rotting on a gibbet by now and I wouldnae have to suffer the stench of ye."

The big man cursed viciously. "Ye havenae got a chance, ye stupid bitch."

"Probably not, but, the question ye must ask yourselves is—How many of ye will still be alive when the battle is o'er?"

They all stared at her as if she was a madwoman. Bridget felt a little like one. She should be terrified and, deep down, a part of her was. Another part of her wanted to howl and throw herself upon these men, nails, teeth, and dagger all slashing away at them.

For a brief moment she wondered if she could hold them off long enough to regain enough strength to start running again. She was feeling a little stronger, the pain in her side had eased, and she was breathing normally again. Then Bridget inwardly shook her head. It was a false strength, one that would be quickly depleted. There was also nowhere to go but up and she had no idea if there was any shelter or safety for her there.

One of the men started to move toward her and she threw her rock, striking him on the shoulder. She quickly picked up another rock, idly noted that she had only four more close at hand, and then tensed. Someone was coming. Bridget looked at the men below her, but they were still standing there watching her and talking low amongst themselves. Yet, she was certain something or someone was swiftly, silently moving ever closer.

Suddenly, out of the corner of her eye, one of the surrounding shadows became a slender, beautiful young man.

She forced herself not to look right at him. He grinned briefly and she nearly gasped, but, before she could decide whether or not she really had seen that wolfish smile, he was gone. A heartbeat later she felt a rush of movement. Dark shapes seemed to fly by her. The men below her looked horrified as the shadows closed around them. Their screams hurt her ears. Bridget felt overwhelmed by the scent and sight of blood for one long, desperate moment, then fell into blackness.

TWO

"Ye said ye were wanting a bride."

Cathal glared at his cousin Jankyn who was perched on the thick, heavily carved footboard of the bed like some raven, one pale slender hand curled around the bedpost. "I didnae expect ye to steal me one."

"We didnae steal her. We saved her."

"Saved her from what?"

As he waited for Jankyn's reply, Cathal studied the woman his cousin had brought into his bedchamber and set upon his bed. She was sprawled upon his furs like a broken doll. Not much bigger than one, either, he mused. Young, he decided, studying her soft, unlined features more closely. Young and stunningly beautiful. A sweet, oval face, a slender straight nose, faintly slanted eyes and light brown brows, luxurious gold-tipped lashes, and a full mouth that was pure temptation. Her figure was slender from her somewhat small breasts to her slim hips. A tiny waist and surprisingly long, beautifully shaped legs were qualities any man with blood in his veins appreciated.

He reached out to touch the thick tangle of hair spread out beneath her. It was like silk, the color a rich, tawny gold, and it flowed in heavy waves to her slender thighs. He was astounded that such a long slim neck could support such a bounty of hair. Then he frowned, noticing a suspicious bruise on the side of her neck.

"Who did this?" he demanded, his fleeting touch enough to assure him that the skin had not been broken.

"It matters not, Cathal. I stopped it. Twas but the blood-lust of the moment, nay more."

Cathal was not sure he believed that, but would not openly accuse his cousin of lying. "Tell me what happened," he ordered as, with as soft a touch as possible, he began to remove what appeared to be a lumpy cloak from around her middle.

"I saw her running. She runs like a young doe, all grace and speed. She came to a halt not far beyond where the forest ends. Not long after, a group of men stumbled out of the trees. It was clear that they had chased her a long way. By then the rest of the pack had seen her and we all began to move closer."

"These men were a threat to her?" Cathal tossed aside her cloak and started to gently remove her soft boots.

"Aye, nay doubt about it. They tried to get her to surrender, but she refused. Three times she hurled a rock at them. Three times she sent a mon to the ground. Then she saw me."

"Are ye sure?"

"Verra sure. She didnae turn to stare at me, but she looked to the side. Aye, she saw me. I got the feeling she had already sensed our approach. Then, when we set upon the men she called murdering thieves, she swooned."

"Set upon them?"

Jankyn nodded. "They are all dead."

"How much do ye think she saw?"

"Enough to send her into a deep swoon, but nay enough to be certain."

"Did the men deserve their fate?"

"Och, aye. We followed their trail back and found six dead

men. There were signs that there might have been another victim of their greed, but we couldnae find the body. We left them where they lay, took what those thieves had already piled up as their prize, and put it in the wee carriage. We hitched the horses up and Raibeart drove it here. I carried the lass here o'er the hill path." Jankyn briefly grinned. "She doesnae weigh much."

"Nay, I suspect she doesnae." Cathal leaned against the bedpost, crossed his arms over his chest, and scowled down at his unexpected guest. "The question is, what to do with her?"

"Wed her. Ye wanted a bride from the Outsiders. Here she is. She is fair enough to look upon, young, and, I can vow it heartily, strong and brave. I am nay sure it would be wise to just send her on her way."

"Nay alone, that is for certain. I cannae just wed myself to the first wee lass through my gates. For all we ken, she is already wed, or betrothed. She may nay feel inclined to wed with me, either."

"Then give her no choice. The moment I brought her within our walls, she didnae really have one anyway."

"Ye said she didnae see much."

"Nay, she didnae, or so I believe. I wouldnae swear to it." Jankyn nimbly leaped off the footboard, walked over to a table near the fireplace, and poured himself a goblet of wine from the decanter set there. "I *am* sure she saw me." He gracefully returned to his perch, sipping his wine as he studied the unconcious woman. "What else she saw, I truly couldnae say, but it matters not. She is a weelborn lass and she is now alone, without kin or older female at her side. Just pausing one night beneath your roof will taint her reputation. There isnae an older, respected kinswoman at Cambrun to stand in place of her kin, leastwise nay one ye could send with her to finish her journey."

That the woman was of good birth or, at least, from a

wealthy clan, could be easily read in the quality of her clothing. More proof could be seen in her soft, clean skin, uncalloused hands, and long nails. If she was not married or betrothed, and he saw no ring to indicate that she was, this visit to Cambrun could cost her dearly. He had never understood why, but certain circumstances could swiftly have people questioning the chastity of a woman, and this was one of them. Cathal doubted there was any way to get her to her destination in utter secrecy. He did not want his clan's name whispered in connection to the suspected loss of some well-born lass' honor, either. They did not need any more rumors swirling about them.

Jankyn was right, although it galled him to admit it. Wedding the woman would solve many problems. It would end any chance that she might find her honor impugned and it would give him the bride he sought. It would also ensure that she did not tell people about anything she had seen, the sort of things that could enflame the fears and suspicions about his clan. Even better, he would gain the bride he sought without having to leave Cambrun. The advantages were almost too numerous to list.

A soft noise from the woman on the bed pulled him free of his thoughts. Even as he straightened up to look at her face, her eyes opened. Cathal drew his breath in so sharply he nearly choked. Her eyes were the most beautiful eyes he had ever gazed into. They were an enticing mixture of blue and green, the color growing more dramatic as the haze of unconciousness fled.

As her now clear gaze went from Jankyn to him and back again, Cathal watched her sleek body grow tense. He stepped back in astonishment when she suddenly hissed and scrambled back to crouch on the pillows, her back against the headboard. Her slender, beautiful hands were slightly raised in front of her, her long slim fingers curled as if she was preparing to claw his eyes out. For a brief moment, there was something intensely catlike in her face, but the look faded so quickly he decided it must have been a trick of the unsteady light from the candles.

"Who are ye?" Bridget demanded, struggling to control the fear surging through her.

"I am Sir Cathal MacNachton, laird of Cambrun," replied the tall man at her bedside. "That mon at the foot of the bed is my cousin Jankyn MacNachton. We mean ye no harm, mistress."

The man had an attractively deep, smooth voice, Bridget decided. His tone was gentle, almost soothing, but she fought its effect. She could not be sure she could trust these men. It was important to remain wary. She did not immediately recognize the clan name or the name of the place. Since he had said the word *mistress* in a soft, questioning tone, she decided to reply. It might help to see if there was any reaction to her name.

"I am Lady Bridget Callan of Dunsmuir." She very slowly began to relax her muscles, seeking to calm herself enough to think clearly.

"Where were ye traveling to, m'lady?"

"My cousin Lady Barbara Matheson's. How did I get here?"

Suspecting the next few minutes of explanations could prove upsetting for her, Cathal fetched her a goblet of wine. She looked a little less frightened, but he was not sure she was calm enough for the ordeal ahead. When he handed her the drink, he almost smiled at the subtle way she sniffed it first, then took only the smallest of sips, obviously trying to judge the safety of the drink.

"I brought ye here," said Jankyn. "Ye had swooned."

"I never swoon."

"Weel, ye did this time."

Bridget sipped her wine and watched the two men. She could sense no threat from either man, yet there was a strangeness about them that roused her curiosity and a hint of unease. A lot of questions needed answering, but she needed a few minutes to think of the right ones. She was not all that eager to hear some of the answers, either. A few minutes to gather her wits, soothe her nerves, and study these men could only benefit her.

The laird was tall, quite possibly a foot or more taller than she was. He was lean yet she was certain there was an impressive strength beneath his slim elegant appearance. She had seen a hint of it in the way he moved as he had fetched the wine. His hair was a deep black and hung in soft waves several inches past his broad shoulders. His skin was a lot paler than she would have expected in a man with such dark hair. Not a wan, sickly pale, either, but a rich, lovely creamy tone that many a woman would envy. The lines of his face were cleanly cut, elegant perfection from his long, straight nose and high cheekbones to the firm jaw. There was a slight fullness to his lips that she found far too attractive. His eyes were strangely beautiful. Set beneath faintly arched brows, rimmed with enviable long lashes, they were a pale golden brown. He was, without doubt, one of the most beautiful men she had ever seen.

Feeling oddly warm, she turned her gaze toward the man called Jankyn. He perched on the end of the bed like some elegant dark bird. A very beautiful bird, she decided. His looks were similar to the laird's, their kinship plain to see, but his beauty was far more refined. The color of his eyes was more golden than brown, a little too similar to those of some beast of the forest. He suddenly smiled at her and she tensed.

"I saw ye," she said. "Ye came from out of the hills, from behind me."

"Aye, just as those bastards readied themselves to attack," replied Jankyn.

Images crowded her mind so quickly they made her head ache. "Those men who were chasing me?"

"And willnae chase ye again. Their thieving, murdering days are at an end."

She shivered and took a deeper drink of wine. Those men had deserved their fate. She doubted her party was the first they had ever set upon. The justice dealt out to them may have been swift and brutal, but so was a hanging. It was, however, probably for the best that she had seen little of that reckoning. The few memories nudging at her mind were too wild to be believed.

"My people?" she asked quietly, tensing for the reply.

"Your men are dead, m'lady," replied Cathal.

"I feared that was so. The last sight I had of them didnae really leave much doubt about their fate. What of Nan?"

"Nan? There was a woman with ye?" Cathal looked at Jankyn who shook his head. "No woman was found."

"But, she was there when I left the camp for a few moments of privacy."

"Which undoubtedly saved your life."

"We searched a goodly distance about the camp," said Jankyn. "We found no woman."

There were a lot of reasons why Nan's body had not been found, most of them too chilling to think about. Bridget decided to cling to the hope that, somehow, Nan had survived. The chances of that were very slim, but, then, Nan was a strong, determined woman.

"Your carriage and belongings were brought to Cambrun," said Cathal.

"Thank ye, m'laird," said Bridget. "As soon as I can find some men to take the place of the ones who were killed, I will be able to continue on my way."

"Ah, now, that may prove to be a wee problem."

Bridget stared at the man. For a brief moment she was confused by his statement, but then she began to get angry. She would never be able to adequately repay these men for saving her life, but she did not think that gave them the right to decide what she should or should not do. This dangerously attractive laird was not her laird or kinsman. Before she could reply to his remark, however, there was a rap at the door and, at the laird's command, a buxom woman of middle years came in carrying a tray laden with bread, cheese, sliced meats, and fruit.

"Ah, good, the wee lass is awake," said the woman as she set the tray on a table by the side of the bed. "No wounds to be tended to, are there?"

Cathal looked at Bridget who shook her head. "Nay, Mora. A bath, mayhap?" he asked, looking back at Bridget.

"That would be most welcome," replied Bridget, "but I dinnae wish to put anyone to any trouble."

"The water be already heating for it, lass," Mora said as she filled a plate with food and set it on Bridget's lap. "Ye eat this now. Ye need some meat on those bones. Are ye certain ye have no hurts?"

"Verra certain," Bridget replied, noticing that Mora looked nothing like the men, being plump, blue-eyed, and red-haired. "I was most fortunate to escape all injury. A few scratches and bruises, but a wash will be treatment enough for those."

Bridget ate her food, watching as Mora served the men. She simply could not shake the feeling that there was something a little odd about these men, and not just because they were so unusually beautiful, so graceful, or had strange eyes. It was almost as if she could scent something different in them. For a brief moment she wondered if they were related to her clan in some way, but quickly shook aside that thought. She would have recognized the name. Her clan kept very precise records of all those connected to them by blood.

When both men sat on the bed to eat their food, she hastily bit back a protest. One quick glance around the room made her almost certain she was in the laird's chamber. It was an odd place to put her, but Bridget fought against the suspicions stirring to life in her mind. These men had saved her life. She owed them the courtesy of at least hesitating before accusing them of something.

An idle glance at the food upon the men's plates gave her a slight start. She quickly ate some bread to hide any hint of surprise in her expression. Her meat was well cooked, but theirs was very rare. It seemed odd that she should be fed something different, but she was glad of it. Meat barely seared over the fire was not to her liking. In fact, she could not think of one person she knew who would like their meat that lightly cooked. She decided it must be some family oddity, rather like her Aunt Mairi who refused to eat cooked vegetables, preferring them raw.

"Why were ye traveling to your cousin's?" Cathal asked.

"She invited me for a visit," replied Bridget. "I just passed my nineteenth saint's day and she felt it was time I saw something aside from the walls and fields of Dunsmuir. She plans to introduce me at court and all of that."

"Ah. Ye seek a husband."

"*I* dinnae seek one. I but seek a look at the world outside of Dunsmuir, to meet people who arenae part of my clan." Feeling compelled to be honest, she added, "I do think my brother wishes me to find a husband, however. He gave me many a lecture on the matter ere I left."

Cathal had to bite back a smile at the look that swiftly crossed her all too expressive face, for it was clear she had found those lectures highly irritating. Although she said she was not going to her cousin's to find a husband, he suspected she held a few hopes of finding one. What interested him most was that she was neither married nor betrothed. As a laird holding good lands and a full purse, he would be a satisfactory choice to her kinsmen. The dark rumors about his clan, which grew more numerous every year, could cause trouble, but marrying her quickly would ensure that those rumors did not reach the ears of her kinsmen in time to cause too much difficulty. Once the marriage was consummated, her clan would have to accept it.

He inwardly sighed. It was a mad plan, but he realized he

had already accepted it. Her brother wished her to find a husband, and Cathal wished to find a wife. He had land and title, as well as enough wealth to silence any objections. Or, any objections raised by her kinsmen, he mused as Mora took his empty plate away. Instinct told him that the delicate woman seated upon his bed could prove to be very stubborn. However, instinct also told him that, out of all the Outsider brides he might choose, he and his clan had the best chance of being accepted by this slim, golden beauty who was now slicing up an apple with an impressive skill and speed. There was no possibility he could hide the truth from a wife and most Outsiders fled in fear of that truth. Cathal simply could not see this woman doing so, but he would be hard-pressed to explain just why he felt that way.

"That was verra good, Mora," Bridget said as the woman took her plate. "I thank ye. Now, if ye could tell me where I might have that bath?"

"Ye will have it here, m'lady," said Cathal. "Please see to it, Mora."

Not wishing to argue with the man before the servant, Bridget waited until Mora left before saying, "Isnae this your bedchamber, m'laird?"

"It is," replied Cathal as he moved to stand by the side of the bed, his hands clasped behind his back.

"Then I should be shown to the guest chambers, aye?"

"Nay, ye will stay here. Tis best if ye become accustomed to these chambers."

Bridget sat up straighter and glared at him. "And just what do ye mean by that?" She saw a grinning Jankyn move to stand beside Cathal and was briefly distracted by the sight of his teeth. "Do ye file your teeth to get those fangs? I had an uncle who did that. Filed all his front teeth so that they were sharp and pointed. Thought it made him look fierce."

Jankyn scowled at her. *"I* have no need of such foolish vanities."

Cathal watched her frown and, before she could think too long on Jankyn's words, he said, "Ye will stay in this bed-chamber."

That command pulled Bridget free from her interest in Jankyn's teeth and she glared at Cathal again. Did he think that, since she owed him her life, she would be willing to warm his bed? The fact that she felt a definite stirring within her blood at the thought made her all the more determined to stand firm against him.

"I am the sister of the laird of Dunsmuir," she began.

"Ah, good. Good." Cathal started toward the door, a chuckling Jankyn close at his heels.

That reply made no sense at all, she thought. "Why is that good?"

"Tis best if the bride and groom are of an equal standing."

"Bride and groom? *What* bride and groom? Who is to be married?"

"Why, ye are to be married, m'lady. To me."

Bridget was so stunned by his words, the two men were several minutes gone before she could utter a word. She spent several minutes more trying to decide if she had heard him correctly. By then, her bath had been prepared. As, with Mora's help, she bathed and dressed in a warm night shift, Bridget convinced herself he had been making a poor jest. When Mora refused to take her to another bedchamber, Bridget climbed into the laird's huge bed. She snuggled down beneath the warm covers and felt exhaustion sweep over her. For a little while she fought it, determined to be alert for the man's return, for any attempt at seduction or worse, but soon knew it to be a losing battle. She told herself no man could take her innocence without waking her up and then welcomed sleep's embrace.

Three

"Ah, 'tis a fine day. I will just get a wee fire going in the hearth to take the chill off this room, aye?"

Bridget opened one eye and peered over the covers at the woman by the fireplace. For a long frightening moment she could not recall who the woman was or where she was and in whose bed. Then her mind cleared enough for her memory to return. She glanced at the pillow next to her, but saw no sign that anyone had shared the bed with her. She inwardly cursed when she realized she felt faintly insulted by that.

Cautiously, she sat up, relieved to find that her ordeal had not left her too sore. She glanced toward the window Mora had revealed and frowned. It was grey outside, grey and raining. That was not unusual, but she did not understand how Mora could think it was so very fine. It made Bridget feel strongly inclined to crawl back beneath the covers and sleep a few more hours.

"Ye are looking much better, lass," said Mora. "A good sleep has brought some color back into your bonnie wee face." Mora helped Bridget out of the high bed and led her over to where a deep basin of hot water was set on a table near the fire. "Ye have a wee wash and I will fetch something for ye to wear. The lads brought your clothes up earlier."

Mora chatted away about how lucky Bridget was to be alive, how lovely her clothes were, and even carried on a lively debate with herself as to whether Bridget would look best in the green gown or the blue. Bridget let the woman talk, listening with only half an ear, and making the appropriate noises when she felt it was necessary to reply in some way. As she washed and cleaned her teeth, Bridget tried to recall everything that had been said to her last night. Just as Mora returned to her side, Bridget finally remembered those startling remarks the laird had made before he had left the room.

"Bride and groom?" she grumbled, her voice muffled by the dark blue gown Mora was tugging over her head. "What is the big fool talking about?"

"Seemed most clear to me," said Mora as she began to lace up Bridget's gown. "He means to make ye his wife."

"How can ye be sure of that? Ye werenae here when he said those things."

"I heard him and Jankyn speaking of it as they left the bedchamber. I was just outside the door."

"Is he mad?"

"Nay. Why would ye think that?" Mora pushed Bridget down into a seat before the fire and began to brush out her hair.

"I dinnae ken," drawled Bridget. "Mayhap 'tis the way he but looks at me once and declares us betrothed."

"A lot of people wed with the wife and husband barely kenning a thing about each other. Ye are the laird's equal in birth, he doesnae need a dowry, and ye are a bonnie, young lass, ripe for marrying. Tis most reasonable. A perfect solution."

Bridget rolled her eyes. "Perfect for him. Mayhap nay so perfect for me."

"Why? He is a braw lad, handsome, has a fine keep and good lands, and is a good laird."

"Weel, mayhap, but why doesnae he go to court himself or visit some other laird's holdings? At least look about a wee bit for a wife?"

"He doesnae like to leave Cambrun. The MacNachtons prefer to stay close to home."

There was a certain tone to Mora's voice that made Bridget feel compelled to ask why. She bit back the words. There could be many reasons why such a handsome man would be reluctant to travel to other keeps or the king's court. It did not have to be anything particularly strange. Nevertheless, it *was* strange to abruptly decide to marry some woman he had just met. Bridget seriously doubted that he had fallen passionately in love with her at first glance.

"*I* wished to go to my cousin's," she said. "I have spent my whole life at Dunsmuir, rarely seeing anyone but the others in my clan. I want to see different places, different people. I want to dance, to see all the fine courtly clothes and manners."

Mora snorted. "A crowd of sly fools who spend their days mocking and betraying others in a bid to gain favor and their nights in all manner of licentiousness."

That sounded wonderously interesting to Bridget, but she was wise enough not to say so. There was a hint of Nan in Mora and such a remark would certainly bring on a lecture. She suddenly felt a pang of sorrow and concern for Nan. The woman had not deserved her fate, whatever it may have been.

"I was told the men who found me searched for my companion, Nan," Bridget said, the hint of a question in her voice.

"Aye, they did." Mora began to braid Bridget's hair. "If they couldnae find her, lass, she wasnae there."

"So strange, isnae it? Where would she go? As I see it, she had but two choices when the thieves attacked. She either died with the others or fled."

"If she had fled, Jankyn would have been able to see that and followed her trail."

"It was dark. He may have missed whate'er trail she left."

"Nay. Jankyn could track a wee mousie in the dark. But, it wasnae so verra dark, was it? Moon was full." Mora moved to stand in front of Bridget. "There. Ye are looking verra bonnie. I will lead ye to the great hall now, aye?"

Bridget's stomach answered the question by growling. As she let Mora lead her out of the room, Bridget wondered what time it was, but was too embarrassed to ask. To judge by the poorly lit hallway they walked along, one would think it was night, but she knew that was not true. Grey and rainy though it had been, it had still been day she had viewed out of the window. The MacNachtons, however, apparently favored the dark. Perhaps they feared the daylight would fade all the fine tapestries and carpets, she mused as she entered the great hall. It, too, was shadowed, the windows thickly shrouded with heavy drapes of burgundy cloth and the room lit by candle and torch.

"Ye awoke just in time to break your fast," said Mora as she tugged Bridget toward the laird's table.

"Oh, so 'tis morning, is it?"

"Weel, nay. Tis the middle of the day. But, ye woke up in time for a meal. Which meal doesnae matter much, aye?"

There was no argument to be made to that so Bridget watched Sir Cathal rise from his seat to bow to her as Mora led her to a seat on his left. He did not look like a madman, Bridget thought as she took her seat. He was too handsome for any woman's peace of mind, calm, and clear-eyed. As she filled her plate with tender lamb, turnips, bread, and cheese, she wondered if there was any way to gently inquire if she had heard him correctly last night. Since Mora had confirmed her rather uncertain memory of that conversation, Bridget was sure Cathal had mentioned marriage. It needed to be discussed, but she was unable to think of a clever way to broach the subject and to discuss it calmly.

She glanced around the great hall as she began to eat. There were not that many people in it. About half a dozen people who bore a distinct resemblance to Sir Cathal watched her closely as they ate. The ones serving looked as if they were related to Mora. Bridget did not think she had ever seen such a clear difference between those who served and those who were waited upon. In her clan there was only one real distinction between the laird's close kin and ones like Mora, but it was not one so easily detected.

Just as she gathered enough courage to begin a conversation with Sir Cathal, two people who immediately grasped her full attention strode into the great hall. A tall, slim man and a slender woman made their way to the laird's table, watching her as intently as she watched them. The woman was strikingly beautiful with gleaming black hair and milk white skin, her bright golden eyes glinting with emotions Bridget could not guess at. The man's hair was a duller black, enlivened by a few streaks of white. There was a similarity in his features to Sir Cathal's, but the lines of his face were far harsher, almost threatening. The look he gave her from his too dark eyes sent a chill down her spine.

"Scymynd, Edmee," murmured Sir Cathal as the couple stopped by his chair. "To what do we owe the honor of your presence? Ye rarely join us in the great hall."

"We have come to meet your guest," replied Scymynd.

Cathal introduced Scymynd and Edmee to Bridget. Although Bridget's replies were calmly said and very polite, Cathal detected a tension in her, as if she sensed a threat was near. He could not blame her. He sensed one as well. Scymynd was the leader of the Purebloods and had made his dislike of Cathal's plan all too plain in the last few months. It was not a good sign that Scymynd would venture into the upper keep to meet Bridget. When he felt Edmee's long, cold fingers stroke his neck, Cathal knew all too well what game she intended to play. He fought the urge to use his power as their laird to send them away. Rebellion was brewing in the caves the Purebloods called home, and he would not aid it by insulting the two most prominent members of that group. However, he would not allow them to intimidate Bridget.

"Are ye to join us for the meal, then?" he asked.

"Nay." Scymynd glanced at the food upon the table, grimaced faintly with distaste, then looked at Jankyn who sat at Cathal's right. "Tis nay to my taste. I am surprised to see ye partaking of it."

Jankyn smeared thick brown honey on a chunk of bread. "I have an adventurous palate."

"So do I," murmured Edmee as she ran her fingers through Cathal's hair.

Bridget was surprised to find herself feeling annoyed by the way the woman touched Cathal. Even more so by the way Cathal allowed it. Edmee was behaving in such an openly lustful, sensuous way, Bridget was amazed she was not blushing at the sight. It did make her think, however, that Cathal's talk of marriage had been some odd jest and nothing more. That, she suspected, was at the root of her annoyance. She did not like being teased. A little voice in her head told her she was lying to herself. Bridget sternly gagged it.

"Cease your games, Edmee," Cathal snapped, pulling away from her touch. "They dinnae amuse me."

"Amusing ye wasnae what I had in mind."

Cathal ignored her and looked at Scymynd. "As ye can see, Lady Bridget has recovered from her ordeal."

"Aye." Scymynd smiled at Bridget. "She must be eager to continue her journey."

It was not easy, but Bridget hid her reaction to Scymynd's smile. It was not a pleasant expression, but coldly threatening. What caused the flicker of alarm she felt, however, was that he had teeth just like Jankyn. She was coming to the unsettling conclusion that those teeth were not the result of some clever work with a file, some odd vanity practiced by some of the MacNachtons. Why someone would have fangs to make a wolf envious was not something Bridget cared to think about. She softly dragged her fingernails over the hard surface of the table to reassure herself that they were still long, sharp, and hard.

Cathal idly noted Bridget's move and inwardly frowned. He suddenly realized that she had rather long fingernails, not one of which appeared to have suffered even the smallest chip from her ordeal, either. Out of the corner of his eye, he caught Jankyn intently staring at Bridget's hands. Cathal decided he would have to discuss Bridget with Jankyn for there was obviously something about the woman that held his cousin's interest. Jankyn knew a great deal about almost every family in Scotland and, if he had some knowledge about the Callans, Cathal wanted to know what it was. But, now, he thought as he looked at Scymynd, he had other problems to deal with.

"She is staying at Cambrun," Cathal announced, taking one of Bridget's hands in his and keeping his gaze fixed upon Scymynd and Edmee. "She was headed to her cousin's to seek a husband. I have decided that she need look no further."

The touch of Cathal's hand sent a warmth through Bridget that startled her. The way he was idly stroking her palm with one of his long fingers was sending small, delightful shivers through her. She had to force herself to pay attention to the confrontation going on between the MacNachtons. One look at the faces of Scymynd and Edmee made Bridget very glad she had been too distracted to immediately gainsay Cathal. Cathal's plan to marry her plainly did not meet with this couple's approval, and Bridget had a strong suspicion it was due to a lot more than Edmee wanting the laird for herself. She had the chilling feeling that she was rapidly being pulled into the middle of some battle for power.

"Ye still intend to marry an Outsider? To sully our bloodline?" Scymynd asked, his voice taut and cold.

A brief squeeze of her hand from Cathal caused Bridget to bite back the angry defense of her clan she had been about to make. The look of cold fury upon Cathal's face, one echoed by Jankyn, told Bridget that she was not the only one who had just been insulted. A quick glance around the great hall revealed that everyone's attention was fixed upon this confrontation. The MacNachtons may have rescued her from one perilous confrontation, but it was increasingly clear to Bridget that the laird had set her down in the middle of another.

"I believe I made my plans verra clear months ago," replied Cathal.

"Ye dinnae e'en ken who this woman is," snapped Edmee. "She could be some thief."

"She *is* Lady Bridget Callan of Dunsmuir, sister of the laird, cousin to Lady Barbara Matheson, and my betrothed." Cathal was pleased Bridget made no protest, that she had the wit to know that now was not a good time to argue his plans for her. "I have found nothing to e'en hint that she may not be exactly who she claims she is. Thus, she is a perfect choice."

"Ye should choose one of your own. Ye put us all at risk, try to destroy all that we are," said Scymynd.

Cathal shifted the grip of his hand upon Bridget's just enough so that he could stroke the inside of her wrist. "Do I? I believe my intentions will save us. Do ye have a son, Scymynd? Does Edmee have a child? Considering how often she *amuses* herself, she ought to have a dozen clinging to her skirts. Where are they?"

"Unlike the Outsiders, we dinnae need to breed like rabbits."

"I wasnae suggesting we do so, but e'en we need the occasional renewal."

"Tis madness. Ye have forgotten who ye are and would try to have us all do the same. Be warned, Cathal," Scymynd said as he started to walk away, "if ye push too hard, those ye try to corner *will* push back. Hard."

Edmee glared at Cathal, then hissed at Bridget. Bridget hissed right back. She had the fleeting pleasure of watching Edmee's eyes widen in surprise before the woman followed Scymynd out of the great hall. Once the pair were gone, Bridget pulled her hand free of Cathal's grasp. She then gave a chuckling Jankyn a stern frown which only seemed to add to his amusement. She forced herself to turn her attention back to her meal, fighting to hide the turmoil in her mind and heart. There really was something odd about the MacNachtons, not the least of which was the way their laird could make her feel all hot and itchy with but a touch of his hand. There were secrets at Cambrun and, although her curiosity was stirred to nearly a feverish pitch, Bridget knew it would be far wiser to ignore them, even wiser to flee them.

Cathal almost smiled at the way Bridget was attempting to act as if nothing had happened. "Ye have naught to say, m'lady?"

"I have heard it said that 'tis best to nay indulge the deluded," she murmured.

"And ye think I am deluded?"

"What else could one call it when ye tell all who will listen that ye intend to marry a woman ye have just met? One who hasnae said *aye,* either."

"And why do ye hesitate to say aye? I dinnae think I am hard to look upon. I am wealthy enough to keep ye weel clothed and fed. I am a laird, have good lands, and those lands are weel protected. Ye couldnae find much better at court, although it sounds vain of me to say so."

It might sound vain, but it was the truth, Bridget mused as she took a long drink of cider to wash down the last of her meal. She had no intention of agreeing with that view, however. Neither did she intend to be dragged into a marriage with a man she had just met, one who was knee deep in plots that were stirring up rebellion within his clan. She slowly stood up and looked at Sir Cathal.

"I was going to court to see a world outside of the walls of Dunsmuir, to be entertained by the elegant clothes and intriguing gossip, and to dance until my feet hurt. If some fine gentlemon decided to woo me, I might have taken a husband. Please note the use of the word *might*. Now, if ye will excuse me, I believe I will go and compose a letter to my cousin to explain my delay and let her ken that I *will* arrive for my visit with her as soon as possible."

"Aye, ye do that, m'lady." Cathal enjoyed the gentle sway of her slim hips as she walked away. "I am certain we can arrange to visit your kinswoman at some time after we are married." He grinned when she clenched her hands into tight fists, hesitated briefly, then continued out of the great hall. Mora flashed him a wide grin and hurried after Bridget.

"She has a temper," murmured Jankyn. "She set Edmee back on her heels for a moment."

"Aye," agreed Cathal. "If Lady Bridget was frightened, she hid it weel. Tis good. She will need courage and strength to be my wife."

"I think she will try to escape."

Cathal nodded. "We will watch for it."

"What if she continues to refuse you? Ye cannae want an unwilling bride."

"She willnae be unwilling."

"Ye sound verra sure of that."

"I am. There is an attraction. I feel it and, when I held her hand, I kenned that she felt it, too. Twill take but a wee while for her to understand and accept it."

"Then I hope ye listened carefully to what she said as she left. There were two words ye must needs remember."

"Aye, woo and dance."

"Exactly. Woo and dance. Do ye ken how to dance?"

Cathal grimaced. "Nay, but if my wooing isnae enough, I suspect I can learn. Lady Bridget can hiss and scratch all she likes, but, in the end, she *will* be *my* wife."

Four

The sound of howling drew Bridget to the window. Moonlight bathed the hillside, softening the sharp edges of rock and shrub. What held her gaze, however, were the dark figures that seemed to fly out of the rocks the keep was built upon. They moved so swiftly she had no time to look carefully at any one figure, but she knew they were human. Despite the feral noise, the swift way they moved, Bridget recognized that she was watching cloaked men and women run nimbly over the rough ground to disappear into the forest. She had heard the sounds last night, her second night at Cambrun, but had not looked out of the window. Bridget heartily wished she had not looked this time.

Bridget let the thick drape fall back over the window. She moved to stand in front of the fireplace, holding her hands toward the flames as she sought to chase away the chill of fear from her body. It was just a hunt, she told herself. Everyone hunted. There was probably some game that was best caught at night.

She cursed and began to pace before the fire. It was time to stop ignoring things and lying to herself. Most people did not hunt at night even if there was a full, bright moon. Most people did not go hunting on foot, racing out of the bowels of a keep, howling like a pack of wolves. Most people did not race across the ground so fast you could miss seeing them if you blinked, once.

Now that she was facing the truth, all the other odd things she had noticed came swiftly to the fore of her mind. People should not have fangs. Bridget was very sure of that. The MacNachtons seemed very fond of the dark. She saw very few of the darkly beautiful MacNachtons about during the day and every window was kept heavily draped. Even though he was at the table for every meal, Cathal did not eat exactly what she did. Jankyn ate very little aside from some alarmingly raw meat. All the MacNachtons were alike in appearance, more so than any other clan members she had ever seen. They all had eyes that would not look out of place on a wolf. The only MacNachton she had seen outside the walls of the keep during the day was Cathal and he had been heavily cloaked. He had also stayed outside for only a short time.

Pausing before the fire, Bridget stared hard into the flames and struggled to recall exactly what she had seen just before she had fainted on the night she was rescued. She had seen Jankyn grinning his fang-baring grin. She had seen those cloaked figures sweep by her, swiftly and silently. Bridget shuddered as she recalled the screams of the men who had been chasing her. The MacNachtons had set upon the thieves, but there had been no sound of swords clashing. There had been blood, however. She could recall seeing it, smelling it. Yet, no matter how hard she tried, all she could recall of that last moment before sinking into unconsciousness was swirling black forms surrounding the thieves, screams, and blood. If she had seen how the MacNachtons had killed her enemies, it was locked deep in her mind and did not want to come out.

One thing did slip out that she suddenly wished she could tuck away again. All too clearly she could hear Nan telling her about the man in the village with eyes and teeth like a wolf, had inhuman strength, wounds that healed like magic, and who only ventured out at night. Demon and witch the villagers had called him, but other words tickled at the edge of Bridget's mind, ones she did not care to even whisper aloud. She had no doubt that that man had been a MacNachton.

And their laird wished to marry her, she thought and shivered. A marriage at least two of his clan were adamantly opposed to. Cathal had spent the last two days courting her. Even more alarming was the fact that she was slowly succumbing to his wooing. He was beautiful and made her knees weak. He was dangerous.

Bridget hurried over to her chest of clothes. She took out her old cloak, piled a few clothes and carefully chosen personal items into the center of it, and tied the four corners together to make a sack. Donning her new cloak, she slipped out of the bedchamber. Silently, but quickly, she crept through the hall, down the stairs, and out the doors into the bailey. She was just about to run out through the gates, surprised but pleased to see them open, when a man dropped to the ground right in front of her. A soft screech escaped her as she stumbled back a step, even as she frantically looked around in a vain attempt to see where he had come from.

"Greetings, lass," the man said in a deep, rough voice. "Ye probably dinnae remember me. I am Raibeart. I drove your wee bonnie cart back here after we saved ye from those thieving swine."

"Ah, weel, I thank ye. Now, if ye will just excuse me," she tried to dart around him, but the man swiftly put himself in her path.

"Now, ye dinnae really want to go out there. Tis dark, aye? Too dangerous for such a wee lass."

"Ye arenae going to let me leave, are ye?" She cursed when he shook his head.

"The laird wants ye to stay here."

"I dinnae care what *he* wants. He isnae *my* laird. He isnae my kinsmon, either." Bridget could feel panic clawing at her insides and struggled to push it aside. *"I wish to go to my cousin's and none of ye have the right to stop me."*

She felt a light touch upon her shoulder. Blindly, she turned and struck out, raking her nails across the face of the man who stood behind her. As her fingernails scored soft flesh the feeling pulled her free of the tight grasp fear had upon her. She looked in horror at the bloody furrows she had left upon Jankyn's cheek. He touched a hand to the cuts as he stared at her, his gaze holding more intense consideration than shock. Mumbling a heartfelt apology, Bridget pulled a square of daintily embroidered linen from a pocket in the lining of her cloak. However, by the time she reached toward Jankyn, intending to clean the blood from his wounds, there was no need for such care.

"Your wounds appear to be closing," she whispered.

"Aye. They were only shallow cuts," he said. "Ye have verra sharp nails, lass." Keeping his gaze fixed upon her face, he slowly licked the blood from his fingers.

"Oh, it needed only that." Bridget closed her eyes, took a deep breath to calm herself, then scowled at Jankyn.

"That was a strange thing to do, lass," murmured Raibeart as he moved to stand beside her.

It was, but Bridget would never admit it. "Nay, it wasnae. I felt a touch and thought I was in danger. Jankyn also crept up behind me when I was feeling agitated." She abruptly made a dash for the gate, not surprised when both men quickly appeared to block her way. "That could become verra annoying."

"E'en if we were inclined to let ye leave," Jankyn said, "we certainly wouldnae let ye march off into the night all alone."

Bridget realized she was no longer afraid. That seemed strange. Nothing had occurred to alter the conclusions she had come to. In truth, what had just happened with Jankyn had only strengthened them. Yet, as she stood before these two MacNachtons, she only felt a very natural annoyance that these men would not allow her to do what she wanted to do. The only expression she could see in their feral eyes was a manly annoyance over a woman not doing as she was told. She felt no threat from these men and, considering what she was now sure they were, that truly made no sense at all.

"Ah, so ye will escort me to my cousin's then, will ye?" she said in a voice so sweet she was surprised it did not make her teeth ache.

"Nay, they willnae," drawled an all too familiar voice from behind her.

Inwardly cursing, Bridget turned to face Cathal. "I have decided 'tis time for me to continue on my journey."

"And ye decided ye had to do it now? Right now? Without most of your belongings?"

"Aye. I got to thinking—"

"A dangerous thing for a lass to do. Ow!" Jankyn rubbed his stomach where Bridget had just hit him with her sack of belongings, and grinned at her.

"Why are ye nay out with the others, howling at the moon?"

"At least I am nay dancing beneath it." He laughed when she blushed.

"Ye were watching me?"

"I heard ye singing."

"That was so rude." If he had been drawn by her singing then he could not have seen her naked, Bridget mused, and relaxed. "I had left the camp to seek a few moments of privacy."

Cathal grasped Bridget by the arm, turning her attention back to him. "Why were ye leaving?"

Bridget could feel the blunt truth on the tip of her tongue, but could not bring herself to speak it. It was as if she feared that, in speaking the words, the truth could no longer be ignored. That was absurd. She knew the truth. By the way the three men looked at her, they knew she had guessed all their secrets. It made no difference. She simply could not utter the dark, terrifying name aloud. In some odd, twisted way, she was actually concerned about offending them.

"I decided I wasnae going to play your game any longer," she replied. "I was going to my cousin's."

"Alone? At night?"

"Tis the best time for an escape." But not here, she realized, and inwardly cursed her own stupidity. At Cambrun high noon on a sunny day would have been a better choice. "I have prepared for a visit with Barbara for months. I want to go to court, to see all the fine clothes, and to watch all the courtiers and their ladies. I want to sit down to a feast and listen to all the whispers about who is sinning with whom. I want to hear the minstrels sing and I want to dance with some fine, courtly gentlemon who will tell me all manner of sweet lies about how bonnie I am. I want—"

A squeak of surpise and outrage escaped her when Cathal suddenly picked her up and slung her over his shoulder. The soft laughter of Jankyn and Raibeart only added to her anger over being so roughly handled. Bridget dropped her belongings and proceeded to pound her fists against his broad back. Cathal did not even flinch as he continued to take her back to her bedchamber and that, too, increased her fury. Under her breath she cursed him and his stubborness.

"Tis nay just me who is blindly stubborn," muttered Cathal as he entered the bedchamber and kicked the door shut behind him. "Tis ye who refuses to give up this plan to go to court. And for what? To hear empty flatteries and malicious tales?" He paused by the bed. "Undo your cloak."

Even as she blindly obeyed that terse command, Bridget wondered why she did so. Such quick obedience was not in her nature. She growled softly when her cloak was pulled from her and tossed to the floor. Before she could say anything, she was tossed down onto the bed. Her body was still bouncing slightly when Cathal sprawled on top of her, gently but firmly pinning her down. Bridget scowled at him, more angry than afraid, and tried not to let the beauty of his face distract her. She had a right to be angry and she would hold fast to that feeling no matter how warm and itchy he made her feel.

"Ye are staying here," Cathal said. "I am going to woo ye and then we will be married."

"Oh! What arrogance! Ye may woo me, but that docsnae necessarily mean ye will win me."

Bridget suspected he had some right to that arrogance for she had been softening toward him, but now she knew the truth. He was a man whose looks made her heart skip and her breath quicken. Feeling his big, lean body pressed against hers was beginning to make her feverish. To her ears, the sound of his voice was like a caress. Unfortunately, he was also a dangerous creature, one whose name she still felt almost afraid to say aloud.

Then again, she mused, he did not feel as if he was a dead man. He felt warm, strong, and alive. There was a glow of health to his lovely skin. He certainly did not smell of the grave. Yet, if one could believe all warnings given and tales told, the devil was prone to trick the unwary with beauty and lust. Cathal was beautiful and Bridget suspected that warm, itchy feeling he stirred within her was lust.

Cathal watched the expressions darting across her lovely face. She had made no accusations, but he was sure she had guessed the truth, or part of it. He took hope in the fact that she was not terrified. There was the occasional glint of fear in her eyes, but no more, and he felt he could deal with that.

"I will ne'er hurt ye, Bridget," he said softly and brushed a kiss over her forehead. "I swear it."

"And why should I accept your vow?" She shivered when he touched a kiss to her right cheek, feeling the warmth of his lips flow through her veins.

"Ah, I think ye do already." Cathal felt the subtle changes in her breathing and knew she was stirred by his kisses. "I think ye ken that ye are safe with me. I think ye also ken that ye are safe with Jankyn, Raibeart, and Mora. Aye, and many others." He lightly rubbed his lips over hers and reveled in the faint trembling of her lithe body.

"And there are others I am nay safe with, ones who wish me gone."

"I willnae allow them to harm ye."

"Ye may try. It doesnae matter. Ye have no right to hold me here."

"Why are ye so anxious to leave, lass? Can ye no spare a week or two for the ones who saved your wee life?"

"How devious ye are to play upon my sense of gratitude."

"Stay. Give me one week. If ye cannae abide marrying me, can see naught to gain, then we can discuss your continuing on to your cousin's."

"A week?"

"Aye, one week."

"I should send word to my cousin. She must be fretting o'er the fact that I havenae arrived yet."

"I will see that she is told that ye are safe and hale."

Bridget was about to tell him that one week would not change her mind about leaving, when he kissed her. His surprisingly soft lips pressed against hers, rubbing and nibbling, quickly robbed her of the ability to think clearly. When he nipped a little sharply at her bottom lip, she gasped softly. For a brief moment she was startled by his tongue in her mouth, but the stroke of his tongue against the roof of her mouth quickly changed shock to pleasure.

A soft growl escaped her as an exciting heat flooded her body. She wrenched her hands free of his grasp and wrapped her arms around his neck. Every part of her suddenly felt intensely alive and needy in a way she did not completely understand. An equally soft growl escaped Cathal and it heightened the pleasure she felt. A wildness was stirring to life inside her and she both feared and welcomed it.

Then, abruptly, he was gone. Bridget felt the loss of his warmth so keenly she shivered and wrapped her arms around herself. She realized she was breathing as if she had just run a long race, her breasts ached, and there was an odd feeling between her legs, a heated blend of pleasure and pain. A quick glance at Cathal, who now stood by the side of the bed, revealed that he was suffering some of the same feelings. She wished she could find more comfort in that. He had awakened something inside of her and she suspected it would be impossible to put it to rest again.

Cathal took a deep, slow breath to steady himself. While he did not indulge in the sensual gluttony some of his kinsmen did, he was no virgin. Yet, no woman had ever stirred his lust into such a swift frenzy with just one kiss. He was not sure if that was good or bad. He only knew he wanted more. There was passion in Bridget Callan and he intended to claim it for his own.

"Enough wooing for now," he said as he strode toward the door. "'Tis late and ye must rest."

"That was wooing?" she muttered as the door shut behind him.

All the warm, exciting feelings he had stirred up faded away, leaving her feeling irritated. Bridget had the sinking feeling that sense of irritation was because he had stopped kissing her. Hissing a curse, she got off the bed and went to change into her night shift by the fire. The man had revealed that there was a lustful side to her and that could prove dangerous. Even more dangerous was that the lustful side of her wanted Cathal to come back—right now.

"A week. I only have to stay out of his reach for a week," she said as she crawled into bed.

That was not going to be easy, she decided. She had let him see that she was stirred by him. There was no doubt in her mind that he would try to take advantage of that weakness. And it was a very big weakness, she thought as she groaned and buried her face in the pillow. She could still taste his kiss. Just thinking about it, of how it felt to have his body pressed so close to hers, revived that delicious heat he had roused inside of her. The man would undoubtedly haunt her dreams, dreams she suspected would no longer be so sweetly innocent.

Flopping onto her back, she glared up at the ceiling of the canopied bed. How she could think she would be safe with people who had fangs, shunned daylight, and had eyes like a wolf, she did not know. But, she did, at least with the ones who did not shun her or openly threaten her. The question was, could she trust Cathal to keep her safe from Scymynd and his ilk?

Bridget quickly pushed that thought aside. It did not matter if Cathal could keep her safe or not. In one week's time she would leave Cambrun. She would not allow passion to blind her to all the very good reasons why she could not marry Cathal MacNachton.

If naught else, she had to consider what sort of children they would breed. The Callans had spent hundreds of years perfecting their bloodline. She could not add MacNachton blood to the mix. Her family would be appalled. And how could she be sure Cathal would even give her children? Apparently, there was already a problem amongst his clan. Did a creature from the grave have what was needed to make bairns? Everything she had seen indicated that the MacNachtons were like those dark creatures who refused to stay dead. Yet, she was sure the man she had just held in her arms was alive. So, if Cathal was not some beautiful demon, what was he? Bridget doubted she could unravel that mystery in a week, but she was certainly going to try.

Five

Cathal slowly licked the life-giving vein in Bridget's long, elegant throat, then gave in to the strong urge to nip her there, very gently. He shifted his body slightly against hers, echoing the faint shudder that went through her. He did not think there was a part of him which did not ache with need. After four days of *wooing*, of pulling her into his arms at every opportunity, he was starving for her. There did not seem to be a single hour of the day when he was not thinking about how much he wanted to be inside her or how badly he wanted to see her naked and willing in his bed.

He kissed the hollow behind her ear and she purred. Cathal could think of no other way to describe the noise she made deep in her throat. It never failed to enflame his desire. He spent far too much of his time thinking about all the things he might do to make her purr like that.

A faint noise yanked him free of the sensual daze he had fallen into. Cathal pulled away from Bridget and realized he had her pinned against the wall not far from the doorway of the great hall. Her feet were several inches off the floor. Her arms around his neck and the press of his body all that kept her in place. He had obviously suffered a complete loss of control. His only consolation was that she looked as dazed and heated as he felt.

Keeping his hands on her tiny waist as she released him and got back down on her feet, Cathal looked around for what had distracted him. He frowned when he saw no one, even though all of his instincts told him that someone had been there. Since most of his people would never think to slip away out of respect for his or Bridget's modesty, he had to wonder if he was being watched. Many of the Purebloods rejected his plan to breed out many of the traits they held dear so it was highly possible that a close watch was being kept on his wooing of Bridget. It was something he had better look into, he decided.

"Are ye ready to say aye?" he asked Bridget, pleased to see that she was still struggling to regain her composure.

"Ye are a verra obstinate mon," she murmured as she fought to calm her breathing.

"Aye, I am." He gave her a quick, hard kiss. "We will have to return to our wooing later."

Bridget blinked and watched him walk away. She remained slumped against the wall for a few minutes as she tried to fully clear her head of the haze passion always filled it with. Idly touching the spot where Cathal had nipped her neck, she felt no wound. It was odd that, when he had scraped her skin with those sharp teeth, she had felt no fear.

Shaking free of the last of her bemusement, Bridget headed out of the keep. There were no MacNachtons around in the sunlit bailey, but there were many of the MacMartins, Mora's people. Bridget knew they would guard her as closely as the MacNachtons did. Their loyalty ran deep. She had learned that much since coming to Cambrun.

Mora smiled at Bridget as she fell into step at her side. "Tis a fine day, aye?"

"Ye say that about every day, Mora," Bridget drawled, then smiled back at the woman. "What do ye consider a bad day?"

"Och, winter brings many of them. I am nay fond of the cold."

Bridget looked around at the people working in the bailey. "There are no children, are there? That first night I dined in the great hall, I heard Cathal speak of the lack with Scymynd, but I dinnae think I really heeded the words. There arenae many MacMartin children, either? Or do ye keep them away from here?"

"Nay, ye are right. There are verra few bairns born to those who work for the laird here. I had but the one, twenty years ago. My David who mostly works in the stable. There hasnae been a bairn born since then. It has been a lot longer since the MacNachtons have borne a child."

"Really? I would have thought Jankyn was only about twenty."

"Och, aye, I forgot about him."

There was an odd, strained note to Mora's voice that made Bridget suspect Mora was lying, but she decided not to remark upon it. "How old is the laird?"

"Wheesht, lass, I cannae recall. Such things are of little interest to me. Ye should ask the laird. Then, again, what does it matter? He be hale and handsome. Blood still runs hot, aye?" Mora chuckled when Bridget blushed. "Has all his teeth, too. Nay, age doesnae matter. Tis the heart of the mon what counts, nay how long it has been beating."

"There is some truth in that. Yet, I *do* wish to have children."

"I am sure our laird will give ye many fine bairns. Tis just that we, MacMartins and MacNachtons alike, have been too much alone. Nay matter how good ye think your bloodline is, ye need to add something fresh to it now and again. When there were more of us it wasnae so verra bad, but, now? Weel, unless my David leaves these hills to find himself a wife, he will ne'er wed. There isnae a woman of marrying age here about who isnae closely related to him, e'en if they were not all older than he is. Ye will give us the fresh blood we need."

Bridget really wished Mora would stop mentioning blood so much. "So, ye think the laird *is* capable?"

"I would have thought ye could answer that for yourself. The way ye two are so often pressed together, the proof of his capability couldnae be ignored, I be thinking."

Another blush stung Bridget's cheeks. She grimaced when she heard Mora laugh heartily as she walked away. It was embarrassing to know that others had witnessed the embraces she and Cathal had shared. She was failing miserably in keeping the man at a distance. It was no wonder everyone who spoke to her seemed convinced she would marry Cathal.

As she started toward the stables, one of the many buildings cluttering the bailey that she intended to inspect very closely, Bridget knew she had to come to some decision about Cathal. Once she had realized how little control she had over her own passions, she had decided to find out everything she could about the MacNachtons. There could yet be some secret to uncover that would cool the heat in her blood. It was becoming clear, however, that everyone kept the secrets of Cambrun very well indeed.

Inside the stable she found clean hay, some very fine horses, and, of course, darkness. It seemed cruel to keep the animals confined in the dark, but then Bridget lit one of the lanterns kept by the door and looked around. There were several iron-barred openings in the walls of the stables, but someone had closed the outside shutters. After walking deeper into the stables, inspecting the horses, Bridget suddenly felt a presence and understood why the stable was so dark. She tensed as she held the lantern up and slowly looked around, wondering which MacNachton was watching her. It was difficult to control an involuntary gasp when the light from her lantern revealed a pair of gleaming yellow eyes. She had to tell herself, several times, that it was simply the light from the lantern which made those eyes seem to glow before her heartbeat slowed to a more normal pace.

"Ye dinnae belong here," said Edmee as she stepped into the arc of light from the lantern.

"Nay? Why shouldnae I be here?" asked Bridget, feigning ignorance of Edmee's warning. "I am nay upsetting the horses."

"Dinnae play the fool. Ye ken what I mean. Ye should leave Cambrun."

"I believe your laird would prefer me to stay."

"Och, aye, to help him fulfill his plan to destroy us."

"Ah, weel, as I understood it, his plan is to save you, to save the MacNachtons."

"We dinnae need saving." Edmee moved until she was barely a foot away. "To think some weak Outsider could save us is laughable. Cathal should stay to his own. He should turn away from the stain of Outsider blood in his veins and return to the fold. He should seek a wife amongst us, one who can help him find his way back to his true heritage."

"And that would be ye, would it?" Bridget realized she loathed the idea of Cathal marrying this woman, or any other woman for that matter. "Yet, if he wished ye for his wife, wouldnae he have chosen ye by now?" Bridget fought the urge to step back from the feral look of fury that tightened the lines of Edmee's face.

"He would if ye left. Without ye about, he would give up this mad plan and turn to me."

"He wants bairns. As I understand it, there is a verra good chance ye wouldnae give him any."

"What do we need those for? Squalling, filthy things."

"Without bairns ye *will* die out, the clan *will* vanish." The smile Edmee gave her made Bridget feel distinctly uneasy.

"Nay, not for a verra long time. There are more years than ye can count left to us ere the lack of bairns becomes a true danger. Tis just his Outsider blood speaking to Cathal, the fear of his own mortality that is the curse of his mother's blood. Cathal will be dust in his grave ere the rest of us, who are *true* MacNachtons, need to fear for our end as a clan."

Bridget had given up the idea that the MacNachtons were the walking dead, yet Edmee's sneered words seemed to imply that they might be. Why would the woman speak so scornfully of mortality, implying it was a curse suffered only by Outsiders? Inwardly, she shook her head. Edmee was trying to frighten her. There was life in the MacNachtons. Bridget was sure of that, could sense it. It might not be the sort of life she was accustomed to, but it *was* there. Then Bridget recalled Mora's evasiveness when she had asked her how old Jankyn and the laird were, and she frowned.

"Are ye saying MacNachtons live a long time?" she asked.

Edmee laughed, but it was not a pleasant, joyful sound. "Ye might say that. We arenae the weaklings ye Outsiders are. We are stronger, faster, superior in every way."

"Including in vanity, it appears."

"We have a right to our vanity. We are in need of nothing from ye or your kind. There is naught ye can do that we cannae do better."

"Truly? Ah me, this lantern grows most heavy. Mayhap we should step outside, into the sun, and discuss this further."

Bridget tensed when Edmee snarled at her and reached for her. Instead of the attack she anticipated, however, her sight of the infuriated Edmee was suddenly blocked by a tall, slim figure. An instant later, Edmee seemed to fly through the air. Bridget gasped as the woman hit one of the posts holding up the roof of the stables, certain that the woman was dead. It took a full minute for Bridget to believe her own eyes when a softly cursing Edmee got to her feet and brushed off her skirts.

"I wasnae going to kill the little fool, Jankyn," Edmee said.

Jankyn shrugged as he stepped back to stand at Bridget's side. "Ye could have. Ye were angry."

A chill went down Bridget's spine. If the ease and speed with which Jankyn had tossed Edmee so far was an example of a MacNachton's strength, he was right. Edmee could have killed her. Bridget was not sure it would have been the accident Jankyn implied, however.

"I am still angry." Edmee languidly combed her fingers through her hair, cleaning it of bits of hay. "Cathal's plan is pure madness. He wants to destroy all that makes us strong. How can ye stand beside him in this?"

"Because he is my laird," Jankyn replied. "Because he is right. We are dying, Edmee. A long, slow death to be sure, but we are still dying. There hasnae been a child born to a Pureblood in two score years."

Forty? Bridget looked at Jankyn, who flashed her a cocky grin before returning his full attention to Edmee. That grin did not soothe her. If no bairn had been born to the Purebloods in forty years that meant Jankyn was that age or older. He looked little older than her. Bridget decided she did not really want to think about that.

"Ye have been of breeding age for at least that long," Jankyn continued, scowling at Edmee. "Despite the many hours ye spend in rutting and the vast army of bed partners ye have had, your womb has ne'er quickened. None of the women of the Purebloods has quickened with child in far too many years. Nay, not e'en those women who arenae so particular about the blood of the mon they rut with. Cathal's father only seeded one child in his Outsider wife. E'en the MacMartins have few bairns. We have bred amongst ourselves for too long, Edmee. None of the gifts we have are worth anything if there is no bairn to carry on the name, the blood, or the traditions of our forefathers. We have become naught but a group of barren women and weak-seeded men.

That *is* death, Edmee. Aye, it might be long in coming, but 'tis still death."

"Better death than to become a weak, puling Outsider," hissed Edmee, and then she was gone.

"She is gone," Bridget whispered, feeling foolish for stating the obvious, yet unsettled by Edmee's abrupt disappearance.

"Aye." Jankyn scowled after Edmee for a moment before turning his gaze upon Bridget. "There are tunnels connecting nearly every building in Cambrun. Ye *are* stirring up a lot of trouble, arenae ye?"

"Me? I just came to explore this building. She is the one stirring up trouble. She wants Cathal, I think."

"She does, e'en though his Outsider blood sickens her. Edmee would like to be the lady of Cambrun. She has ne'er been able to convince Cathal of that, however. It doesnae help her cause that she makes her contempt of his mother so verra clear. Cathal has ne'er intended to wed with a MacNachton, either. He wants bairns."

Bridget frowned at him. "There is a wee bit more to me than a womb, ye ken."

"Och, aye, a wee bit." He laughed when she softly hissed in annoyance, then grew serious. "O'er the last few days 'tis evident neither of ye will suffer in the making of a bairn." He only briefly smiled at her blushes. "Tis a blessing, that. And where is the insult in a mon thinking a woman a good choice as mother to his bairns?"

None, she supposed, but she was not about to admit it. "There should be more."

"Ah, poor lass, so unsure of yourself." He nimbly danced out of her reach when she tried to hit him. "The only thing I will say is that, compared to the rest of us, Cathal is nearly a monk. He isnae one to be caught in embraces with a lass round every corner. And, aye, mayhap he thinks too much on a bairn, but 'tisnae just an heir he seeks, is it? Tis the salvation of his people. Tis no small thing that. So, do ye cease teasing the fool and say aye?"

Bridget sighed. "Tisnae an easy thing to decide. Tisnae just my fate, but that of my children I must consider and ye ask me to do it in but a week."

"We are but a wee bit different."

"Och, aye, ye are that."

"But, that shouldnae trouble a Callan, I think." He sighed when she did not respond to that remark. "We arenae what ye think we are, lass. Nay exactly. I dinnae believe the soulless dead breed bairns." He smiled gently at the look of consternation that briefly crossed her face. "We are but different. Cursed in some ways, blessed in others, but 'tis Cathal who must tell ye the tale." He tensed at the sound of a bell. "Later, lass," he murmured and disappeared into the shadows.

A moment later Bridget understood his abrupt leavetaking. One by one the shutters were opened, filling the stables with sunlight. She sighed and extinguished the lantern, returning it to its hook by the door. As she walked back to the keep, she absently returned the greetings of the MacMartins she passed. Once inside the keep she made her way to the doors of the great hall and stared at Cathal where he sat at the laird's table talking to two of the MacMartins and a man called Manus, one of all too few MacNachtons who were like Cathal.

Cathal was so beautiful he made her heart ache. His touch set her blood afire. He was a wealthy laird, something which would greatly please her kinsmen. Unfortunately, this particular matrimonial prize came with a few less than acceptable characteristics. He couldnae abide the sun, had fangs, was a little too fond of undercooked meat, and it appeared that most of his kinsmen lived in caves beneath the keep. All of that worried her, but not enough to make her walk away from him.

She softly cursed as she walked toward him. She loved

him. It was that simple and that complicated. Bridget was not sure when she had lost her heart to him, but suspected it explained why she had not fled Cambrun screaming in terror when she had first begun to suspect what the MacNachtons were. She had made only one rather weak attempt to escape. She stopped by his chair and placed her hand over his heart.

"Ye *are* alive,"she murmured and felt him tense.

Cathal studied her face closely and felt his hopes rise despite her words. "Aye, lass." He put his hand at the back of her neck and pulled her close to him to add softly, "And the only one who can put your wee bonnie soul at risk is ye."

"Weel, that is a comfort, I suppose."

"So, have ye decided ye will have me then?"

"Aye." She did not resist when he tugged her down onto his lap and kissed her while the other men cheered and hooted.

"Might I ask what changed your mind?"

Bridget had no intention of telling him what was in her heart, not until she got some hint as to what he felt for her. "Ye kiss weel."

"Thank ye, but I think there is another reason."

"Aye. I recently decided that I best take ye as I dinnae seem to want anyone else to have ye."

He kissed her again. It was a start. Cathal finally admitted that he wanted more, much more, from her, but he could be patient. She would soon belong to him in body and name. He was willing to work for the rest, for her heart and soul.

Six

"Are ye verra certain about this?"

Cathal frowned and looked at Jankyn even as he continued to brush his hair. As always, Jankyn was perched somewhere, this time upon the ledge of the deepset window in the room. In the two days since Bridget had agreed to marry him, Cathal had seen little of Jankyn. Until the man had entered the ledger room Cathal had been using as his bedchamber, he had feared Jankyn would not stand up with him at his wedding.

"Aye, I am certain," Cathal replied. "I had thought ye agreed with this, as weel. Wheesht, ye were the one to suggest it."

"I ken it, and I havenae changed my mind about your plan. Tis a good one."

"But ye have changed your mind about Bridget?" Cathal carefully set his brush down, knowing he should heed whatever Jankyn had to say, but deeply reluctant to hear it.

"Aye and nay." Jankyn sighed and dragged his fingers through his hair. "I like the lass. She doesnae shy from the truth about us. Aye, she tried to flee once, but I am nay sure that was only because of what she thought we were. She wasnae in a blind terror, either. Tis just that, weel, have ye noticed anything a wee bit odd about her?"

"Aside from the fact that she has agreed to marry a mon who avoids the sun and whose kinsmen live in caves?"

"Aye, aside from that," Jankyn said, the hint of laughter in his voice.

Cathal suddenly recalled the way Bridget had acted when she had awakened her first day at Cambrun, that odd fleeting vision he had had of something different in her face. He inwardly shook his head. It *could* have been some odd shadow caused by the candlelight. It was not something he wished to speak about, either.

"Odd in what way?"

"She hisses and verra weel, too. She scratches, swipes at one with those verra sharp nails of hers when ye startle her. Ye didnae see her run, but, trust me, she is verra swift and sure of foot. E'en with the full moon, most Outsiders move cautiously. The night and the shadows didnae slow her down at all. She kenned I was there ere she saw me. And, the fact that she saw me in the shadows is, weel, unusual. She dances in the moonlight. E'en though there was no sound to warn her, she kenned something had happened to her people. I watched her tense, crouch, and look about. Tis as if she scented danger upon the air."

And she purrs, Cathal thought, but only said, "Some people have keener senses about such things."

"There is something about the name Callan that picks at me, rouses my curiosity. I havenae been able to find out why, however. It may take some time."

"So, what are ye asking? Ye wish me to wait ere I marry her?"

"It might be best. Give me time to find out about the Callans."

"It might weel be for the best, but I willnae wait."

"Ye want her."

"Aye, I want her. I cannae rest for the wanting of her."

"And if there is something, weel, different about the Callans, something in the bloodline?"

"As there is in ours? I doubt that. Bridget is much akin to the MacMartins. She eats what they do, walks about freely in the sun, and all the rest. If there is something odd in the Callan clan, 'tisnae that which will alter my plan. The Callans obviously dinnae hide away at Dunsmuir as we hide here."

Jankyn nodded. "Fair enough. Do ye want me to continue to discover all I can about the Callans?"

Cathal hesitated only briefly. He hoped Bridget would tell him if there was something he ought to know about her clan, but he understood the habit of secrecy all too well. It would be best, however, if he knew all about the Callans. If nothing else, it would be best to be armed with such knowledge, good or bad, when he finally met her family.

"Aye, continue. I cannae be sure my bride will tell me all, or if she e'en kens that there is aught different about her family. We ken all too weel the importance of holding fast to our secrets. Yet, I dinnae really like surprises, either."

"Agreed. Take heart in the fact that she kens your grand plan for the future of the MacNachtons yet clearly sees no hindrance in helping ye fulfill it. I do. As ye said, in the important ways, she could be one of the MacMartins. Far more fertile, though. I did learn that her cousin Barbara has been wed but four years and has four children."

"A bairn a year?" Cathal wanted children, badly, but he did not think such constant breeding could be good for a woman.

"Nay. Two sets of twins. Fat, healthy bairns. One pair of lads and one of lasses. As I said, fertile stock."

Cathal briefly closed his eyes and fought down a sudden swell of emotion. He wanted Bridget for many reasons, her ability to give him children no longer his prime concern. Yet, he would be lying if he did not admit that the possibility of her being very fertile indeed thrilled him right down to his toes. He shook free of the feeling and idly brushed his hands over his black-and-silver doublet.

"Ye look verra fine," drawled Jankyn. "I am sure your wee bride will have no complaint." Jankyn nimbly jumped down from his perch and started toward the door. "Shall we go to the great hall now?"

"What of the Purebloods?" Cathal asked as he followed Jankyn out of the room and walked by his side to the great hall.

"Ah, weel, none of them are much of a mind to celebrate this wedding," replied Jankyn. "Some understand, but wish it wasnae so, some understand but doubt the need, thinking all will right itself in time—"

"Blind fools," muttered Cathal.

"True, sadly true. Some dinnae care one way or t'other. Some hate it, but feel 'tis your choice. And then there are the ones like Scymynd and Edmee. They talk, a lot, and none of it good for you. I just cannae say which of the other wee groups are listening and agreeing. Tis weel kenned that I stand by ye in this and that makes some hesitant to speak honestly with me."

Pausing in the doorway of the guest hall, Cathal studied the people gathered there. He could feel the tension in the air. It was also clear that everyone had gathered in groups, people staying with those who thought as they did. At the moment it appeared that his plan was breaking his clan apart instead of saving it. He could only pray that this lack of unity was temporary. Nodding at each person who greeted him, Cathal made his way toward the priest, his cousin James, a man of two worlds as he was.

"A storm is brewing," said James.

"Aye," agreed Cathal. "Change often stirs unrest. My father had some trouble, too, though nay as much as this."

"The occasional such marriage can be shrugged aside as

an aberration. Ye have made it clear that ye intend to make this custom. I also think Scymynd feels a halfling isnae good enough to be the laird here. He has always coveted the position. Ah, and Edmee cannae swallow the thought that ye would prefer an Outsider to her in all her bonnie purity of blood."

"And what do ye think, Cousin?"

"I think they have all gotten too blood proud, too vain, thus blind to the truth. I can understand how hard it must be to consider the loss of some of the gifts our forefathers gave us. Yet, one oftimes has to give up something to survive. What ye do now, ye do for their sake."

Cathal heard a noise behind him and saw Bridget enter the great hall. "Weel, nay *all* for their sake."

He ignored James's soft laughter as he watched Bridget walk toward him. Lithe and lovely, she moved with a sensuous grace. Her tawny gold hair had been left loose, hanging in long, thick waves to her slim hips and decorated with green silk ribbons to match her gown. She was so different from him, in size, in looks, in heritage, and in blood, but he was certain they were a perfect match. Cathal intended to make her see that truth as well.

After one quick glance around the great hall, she kept her gaze fixed upon him. Cathal could sense her unease. She had enough sense to know that not many of his kinsmen wished her well. He wanted to promise her that everything would be well, but he could not lie to her. He could not be sure it would be or that she would believe some soothing but empty words. Bridget was risking a lot to marry him. She was too quick-witted not to know that. Cathal was not only flattered by that; he felt hopeful. For Bridget to do this had to mean that she cared for him, felt more than lust for him. There was a good chance that the seed of affection had already taken root in her heart. Cathal prayed he had the skill to nurture it well and make it grow.

Bridget slipped her hand into Cathal's and felt Mora move to stand beside her. She wished someone from her own family was with her at this important time, yet was also pleased that she faced this alone. It had taken but one look at the gathering of MacNachtons to know trouble was brewing. There was no telling what form that trouble would take or how dangerous it could become. She could not drag her family into the middle of it all. She was willing to put herself at risk to stay with Cathal, but not her family. When the conflict was resolved, she would invite her family to Cambrun to celebrate her wedding and not before.

She knelt with Cathal before the priest. It was obvious that Father James had MacNachton blood in him. The fact that one of their ilk could hold a place in the church eased several of her lingering concerns. She repeated her vows and struggled to ignore the whirlwind of conflicting emotions she could sense in the air around her. When the vows were made and Cathal had kissed her, there was some cheering and Bridget tried to find some comfort in that. That the clan was divided by her marriage was not good, but at least it was not united against her.

The MacMartins soundly congratulated her and Cathal, as did the half dozen people Edmee scornfully called halflings. Some of the Purebloods did as well and some were merely polite. It was the group with Scymynd and Edmee that troubled her the most. They did not even pretend to welcome the marriage. When toasts were made, that group was bold in their refusal to join in them. Bridget began to wonder why they had even attended the wedding and had the sinking feeling that their reasons would only stir up more trouble.

"I should ask them to leave," murmured Cathal as he took Bridget's hand in his and held it against his thigh while he watched Scymynd spread his poisonous opinions through the crowd.

Bridget knew Cathal was tense despite the languid way he

sprawled in his seat at the laird's table. "I think that would be seen as an insult and, mayhap, be used against us."

"Tis what I think as weel. Tis all that binds my tongue. Though it galls me to ignore his insults to ye, and me, I see no gain in acting against them right now."

"Nay. In truth, it may cost him more to act so poorly at his own laird's wedding, to behave so ungraciously whilst ye behave graciously." She grimaced when Cathal looked at her and cocked one eyebrow. "Tis a possibility."

"Aye. Mayhap. A wee one. Now, I must go speak to James."

"Twas good of the church and Father James to allow us to marry at night."

"Verra good. And verra expensive," he drawled. "I will be but a moment."

Cathal had only just disappeared into the crowd and Bridget was just turning to speak to Mora when she sensed someone standing behind her. She did not really need to hear Mora's whispered curse to know that this someone was not there to wish her a long life and much happiness. It was no surprise when Edmee moved from behind her and sat down in the laird's chair.

"Ye are a fool if ye think ye are woman enough to satisfy such a mon," said Edmee.

"He must think I will serve him weel enough or he wouldnae have chosen me," replied Bridget.

"He didnae choose ye. He chose your womb."

That stung, but Bridget swiftly pushed aside that twist of pain. She would not give this woman the satisfaction of knowing her dart had drawn blood. Bridget had to believe there was more, if only a strong passion. It was what she was gambling her whole future on.

"There isnae a mon alive who doesnae consider such things when choosing a bride." Bridget took a sip of wine only to nearly choke on it when Scymynd appeared beside Edmee, his feral eyes aglow with hatred and fury.

"The mon doesnae deserve to be our laird," hissed Scymynd. "He befouls our nest by taking ye as his bride."

Bridget slammed her goblet down on the table and leapt to her feet, enraged by this insult to her name, to her clan. "The blood of a Callan is every bit as good as yours. We have held our lands since before the Romans built their walls to affirm their grasp upon the Sassenach lands. And no Callan has e'er had to spend his life huddled in a cave."

The moment the words left her lips, Bridget knew she had gone too far. Fury changed Scymynd's face into something that was still beautiful, but also frightening. He snarled and bared his fangs. If the man those villagers had caught and killed had looked like this, it was little wonder they had believed him to be a demon. She could not fully suppress a squeak of alarm when suddenly he had her by the front of her gown and was holding her several feet off the ground.

"Ye *dare* to lay hands upon my bride?!"

Bridget was just realizing that that furious growl had come from Cathal when she was abruptly released. Strong hands caught her around the waist, preventing her from falling to the floor. She caught a brief glimpse of Jankyn as he set her aside. Stunned, she watched a man who was Cathal, but was not, toss Scymynd halfway across the great hall as if the man weighed nothing. Could that snarling, fang-baring man truly be the man she had just married?

A melee erupted and Bridget watched in horrified fascination as the beautiful, elegant MacNachtons changed before her eyes into a snarling pack of wild animals. The way they set upon each other was alarming. It should have left the great hall soaked in blood and cluttered with the dead and dying, but, time and again, the MacNachtons shook off mortal blows and returned to the fray.

Mora and her son David grabbed Bridget and dragged her beneath the table where several other MacMartins hid. Bridget huddled there watching the battle from beneath the edge of the linen cloth covering the table. Here was the truth she had only guessed at. Here was the feral beast hidden beneath the beauty, the inhuman strength that allowed a man to toss another across a room as if he weighed no more than a bairn. The speed with which they moved, the sounds they made, and the way they rose up uninjured from blows that would have put any mortal man into a grave, all revealed the truth she had tried so very hard to ignore. She would not be able to ignore it now and she feared what that might do to her future with Cathal.

Then two men rolled by in front of her eyes. One man sank his long teeth into the neck of the other, who howled out in fury and pain. Bridget gasped as her memory of the night her party was attacked abruptly returned. Now she could see clearly beyond the lingering image of swirling shadows and blood, and heartily wished she could not. She was no longer surprised she had fainted. Now she understood the terror, the horror, upon the faces of those thieves before they died.

"Now, m'lady, ye dinnae need to worry o'er our laird," said Mora, patting Bridget on the back. "He can hold his own."

"Do they do this often?" Bridget asked, surprised at how normal her voice sounded for she was cold and trembling inside.

"Nay. Oh, there are fights here and there, now and then. Tis what men do, aye? They like a wee punch and wrestle from time to time. And, weel, these lads can really only have a fair one with each other. This will knock a wee bit of sense into some of them."

"Tis because of me. I am nay saving Cathal's clan as he wished," she whispered, "but destroying it."

"Nay, nay. Tis but the changes that must come which stirs this up. Change ne'er sets easy on a person's shoulders. Most all of them have the wit to see that 'tis necessary, but they will fight it for a wee while ere they settle to it. Tis only natural."

Natural was an odd word to use when talking about the MacNachtons, Bridget thought.

"Ah, there ye be, now. Father James be seeing an end to it."

Bridget watched the priest stride through the melee, a half dozen men at his side. He knocked men down, tossed men aside, and bellowed for calm and good sense. Despite all she had seen, she still found it startling to see a man of God acting very much like the ones all others would swiftly curse as demons. Then, as suddenly as it had begun, it was over. Scymynd, Edmee, and their allies were gone. The Purebloods who remained stood looking uncomfortable as Father James lectured them. Bridget saw her husband look for her and shivered. The memory of how the MacNachtons had dealt with those thieves was still clear in her mind, clear and terrifying. This incident had given the chilling memories credence, ensured that she would not be able to dismiss it all as a bad dream. She now knew exactly what her husband was, what he was capable of. How could she live with that? And, yet, how could she not?

Seven

"Weel, this was a fine show to put on afore your new bride," grumbled James as he frowned at Cathal and Jankyn.

Cathal winced and noticed Jankyn did as well. "Scymynd put his hands on her," Cathal said. "Ye saw what he did. Ye ken weel what he is capable of. He could have killed her with but a flick of his wrist."

James sighed and nodded. "I ken it. I but pray ye werenae thinking to introduce her to our ways gently, slowly."

"Bridget has guessed what we are," said Jankyn.

"There is a sharp difference between guessing at something and seeing the hard truth of it, lad," said James.

"Where is she?" asked Cathal, recognizing the truth of James's words and suddenly feeling a chill of fear.

"Beneath the table with Mora and her lad waiting to see if it is safe to come out," replied James.

Cathal gently strode over to the table and crouched down to look at Bridget. She was pale and trembling slightly, her beautiful blue-green eyes wide with shock. He could see her struggling with her fear of all she had just seen and felt his own fear grow stronger. The thought of losing her was terrifying, more so because she would be fleeing *who* he was. There was no way he could change that to keep her at his side. It would be a battle lost before it had even begun. He held his hand out to her.

"Come, lass, 'tis all quiet now," he said.

"They tore their throats out," Bridget whispered, staring into her husband's beautiful face.

"Nay, sweetling. Look about. There are no dead here."

"The thieves. I remember it all now. Your kinsmen tore their throats out."

The pain of losing her began to creep through his body, but Cathal struggled to fight off that encroaching sense of defeat. He knelt down and rubbed his suddenly sweaty palms over his thighs. There was no point in lying. Even if he could bring himself to start his marriage with a lie, she would not believe him. She was too clever and had seen too much.

"Aye, I suspicion they did, or something verra like that. Those men sought to kill ye, Bridget. They did kill the others who traveled with ye. Come." He held his hand out to her again. "Again, I swear to ye, I will ne'er hurt ye."

A part of Bridget told her to get up and run, very fast and very far. It would be the sensible thing to do. She had just been shown how little she really knew this man and what she had learned was hardly comforting. That sensible part of her had every right to urge self-preservation, but the voice of her heart proved louder and more demanding. Uttering a soft cry, she flung herself into his arms, clinging to him in the blind belief that he would keep her safe. He wrapped his arms around her and held her almost too tightly as he stood up. He kissed the top of her head and rubbed his hands up and down her back, his touch smoothing away her lingering fear. Cautiously, she lifted her head from his broad chest, looked around the great hall, and sighed.

"This wasnae quite the celebration I had anticipated,"

she murmured as she watched the MacMartins and the MacNachtons who had stayed behind begin to clean up the mess.

"Dinnae worry, m'lady," Mora said as she moved to stand beside Bridget. "We will set things aright and still have our feast." She looked Bridget over carefully. "Why dinnae ye and the laird hie yourselves off to your chambers? I will bring ye up a full tray of food and drink in a few minutes. Ye have said your vows and heard the toasts." She grinned and winked. "We can celebrate without ye right enough, aye?"

Keeping one arm wrapped firmly around Bridget's slim shoulders, Cathal nodded and started out of the hall only to be stopped by a grinning Jankyn. Despite the large smile Jankyn wore, Cathal could see the concern and unease in his cousin's eyes. He felt the same. Bridget had come to him, but he knew everything was not as it had been before the fight.

"I havenae yet kissed the bride," Jankyn said.

Bridget looked up at Jankyn as he grasped her hands in his. He was the beautifully, annoying, often smiling, Jankyn again. Then she looked into his eyes and nearly gasped. He was nervous, uncertain. She had seen what he was all too clearly and he was no longer certain of her acceptance. She rose up on her tiptoes and kissed him.

"Enough," said Cathal, nudging Jankyn aside just as his cousin began to wrap his arms around Bridget, clearly intending to help himself to a very hearty kiss.

Jankyn's actions had started something, however, and Cathal had to endure several more interruptions before he got Bridget out of the great hall. He understood that his brethren who remained in the great hall sought to reassure him of their support. Some probably even hoped to reassure Bridget, to soften the sting of Scymynd's scorn and dislike. None of that made him pleased to watch his bride being kissed by other men and he was relieved when he finally got her safely behind the door to his bedchamber. Then he recalled all she had seen tonight and inwardly grimaced as he urged her into a seat before the fire.

"Ye *are* safe with me, Bridget," he said as he sat down in the chair next to her, turning it slightly to face her squarely.

"Ye dinnae have to keep saying that, Cathal," she replied. "I do ken it or I wouldnae be here, would I?" She realized she needed to believe that, needed to have complete confidence in her own judgment about this man. It was the only way she could survive the trials ahead of them.

"Thank ye for that." He sighed and dragged a hand through his hair. "I ken ye had guessed a lot about us ere ye agreed to marry me."

"Aye, I had. One doesnae have to be at Cambrun long to see the differences. I tallied them and, mostly, ignored them."

"Except for the time ye tried to flee." He took her hands in his.

"Ah, aye. Weel, that wasnae only because of those differences. I was feeling a wee bit cornered, too, ye ken. There was the strangeness, the threatening conversation with Scymynd and Edmee, your persistent talk of marriage, and, then, that night, I heard the howling. Watching your kinsmen race out into the night was one thing too many at that precise moment." She shrugged. "So, I decided to leave."

Cathal released her hands, stood up, and leaned against the rough stone encircling the fireplace. He had to wait to try and explain things, however, for Mora arrived with food and drink. Once it was set out on the table placed between the chairs and Mora had left, Cathal poured himself and Bridget some wine. He returned to his place against the wall and took a deep drink to steady himself.

"The MacNachtons have lived in these hills for hundreds of years, so long that I am nay sure I believe the tales of how we came to be here or be what we are. The how or why isnae really important. We arenae the walking dead, soulless creatures who refuse to stay buried and feast upon the blood or flesh of the living."

"I was ne'er able to hold firm to that thought," Bridget said, smiling faintly. "Ye just seemed too, weel, too alive. Alive and warm."

"We are simply a different breed. We are stronger, faster, and live longer."

"How much longer?"

"Weel, there havenae been many like me, ones bred of both worlds. Only half a dozen of us now and far fewer in the past. The ones who did come before me all seemed to live more than a hundred years. Some many more, some but a few more. I just cannae say for certain."

"Ah, a great age, nonetheless."

"Aye. Tis one reason I hesitated to take a wife from outside the clan. There seemed little doubt that I would long outlive my mate. I am but one-and-thirty now. When my mother died, the grief my father endured was hard to watch. Worse, he kenned he would endure being alone for many, many years. He didnae kill himself, but he risked death at every turn and finally met it five years ago."

"He loved your mother so verra much?" she asked softly.

"Aye, I believe he did, but 'tis more than that. We mate and, if 'tis a true mating, the loss of that mate is like losing part of one's soul." He grimaced. "It sounds most strange, yet 'tis difficult to put into words. My brethren can behave most promiscuously, but ne'er after they mate."

Bridget suspected there was something he was not telling her, but she decided not to prod him. "How long do the Purebloods live?"

"A verra long time. A MacNachton ages slowly. Tis because we heal so quickly. There are verra few ways to kill a Pureblood MacNachton. A broken neck, or a wound that causes the blood to flow so swiftly e'en our ability to heal quickly might not be enough to save us. A wound directly to the heart. Beheading, burning. Weel, ye must see what I mean."

"Aye. It takes work. But, ye arenae a Pureblood."

"Nay, but 'tis much the same. I heal a wee bit more slowly 'tis all and I age verra much as an Outsider does. I think the Purebloods fear that most of all, fear losing all those years of living and facing a greater risk of mortal wounds, nay matter how small. I confess, when I first realized that I wouldnae live as long as Jankyn or Scymynd, I was angry, felt I had been cheated of something most grand. My father asked me to tell him one thing our brethren had accomplished with that gift. I had no answer for there was nothing. He said 'twasnae the length of one's life that mattered, just what one did with those years. And, I can still hear him say, as he stood beside my mother's fresh grave, that a long life was naught but a curse if one was alone."

He set his wine goblet on the table, knelt by Bridget's feet, and took her hands in his, pressing a kiss upon each small, soft palm before looking at her. "What ye saw happen to those thieves and what ye saw tonight is a part of me. I cannae deny it. I cannae deny that there have been MacNachtons who have behaved verra much like the creatures of some nightmare. There *is* a feral part of me, of us. It comes out in the hunt, in battle, in anger. It has been a verra long time, however, since MacNachtons were a threat to innocent Outsiders, although I fear Scymynd would like to be so again. They used to call us the Nightriders because we raced out of these hills at night and death always followed, though nay in the ways and numbers the tales would have ye believe. I think Scymynd wants those days to return."

"What of the sun, Cathal? Can that kill ye?"

"Aye, eventually. Tis as if the sun feeds upon us, steals the life right out of us. It burns us up. A Pureblood can die rather quickly if caught out in the sun. I can endure it for a while, but it does leave me feeling weak and ill."

"And what of whatever children we may be blessed with?"

"I cannae say. There isnae any way to ken what traits will weaken, which will linger, and which will disappear. My cousin Connall is of the same paternal and maternal bloodline as I am, but is different. James is born of a halfblood and an Outsider. He can endure quite a lot of daylight, but he still suffers a wee bit."

Bridget slipped her hands free of his grasp and took his face in her hands. "It matters not. I chose ye. I have said vows afore God. Tis good to ken that I deal with people, nay demons, but it still doesnae matter. Ye are my husband."

There was a lot more she wanted to know, but decided now was not the time to ask too many questions. She would let him cling to a few of his secrets. She was clinging to a few of her own.

Cathal rose up on his knees and kissed her, gently at first, but his desire for her quickly grew hot and strong. He picked her up out of the chair and stood her in front of the fire. Slowly, pausing now and then to give into the urge to kiss her again, he undressed her. Smiling faintly at her blushes when she finally stood naked before him, he looked her over. Her breasts looked just big enough to nestle sweetly into the palms of his hands. Her waist was small, her hips gently rounded, and her legs long, slender, and strong. There was a hint of gold to her beautiful skin that had him aching to touch it, taste it. His gaze settled upon the neat vee of gold between her slim thighs and he quickly began to shed his own clothes.

The embarrassment Bridget felt over standing naked before Cathal began to rapidly fade as he undressed. By the time he stood as naked as she, Bridget was nearly shaking with the need to touch him. She would never have thought that a man as beautiful as Cathal could look even more beautiful naked, but he did. He was all lean, taut muscle from his broad, smooth chest to his long, well-shaped legs. And all of it covered with that lovely fair skin. A thin line of black hair started at his navel, thickened at his groin, and thinned again to lightly coat his legs. Her gaze went to his groin again and she felt a tiny flicker of uncertainty. That particular part of him looked a lot larger than she had anticipated and she became acutely aware of how much smaller she was than Cathal.

"Twill be fine, love," Cathal said as he picked her up in his arms and carried her to the bed. "I cannae promise ye that there will be no pain, but I will do all I can to make it but a small one, quickly done and quickly forgotten."

"It must be done." She trembled with delight when he joined her on the bed and took her into his arms. "I just suddenly felt rather small."

"Ye *are* rather small," he teased. "Small but exquisite. Utterly beautiful. Trust me, sweetling. We will fit together perfectly. I kenned it almost from the start."

Bridget wrapped her arms around his neck when he kissed her. The feel of his warm skin against her, the sensuous strokes of his tongue within her mouth, soon had her blood running hot. She cautiously teased at his tongue with her own. His low growl of approval prompted her to be even more bold. When he pulled his tongue back, but left his mouth open against hers, Bridget took it as an invitation and quickly accepted it. Bridget soon discovered that she loved the taste of him, enjoyed the fine tremors that went through his strong body with every stroke of her tongue. Just as she thought about touching those very sharp teeth with her tongue, he abruptly ended the kiss. He pressed his forehead against hers as he struggled to catch his breath. This sign that she had stirred his desire so fiercely gave Bridget a sense of pure feminine power. Something distinctly wild began to stir inside of her.

"Lass, ye learn much too quickly," Cathal said when he finally regained some semblance of control.

"That is a bad thing, is it?"

"Nay, a verra good thing." He began to kiss her throat. "But nay this night." He gently nipped her soft skin at the place where he could see the rhythm of her pulse. "Tonight I need to be gentle and kisses like that dinnae make me feel verra gentle at all."

Even as Bridget opened her mouth to speak, he covered her breasts with his elegant hands and she gasped. Beneath the light teasing caress of his long fingers her nipples grew taut and aching. When he slowly drew the hard tip of one deep into his mouth and suckled her, she buried her fingers into his thick hair and held him close. She suffered one brief moment of fear over the strength of the feelings he was stirring within her, then gave herself over to them.

Cathal was both astonished and delighted by the passion his new bride was revealing. He feasted upon her breasts, stroked her slim legs, and rubbed himself against her in a growing urgency. Every touch of her small soft hands, every slow scratch of her sharp nails, threatened to break the tight control upon his desire he struggled to maintain. He had wanted their first loving to be a slow, gentle union, but her every little purr, the soft growls that escaped her, increased his aching need to be one with her. He slid his hand down between her legs to stroke her, ready her for his possession, and her lithe little body arched off the bed at the first caress of his fingers. Cathal did not believe he had ever had a woman who was so responsive to his touch, so openly passionate.

Knowing he could not wait any longer, and beginning to think she was as desperate for their joining as he was, Cathal slowly entered her. He gritted his teeth, fighting the strong urge to thrust himself deep inside her tight heat again and again. When he reached her maidenhead, he hesitated, his whole body shaking with the strain of holding back. Taking a deep breath, he broke through that barrier and felt those sharp fingernails of hers dig into his back.

"The pain," he began, surprised he had enough wit to speak. "Bridget, have I hurt ye too sorely?"

It had hurt, but that sharp pain was already fading away. She wrapped her legs around him, felt him go deeper within her body, and echoed his gasp. Slowly, enjoying his warm skin beneath her hands, she stroked his back.

"It was but a brief hurt," she whispered. "Now, husband, I think ye need to show me it is worth it."

He laughed shakily and began to move. The brief dimming of her passion was short-lived, and she was soon moving in perfect harmony with him. Her response to him was so swift, her passion so hot and inviting, he lost control. When she cried out his name and her body shuddered and clenched around his, he poured himself into her. His release was so powerful that he barely stopped himself from indulging in the full mating many a MacNachton male craved. He swiftly moved his mouth from her neck and buried his face in her breasts. It seemed a long time before he began to come to his senses again. The gentle way she ran her hands over his back smoothed away his fear that she had been aware of what he had nearly done.

"Ye bit me," Bridget murmured, touching her neck, but finding no wound there.

Since there was no anger or alarm in her voice, Cathal relaxed. "Ye scratched me."

Bridget peered over his shoulder, but saw only a few faint marks. "Either I didnae scratch ye verra hard or ye have healed already." She ran her feet up and down his well shaped, strong calves as she savored the lingering tingles of passion in her body.

Cathal slipped from her grasp, dampened a cloth in the bowl of water set out on a table by the bed, and washed them both clean of the remnants of their passion. He smiled faintly at the way she blushed, charmed by the hint of modesty and heartily pleased that it was not strong enough to dim her desire when they made love. He sprawled on his back and pulled her into his arms, savoring the way she curled her body around his. Some benevolent spirit must have been smiling down on him the day Jankyn had set Bridget in his bed.

"So, lass, was it worth it?"

Bridget smiled against his shoulder. She could not believe she wanted him again, but she did. "Weel, 'tis hard to say," she murmured as she stroked his taut stomach. "A person shouldnae make a judgment too quickly and on so little evidence. Of course, if ye are too weak and weary—" She laughed when he abruptly reversed their positions and proceeded to show her that he was more than capable of giving her more "evidence."

Eight

Bridget caught herself humming as she strode through the village at Mora's side and shook her head. She was so happy, she made herself uneasy. Yet it was difficult to subdue the joy warming her heart. She had a beautiful husband who made her wild with desire, there had been no sign of trouble from the Purebloods for a month, and today was a sunny, warm day. The little village she strolled through was beautiful, the narrow valley it sat in was too lovely for words, and its fertile fields were plowed, planted, and already showed signs of a growing crop. She was so pleased with herself and her life, she could easily believe she was blessed.

She knew there were problems that still needed to be solved. Despite their silence, she doubted that all the Purebloods had accepted her or Cathal's plans for the clan's future. Although Cathal obviously shared her passion, there was no sign yet that he returned her love. She knew there were a few secrets remaining about the MacNachtons that Cathal did not seem inclined to share with her. She still had not gained the courage to share all of her secrets with him, either, and it often made her feel painfully guilty. At times, even when they were sprawled in each other's arms, limp, sated and sweaty, she got the feeling Cathal was not completely satisfied, that there was something he needed or wanted that she was not giving him.

"Wheesht, lass," Mora said, "your moods change near as often as the weather. One minute ye are all smiles, the next ye look as if ye have a pain in your belly."

Bridget was surprised into a laugh as she paused by a rough table where several bolts of cloth were displayed. "I was just thinking about how wonderful everything is. I was feeling so happy, it was nauseating." She smiled when Mora laughed. "I must say," she murmured as she ran her hands over some soft linen, "there are some verra fine goods for sale in this wee village."

"Aye, the MacNachtons have a taste for fine things and the coin to buy it. We have some verra skilled people, too." Mora frowned. "The word begins to spread. Tisnae so rare now to find people from outside the valley traveling here to buy our goods. Our weavers are much admired, ye ken."

"Oh, dear. Good for the people of the village, but—" Bridget hesitated, not sure how to express her concern.

"Aye. But. Tis why the laird seeks a few changes."

"Changes nay welcomed by all, although it has been verra quiet for a month."

"Verra quiet. I would like to think 'tis all settled, but I cannae. That Scymynd has always coveted the laird's chair and now he feels he has the cause needed to pull others to his side. He and a few others are verra prideful, e'en vain."

"Like Edmee." Bridget was pleased she had not even caught a glimpse of the woman since the wedding, but could not convince herself that Edmee had given up her desire to have Cathal for her own. Worse, Bridget had never garnered the courage to ask Cathal if Edmee had any good reason for thinking that she had some claim on him.

"The laird doesnae want that woman."

Bridget was a little startled at how well Mora had guessed her thoughts. "Ye read minds, do ye?"

"Nay. Tisnae hard to guess what any woman would think or feel when a woman like Edmee eyes her mon. When the laird was a randy wee lad, just coming into his monhood and all, he and Edmee tussled about some. But, then, Edmee has tussled about with near every mon at Cambrun. It didnae last long. She couldnae be faithful if she tried and I think she made her contempt of Outsiders too sharp and clear to see. She could ne'er seem to understand how that insulted the laird's mother, may God bless and keep her sweet soul, and the laird. And now Edmee insults ye, the laird's chosen wife."

"I would have thought she would be cleverer than that."

"Ye would think so. But, nay, she has that arrogance, that blind pride of blood. She thinks the laird ought to renounce his Outsider blood, seems to think he cannae help but do so. What worries me is that she will see his choice of bride as an insult to her."

"Aye, I suspect that she will, or already has."

"Tis all blind pride, for she kens all is lost now that ye and the laird are mated. He willnae, probably cannae, be hers now."

"I should like to believe that is the way of it, but, weel, she is verra beautiful." Bridget frowned when she saw how intently Mora was staring at her. "What is it?"

"Didnae the laird explain the mating ere he did it?"

Bridget blushed. "Weel, nay, but it wasnae really necessary."

"I dinnae think we are speaking of the same thing." Mora grasped Bridget by the hand. "Ye and I need to have a wee, private talk, a *verra* private talk." She saw the woman whose cloth they had been examining watching them from the doorway of her cottage. "Dinnae frown, Jean. We will be putting some coin in your palm ere we leave today, but I must have a wee private talk with my lady."

Jean smiled and nodded. "A new bride needs counsel now and again, aye? Go inside. I will make sure no one troubles ye. Have yourself a wee drink, too. I have some verra fine cider."

Mora nodded and led Bridget into the small cottage that obviously served as Jean's shop as well as her home. She let Mora pull her along until they reached a room at the rear of the cottage which served as the family's main living quarters. Bridget sat down at a large well-scrubbed table while Mora poured them each a tankard of cider. When Mora set a tankard in front of her, Bridget started to thank her only to be startled into silence when Mora closely examined her neck.

"Aye, I feared as much," muttered Mora as she sat down across from Bridget and took a hearty drink of cider. "That big fool. He hasnae completed the mating. Tisnae good. Nay, 'tisnae good at all. Especially if that bitch Edmee finds out."

"Mora, what are ye talking about? The marriage has been consummated. Quite thoroughly."

"Ah, lass, the laird obviously waits to be sure ye have fully accepted him, accepted him for what he is, *all* that he is. He hasnae given ye the bite yet."

Bridget frowned, not certain she liked the implications of that. "He does bite me."

"Love bites, wee nips, but nay *the bite.* Being that he is a halfling, mayhap he doesnae have to. I hadnae considered that. Halflings are always different in some way from Purebloods."

After taking a long drink of cider to calm her rising temper, Bridget said, "Tell me, Mora, what ye mean by *the mating* and *the bite.* Ye keep starting to tell me, then wander off the subject, and, weel, end up talking more to yourself than to me."

"Pardon. Tis nay widely kenned. Tis one of the Mac-Nachtons' most closely guarded secrets. I learned of it because, weel, a wee bit o'er twenty years ago I was in love with a Pureblood. Ye ken my son David, aye?"

"David is the son of a Pureblood? But he has reddish hair. I have seen him about during the day as weel."

"Aye, he is more our kind than theirs, but the MacNachton blood is in him. He is a strong, healthy lad, always was. And, though he can go about in the daylight, he has to be most careful, avoiding the full heat of the day and such as that. Seems way back in his father's line one of his ancestors mated with a halfling. The wee added bit of our blood is what has made my David so blessed. The laird has seen that my lad is educated and he will be verra important to the clan. Already is in many ways."

"Can ye tell me who his father is, or is that a secret?"

"Jankyn." Mora laughed briefly at Bridget's obvious shock, then sighed. "Aye, Jankyn doesnae look a day older than our son, aye? But he is my age. And that was some of the problem. Oh, I did love that lad."

"Jankyn is easy to love, e'en when ye wish ye had a thick stick in hand to clout him o'er the head."

Mora grinned and nodded, then grew serious. "It was both wondrous and awful, heaven and hell. Twas a delight when I was with him and a pure torment when I thought on the years ahead. I could see it as it is now all too clearly, with me as I am and him still looking like a bonnie lad of twenty. Ah, but he said he wished to marry me, and I was sorely tempted. Was near to saying aye when he told me the secret about the mating, about the bite." Mora nodded when Bridget touched her own neck. "Aye, for ones such as us, 'tisnae just a wee thing, is it? We cannae heal as they can. We arenae as strong. Mayhap I just didnae love him enough. I couldnae do it. My heart, my body, aye. My blood? To let him feed on me, e'en just a wee bit? Nay, I couldnae. E'en when I kenned I carried David, I couldnae, and, being a Pureblood, Jankyn couldnae swear that he wouldnae do it. He couldnae be sure he would be able to stop himself from completing the mating."

"It has to be the neck? He couldnae just take a wee sip from somewhere else?"

"Nay, I dinnae think so. Tis like this—when ye are together as mon and wife, just as he spills his seed, he bites ye and has a wee taste."

"Every time?" Bridget asked in alarm, thinking of all the times Cathal had nipped at her neck while they made love.

"Wheesht, nay. Just the once."

"Oh, thank God. If 'twas every time, I wouldnae last out the week." She blushed when Mora laughed heartily.

"Aye, the laird does have the fever for ye. Nay, lass, 'tis just the once. Tis done on the wedding night. As the mon gives ye his seed, gives ye a part of him as it were, he takes a wee bit from ye. Tis a blending and 'tis what binds him to ye as a mate."

Bridget sipped at her cider and thought over all Mora had told her. It explained Cathal's talk of mating. It certainly explained the way he always nipped at her neck as his body shuddered with release, as well as the way he seemed to tear himself away from there. Maybe all halflings did not need to do it, but she now felt certain that Cathal had that urge. It explained that odd feeling she kept getting that she was failing him in some strange way. And, yet, to allow him to sink his teeth into her flesh, to drink her blood? Could she still think of him in the same way if she allowed him to do that? Could she still feel the same way about him?

"Despite the odd choice of food, I had decided that the MacNachtons didnae drink blood," she said.

"They dinnae do it verra often. Many, many years ago they werenae so, weel, controlled. When they would go on a hunt, it wasnae always for animals. They fought a lot of battles, too, and were verra savage. Tis said they used to ride out at night to fight or hunt. They must have been a chilling sight with their black cloaks and black horses. They were called the Nightriders."

"Aye, Cathal mentioned something about that once."

"Weel, the name is still whispered from time to time, but it has been so verra long, 'tis little more than a myth now, a tale of the old, frightening times. Their laird put a halt to the harming of people save those like your thieves or enemies of the clan. The Nightriders had become too weel kenned, aye? Too many eyes had turned this way. There were hunts for them and killings done. From then 'til now, the habit of staying within these hills has held fast."

"But they still have a hunger for blood, dinnae they?" Bridget had suspected as much, but she was not sure how she felt about it.

"Not as they used to. The Purebloods prefer verra fresh meat, but ye ken that. Most of the time they are content with what they can get from an animal. Dinnae drink the wine they mix especially for themselves," Mora said with a smile. "They will occasionally have a wee taste of each other if the need arises. If they are verra badly injured or weakened, 'tis the surest way to make them strong again. It can e'en save their lives. I dinnae have much to do with the Purebloods save for a few like Jankyn, but I *can* swear that they dinnae go about dining on people anymore. An enemy or someone like those thieves who were hunting ye down are fair game, however, and they do take full advantage of that. Used that way, weel, 'tis verra much like just another weapon, isnae it?"

Bridget slowly nodded. "Aye, one could think of it that way, I suppose. As for the odd diet, weel, I already accepted the barely seared meat, so I believe the rest willnae trouble me so verra much. Tis much the same fare as we eat, save that we cook our meat a wee bit more and put the other, er, bits into puddings and stews."

"But, ye *are* troubled about the bite, arenae ye?"

"A wee bit. I shall have to think about it. One doesnae protect such a vulnerable spot all one's life then turn about and offer it to someone with ease, e'en if that someone is the mon ye love. Then again, I *do* love him so I should trust him to do it without harming me."

"Tis a hard thing to decide." Mora finished her cider, then stood up even as Bridget finished hers.

"It might be easier if I was certain he loved me as I love him," Bridget said as she stood up.

Mora hooked her arm through Bridget's and started to walk her back outside. "He wants to mate with ye, lass."

"Tisnae the same thing. At least nay in my mind. Mayhap I need to consider that as weel. Of course, we didnae do it on our wedding night, so mayhap it doesnae matter any longer. Mayhap it wouldnae work."

"Of course it would work. Tis just tradition to do it on one's wedding night."

They reached the outside where Jean still waited. As Bridget chose the cloth she wanted, she found herself a little surprised at the ready acceptance the village women showed her. She had to wonder if, even though she was the laird's wife, she was still seen as one of theirs. It would not surprise her to discover that her husband had considered that as well. Instinct told her that when Cathal made a plan, he was meticulous about it. She was probably the only part of his grand plan that had not been plotted out most carefully.

But a few feet from the castle gates, Bridget abruptly stopped. She had been considering what she should or should not do about *the bite*. Once she had recovered from the shock over what Mora had told her, Bridget had discovered that she was not as troubled by it as she had supposed she would be. If she was going to allow it, however, she wanted it to be a somewhat special occasion, rather like a second wedding night. It was a wonderful plan and she had just begun to sort it all out in her mind when she recalled one very important possibility she had not considered.

"Mora, I have but one more question," Bridget said, her gaze fixed upon the high, dark walls of the keep.

"Then ask it, m'lady. I have told ye all I ken about the matter, but I might still be able to help ye."

"Ye say he will take but a wee sip, aye?"

"Aye. Tis what Jankyn said. Although, his idea of what a wee sip is could be a great deal different from ours. He was most firm, however, in saying that it willnae kill ye. Could be a wee sip quickly over and finished with, or could be one big enough to leave ye a wee bit unsteady for a few days. It was ne'er really a fear of dying that made me refuse to be a part of it. I did, and do, believe in Jankyn's word that it willnae kill ye."

"But could it—" Bridget grimaced and forced the question out. "Weel, if I was with child, could it harm the bairn?"

Mora clasped her hands together and pressed them against her large breasts. "Oh, m'lady, do ye think ye might be carrying? So soon?"

The absolute joy upon Mora's face made Bridget realize that it was not only Cathal who was eager for the return of children to Cambrun. "My woman's time is nearly a fortnight late in coming."

"It could be late for many reasons, m'lady," Mora said. "A change in your food, and, weel, ye are but newly wed, and then there is all this trouble with the Purebloods. Oh, so many things could upset such a thing."

Mora was trying so hard to dim her own hopes it was almost painful to watch. "Nay, Mora, I dinnae believe it is any of those things. Callan women are verra precise, shall we say. I have always been so. Callan women are also notoriously fertile." She grimaced. "It wasnae something I felt inclined to tell Cathal when he seemed to be marrying me for my womb."

"Och, lass, I think ye ken there is more, aye?"

"Aye. I am just nay sure how much more. But, what about letting him give me this bite whilst I am with child?"

"Ye will have to tell him first. He will ken what to do or not to do. When will ye tell him, m'lady? Soon? Oh, 'twill be verra hard to hold fast to this news for verra long. That is why ye bought all that lovely linen, isnae it?"

"Aye, it is. And, Mora, ye had best hold fast to this secret," Bridget said, trying to sound very firm.

"Oh, I will, m'lady. I will. The laird must ken it first, from ye, and nay from gossip. The mon will be wanting to make a grand announcement and all. I suppose ye will have to wait until ye have missed your woman's time again, and, mayhap, a third time just to be sure."

Bridget sighed as she started on her way again, Mora nearly skipping along beside her. "I will ken for sure in about a fortnight for I will have missed a second bleeding. There will be no doubting it then. In truth, I have no doubt now, but I will wait the fortnight ere I tell Cathal. I want that time to try and become more certain in heart and mind that I truly am more than a womb to the mon."

"I think ye are, but I understand that *ye* need to believe it."

When they reached the steps leading up to the heavy doors of the keep, Bridget felt Mora take her by the arm as if to help her up the steps. Bridget silently cursed as she realized why Mora was doing that. She had the sinking feeling that her pregnancy was going to prove to be a very long one indeed.

Nine

Cathal smiled at Bridget as she entered his ledger room. He felt his body tighten with interest as he watched her walk toward him and almost laughed. After six weeks of making love to her every chance he got, he was a little surprised at his own greed. She was a fever in his blood which was both a delight and a torment. He saw her passion as a glorious gift, but he needed more. It was also getting harder to stop himself from performing that final act of mating. He craved it more than he had suspected. Indeed, he had hoped it was one of the MacNachton traits that had been bred out of him. Unfortunately, the need was there and growing stronger every day, yet, each time he tried to tell her about it, cowardice silenced him. He feared bringing a look of disgust, even a chilling revulsion, into her lovely eyes.

Shaking away that concern, he waited until she got close enough, then tugged her down onto his lap. "I am pleased ye sought me out, wife, but, truth tell, I was about to send for ye."

"Oh, why? Is there trouble?" Bridget wondered if the peace they had enjoyed was about to end.

"Nay, all remains quiet. I thought ye might wish to see what your cousin and your brother replied to my letters."

Bridget cautiously reached for one of the two letters he pointed to. She was pleased to see that it was the one from Barbara. It would take her a few moments to build up enough courage to see what Duncan had to say. Barbara's letter soon had her smiling. She could almost hear her cousin's voice. Feeling warmed by Barbara's expression of concern, her hearty congratulations on the marriage, and an insistence that they must visit soon, Bridget set the letter down and warily picked up the one from her brother.

"Tisnae so bad," said Cathal. "Ye act as if it will singe your fingers. There is a hint of anger in there, but 'tis directed at me, as is just."

"Oh, dear," muttered Bridget as she read the letter. "He means to visit soon."

"Aye. I cannae refuse him, lass. I dinnae believe the Purebloods will cause trouble and he isnae arriving on the morrow, is he. Who is this Effie he says will be with him even though he means to tell her she cannae come?"

Bridget smiled as she set the letter down. "My younger sister Efrica. She is just turned sixteen. And Duncan is right. He will tell her she cannae come, but she will find a way to do so." She frowned. "Are ye sure it will be safe for them to come here?"

"Aye, e'en if I must seal the Purebloods in their caves. But, I truly dinnae think there will be trouble. The Purebloods dinnae want the eyes of the Outsiders turning too keenly upon Cambrun, do they. Naught would cause that to happen more swiftly than doing harm to an Outsider laird. Unlike ye, who was left alone and brought here in the night, your brother's presence here will be no secret to his people. Questions would be asked if he didnae return to Dunsmuir, more Outsiders would come here, and so forth."

"Of course. Doing any harm to such a visitor would bring more trouble than it is worth."

Cathal began to slip his hand beneath her skirts. "So, why did ye seek me out?"

Slipping off his lap and grinning at his frown, she replied, "To ask ye to come with me, to tryst with me beneath the stars."

"Intriguing. Isnae that the sort of thing one does beneath a full moon?"

"Aye, but the weather wasnae so verra fine then. Tis still quite light out and I have a few lanterns. I also have some verra fine wine, sweet cider, honey cakes—"

"Honey cakes?"

Bridget giggled when he stood up and took her by the hand. "The honey cakes turned the key, aye? I think my vanity has just been dealt a mortal wound," she drawled as she led him out of the ledger room.

"Ah, lass, ye wouldnae ken what vanity was if it stomped up to ye and twisted your wee nose."

"Was that a compliment?"

They continued to tease each other as Bridget led him out of the gates of Cambrun. He soon realized where they were headed and silently commended her choice. Cathal had just noticed the flicker of light when he heard the rustle of movement through the small grove of trees where he and Bridget walked. He tensed and settled his hand upon the hilt of his sword.

"Did ye hear that, lass?" he asked.

"Aye, 'tis just Mora and David leaving. I wanted everything to be readied for us and they kindly offered to help. Oh, my, they did do a fine job." Bridget smiled with delight as she looked around the small glade, the light of the moon and the lanterns adding a certain magic to it. "Tis a wonder to find such a place amongst the rocks."

"Tis a hint of the promise of the valley below." Cathal crouched by a small pool and lightly swirled his fingers in the cold water. "One of my ancestors made it more than it was when he found it. From his writings, I gather 'twas but a brief break of lusher growth amongst the rocks, stunted trees, and prickly bushes. He had this pool cut to hold some of the water which trickles out of the rock and continues down into the stream in the valley. Where there was a break in the rocks, he brought up dirt from the valley, widened the break, and replaced gnarled or prickly growth with something a wee bit softer."

"Ah, and thus gave himself a wee piece of the valley closer to the keep," Bridget said as she sat down on the blankets that had been spread out on the ground. "Tisnae all rock and thin, gnarled growth upon your hill, Cathal. Your keep sits square on the barest, rockiest part, but there is green enough about to soften the rest. And, weel, stone does have its own beauty, doesnae it?"

He sat down beside her and kissed her cheek before grabbing one of the honey cakes set out with the rest of the food in the center of the blankets. It pleased him that she could see the beauty of Cambrun. Visits from Outsiders were few, but all of them recognized the fertile beauty of the valley while seeing only the harshness of the keep and the land it sat upon. They saw its value as a stronghold, and little else. Bridget's appreciation of the subtle, often hidden beauty of Cambrun also meant she could be content with the home he offered her and that soothed a fear he had not fully realized he had suffered.

"E'en the keep itself is quite beautiful," Bridget said, then cast him a slightly wary glance. "A few lighter colors might be nice, though. To ease the darkness?"

"If it pleases ye to change a few things, do so. Tis your home now." He poured himself some wine and took a sip. "Aye, now that I think on it, 'tis a fine idea. The darkness of the keep is too noticeable, isnae it. There are few visitors, but they have all remarked upon it. It might be best if it wasnae quite so obvious. Such things stir questions, a curiosity, and we need no more of that."

"It *was* one of the first things I noticed. I ken ye must have the darkness, if only so that *all* your clan can feel welcome, but one doesnae need to bare all the windows to bring a wee bit of light into the place."

Cathal set down his goblet, pulled Bridget into his arms and kissed her, too moved by her words to speak. She understood. Even more important, her words revealed an acceptance of the MacNachtons that was far more complete than he had realized. She was a creature of light and he had begun to feel guilty over forcing her to share his dark world, but she offered no complaint. Instead, she sought a way to give them all what they needed, a lightness for herself without truly stealing away the shadows he and his brethren needed. It was all more than he had dared hope for and he felt almost frightened by so much good fortune.

"I thought ye came here for the honey cakes," Bridget said a little breathlessly as he began to undress her, warming each newly revealed patch of skin with his heated kisses.

"I suddenly had a hunger for a sweeter, hotter honey," he said, his gaze fixed upon her lithe body, her skin turned quite golden by the soft light, as he shed his own clothes.

Bridget was glad he wore only a shirt and his plaid for he was quickly just as naked as she was. She welcomed him into her arms with a murmur of appreciation as his flesh met hers. Although she had planned to discuss the mating Mora had told her about, she decided it could wait. They had all night.

His kisses and caresses soon had her feverish with need for him. She tried to stir him to an equal need, but he neatly eluded her attempts to touch him in all the places she now knew could rend his control. When he lightly but firmly pinned her hands to the blanket, she hissed in frustration, but also felt a shiver of excitement run through her. She then tried to caress him with her body, but he proved adept at thwarting her in that, too. When he ceased feasting upon her breasts, the night air both chilled her and added to the ache he had left behind. The kisses he spread over her belly soon warmed her, however. He gently nipped the inside of each of her thighs and she opened to him, but, instead of the anticipated touch of his long fingers, she felt the heat of his mouth. She briefly tensed in shock at such an intimate kiss and tried to pull away.

"Nay, lass, dinnae deny me," he said. "Here is the honey I crave the most."

With but a few strokes of his tongue, he banished her uncertainty, replacing it with ecstasy. When she felt her release at hand, she cried out for him to join her, but he ignored her pleas, taking her to those dizzying heights with his mouth. She was still trembling from the strength of her release when he thrust himself inside her. There was a wildness in him, but she welcomed it. It stirred an equal wildness within her and her passion soon rose again until her cries of completion blended perfectly with his. For several moments she could do no more than hold him close, stroking his back with unsteady hands, but with the return of her senses came the sting of embarrassment.

Cathal smiled and kissed the blush that had started to spread across the breasts he nuzzled. "Now, lass, dinnae spoil the enjoyment we can share by getting all shy and modest afterward." He gave her a quick, hard kiss on the mouth, then rose from her arms.

Although she agreed with him, she still felt a lingering embarrassment as she tugged on her shift. "I am nay accustomed to such abandonment," she murmured.

"Ah, then I have obviously failed as your husband," Cathal began as he donned his plaid.

"Aye, as her husband, but nay her mate. Ne'er her mate."

Bridget watched in horror as Edmee appeared out of the shadows. She barely finished blinking in surprise when she saw the woman toss Cathal aside. He slammed into a large boulder at the far side of the glade and sank to the ground. Certain he was dead, Bridget flung herself at Edmee. The woman screamed in fury and pain as Bridget tore at her with her nails. A cry of frustration escaped Bridget when Edmee finally got a firm hold on her. For one brief moment, as Edmee lifted her up, they were face-to-face.

Edmee's eyes widened and Bridget knew what she saw. She gave the woman a feral smile and then twisted her body in an attempt to break free of the hold the woman had on her. Edmee quickly adjusted to the move, holding her even tighter. Knowing what was going to happen next, Bridget grasped two handfuls of Edmee's hair just as the woman threw her. She savored the scream that escaped Edmee as that hair tore free, then she rolled herself into a ball in a desperate attempt to protect her womb from the fall that was coming.

When she hit the ground, she felt as if all the air was abruptly yanked from her lungs and pain exploded in her head, but she found most of her fall cushioned by a thick growth of heather. Tossing aside the gruesome trophies of Edmee's hair that she still held, Bridget staggered to her feet. Through a haze of pain she watched the woman start toward her and knew she would not be so lucky next time. Then she saw Cathal rise up from the ground, but hid both her surprise and delight from Edmee. Cathal looked as feral as she had ever seen him, his eyes glittering gold in the light, the elegant lines of his face now turned predatory, and his fangs well exposed by his furious, silent snarl. At that moment, knowing he was about to kill this woman who sought to kill her and the child she now knew she carried, Bridget thought him utterly beautiful.

"What *are* you?" demanded Edmee, staring at Bridget with a look that held both cold, deadly fury and curiosity.

"My wife," snarled Cathal as he grabbed Edmee from behind and lifted her up. "My mate."

Edmee was thrown several yards, but she was quickly back on her feet and charging Cathal. Bridget tried to watch the fight that ensued, but the pain in her head made her vision cloud. She felt her knees buckle, but, even as she started to sink down, strong hands caught her around the waist. As she was steadied against a strong, lean body, an arm around her shoulders, she looked behind her to see Jankyn and Raibeart. She grimaced when Raibeart picked up the hanks of Edmee's hair and looked at her with a mixture of astonishment and amusement.

"Wheesht, lass, ye may be but a wee thing, but ye can be vicious, aye?" Raibeart drawled.

"I thought she had killed Cathal." She looked toward the fight, unable to tell who was winning. "Are ye here to help him?"

"Only if it looks as if he is losing," said Jankyn.

Bridget was not sure how he would be able to judge that until it was too late, but said nothing. She struggled against unconciousness even though she knew it would release her from the pain she felt. Then, suddenly, it was over. Edmee lay on the ground with a dagger in her heart. The way Cathal remained beside the woman on his hands and knees, bloodied and breathing hard, worried Bridget, however. To her utter astonishment, she saw the woman's lips move, but the pounding in her head kept her from hearing what was being said. She tensed and struggled to clear her vision when Edmee grasped Cathal by the front of his plaid and pulled him close. Since neither Jankyn or Raibeart moved, she prayed that meant they could hear well enough to know there was no chance of some final treachery.

Cathal stared into the dying Edmee's eyes and felt the exhilaration of victory rapidly fade. "This was unnecessary."

"Mayhap," agreed Edmee. "My temper, ye ken. I was always warned that it would be my doom. I wanted her dead. She stole ye from me."

"Edmee, I was ne'er yours. And, ye didnae really want *me,* did ye. Ye wanted a laird. Bridget is my wife, my mate. I begin to think it was fated."

"She isnae your mate yet, is she? Or dinnae ye feel that need, halfling?"

"I but wait until I am certain she will be willing. She is an Outsider." He struggled against the weakness swamping his body and decided his loss of blood had been greater that he had realized. "I need to be sure she can understand, willnae be too shocked." He frowned when a soft laugh escaped Edmee, but he was too dizzy to speak, to ask her what she could possibly find so amusing now.

"Oh, my braw, bonnie fool, I think ye are due for a few surprises. Tis a shame I willnae be here to see it all." Edmee raised one badly shaking arm, clamped her hand at the back of his head, and pressed his face against her neck. "But, I do mean to be sure ye will live to suffer Scymynd's revenge. Drink, my laird. I am dying. Ye kenned this would be a fatal blow when ye dealt it. Take what little I have left to offer. Just dinnae mistake this for a kindness."

It was an offer Cathal did not have the will to resist. The way Edmee stroked his hair as he drank the last of her strength told him her harsh words were not true, not completely. He knew he would not mourn the woman's death, but he would long regret his part in it.

Bridget watched Cathal and gasped when she realized what he was doing. "Oh! That had better nay be *the* bite." Stunned by her own words, she put a hand to her throbbing head, "Oh, I should have guessed this would happen. Ye Mac-Nachtons have finally driven me utterly mad," she muttered and let the darkness take her. Jankyn and Raibeart's startled laughter was the last sound she heard.

When Cathal closed Edmee's eyes and stood up, he looked

toward Jankyn and Raibeart. The sight of Jankyn holding a limp Bridget in his arms chilled him to the bone. "Bridget?"

"Has a lot of bruises and a lump on her head, but is alive," replied Jankyn as he carried Bridget to the blankets and set her down.

"What brought ye two here?" Cathal quickly washed up in the pool then moved to help get Bridget into her gown.

"We have been watching Edmee," replied Raibeart. "Followed her here." He bent and picked something up from the ground. "What is this?"

Cathal took the golden, intricately carved medallion from Raibeart. "Bridget's medallion. Her grandmother gave it to her. The chain must have been broken when she struggled with Edmee." He noticed Jankyn staring at the medallion. "'Tis but a pretty fancy. A cat with amber stones for the eyes. Bridget is most fond of it. Did she see me feed?" he abruptly asked the men.

"'Twas the pain in her head that made her swoon, Cathal," Jankyn replied. "Take her back to the keep. Raibeart and I will tend to Edmee. There will be trouble o'er this, I fear."

"Aye," agreed Cathal as he picked Bridget up in his arms. "Despite what she tried to do, Scymynd will think a reckoning is due and may convince others of it. I will be ready. Edmee kenned how it would be. Tis why she offered me the last of her strength. Of course, she denied that it was a kindness, or e'en for my sake."

"Snarling until the end. Aye, that was our Edmee. Go on, Cathal, and dinnae chastise yourself o'er this. She gave ye no choice."

Cathal was still trying to convince himself of that as, several hours later, he sat by his bed and watched Bridget begin to wake. He had killed one of his own and, no matter how that had come about, it was a loss that would take time to accept. When Bridget opened her eyes and looked around, he quickly grasped her hand to ease the fear he could see on her face.

"Oh, thank God," she whispered, briefly clutching his hand more tightly in hers. "I feared ye had died. Why are ye sitting there?"

"I wished to be right here when ye awoke in case ye woke afraid."

"And, I did."

"Aye. I also wished to reassure ye that ye are safe."

She smiled faintly. "Ye did. Of course, I would feel e'en safer if ye were a wee bit closer."

Cathal laughed softly, shed his plaid, and got into bed. He pulled her into his arms and murmured his pleasure when she curled her body around his. He wondered if she found the same comfort in his arms that he found in hers. She was not really safe yet, however. Scymynd would strike out soon. Cathal had no doubt about that. As he stroked her back and felt her relax in sleep, he silently swore that he would keep her safe. He had no other choice. Duty demanded it. Honor demanded it. And most of all, he realized as he pressed a kiss to the top of her head, love demanded it.

Ten

"Have ye made her your mate yet?"

Cathal looked up from his work to frown at Jankyn even as the man strode across the ledger room to stand before his worktable, his hands on his hips. "Why would ye ask me that?"

"I happened to get a good look at your bride's wee, bonnie neck a week ago as ye fought with Edmee. No mark. We may heal from a bite without a scar, but an Outsider cannae. Your mother wore your father's mark. Proudly. Do ye nay feel the need or are ye ashamed of it, try to deny it?"

"The need *is* there," confessed Cathal, "although I had hoped it was one of the MacNachton traits I didnae inherit from my father. As ye ken weel, every halfling is different in what remains, what weakens, and what disappears. I am nay ashamed of it, however. I but worry about how Bridget will react to it. Cowardice has held my tongue, but I must gird my wee loins and tell her soon. The need grows too strong."

Jankyn moved to where a jug of wine was set on a table along with several goblets. He poured out two drinks, served Cathal one, and sat on the edge of the worktable to sip his. Cathal took a drink as he eyed Jankyn warily. Something else was weighing on his cousin's mind, something other than the fact that Bridget did not yet wear his mark.

"Mayhap that is a good thing," Jankyn said. "Ye may e'en decide ye dinnae want to do it. I have finished searching out the truth about the Callan clan."

The look Jankyn gave him made Cathal feel distinctly uneasy. "What did ye find out?"

"Weel, most of your brethren would still consider your bride an Outsider, but she isnae, nay completely."

"Oh, nay, dinnae tell me she has MacNachton blood."

"Nay, but it appears the Callans have a wee oddity of their own. I did wonder at times why Bridget was so quick to accept us. A Callan *would* be. In truth, I believe ye couldnae have found a more perfect match, but ye may feel differently."

Cathal growled a curse. "Just tell me. What is odd about the Callans? Something that is carried in the blood?"

Jankyn nodded. "Cats. The original source of the, er, taint is a wee bit obscure. Twas either brought back by a Crusader or from some ancient Celtic bride, a priestess in the old religion, a shape-shifter." He shrugged. "Despite what I am, I find that a wee bit difficult to imagine. But, there it is. The Callans appear to have done what ye plan to do—bred it out. There are tales from the old, misty past that hint at some difficulties because of this trait, but the Callans began to be verra particular in their mates. Their family lines are kept meticulously complete right to the most distant of cousins. Intermarriage, no matter how rich the prize, is strictly forbidden for fear that this trait will blossom in its full glory again and pull them all back into danger."

"So, they have bred it out then?" Cathal could understand why Bridget might hide this fact about her clan, but still felt hurt and angry that she would hide it from him.

"Most of it. There lingers a hint, though. In the coloring, for example. Twas the medallion that set me on the right path. It reminded me of a tale I had once been told. I found that and soon tracked down the rest. It also explains a lot of things such as how your wife hisses and scratches, how she can run as she does."

"How she purrs," Cathal whispered.

"Does she? How intriguing." Jankyn met Cathal's scowl with a sweet smile. "The way she seems to sense danger, her keen eyesight, especially in the dark, and that certain grace she has. All Callan women are rumored to be small, lovely, graceful, passionate, and fertile. Verra, verra fertile. Your wee wife comes from a verra big family."

"Do ye recall the first night she was here? The way she acted when she first awoke?"

Jankyn nodded. "Verra like a cat."

"Aye, but for one fleeting moment there was something in her face, something verra catlike."

"Why didnae ye say so?"

"I thought it a trick of the light. Now I think not. It also means it might be impossible to breed out all our MacNachton traits. The Callans havenae fully succeeded, have they?"

"Would that be such a bad thing? I can think of a few that would only serve us weel and would only raise envy, nay fear."

"True. I suspicion some of the things in the Callan bloodline do the same. The more I think on it, the more I curse myself as a blind fool. Aye, some of what Bridget does could just be considered, weel, a female's ways. But nay all of them. Certainly nay the way she fought Edmee. I was but stunned when Edmee tossed me aside. Couldnae move, but I could see how Bridget leapt at Edmee. She used those cursed long nails of hers on Edmee and it took Edmee a few moments to get a firm grasp on Bridget. I can now see that the way Bridget moved to try to stay out of Edmee's grasp was verra like a cat. Then Edmee threw Bridget and, somehow, e'en as she was flying through the air, she curled that wee body of hers into a ball. That and the heather saved her."

"Aye. Raibeart and I were close enough to see that. Raibeart still mutters about it. That and the fact that your wee wife made sure to take a few large hanks of Edmee's hair with her when she was thrown. Of course, a cat is said to land on its feet. For one wee minute, I truly thought she was about to perform that wondrous feat, but then she curled up into the ball. I wonder why."

"Mayhap when I have finished bellowing at her, I will ask her that question." He smiled faintly when Jankyn laughed.

"So, ye will keep her?"

"Aye. E'en when I feared ye were about to tell me she had MacNachton blood, something that would near ruin all my grand plans, I meant to keep her." He sighed, finished off his wine, then rose to refill his goblet. "I had best send for her, confront her with this, and hear what she has to say for herself."

"No need. I believe I hear the patter of wee paws approaching."

Cathal gave Jankyn a disgusted look as he retook his seat. "I would be wary of teasing her too much. Dinnae forget those nails."

"Cathal?" Bridget called even as she entered the room. "Oh, greetings, Jankyn. Am I interrupting something?"

"Nay," replied Cathal. "In truth, I was about to send for ye. Have a seat, please." He waved her toward the chair facing him on the opposite side of his worktable. "There is something we need to discuss."

The somewhat cold tone of Cathal's voice made Bridget nervous. She found no comfort in the unusually serious look upon Jankyn's face, either. Clutching tightly to the scraps of material she had brought to show Cathal, Bridget moved to sit in the chair.

"Has something gone wrong?" she asked.

"Nay. I wished to ask ye a few questions about your family, about your clan," replied Cathal.

"Oh. Has Duncan written again?" Bridget began to get the sinking feeling that Cathal had discovered something about her clan before she had been able to tell him herself. "Has he refused to give o'er my dowry?"

"Nay. This has naught to do with that, or with Duncan. Nay, I am interested in your ancestors." Cathal watched her pale slightly and felt both sympathy and anger. She should have realized she could trust him with this secret. "Let us say, the ones who went on the Crusade. Or, mayhap, an ancient Celtic priestess?"

"Ah, ye ken it all, dinnae ye." Bridget was almost relieved that her secret was out, but the anger she sensed in Cathal made her uneasy, even a little afraid. "Did Duncan send another letter confessing all?"

"Nay, Jankyn discovered the truth. One of my ancestors was convinced there had to be others like us so he began to collect all manner of fact and rumor about every clan in Scotland. In the generations to follow there was always someone who held the same fascination. Jankyn does it now. He saw your medallion and that sent him down the right path to uncover all the Callans's dark, wee secrets. Did ye nay think I ought to ken about this?"

"I didnae see how it would make any difference to your plans. Ye arenae one of my bloodline, either." It was a weak defense for what had been pure cowardice on her part, but his anger was starting to stir up her own.

"Nay? Ye kenned what my plan was. Here I am trying to breed things out of my bloodline and ye neglect to tell me that, in marrying ye, I could be breeding other odd traits right back in? Did ye nay consider what sort of children two people such as we are might breed?"

"Nay, I didnae, but now that ye mention it, 'tis an intriguing thought. Mayhap a lad who can tear his enemy's throat out then lick himself clean afterward."

Bridget heard Jankyn's laughter, but ignored it. She kept

her gaze fixed upon Cathal who looked an even mix of outrage and shock. She knew she had been wrong in not telling him about the Callans, but if he thought he could now cast her aside because of her bloodline, he had better think again. It was not easy, but she pushed aside the pain and fear that possibility bred in her and faced him squarely. And, she mused, he had no right to chastise her for keeping secrets. That thought increased her anger and she welcomed the strength it gave her.

"That wasnae funny," he snapped. "Now, tell me about your clan."

"Aye, it seems that hundreds of years ago a Callan bred a child on a woman with a few unusual qualities. He wed her, brought her to Dunsmuir, and proceeded to breed a lot more bairns. I tend to think it was a Celtic woman. The women in the lands the Crusaders roamed were mostly dark, I believe, and Callans arenae dark. Ne'er have been as far as we can tell. Tis said she could change into a cat and I dinnae mean the kind ye have in the stables, either."

"Do ye believe that?"

Bridget shrugged. "Tis difficult to imagine and, if she could, if any of her children could, that skill disappeared o'er the following years. There was something there which caused some trouble, however, so, about two hundred years ago or more, the laird at that time decided to breed it out. A few times cousins married, but 'twas quickly decided that wasnae a good idea. So, e'en more care was taken. When a Callan reaches an age to marry, he, or she, must memorize a list of the names of families we cannae marry into. Or, at the verra least, we will need to pause to be sure our choice isnae from the branch which might concern us. The name MacNachton wasnae on the list."

Cathal ignored that. "But, whatever it was hasnae completely disappeared, has it?"

"Nay, but ye need nay worry that I will suddenly grow

fur." She sighed when he just glared at her. "We just have a few catlike qualities. Like strong, sharp fingernails, a lot of hair, keen eyesight, an ability to run fast, and the like. Some of us seem to have more such qualities than others, or stronger ones. It simply refuses to be completely bred out, which is why the strict rules on who we may marry continue to be applied. What of it? Do ye think to end this marriage because of it?"

"Of course not. Why would ye think that?"

"Oh, I dinnae ken. Mayhap because ye are acting as if I have grossly betrayed ye."

"Ye should have told me the truth," Cathal nearly yelled. "Ye have been keeping secrets from me, your husband."

Bridget jumped to her feet, ignoring the cloth scraps that fell to the floor. She was furious that he had made her feel so afraid, so hurt, and that he would act so outraged when he still clung to a few secrets himself. "Ye, sir, have no right to be waving a scolding finger at me." Not sure if she wanted to hit him or weep and feeling like doing both, Bridget started out of the room. "There are still a few secrets ye havenae told me, I vow." She yanked open the door.

"Where are ye going?"

"To the stable, I think. I saw a rat there yesterday." She slammed the door behind her.

"That went weel," murmured Jankyn. "Why do I suspect that ye were in the stables yesterday?"

"Because I was," grumbled Cathal, then he glared at Jankyn but it failed to dim his cousin's grin. "I wonder why she thinks I am keeping secrets."

"Because ye are. Ye havenae told her about the mating, have ye?"

"Weel, nay, but she doesnae ken that."

"Ye would be surprised at how easily a woman can root out a mon's secrets."

"Aye, I suspicion I would be. Weel, there *is* one good

thing about all this. Twill make the meeting with her brother easier."

"How so?"

"His clan is in much the same position as ours. I was worried about how to let Bridget remain close to her family yet hold fast to our secrets. Now I may deal with the mon on more even ground. We both keep secrets to protect our people."

"True. Of course, he may still feel inclined to object to one of his wee cats marrying a mon who is a wee bit like a wolf."

"I dinnae think so. And, after all, I am nay on the list." He exchanged a brief grin with Jankyn.

Jankyn picked up the scraps of cloth Bridget had dropped. "I wonder what she brought these here for?"

Cathal took the bits of cloth from Jankyn. "Ah, I suspicion she sought my approval. She wishes to change a few things. Just before Edmee attacked us Bridget talked about using some lighter colors around here to ease the darkness. She said she kenned we have to have the darkness so that *all* our clan can feel welcome, but that one doesnae have to bare all the windows to bring a sense of light into the place."

"Ah, Cousin, such a sweet acceptance she reveals, e'en when so many of our brethren scorn and reject her. Tis uncomfortably moving."

"I ken it. I was moved enough to have to make love to her there and then. Tis probably why Edmee was able to sneak up on us."

"It may have helped her, but, then again, Edmee was always good at that. Go, Cousin, and soothe your wife's feelings. Ye dinnae wish to lose this one. She is good for ye, good for all of us. And, for sweet Mary's sake, since ye *do* feel the need, get the mating done."

"Aye," agreed Cathal as he got up and started for the door. "Tis time. I but need to plan it out a wee bit. Something a wee bit special. After all, 'twill be as if we are marrying again."

Cathal stepped into his bedchamber and looked at his wife. She stood in her shift before the fire brushing out her hair. The brief look she sent him was not welcoming. He sighed and went to stand behind her.

"I dinnae ken why ye thought it, but I ne'er once considered ending our marriage. Nay, not e'en when I feared Jankyn was about to tell me that he had discovered ye had MacNachton blood." He took courage in the fact that, after only a brief hesitation, she let him take the brush from her hand and brush her hair. "Considering all I have asked ye to accept, how I held ye here just to get ye to marry me, and all I hid from ye until after the vows were said, ye are right in saying that I have no right to scold ye about having a secret." He set the brush down on the table, took her by the shoulders and turned her round to face him. "That was the only secret ye are keeping, isnae it?"

Bridget did not know whether to laugh or hit him. However, since there was one secret she was still keeping, she did neither. Her first attempt to have a special place and time to discuss this mating business and the child she carried had been brutally ruined, but she was already preparing another. She would not try to have that last exchange of secrets now.

"Nay, that was the only one," she replied, telling herself she was not truly lying, just making a small delay in telling the truth.

"So, ye have a wee bit of the cat in ye," he murmured as he pulled her into his arms. "I should have guessed. Ye purr. No one purrs."

"Tisnae such a strange sound," she said as she undid his plaid. "I suspect I could make ye purr."

"Ha! Men dinnae purr." He helped her remove his shirt and quickly tugged off her shift before pulling her back into his arms. "They make monly sounds."

His eyes widened slightly as Bridget kissed the hollow at the base of his throat. She was always free with her passion, but she had never made the first move before. Cathal forced himself to let her continue to take the lead. He quickly decided it might prove to be one of the hardest things he had ever done as she kissed her way down to his stomach. A shudder went through him when her silken hair brushed against his groin as she kissed and gently nipped at his thighs.

The soft warm touch of her mouth against his erection sent such a wave of pleasure through him that he jerked and cried out. She started to pull away from him and he finally moved. Threading his fingers through her hair, he tugged her back, growling his delighted approval as she stroked him with her tongue. When the moist heat of her mouth enclosed him, Cathal knew he would not be able to enjoy this delight for very long. It was but moments before he knew he had to be inside her. Yanking her up into his arms, he raced to the bed, tossed her down on it, and fell on top of her. Her soft husky laugh echoed in his ears as he thrust himself inside her.

Bridget idly combed her fingers through Cathal's hair as she slowly recovered from his lovemaking. He had not even nipped at her neck this time, but buried his face in the pillow as his release tore through him. She was not sure if she was pleased by the way he had clung to that last thread of control or not. There was no doubt in her mind that she had made him crazed with desire and she wondered if, in some small part of her, she had been trying to push him to just do it. Now they still had to dicuss the matter and he was proving very reluctant to do so. When he raised his head to look at her, she smiled at him.

"Ye purred," she said, "just like a big tomcat." She laughed softly at the way he scowled at her despite the laughter brightening his eyes.

"It wasnae a purr," he said. "It was a verra monly growl."

Bridget laughed again as she slid out of bed and hastily donned her shift. "Weel, there will soon be some verra loud growling coming from me if I dinnae get some food."

Cathal realized that it was time for the evening meal and got out of bed. As he dressed and then helped Bridget, he swore that he would see the trouble with Scymynd and the rebellious Purebloods ended soon. He wanted all that behind him so that he could turn all of his attention to his wife and his marriage. He loved her. He knew that now. A part of him suspected she cared deeply for him, might already love him, but she was as secretive about that as he was. Once he cleared away the last of their troubles, rid them of the last threat to their peace and safety, he intended to woo his wife as unrelentingly and avidly as any man had ever wooed a woman. She gave him passion and laughter with ease. Before too much longer he was determined that she would give him her love as well.

Eleven

"This will do perfectly," said Bridget as she looked around the bedchamber.

"I dinnae ken why ye must do all this just to talk to the mon," said Mora as she quickly wiped off the wine goblets and set them back on the table.

Bridget sighed. "What Cathal and I must speak about is verra important, to both of us. This, weel, this is also to give us a sense of celebration to what will be said and done and shared between us. He will finally make me his mate and I will tell him that he is to become a father. I waited ten days after Edmee's attack on us to see if Scymynd would do something. I didnae want this momentous occasion interrupted or ruined. Weel, Scymynd hasnae done anything and I cannae wait any longer."

"Nay, ye cannae. If naught else, the laird might finally realize that ye havenae had your woman's time since ye were married. Any fool kens weel what that means and ye dinnae want him guessing the truth."

"Och, nay, certainly not. Especially since he will quickly suspect that I have kenned it for a while and wonder why I didnae tell him. I might be able to talk my way round that,

but I would just as soon nay have to try." She took one last
look around the room, at the softly burning candles, the food
and wine, the new pale blue draperies, and the vast profusion
of bed furs. "Just give me some time to get into my lovely
night shift and then send my victim up here."

Mora rolled her eyes. "He sees ye in that night shift and I
suspicion it will be a while ere ye do any talking."

"That is the plan."

"'Tis the middle of the day!"

"I expect this to take a while. Best to start early."

Shaking her head, Mora left. The moment the door shut
behind Mora, Bridget giggled. The woman had looked a little scandalized. It probably was a little scandalous to be
planning a long afternoon of lovemaking, but Bridget was
determined to clear away the last little secrets in her marriage. She also wanted Cathal to make her his mate. It meant
a great deal to him and she knew their marriage would not
be complete in his mind until that last step was taken.

Just as she reached for the delicate night shift she intended to entice her husband with, Bridget sensed that she
was no longer alone. She started to turn around and was
quickly caught up in a pair of strong arms. The feel and
scent of the man who held her was not one she recognized.
Before she could cry out, a hand was clasped so tightly over
her mouth she was sure she would have bruises. She tried to
fight her captor's grasp, but the arm wrapped around her ribs
tightened until she was struggling for each breath she took.

"Be still, ye wee bitch," snarled a voice in her ear. "Dinnae
e'er forget. I could snap your wee neck in a heartbeat."

Scymynd, her mind screamed as he walked toward an
opening in the wall. Their enemy had finally made his move.
She frantically wondered if she was inadvertently cursing
herself when she prepared these little celebrations, then decided the lack of air and fear were making her daft. When he
stepped through the door, pulling it shut behind them, she

tried to make use of that brief moment his hold was eased to wriggle free, but he was quicker. He held her even tighter and Bridget feared she would soon lose conciousness. As he started down a dark, narrow stairway, she had to wonder if that would be such a bad thing after all.

"Ah, there ye are, m'laird," said Mora as she hurried across the great hall to where Cathal sat at the laird's table with Jankyn.

"Ye need to speak with me, Mora?" Cathal asked, idly wondering why Bridget had not yet appeared for the meal that was being set out.

"My lady would like ye to join her in your chambers for a meal."

"Oh? Is she feeling ill?"

"Nay, m'laird," Mora replied, blushing deeply.

Cathal lightly punched a snickering Jankyn on the arm. "Thank ye, Mora. I will join her there in a few minutes."

"Why are ye waiting a few minutes?" asked Jankyn the moment Mora left the room.

"Anticipation."

"Yours or hers?"

"A wee bit of both I hope."

"Lucky mon." Jankyn frowned as a MacMartin came running into the great hall and headed straight for them. "Trouble, I wonder?"

"M'laird," the man cried as he stumbled to a halt near Cathal's chair. "We have visitors."

"I can see that," Cathal murmured as he studied the group of people who now filled the doorway to his great hall.

It was Bridget's family, of that he had no doubt. Three men stood to the fore of the group and their similarities to her were more numerous than their differences. Hair in varying shades of tawny gold, eyes slightly slanted, and, although they were all much taller than she, the same lean graceful forms. There was a plump older woman with them and what appeared to be a rather small, bone-thin man hiding behind her skirts. Suddenly a dainty girl who was obviously on the cusp of womanhood, shoved her way to the fore of the group and scowled at him.

"Where is my sister?" demanded the girl, shoving a stray lock of honey gold hair from her small face.

"Ah, ye must be Effie," said Cathal. "Your sister is fine. Come, there is ample food and drink here. Since Bridget is not here to do the honors, might I ask ye to introduce yourselves?"

The tallest of the three men strode toward the table, the rest of the group falling into step behind him. Now Cathal could see the subtle differences in the shades of hair and eyes. Duncan had hair and eyes the color of amber, his twin brothers, Kenneth and Osgar, had hair a shade darker than Bridget's and eyes more green than blue. Efrica was beautiful, despite the scowl she wore as she studied him with blatant mistrust easy to read in her soft amber eyes. When Duncan introduced Nan, Cathal moved to kiss the woman's hand, causing the skinny little man behind her to come forward and demand he release his wife.

"And the wee skinny mon is her husband," said Duncan. "He found her where the thieves had left her for dead and, whilst they robbed the dead men, Malcolm here got our Nan out of their reach. Once Nan woke to find herself residing in a cottage alone with a man, she knew she had to marry him."

It was difficult, but Cathal fought back the urge to grin over that introduction, all slowly drawled out in a bland tone of voice that completely belied the high gleam of laughter in the man's eyes. "Please, sit." He signaled to one of the Mac-Martins as he retook his seat. "Have someone fetch your lady to the hall. Tell her she has visitors."

"I could go and get her," said Effie even as the servant

hurried away. "Ye tell me where she is and I will go to her."

"Sit down," Duncan ordered his sister even as he and the others sat down. "I should have left ye to rot in that trunk."

"Trunk?" asked Jankyn, briefly glancing at Effie as she sat down next to him.

"I thought I was bringing Bridget some of her belongings," replied Duncan. "Instead, I was bringing this wretched torment. I still cannae understand how she managed to stay quiet in there for two days." He glared at Effie. "When I heard the rapping, I ignored it for a wee while. I kenned it was her and I was that angry. I should have stayed angry."

"M'laird!" cried Mora as she raced into the hall. "The lass is gone!"

Mora's cry had not ceased echoing in the great hall, before Cathal was up and racing toward his bedchamber. He could hear others behind him, but paid them no heed. He strode into his bedchamber and looked around. There was no sign of a struggle. It looked as if all was readied for the private meal Bridget had invited him to. He touched the lovely linen night shift on the bed and fought down a surge of fear. He had to think clearly.

"Scymynd," hissed Jankyn.

"Aye, so I think, but how would he get hold of her? She wouldnae go with him willingly."

"There must be a way for him to get into this room."

"My laird," panted Mora as she stumbled into the room. "Ye didnae wait for me to give ye the note I found."

Cathal urged Mora into a seat by the fire to rest and took the note she held clutched in her hand. It was simple and to the point. He was to go into the caves and meet with Scymynd if he wanted his wife back. He cursed as Jankyn took the note from him and read it.

"Ye willnae go alone," said Jankyn. "It doesnae say ye must. I dinnae trust Scymynd to act with honor."

"Who has my sister and where?" demanded Duncan as he stepped up to Cathal. "E'en better—why? Have ye put her in the path of your enemies?"

"Aye, although I ne'er thought it would go this far." Cathal shook his head. "If naught else, this mon thinks of your kind as nay better than the animals we kill for food."

"Then we had best go get her. I ken that ye are aware of where she is, and with whom."

The thought of Bridget's brother going down into the caves, of getting a very clear view of all of Cambrun's dark secrets, was a chilling one. The man would see things down there which would have him dragging Bridget out of Cambrun as fast as he could. He had thought the Callans's past would shelter him from criticism, but had never anticipated this.

"I ken the who, the where, and the why. There is nay need for ye to come with us."

"Allow me to be the judge of that. Where ye go, I follow."

"I cannae protect ye where we must go. It isnae something ye should see."

"All the more reason to look at it." Duncan stepped close to Cathal and said in a soft, hard voice. "I ken who ye are, what ye are. I am thinking ye ken who we are, what we are. Ye have been with my sister too long and too closely nay to have grown curious. And what little I have seen of Cambrun has only confirmed what I learned of the MacNachtons. We are alike in that we both must keep our secrets. Ye will keep ours and I will keep yours. I *will* go with ye to fetch my sister back." Duncan stepped back and brushed off the front of his doublet. "I will, of course, allow ye the privilege of killing him."

"E'en if ye didnae wish to, I would insist. Ye may think ye ken what we are, but ye cannae imagine what sort of fight ye would be caught in, and lose, where we are going." His eyes widened slightly when Duncan pulled his dagger and smiled in a surprisingly chilling way for such a fair, handsome man.

"I may nay have the teeth for the job, Sir Cathal, but I am verra good with this. And, nay matter what ye may be, your heart is in the same place as mine."

Cathal nearly echoed Jankyn's soft whistle. It seemed that his new brother knew a great deal indeed about the Mac-Nachtons. Later, he would have to find out how that could be, for the MacNachton secrets were not easily uncovered.

"Then come, but only ye." He turned to Jankyn as Duncan told his brothers to stay behind and tie their sister Effie down if they had to to keep her from following. "Find out how he got into this room, for I am certain he took her from here."

It did not take long for Jankyn to find the doorway Scymynd had used. Cathal had a strong feeling that the man had undoubtedly been spying on him for a long time. If he survived this confrontation, he was going to hunt out every door like this and make sure it was secured from his side. He was sure they had been built for escape, not spying and treachery. Just as he, Duncan, and Jankyn prepared to enter the narrow passage behind the door, Raibeart hurried into the room. Cathal silently nodded his gratitude for the man's support and entered the passage. As he made his way down the narrow steps, he prayed Bridget was safe, that she was only being used as bait. It calmed him only a little for he knew he could not trust Scymynd's word. He vowed he would make the man pay for every bruise Bridget had suffered and, this time, there would be no truce, no tolerance, and no mercy.

Bridget bit back a cry of pain when Scymynd tossed her onto a flat rock jutting out from the smooth stone wall of a large cavern. She sat up and looked around. It was probably a great hall of some sort for there were tables and benches pushed to the side. She suspected every Pureblood of Cambrun was gathered there and they were all staring at her.

Slowly, Bridget looked from face to beautiful face. A few held the same look of contempt and dislike she had seen on Edmee's face and Scymynd's. Some had little expression at all. Too few looked uneasy, revealing their reluctance to go along with this latest act of betrayal against their laird. The opinions and loyalties of this crowd were not easily read and Bridget sighed. There might be some allies amongst this crowd, but it would take more than a look to guess who they were. She did not have the time for anything else, however.

"Do ye think he will come for her?" asked a man as he held a bowl of water for Scymynd to wash his hands in.

The implication that he needed to wash after touching her, made Bridget so angry that a little of her fear was burned away.

"Aye," replied Scymynd. "He will be here soon. The silly wench had sent for him just before I took her. Considering how our great laird has been chasing after her skirts since before they were married, I believe he would answer any summons from her with a pathetic speed."

She felt her fists clench as she fought the urge to strike the man. Bridget knew that would give her only a very small moment of satisfaction. After that, she would be very lucky if Scymynd allowed her to live. She was not so sure he intended to do so anyway.

"Edmee would have liked to see this," Scymynd said, sounding almost tender. "She had hungered for his humiliation and the Outsider's destruction since the first moment the little bitch stumbled into Cambrun. It is still difficult to believe that halfling had the strength to kill her, but he will pay for her murder."

That, Bridget decided, could not go unchallenged. "Cathal didnae murder Edmee. She attacked us and tried to kill both of us. He but defended himself. If ye wish to betray your laird, or to take his place, at least have the courage to do so with the truth."

Scymynd raised his arm and Bridget braced for the blow, but it never came. An older woman moved between him and her as if she had not realized she was interfering with anything. She gave Bridget a kind smile as she handed her a goblet of cider. Bridget gave her a smile of gratitude, for the drink and the interference, for she sensed that the woman had known exactly what she was doing.

"Agnes," growled Scymynd, "the wench isnae some honored guest."

"She isnae a criminal, either," replied Agnes as she moved away. "She is a weelborn lass, sister to a laird, and deserves the courtesy."

Scymynd glared at Bridget. "An Outsider laird. Little better than a peasant."

Bridget sipped her cider wondering why Scymynd taunted her so, seemed to actually want to make her act or speak out in a way that demanded retribution. She had the chilling feeling that he was trying to make her give him an excuse for killing her. This, she decided, was a trap for Cathal, and for her, although she suspected many of the Purebloods gathered there might not be fully aware of that. Scymynd intended to end this confrontation with her and Cathal dead and Scymynd himself sitting in the laird's chair.

The man could not be so vain or so stupid as to think it would all be so easy. Bridget doubted that all of the Purebloods would wish to be part of that. There was also Jankyn and Raibeart to contend with, plus a half dozen halflings who would not tolerate the murder of one of their own. She doubted that all of the MacMartins would be so complaisant, either. The man was going to plunge Cambrun into a war and, considering who would be fighting in it, it would be a long, brutal, and very bloody one.

"What are ye thinking, Outsider? That ye are soon to be gallantly rescued?"

The condescension in his voice made her clench her teeth, but she replied sweetly, "Nay. I was but wondering why ye are so eager to destroy the verra place ye claim to want to save." Bridget sensed someone slip up behind her, but felt no threat, so did not turn around.

"What nonsense are ye spouting?"

"Tisnae nonsense. I think ye have no intention of allowing me and Cathal to leave here alive. Do ye think ye can then sit your arse in the laird's chair and have all welcome ye? Not everyone is displeased with the laird they have. Halfling or nay, he is still the son of the laird who came before. And then there are my kinsmen to consider. They are plentiful and willnae allow my death to go unpunished. Ah, and Cathal's cousin Connall may have an objection or two. Nay, I think for all your talk of wanting what is best for Cambrun, for the Purebloods, the only one ye want the best for is yourself."

She sipped her cider, refusing to quail before his glare. There was a soft noise behind her and she realized there were now two people at her back. Cathal obviously had a few allies amongst the Purebloods, or, at the very least, there were some who felt Scymynd needed some sort of control. A quick, sly glance around the chamber revealed a few frowns directed at Scymynd. It seemed she might have caused a few people to start thinking. It was not much, but it would do for a start.

"Halflings and Outsiders. I dinnae need to fear them." Scymynd looked behind her. "And a few traitors to their blood."

"But, e'en though Cathal is a halfling, isnae he of your blood?"

"His father fouled the blood of his son when he bred with that Outsider. Now the son thinks to befoul what little MacNachton blood he carries e'en more as he tries to pass it along to a son. Tis enough, more than enough. If Cathal had his way we would all be consorting with Outsiders. He may as weel ask us all to wallow in the mire with the swine."

Bridget hissed, tired of his constant insults. Her action startled him and she gained a small measure of satisfaction from that. "So proud ye are, so certain of your utter superiority. Och, aye, ye are prettier than anyone ought to be allowed to be, ye live to some great age, ye are strong and fast and heal as if by magic, but ye can still be killed. Ye told Cathal that he shouldnae push ye too hard or ye will push back hard, mayhap harder. Weel, for all ye spit on those who arenae so wondrously pure as ye, the same rule follows."

"Let them push. They will die."

"Aye, nay doubt, mayhap e'en in great numbers. But, they have one great strength ye dinnae have. If one of them dies, there is another, and another, and another. They can breed, sir. They can rebuild their armies. There are also far more of them than there are of ye and there always will be. Go ahead and push, sir, and kill and feast until ye are as fat as a piglet, but in the end it will be a hollow victory and it cannae last. In the end, we poor, weak, pathetic Outsiders will win if only because ye cannae replace your losses and we can."

He took a step toward her and Bridget braced herself. She felt the people at her back do the same. Whatever he intended to do never happened, however. In the tense silence of the hall came the soft sound of someone approaching.

"I believe my gallant rescue is about to begin," drawled Bridget, sounding far more confident than she felt as she prayed that Cathal had a very clever plan to get them out of this mess. Or a very large army.

Twelve

"Release my wife, Scymynd."

Bridget felt both relieved and terrified when Cathal appeared out of the shadows. A moment later Jankyn was at her side, nodding to the others gathered behind her even as he nudged her to a point slightly behind him. She peered around him to see two men step forward to flank Cathal and she gasped.

"What is Duncan doing here?" she asked, knowing what her brother might soon see and wondering why Cathal allowed him to come along.

"He insisted upon coming," replied Jankyn, never taking his gaze from Scymynd. "Did he hurt ye?"

"Nay, I am fine. Weel, except for the fact that he is using me to get to Cathal."

"Ah, lass, he would have found another way. Scymynd has hungered for this battle e'er since the day Cathal was born and ended all chance that Scymynd had of becoming our laird."

"Nay, I think not," Scymynd replied to Cathal. "She might still have her uses."

Cathal stepped closer. "Ye said ye would release her if I

came to ye. Here I am and here I will stay until this is finally finished. Bridget cannae be of any further use to ye. Let her go."

"No matter what happens between us, it willnae end here, will it? Nay, ye fool. Ye have destroyed us with your plots to weaken our blood, to befoul our nest with the child of an Outsider. Twas hard enough to watch ye, a halfling, sit your arse in the laird's chair, but your get bred upon this woman willnae e'en be half, will they?"

"Ye speak of insults to your vanity that havenae e'en been made yet."

"Dinnae lie to me. Ye do it poorly. That bitch carries your whelp! I heard her and that cow Mora talking about it."

Bridget blushed beneath all the gazes that were suddenly fixed upon her. This was not the way she wanted Cathal to find out he was soon to be a father. The poor man looked shocked and somewhat terrified. It was a horrible time for him to know that far more than his wife, his position as laird, and even his life was at stake. As a laird, a warrior, those were risks he was born and bred to accept. Now, added to that tally was the one thing he wanted most of all—a child. She could not help but think that Scymynd knew that, had blurted out the truth in the hopes of weakening Cathal's resolve.

"Is it true, sweetling?" Cathal said even though he could tell by the look upon her face that it was.

"Aye," Bridget replied. "I was planning on telling ye. Tis why I planned a fine, and verra private, meal in our chambers today."

"Ah, aye, I noticed the preparations. How far along?"

"Two months, mayhap a wee bit less."

"But, we have only been wed about that long."

Bridget shrugged. "I told ye I was fertile," she mumbled.

"So, ye see?" Scymynd looked around at the Purebloods gathered in the cavern. "If this isnae stopped here and now, we will find ourselves ruled by a puling Outsider brat. That child, his heir, will be more one of *them* than one of us. Ye must see how wrong that is, what a foul abomination it is. It simply cannae be allowed. It *must* be ended here."

"Scymynd, ye had best nay be suggesting what I think ye are!"

Cathal looked toward the tall, elegant, white-haired Agnes, one of the oldest of the Purebloods. She looked outraged. A quick glance around at the others told him that the tide might be turning against Scymynd. He was strongly suggesting the breaking of an ancient rule, the one that forbid a MacNachton from harming a woman with child, or a child. Scymynd did not seem aware of the fact that he was treading down a path that could quickly lead him to a place where he would stand alone or nearly so.

"What do ye ken about it, old woman?" snapped Scymynd. "Ye fawn upon the Outsiders, tending their hurts and illnesses. Tis because of this bitch that Edmee is dead."

"Edmee is dead because she tried to kill the laird's wife," said Agnes. "Nay more, nay less. Dinnae try to use her foolishness to stir up anger and hatred. And dinnae ye dare ask us, any of us, to stain our hands with the blood of a bairn, born or unborn." There was a soft rumble of agreement from many of the Purebloods. "Twill be the first birth of one of our own, pure or nay, and aside from the laird, in two score years."

"And ye see that as reason enough to let this filth into our line?"

"His insults are growing verra tiring, Cathal," murmured Duncan. "I do hope ye are planning to shut him up soon."

Scymynd glared at Duncan. "Another Outsider. Do ye mean to surround yourself with such weaklings?" he demanded of Cathal.

A low growl escaped Duncan and it echoed around the cavern. Cathal quickly placed a hand on the man's arm to steady him, but nearly grinned at the way all the Purebloods looked at him. After a quick look himself, Cathal could understand the surprise, confusion, and curiosity upon their faces. When Bridget was angry or cornered, she looked like a hissing cat. Duncan looked far more impressive, like one of those great lions he had read about.

"Oh, dear," murmured Bridget, looking at her brother. "Duncan is starting to lose his temper."

"I believe I noticed that, lass," said Jankyn, laughter rippling in his voice.

"Enjoy your wee giggle. If he gets any angrier, it willnae be pretty."

"Does he rip out his enemies' throats and then lick himself clean afterward?"

"Oh, hush."

"'Tis time we ended this, Scymynd," said Cathal. "I challenge ye. If I dinnae survive, then let it be kenned that I select Jankyn as the protector of my wife and bairn. If aught happens to them, then I select Jankyn as my heir and Raibeart as his first."

Cathal almost smiled at the look that crossed Scymynd's face. The man recognized the importance of those choices. Both men were Purebloods. By choosing them he had stolen most of the power from Scymynd's claim that they were being taken over by those that too many Purebloods considered inferiors. The fact that so many called out their agreement only dug the knife deeper into all of Scymynd's plans.

Bridget leaned around Jankyn even as he turned slightly to speak to one of the men behind them. For a brief moment, she had no shield and she knew the very moment Scymynd saw that. He moved swiftly. His dagger was sailing toward her before she had even accepted the fact that he had drawn it. Suddenly she found herself at the bottom of a pile of bodies. One of the ones who had so swiftly thrown themselves in front and on top of her grunted and she realized Scymynd's dagger had found a target.

"Bridget!" called Cathal and Duncan at the same time.

"I am fine," she called back as she struggled to get out from under all her protection and too many hands reached out to help her.

Once free she looked to see who had taken the dagger and gasped when she saw that it was Jankyn. Bridget moved quickly to his side, only faintly aware that she had several shadows encircling her, following her every move. To her relief, the dagger had entered high on his back. Taking a deep breath, she yanked it out. As Jankyn cursed she watched in fascination as the wound slowly but surely healed itself.

"That is truly wondrous," she murmured.

"I am surprised it is healing so weel," muttered Jankyn, "after ye nearly killed me whilst yanking the knife out."

"One more word and I will put it back in." She heard several of her protectors laugh.

"Kill him, Cathal, or I will."

Bridget recognized that snarl and tried to see where Duncan was. "Duncan sounds verra angry now."

"And looks it," said Jankyn. "Ye Callans may nay change any more but ye certainly come as close as anyone I have e'er seen."

"I cannae see. Does his hair look weel, fatter or higher?"

"As if his fur is standing on end?"

Jankyn was obviously going to torment her about her heritage every chance he got. "Aye, something like that."

"Aye, but Cathal is sending him over here. Stay behind me, lass. I dinnae think ye will want to see this fight."

After exchanging a brief touch of hands with Duncan, Bridget tried to wriggle herself into a position amongst her ring of protectors. She did not want to see the battle to come, but she needed a chance to be able to peek at it once in a while. Finally, placed between and behind two Purebloods, she found that she could see just enough between their broad shoulders.

Cathal moved to the center of the cavern which served as a great hall for the Purebloods. There was utter silence in the cavern. With that one rash act, Scymynd had not only lost all chance of being laird, but of being the leader of the Purebloods. Even the very few men who seemed inclined to stand by him, would prove no trouble for they were being held in place by several of their brethren. Cathal doubted it had been Scymynd's plan, but the battle would now be between just the two of them. He might not have the full support of the Purebloods, but Scymynd now had little or none.

"This has been a long time coming, halfling," growled Scymynd.

"Only because ye pressed for it, Scymynd," replied Cathal.

"If naught else I must make ye pay for killing Edmee."

"Edmee's vanity and temper killed Edmee. I was just the selected weapon. No one tries to hurt my wife without paying dearly."

"She was worth ten of that Outsider bitch. When I am done with ye, I will see her gutted and that foul thing she carries tossed upon the midden heap where it belongs."

It was not easy, but Cathal closed his ears to the filth coming from Scymynd's mouth. He knew what the man was trying to do and he could not let himself be stirred to a blind anger. That would make him act foolishly and that would get him killed. He intended to survive this battle. He had a wife to woo, a mating to perform, and a child to meet. Never had he felt such a deep need to survive.

Scymynd's attack came swift and hard. Cathal used every trick he had ever learned to hold his own, to compensate for the fact that he did not heal quite as fast. Even so, he was soon suffering from several small wounds. His only compensation was that Scymynd was suffering from more, his blood loss already severe enough to slow his ability to heal. Cathal shut his mind to his own weariness as the fight wore on, to his own pain and blood loss, and concentrated only on giving Scymynd as many injuries as possible, keeping the man's teeth away from his throat, and his dagger out of his heart.

The end came quickly, almost too quickly. Unused to such punishment, Scymynd staggered. For one brief moment, Scymynd's chest was unprotected, his dagger on the ground. Cathal sank his dagger deep into Scymynd's chest, so weak himself that he barely kept himself from falling on top of the man he had just killed. Sprawling on his back beside Scymynd, Cathal became all too aware of his injuries. He began to fear that his blood loss was too severe. Then a young man named Tomand knelt by his side and offered his neck, then another man, and another.

"What are they doing?" asked Bridget as she tried to see between her two protectors only to discover they had pressed their shoulders together and effectively closed her window.

"Cathal is verra weak, lass," Jankyn said quietly. "Nay, dinnae look. If naught else, there are so many of his brethren offering him what he needs to recover ye willnae be able to see him."

Duncan took the place of one of Bridget's protectors when the young man moved away. "Weel, mayhap I didnae ken everything about the MacNachtons," he murmured. He looked at Bridget. "I will take ye back to Dunsmuir, if ye want."

"She stays here," snarled Jankyn.

"'Tis her choice, lad, so tuck away the teeth."

It appeared that Duncan was not very troubled by what he had just witnessed, or suprised. Bridget wondered where and how he had learned about the MacNachtons before he had come to Cambrun. "I dinnae want to leave, Duncan," she said, and kissed his cheek, "but thank ye for the offer."

"Are ye sure, lass? I am nay sure ye will e'er be fully accepted by these people. The way they talked about anyone who wasnae one of them reveals a dangerous arrogance."

"I think Scymynd was the worst of them, Duncan. He is the one who did most of the talking. I ken that it will be a long time ere I am accepted, but, this is my bairn's home, the home of his father, the home of his people. And, aye, for all that ye could find something wrong with Cambrun and its people, I could find something right." She winked at her brother. "Weel, except, perhaps, for Jankyn."

He grinned over Jankyn's muttered curses, then grew serious again as he closely studied Bridget's face. "And whate'er I might say is wrong with the laird? Ye will find something right to counter it?"

"Aye, or hit ye about the head with a stick."

"Ah, I thought it might be like that."

She leaned very close to him and whispered in his ear, "I am quite stupidly in love with him."

"MacNachtons have verra keen hearing, ye ken," drawled Jankyn.

"One particular MacNachton had best be feeling verra deaf at the moment, or verra forgetful," Bridget said, fighting the urge to smile at the face Jankyn pulled before he left her alone with her brother. "I have some good friends here, Duncan. When ye have good friends, ye dinnae need quite so many, do ye."

"Verra wise, lass," said Agnes as she came to stand beside her. "I do hope ye will tolerate one or two more. Do ye ken, the way ye spoke to Scymynd, the things ye said, opened many an eye. Scymynd told a good tale, but, for all its pride and glory, it was an empty one. Now, I am a healer, ye ken, e'en though my hours be strange." She briefly grinned revealing very sharp, and very strong teeth. "Howbeit, I would be most honored if ye would allow me to be your midwife. Ye can ask Mora about me. I was at David's birth."

"Thank ye, that would be most kind. I confess, I have been much taken up with trying to figure out how and when to tell Cathal, that I have given no thought to the birth itself."

"Best ye tell her everything, lass. Tis always best if the midwife is warned," said Duncan.

"Is there a history of birthing troubles in the family?" asked Agnes.

"Nay," replied Bridget. "We are disgustingly fertile, have disgusting ease in the birthing, and, weel, we are verra apt to have more than one." She was a little startled by the wide grin Agnes gave her.

"Och, lass, I will but see that as a double blessing, but I think 'tis something we best keep to ourselves. I have a feeling the laird will have enough difficulty adjusting to the thought of one, as will many another here. Aye, let it be a surprise." She patted Bridget's hand and walked away humming softly.

Before Bridget could wonder long on that, however, Cathal approached her. She quickly threw herself into his arms, breathing a sigh of relief over the strength she could feel in his embrace. Hearing the steady beat of his heart beneath her ear was as sweet to her as any music she had ever heard.

"Are ye weel, sweetling?" He asked as he slipped his hand beneath her chin and turned her face up to his. "Are ye hurt?"

"I am weel and I am unhurt," she reassured him.

He rested his forehead against hers. "Are ye sure, lass?" he whispered.

"Verra sure," she whispered back. "I was sure after the first time something, er, went missing, but waited just a wee bit longer. Then each time I tried to prepare something special so I could tell ye, it all went wrong. I had wanted us to have a wee celebration, ye ken."

"Weel, we are about to have us a grand one, if ye arenae too weary."

"Och, nay. I do think I had best go and clean up and all."

"I will take her back to her room," offered Duncan. "The others will be wanting to see that she is all right."

Cathal nodded and watched Duncan escort his sister away. He grinned when he heard her joyous screech and knew Duncan had told her that Nan had survived. A soft touch on his arm drew his attention and he smiled down at Agnes.

"Your lass has agreed to let me be the midwife, if that sits weel with ye, laird," she said.

"It sits verra weel, Agnes," he replied and kissed her cheek. "I fear it will be a while ere I dare believe it. I ne'er expected it to happen so quickly."

Agnes grinned. "Weel, the lass did tell ye she was fertile."

"Aye, she did at that." He looked around at the Purebloods still lingering in the cavern. "I think the trouble has ended, too."

"Aye, lad. Your lass has a clever tongue and she had already turned a few minds by the time ye arrived." When Cathal quirked one brow at her, she quickly told him all Bridget had said to Scymynd and nodded at his look of pride and astonishment. "Twas the pure truth, too, and that is hard to fight, aye?"

"Aye, Agnes, verra hard to fight. I think God smiled on me a wee bit when He set her down within my grasp."

"Och, aye, lad, He did indeed. Now, get ye back up the stairs and start preparing for this grand celebration. I expect a lot of fine food and plenty of wine. I am thinking there will be a lot of toasts drunk to our future. Tis looking verra bright indeed, isnae it?"

"Aye, Agnes, verra bright indeed."

Thirteen

Cathal looked around his great hall, crossed his arms over his chest and smiled. It was a grand celebration. Scymynd was dead, the clan was united again except for one or two discontents whom no one paid any heed to, and he was going to be a father. He could understand Bridget's disappointment that such news had been told in such a way, even shared it some, but that news had changed everything. Scymynd's support had faded away. Even most of the ones who had stood firmly by Scymynd had deserted him in the end, appalled that he would even speak of harming a woman carrying a child, let alone attempt to murder her. They had suddenly begun questioning everything he had said or done. There also seemed to be some who saw the speed with which he had bred a child on his new Outsider wife as a sign that he was right. Like it or not, change was necessary if they were to survive. Many another had heard and heeded all that Bridget had said to Scymynd which had, in many ways, added a great deal of weight to his own warnings. Leave it to a woman to point out that the greatest weapon your enemies have is that they can just keep making more of themselves.

He looked toward where Bridget's three brothers were encircled by half a dozen Pureblood women and grimaced. They probably hoped the Callan men would prove as fertile as the Callan women. If they did, there might well be a few bastards born at Cambrun in the spring. He doubted marriage was on the minds of any one of them and Duncan was very careful concerning the bloodlines of all who thought to join with the Callans through marriage. The man had accepted his marriage to Bridget, but Cathal was still not certain why, except that the marriage had been consummated. And, of course, there was a child on the way.

If he did not stop smiling, people would think he was drunk or had lost his wits, he mused, but he could not seem to stop. Just the thought of Bridget carrying his child had him grinning like an idiot. Matters were not completely settled between him and his wife yet, but even that thought could not dim his joy.

"I am thinking it might be time for me to marry," said Jankyn as he stepped up beside Cathal.

"Ye? Have ye finally settled upon one of your harem?"

"I dinnae have a harem," objected Jankyn. "Nay, I think I am finally starting to age. I found a grey hair."

Cathal looked at Jankyn's thick black hair, then caught the hint of a blush upon Jankyn's cheeks. "Ah. Not there."

"Nay. Not there."

"Mayhap ye are only partly aging." Cathal had to bite the inside of his cheek to stop himself from laughing when Jankyn cast a horrified glance at his groin. "So, ye think ye are getting older and wish to have a loving companion." He grew serious. "Best ye choose carefully, Jankyn. If nay a Pureblood, then ye will outlive your mate for many years. Recall what that did to my father. Worse, I believe he began to fear that he would outlive me as weel. Ye do have a wee touch of Outsider in your blood, but it doesnae seem to have changed ye from the Pureblood as far as years to live is concerned."

"So I thought, but I begin to wonder. I am going through my bloodlines. Och, I am nay like ye, but it begins to look as if I am nay a Pureblood, either. Once the other blood gets into your lineage it doesnae leave." He shrugged. "I still have weeks of writings and lineage charts to go through, however."

"Does it bother ye? One way or t'other, I mean."

"Only in that, if I have been told I am something I am not, a Pureblood, I may have wasted years I didnae have to waste."

"Ah, weel, take heart. E'en if ye are much akin to me, ye still have many years left. Many more than the lifetime of many of the Outsiders." He caught Jankyn staring at Efrica Callan who was laughing at something Bridget said. "She is only sixteen years of age, Cousin."

"I ken it. I was just wondering if she purrs." He exchanged a brief grin with Cathal before wandering off into the crowd.

Cathal decided it was time to find his wife. He had in mind a more private celebration. When Duncan stepped into his path, he grimaced. The man had said nothing since the battle with Scymynd, but he had a feeling that reprieve was over.

"Aye, I am going to ask ye about that," Duncan drawled and smiled. "I but need to ken that 'tis as Bridget says, that ye dinnae do that all the time, dinnae need a human's blood to survive."

"She told ye true. E'en after the fight, I could have had an animal's blood and it would have helped a wee bit, kept my blood loss from inflicting me with a fatal weakness. Tisnae the same, as ye can see. And, as ye saw, it wasnae asked for, wasnae just taken, it was offered. Unless 'tis an enemy in battle or murdering thieves such as those who set upon Bridget, 'tis always only at invitation and ne'er done to harm or kill. The laws were set down many years ago and anyone of us who breaks them, weel, let us just say that the punishment befits the crime."

"But the hunger is there."

"Aye and nay. I willnae be feeding on Bridget or any of my new kinsmen. Blooded wine, near raw meat, and such as that serves as weel."

"Tisnae my way and I cannae say I am comfortable with it, but who can say what is right?"

"I suspicion there are a few things ye try hard to keep under control."

"Och, aye. I dinnae purr. Tis too cursed unmonly," he drawled as he walked away.

Cathal laughed and continued on his way to collect his wife. He smiled at Efrica as he stepped up next to Bridget and slipped his arm around her waist. Efrica was definitely going to give Duncan grey hair, he mused.

"I suppose ye are intending to take her away," said Efrica.

"Aye," he replied. "I am. Ye can see her on the morrow."

"Ah, there ye are, my bonnie child," said Agnes as she walked up and slipped an arm around Efrica's slim shoulders. "Ye promised to show me that chess move ye used to so soundly defeat Marcus. I could use a few clever tricks. Twould be pleasant to win now and again."

Bridget watched Agnes listen most intently to Efrica's chatter, her pale white hand gently stroking her sister's hair or touching her cheek. "Children have been missed, havenae they?"

"Och, aye," agreed Cathal as he led her out of the great hall. "E'en at our worst, in the days when we rode through the night and caused far too many deaths, a child was always treasured, protected. I was spoiled. So was David. It has been so long since a child was born to the Purebloods that I think many of them had convinced themselves it didnae matter. And, they could barely remember what it was like to have one about."

"Tis sad. Tis as if that bloodline can nay longer renew itself."

"Aye, that is sad, but it can continue in others. One just has to accept that it must be mixed with others. I believe that acceptance is already there in some of the Purebloods and coming in others."

Once inside the bedchamber, Cathal moved to stir up the fire. It was time, he decided. He had to take the chance and tell her what he needed to tell. It was a night for endings and beginnings. He felt sure that Bridget would not reject him for wanting the mating, even if she did not wish to participate. A soft smile touched his face when he turned to find she had slipped behind the privacy screen, her gown already crookedly draped over the top.

"I need to ask ye something, wife," he began. "I suspect I will have to explain a few things as weel. I didnae think I would as I am only half, half Outsider, half Pureblood, but I find I must."

Bridget felt her heart skip as she tugged on her night shift, but she stayed behind the screen. It was possible Cathal would find it easier to speak if he did not have to look her in the face. She knew she would.

"Tis about the mating, aye?" she asked.

"Aye. Who told ye about that?"

"Mora. She noticed I didnae have the mark."

"Ah. Weel, that might make it easier. Did she tell ye what happens?"

"Aye. Instead of bellowing in my ear at a certain point in our lovemaking, or burying your face in the pillow, ye will bite me on the neck and, weel, have a wee sip."

Cathal reached around the screen and tugged her out. "Bellow in your ear?"

"Loud enough to make my ears ring."

He grinned briefly, then took a deep breath and asked, "So? Are ye willing? Dinnae say aye unless ye are absolutely sure."

"Cathal, I have kenned about it for weeks. I was going to

try to get ye to tell me about it when Edmee attacked. Again tonight, weel, whilst we dined in the room at midday. I am nay sure I understand how it all works, but ye need it to feel truly mated, aye?"

"Aye, and I dinnae understand it, either. It just is."

"And 'tis only the once. Ye do it, and that need is gone."

"Exactly. And, after what happened today, I have nay fear at all that it will be any more than a verra wee sip indeed, nay matter how sweet ye taste." He picked her up and carried her to the bed. "And, ere ye ask, nay, it willnae hurt the child. In truth, this is a perfect night for this."

"Because ye have already had some," she said quietly as he shed his clothes.

"Aye." He sprawled on the bed beside her and tugged off her night shift. "I plan to have ye so wild with desire ye will probably miss the whole thing."

Within moments she began to think he would easily live up to his promise. He left no part of her untouched or untasted. Bridget was panting his name by the time he joined their bodies. She cried out with her release, and heard herself babbling all manner of things. She felt him tense within her arms, and then felt a sharp pain on her neck even as his seed warmed her womb. To her utter astonishment, she felt her barely ebbing passion race to the heights again. She clung to him as she felt herself shatter for a second time and had the brief, sinking feeling that she had just said things she had not intended to all over again.

It was several long moments before she gained the strength to open her eyes. The way he was looking at her as he gently brushed the hair from her face made her heart race. Bridget smiled faintly, a little disappointed that he was not whispering sweet words of love.

"Ye love me, lass," he said, and grinned at her wide eyed look. "Aye, ye do. Ye were screeching it there at the end. Twice."

So that was what she had said, she mused. "Aye, I do. I have for a long time. Why do ye think I said aye?"

"Ye wed me because ye loved me?" he asked in surprise.

"Aye, but ye dinnae have to fear that I will pester ye for the same. I understand 'tis different for men."

"Lass, I will confess that I was nay so quick as ye to see the truth, but I do love ye. I have for a while. I have been trying to think of ways to make ye love me." He laughed softly when she threw herself into his arms. "In truth, since ye told me ye loved me just as I was about to bite ye, I cannae be sure which has me feeling most bound to ye. I may have e'en been mistaking a need for those words for the need for the mating."

"Weel, it doesnae matter. The need is gone, aye."

"Completely. Ah, love, ye have given me so much. Passion, laughter," he slid his hand down to her stomach, "the future."

"And ye have given me many things as weel, Cathal."

"A lot of trouble."

"And a lot of passion. Aye, it wasnae always pleasant to love ye and think ye didnae love me, but, there was joy in the loving. Truly." She grinned and ran her feet up and down his legs. "'Tis better to have the joy be in the loving and in being loved."

"Ah, my wee wife, I wish I was a poet or a minstrel. I would like to drown ye in pretty words. There is so much inside of me that I feel, but I dinnae have the words."

She touched her fingers to his lips. "I love ye."

"I love ye, too."

"Ye dinnae need any other words than those, Cathal. Not ever."

"Not ever. I will be living for a verra long time yet."

"We Callans are verra long lived as weel."

"Oh, I do hope so, love. I do hope so. For I need ye. Ye are my sun, my joy."

Bridget brushed her lips over his, deeply moved. "Ye are getting much better with your words, Cathal," she whispered.

"My wife, my mate, forever."

"Do ye ken, I think those are the finest of all. My husband, my mate, forever."

Epilogue

Spring 1476

Cathal frowned as he woke to a faintly familiar sound. He looked at his wife who was sprawled at his side sound asleep. As she should be, he mused and grinned, thinking of the long hours they had spent making love. He then frowned because the noise was not coming from her. He sat up and looked around to see if she had let in one of the cats again. Then he tensed and looked toward the window, beneath which sat the large cradle holding his twin sons. Mora had obviously slipped into the room and tied back the draperies just enough to let the sunlight fall into the cradle.

Cursing softly, he slipped out of bed, threw on his plaid, and approached the cradle. He was able to stand close by it yet stay out of reach of the sunlight as he studied his sons. The sound was definitely coming from them.

"Is it time for them to be fed?" Bridget called out in a sleepy, husky voice.

"Nay," Cathal replied. "They are just purring."

He continued to stare at his sons as he heard the rustle of the bedclothes and, a moment later, Bridget appeared at his side wrapped in one of the bed furs. "My sons are purring, Bridget."

Bridget looked down at her lovely, perfect little babies. They were both on their backs, letting the sun warm their plump little bellies. They were also, most definitely, purring. She bit the inside of her cheek to keep herself from laughing.

"Ah, so they are."

"Men dinnae purr."

"They arenae men. They are wee bairns."

Cathal draped his arm around her shoulders, turned her to face him, and pressed his forehead against hers. "Bridget, my sons are purring."

Seeing the amusement glinting in his eyes, she grinned up at him. "Aye, and loudly, too. And they are doing it whilst lying in the sun's light like the fat, wee piglets they are."

He grinned back at her. "So they are. Indeed, so they are. Might I ask when ye kenned that they could abide the sun?"

"I needed to be sure ere I told ye. I wanted to do one more wee test." She briefly glanced into the cradle. "That will do." She squeaked in surprise when he picked her up, carried her over to the bed and tossed her down on top of it. "They will soon be squealing for their food," she said as he tossed aside his plaid and sprawled on top of her.

"Then they can wait a wee while. Their father needs to make love to their mother."

"He does, does he?" She wrapped her arms around his neck.

"Aye, he needs to thank her for giving him the gift of children. He needs to thank her again for giving those children the gift of sunlight."

"Cats love the sun," she whispered.

He kissed her again. "And he needs to thank her yet again for giving him the gift of sunlight, too." He brushed a kiss over her lips when she frowned slightly. "Ye are my sunlight,

Bridget. Ye and your love have pulled me out of the shadows. And, to ken that my sons will ne'er have to hide in them is the greatest gift of all."

"The shadows arenae so verra bad, Cathal. I found ye there, didnae I?"

"Aye, ye did, and, now, to show ye how grateful I am for that, too, I am going to make ye purr."

"Oh, how lovely," she murmured against his lips just before he kissed her.

Cathal soon heard her make the sound that never failed to heat his blood. It was funny in a way, he thought as he began to sink into the sheer joy of loving and being loved. He had never really liked cats.

THE
HIGHLAND
BRIDE

Lynsay Sands

One

"It will be fine." Eva leaned forward to run a hand between her mount's ears, and down its neck as she spoke. "Everything will be just fine. Those rumors about the MacAdies and Mac-Nachtons having a lust for blood are just so much nonsense. Really," she assured the beast. "And even if they were true . . . Well, the MacAdie laird would hardly pay Jonathan all those coins to marry me, merely to bring me to Scotland and drain me of my lifeblood. Surely, there are cheaper ways for him to feed."

The mare snorted as she took the last few steps necessary to gain the hill they had been traversing. It was questionable whether the sound was a comment on her rider's words, or simply indicated her relief that the hill was behind her, but Eva suspected it was the latter. Her words—with their hint that she might actually believe the rumors about the MacAdie clan—hardly deserved comment. Eva was almost embarrassed that she had dared voice them. Even if only to her mount. Not that she had anyone else to talk to.

Her gaze slid over the men riding with her; two in front, two behind, and one on either side. Six men in all and every last one stoic, grim-faced, and unapproachable. She made a face at the backs of the pair riding before her, knowing it was childish and rude, but they were rude, taciturn men. Scots all. Not one of them had said a word to her that wasn't merely an order or instruction since leaving Caxton keep. Not that there had been much opportunity to speak. Their party had been riding nearly nonstop for two days now; traveling up hills then down again, sticking to the wooded areas and rarely moving at less than a trot. It had been a very long two days for Eva who had managed well at first, but had dozed off in her saddle several times today, and each time she had, it was only to awaken later to find herself seated before Ewan on his horse. Obviously in charge of this trip, he had apparently managed to ease her from her own horse to his without waking her, then had cradled her in his arms like a child while she napped.

Eva had been embarrassed the three times she had awoken to find herself so, but once aware that she was awake and alert, the Scot had merely stopped long enough to shift her back to her own mount and continued on. It was difficult to sleep on a rocking horse. Eva was sure those naps had only been short ones and that while exhaustion had allowed her to drift off into sleep, once she'd gained an hour or so of much needed rest, she hadn't been able to stay asleep. She was exhausted and in desperate need of a good eight hours of uninterrupted rest, something she feared that she wasn't likely to get soon.

Which was a terrible shame in her mind as her exhaustion was making it difficult to keep her usually positive perspective on things. Instead of thinking of this as a grand adventure as she probably would have were she not so tired, Eva found herself feeling lonely and frightened. She had left everything she knew and loved behind, and was heading toward a life in a foreign land amongst complete strangers, with nothing but the clothes on her back and the small satchel hanging from her saddle. The satchel contained another threadbare gown, a small painted picture of her mother, her father's small blade, and little else. It was all Eva possessed in this world.

Not that she minded her lack of possessions, Eva was used to that, but she did wish she'd been able to bring Mavis with her. The little kitchen maid, who was sometimes pressed into service as Eva's lady's maid, was the only friend that she had. Eva had been closer to the girl than to her own brother. Mavis was the only person she would really miss. But Jonathan had refused to release the girl, and she doubted that these men would have welcomed another burden besides herself on this journey.

Eva grimaced at the thought of being seen as a burden by these men. She didn't care for the designation much, but her brother had made no bones about the fact that a burden was all she had been to him since her parents' deaths when she was nine. Despite all of her efforts to stay out of his way, her directing the servants for him, and even pitching in and helping them when necessary in an attempt to make up for what little food she ate . . . All of it had been for naught. Jonathan had found her presence unbearable to the point that when he was unable to find her a husband, rather than allow her to live out her days at Caxton, he had been preparing to send her to a nunnery. Then these men had arrived with an offer to bride her.

Eva shook her head at the way her life path had changed so abruptly. Two days ago she had awoken with the glum realization that this was the last full day she would spend in her childhood home. The very next morning, she was to be sent to the abbey to join her next older sister as a bride of God. Something Eva didn't really think she was suited to. She had always thought of nuns as serene and graceful brides of the lord. And even Eva had to admit that she was anything but serene. As for graceful, it was not a word that had ever been used to describe her.

But that had been two days ago. By midmorning of that day, her future had been put into question when Mavis had sought her out in the gardens to inform her that six Scots had arrived and were bartering with Jonathan for her hand in marriage. Eva had—at first—been sure the girl was wrong about this. Her brother had told her repeatedly that he had nothing to offer as her dower, so there was nothing over which to barter. But, as it turned out, they weren't bartering over what Jonathan would pay to be rid of her, rather what the Scots would pay to have her.

Eva had still been reeling in shock from that news when Mavis had informed her that they were MacAdies. Never having paid much heed to gossip, Eva hadn't understood the relevance behind this news. Mavis had recognized this at once from her blank expression and had taken an unseemly delight in telling the tale of the nightwalking, blood-lusting vampires the MacAdies were claimed to be, adding a horrified "Oh, 'tis too awful m'lady. *You,* married to one of those monsters!"

Eva had shushed the girl, telling her it was all stuff and nonsense, but the maid's words had plagued her ever since. It *was* nonsense, of course. Wasn't it?

"Of course, it is," she assured herself stoutly for probably the hundredth time in two days. After all, hadn't Ewan and the five MacAdie men with him arrived at Caxton at midmorning? In clear daylight? According to the rumors Mavis had repeated, they shouldn't have been able to manage such a feat were they vampires who would perish at the touch of the sun's light.

Of course, when she'd said as much to Mavis, the girl had explained that Cook had said that the MacAdies weren't all vampires. That the laird had married a MacNachton woman who was one and some of the people of MacAdie had followed suit. Their offspring were half-breeds, but that there were still mortal men among them, a necessity to accomplish what the soulless bloodlusters could not. These men, she had announced, were obviously the mortal helpers, servants to the vampire, sent to collect her for their laird who was a son of the MacAdie laird and his soulless bride and therefore, unable to travel in daylight.

Eva had been less impressed with this news. Her only response had been a snort of disbelief which hadn't been as convincing as she would have liked. The maid had managed to plant the seed of doubt in her mind with her tales.

"It's silly, really, Millie," Eva assured her mare. "There is no such thing as vampires. Tis a myth. Like sirens of the sea."

"She's talkin' to hersel' agin."

Ewan managed to restrain the sigh that wanted to slip from his lips at Domhall's words. He had rather hoped that the men wouldn't notice that Lady Eva was again talking to herself. An unlikely feat when he and Domhall rode behind the woman with a perfect view every time she took the trouble to start mumbling away.

The lass had been doing so since they'd ridden out of the gates of Caxton keep that first afternoon on the long journey from Caxton on the northern coast of England, to MacAdie in northern Scotland. And the men had been pointing it out in worried tones ever since. It was obvious that they worried that their new lady was mad.

"The MacAdie willnae be pleased to find hissel' landed with a mad wife," Domhall commented.

Ewan sighed at these words.

"Nay, he willnae be pleased," Keddy agreed. He'd been riding on the woman's left, but now dropped back to join the conversation. "And nae doubt he'll be blamin' us fer it."

"Nay," Donaidh protested, dropping back from his position on their new lady's right to join the conversation as well. "He'll no blame us."

"Aye. He will," Keddy insisted. "He'll think we drove her mad with tales of what to expect."

"He kens none of us would do that," Ewan said calmly. "Besides, she isnae mad."

"Oh. Aye," Domhall agreed. "And every sane woman talks to herself, then?"

"Sane Scots, nay," Ewan allowed. "But a Scot, she isnae, is she? 'Sides, who's to say she be talking to herself? Mayhap she's merely soothing her mount."

"Soothing her mount, is she? From sun up to sun down?" Domhall snorted at the very idea and Ewan had to grimace. The argument hadn't sounded very convincing even as he'd spoken it, but the closer they got to MacAdie the more he began to fret on the situation. As Connall's first, it was his place to look out for his laird's best interests. And it didn't seem to him that having the men arrive thinking the lass mad—and spreading that rumor to everyone else—was a good thing for Connall. He thought it might be a good idea to nip that tale in the bud ere they arrived, but suspected he could talk to the men until he was blue in the face, unfortunately, so long as the lass continued to talk to herself, his talking wasn't going to do a great load of good. It was time to have a word with the lass himself and see if he couldn't sort out whether she was insane or not. If she wasn't, all well and good. If she was . . . well, Connall had a problem. But the least Ewan could do was see if he could keep her from talking to herself and putting that worry into the men's minds.

Digging his heels into the sides of his mount, he urged his horse to a trot that sent him out in front of the men and to his new lady's side. The woman glanced at him with surprise, then offered a tentative smile and Ewan really wished she wouldn't. There was little enough to cause good cheer in this hard life, especially after two days in the saddle, and he was sure the men would see her constant smiling as another bad sign. He scowled to discourage it and was satisfied when it wilted away and her lips turned down. Ewan then began to search his mind for an inoffensive way to broach the subject of whether she were mad or not.

* * *

"Are you mad?"

Eva blinked at that abrupt question. "I beg your pardon?"

"Yer talking to yerself, lass. Are ye mad?"

Eva stared at the man who—by her estimation—had seen at least forty summers. She could hardly believe he'd had the temerity to ask such a question of her, or the question itself, really. It had never occurred to her that they might think her mad because of such a small thing.

"I wasn't talking to myself," she said finally.

"Nay?" It was a polite sound of disbelief. She supposed he had a right to it, since he must have seen her talking.

"Nay. I was talking to Millie," Eva explained, aware that the other three men had moved up to listen to the conversation. The two who had been riding in front were also slowing and falling closer. She offered each of them a smile now, feeling sure it was important she not leave them thinking her mad.

"Millie?" There was open worry on Ewan's face and he glanced around as if expecting to see some unknown woman pop up out of nowhere.

"My horse," Eva explained patiently.

"Ah." He relaxed at once, tossing a triumphant smile to the men around them. They looked less impressed.

"And would ye be expecting the horse to answer ye?" One of them asked, drawing a frown from Ewan.

"Keddy," he said the name in warning tones.

Determined to remain unruffled, Eva merely smiled at the red-haired young man with the freckled face and shook her head. "Nay, do not be silly. Horses cannot speak."

That seemed to be the right thing to say, Ewan had relaxed again and the other men were nodding solemnly in agreement.

"Nevertheless that does not mean she cannot listen," Eva added.

"Ah." The larger, dark-haired man who usually rode on

her right gave a considering nod. "That's true enough, Keddy," he pointed out to the redhead.

Eva offered him a smile for supporting her, and tried to recall what his name was. She thought Ewan had called him Donaidh when giving orders.

"Why would you be talking to her, though?" The man who usually rode behind her on Ewan's right asked. Eva thought he was called Domhall.

"Other than one trip to your court, she's never been off Caxton land," Eva said solemnly. "I fear she finds all of this just a bit unsettling, so I talk to her to soothe her."

Millie—as well as Eva herself—had only been off Caxton land once, during the trip to the Scottish court where Jonathan had attempted to find a man who would take her without a dower. He had claimed to have chosen the Scottish court over their English one for two reasons; first, it was closer and less of a troublesome journey to make. The second reason had been that, thanks to King James's present efforts to encourage Anglo-Scottish marriages in an effort to further firm the truce the two countries were presently enjoying, her brother had thought it might be easier to marry her off there despite her lack of dower. He'd been wrong. Whether the intended husband was English or Scottish, Eva wasn't pretty enough, or accomplished enough to be desirable without a dower. Not that she minded. God had given her a fine mind and that would serve her well, long after age had stolen whatever looks she had been given.

Aware of the silence that had fallen among the men, Eva glanced about. The Scots were once again riding in formation. Satisfied that she wasn't talking to herself, and therefore perhaps wasn't mad, it would appear that they were now simply going to fall back into their usual surly travel silence. This was a disappointment to Eva who had found it quite pleasant to speak to these men, to anyone really.

Eva was as unaccustomed to long lengths of silence as

she was to long journeys. There had always been someone to talk to at Caxton; the maids, the blacksmith, the stable master, the children, the priest . . . Any one of them would have taken the trouble to speak to her had she stopped by to see them, yet these men had ridden at her side for two days in silence. It had made a long, wearying and monotonous journey even longer, more wearying, and more monotonous, and frankly, Eva was tired and cranky enough not to be too appreciative at the moment. In fact, she was beginning to grow irritated with the man responsible for this journey; her husband, Connall MacAdie.

She muttered the name with a sigh. It was her considered opinion that by sending his men to collect her like a cow he wished purchased, her husband was showing her very little in the way of care and concern. Eva supposed this meant she could expect to be considered of little more value at MacAdie than she had been at Caxton. Had it been so much to hope that she might have gained a husband who valued her at least a little? It seemed Connall MacAdie wasn't likely to.

"M'lady?"

Eva glanced at the man on her left distractedly. Keddy, the redhead with an unfortunate blanket of freckles on his face, had urged his mount closer again to address her. "Aye?"

"Why are you talking to your horse about our laird?"

"Was I?" Eva asked, taken aback at the realization that she must have been muttering her displeasure with her new husband aloud.

"Aye," Keddy assured her, then glanced to the man riding on her other side. "Was she no', Donaidh?"

"Aye." The large, dark-haired man urged his own mount closer again so that Eva was sandwiched between the two of them on Millie's back. "And ye werenae soundin' too pleased with him. Are ye no pleased to be the MacAdie's bride?"

Eva considered lying to avoid offending these men, but lying wasn't in her nature. "I would be more pleased had he bothered to collect me himself, rather than having you collect me like a new cow for the fields," she admitted bluntly.

"Ah." Ewan and Domhall had moved up again so that the four of them were crowding her once more. It was Ewan who decided to address this matter now, "Yer English, so ye wouldnae be understandin', but Connall wouldnae send the six of us to collect a cow. He'd send one man, and it wouldnae be any o' us."

"Aye," the other men nodded their agreement.

"So I should be flattered that he could not be bothered to come fetch me himself, but sent the six of you?" Eva asked dryly.

"Aye." Ewan nodded.

"O'course," Keddy agreed. "After all, he couldnae collect ye himsel', so sent us in his stead. *Six* of us in his stead. It shows how important ye are. He even sent Ewan."

The way he said it made it sound like it was a huge honor, an opinion that was verified for Eva when Domhall added, "Aye, and Ewan is his first."

The way he said that suggested it was an important position to hold. Eva was less interested in that, however, than why the man couldn't collect her himself, so asked, "Why could he not collect me himself?"

"Well . . . That'd be difficult to explain, lass," Ewan began slowly even as Keddy said, "It's his condition."

"Condition?" she asked with a combination of concern and interest.

"Aye, his condition," Ewan muttered, but he was glaring at Keddy for interfering.

"What condition, pray tell?"

Ewan's scowl became even more fierce on Keddy at this question, then he finally glanced at her and said, "Tis best to ask him that."

Eva frowned at that unsatisfactory statement, but couldn't think of a way to force a proper answer out of him. Giving up on it, she glanced at these men, her men now, she supposed. They had gone quiet again and Eva didn't wish to return to the solemn silence that had marked most of this trip so far, so sought her mind for something to draw them into conversation again and keep them talking. She'd like to get to know them. She'd like to get to know someone. Eva was very aware that she was completely and utterly alone and deep in a foreign land that was now to be her home.

She recalled dreaming of marrying and moving to her own home, and how wonderful that would be, but the reality was something else entirely, scary where she hadn't considered it might be. Why had she never considered that it would be so scary and lonely?

"Tis a lovely day, is it not?" she asked desperately as the men began to ease their mounts away, obviously preparing to return to their usual positions with their usual silence.

Her comment stopped the move away from her, but the silence continued for another moment as the men glanced at each other. Eva bit her lip as she realized that it wasn't a lovely day at all. It was late summer, but the sky was overcast and the air had a nip to it. It was too late to retract the statement, however. Aware that her face was flushing with a blush of embarrassment, she raised her chin a bit and stared straight ahead ignoring their rudeness in gawking at her as they were.

"Er . . . A lovely day?" Ewan queried finally.

"Well, 'tis not raining," she pointed out defensively. It could be worse after all, she told herself.

"That's true enough," Donaidh allowed judicially and Eva relaxed a little, but then silence fell again. She supposed that was all that her comment on the weather deserved, and decided she'd have to come up with something more interesting to discuss. Eva contemplated her options, but nothing was really coming to mind. Politics were out of the question. These were Scots. She was English. Dear God, they were practically enemies by birth alone, and surely wouldn't agree on anything political.

Oddly enough, it was Ewan who prolonged the conversation by announcing, "Tis no far to MacAdie now."

Eva felt herself stiffen at this news. Much as she would be grateful to get off her horse, she was suddenly anxious at the idea of coming face-to-face with her husband.

"Will my husband be there when we arrive?" she asked, wondering how awful she looked after traveling for two days without stop, and suspecting she must look as travel worn and weary as she felt. It was surely no way to first meet your new husband.

"If we arrive after dark, he'll be there, but if we arrive while it's still light out, he may still be . . . about his business," Ewan concluded after a hesitation. "He didna ken how long it'd take to negotiate the marriage, or if we'd even succeed, ye understand," he said, excusing the man.

"Nay. Of course not," Eva agreed absently, but her mind was on what he had said. If they arrived before dark he might not yet be there, which would give her the opportunity to at least change into her other gown and possibly tidy herself a bit, if not to take a bath and make herself properly presentable for this man she was to spend the rest of her life with. First impressions were very important, at least her mother had always said it was so. "And do you think we shall arrive ere dark, or after?"

Ewan considered the matter, then decided, "We should be arriving near to when the sun sets."

Eva felt her shoulders sag with disappointment at those words, but quickly forced them back up. "Near to" meant they might yet arrive before her husband, which meant she might at least have a couple of minutes to try to repair herself before meeting him. More if he should happen to be later than expected. That was better than nothing.

Two

Eva stared down at the castle below and swallowed a sudden lump in her throat. The keep crouched at the base of the surrounding hills, shadows falling across it like a cloak. It looked a dark and gloomy place. In comparison, Caxton Hall seemed a sunny abode, at least in her memory. To her mind, the gloomy structure below went a long way toward explaining the attitude of the men she rode with. Who could be happy and full of good cheer while abiding in such a dismal place?

"The sun is setting."

Eva stirred herself to glance at her companions at that comment from Donaidh. The man's words had sounded concerned to her. That concern was echoed in the expression of every man around her, she saw and wondered briefly if they worried that their lord would be displeased with their late arrival. Eva wasn't too pleased with it herself, as she'd really rather hoped to have at least a few minutes to clean up and prepare herself before meeting her husband. But she was guessing that the man would be about by now, or at least would be ere they managed to make their way down the rather steep hill they had crested and to the castle.

"Stay close," Ewan ordered the men and Eva was surprised to hear the sudden tension in his voice. She was even more surprised when he gestured to Donaidh and the large man suddenly lifted her off her mount and onto his own, settling her before him as the other men now closed ranks, surrounding them on all sides.

Eva didn't struggle or protest, but she did crane her neck to try to peer back down at the castle again. She was sure that just before Ewan had blocked her view by urging his mount out before the horse she now sat on, she had glimpsed dark figures moving in the deepening black valley below. All she'd had was a quick glimpse, but Eva thought she'd seen a couple of darker shadows moving away from the castle. No matter how she craned her neck, however, she couldn't now see past the mounted men surrounding her.

The ride down into the valley seemed to take forever to Eva. It probably wasn't that long a ride, but the tension in the men around her was infectious, and that and the fact that she couldn't see a single blasted thing past the backs of her surrounding guards made it seem unending. Her vision was so obscured that it wasn't until the starlight overhead was suddenly blocked out entirely and she glanced up to see that they were riding under the parapet and through the castle gates, that she knew they had arrived.

The moment they were past the gates, sound exploded around them. It was as if someone had removed a muffling cape from her head, still, Eva could see nothing and she wished she could. The bailey here sounded as busy as Caxton bailey would be during the busiest mid-afternoon hours, yet it was nighttime and should have been much quieter.

At first distracted by the noise, it took Eva a moment to realize that the men surrounding her had now relaxed. The difference was notable. Eva felt herself relax in response, but didn't give up attempting to see her surroundings—as impossible as that was at the moment with the men still riding clustered close around the horse she and Donaidh were astride. Eva was able to catch a flash of color here and there in the light of torches that were spread liberally about. There must have been hundreds of them to emit such light, she guessed and thought it a dreadful waste. Such resources would have been carefully preserved at Caxton, but then her childhood home was a poor hold. Eva supposed her new home was in much better shape. The fact that the MacAdie had not only taken her without dower, but had actually paid one for her, should have told her that, she supposed, and wondered if she should tell her husband that he needn't have bothered buying her. Jonathan had been willing to give her away, at least he had been before the Scots had made mention of offering a dower for her.

Nay, she decided. Perhaps the fact that he'd had to purchase her would give her some small value in his eyes.

A barked order from Ewan brought the party to a halt, while a second bark had the men dismounting. This would have been Eva's opportunity to get her first glimpse of her new home, were it not for the fact that Donaidh lifted her down from the saddle even as the other men shifted and stepped down themselves. The man was quick to follow her to the ground and Eva found herself once more surrounded. Now she stood in a forest of bodies, both men and horses, and once again, she couldn't see a thing. It was becoming damned annoying.

"Ewan."

Eva glanced around sharply at that call, the ring of authority in it and the way the men around her suddenly stiffened to attention told her that it was most likely their laird, her husband. Biting her lip, she quickly tried to brush the wrinkles and dust out of her gown with one hand, while attempting to push the stiff wind-ratted mass that was her hair into some semblance of order as she listened to the men talk and awaited the introduction that surely would come.

"M'laird," she heard Ewan's baritone greeting.

"Any trouble?"

"Nay. We rode through the night as ye ordered, rested on the edge of Caxton land, collected her and rode through the night on the way back. The trip was without incident, m'laird."

"Good. Magaidh—Oh, there ye are. The lass'll be exhausted, could ye—"

"Aye, I shall see to 'er," a woman's voice assured him.

"Thank ye. Ye men see to yer horses, then report to me."

Eva stilled at that order and the sudden shifting of men around her as they moved to collect the reins of their horses to lead them away. They took Millie with them as well, leaving Eva standing alone to stare after them with bewilderment. For a moment, she felt rather like a lost child abandoned at market, then she gathered her wits enough to glance sharply around in search of the man who was her husband. The only person still standing near her was a woman; a beautiful, dark-haired creature with a welcoming smile.

"Eva?"

"Aye," she acknowledged uncertainly.

"I am Magaidh. I'll take ye to yer room and see ye taken care of." She held a hand out and clasped Eva's in welcome, then drew it through her arm and began walking her to the castle door.

"My husband?" Eva asked in a small voice as they entered the building. It was finally sinking in that after all her worry about her appearance on first meeting him, the man hadn't even troubled himself to look on her. He'd ordered this woman to tend to her, then had wandered off without even a greeting.

"Connall has business to attend to. 'Sides, he was aware that ye'd be exhausted and would want little more than hot food, a warm bath, and a soft bed to rest in. He'll greet ye proper in the morning once ye've recovered from yer journey," the woman assured her with a pat of her hand, then called several soft orders in a language that sounded like so much jargon to her untrained ear. Gaelic, Eva supposed as she was led up the stairs.

"Ye must be exhausted. A bath'll reinvigorate ye ere ye eat, will it not."

Despite the couching of the words, it wasn't a question, the woman was informing her that she would be bathing before dining. Eva merely nodded. She hadn't a clue who Magaidh was, but she was dressed in a fine silk gown and had a definite air of authority about her. All in all, Eva supposed the other woman fit the image of a fine Lady of the Castle, more than she did herself.

"Are you the MacAdie's sister?" she hazarded the guess as they had ascended the stairs and started along the hall.

"Mither," the woman corrected with a smile, her eyebrows rising when Eva abruptly stopped walking and gaped at her in horror.

"Dear God, I've been married off to a boy," Eva breathed and the woman laughed.

"Nay."

"But I must be! You are not old enough to have a child more than ten."

"Connall is well past ten, lass."

"But—" Eva paused as realization claimed her. Of course, this woman was MacAdie's stepmother, that was the obvious explanation. The voice she had heard in the bailey, the one she had assumed was her husband's, had held the strength and timber of a man of at least thirty, and a man used to carrying responsibility.

"Here we are." Magaidh opened a door and led her into a large bedchamber. Eva gaped at the room. To a girl used to bare walls and sometimes even bare floors, the grandeur that met her eyes here was rather dazzling. This room was at least four times the size of the tiny bedchamber she had occupied at Caxton, and, these walls were not bare. Fine tapestries lined each wall, fresh smelling rushes carpeted the floor and a cheery fire burned gaily in a huge fireplace making it obvious that they were not stingy with their wood here, as they were at Caxton.

Eva moved to the bed and ran her fingers lightly over the fine silk material that hung around it. It was pulled back now, but would be lovely when drawn around the bed to block out the cold and draft, she thought with a sigh of pleasure. "Tis lovely."

"I'm glad ye like it."

Eva turned to smile shyly at the woman, then glanced to the door she had forgotten to close as servants began filing through it. Two men came first, bearing a huge tub which they set near the fire. Several women followed with pail after pail of steaming water. These were poured into the tub, along with a small jar of sweet smelling flowers and herbs. Once this was done, all but one servant left.

"Glynis will help ye with yer bath," Magaidh announced moving toward the door as she spoke. "I'll have yer meal sent up once ye've finished."

"Thank you," Eva said with a sincerity she couldn't possibly express properly.

Magaidh glanced back with a smile that seemed to warm her from the inside out. "Yer more than welcome, child. Yer home now."

Eva shook her head as the door closed behind the lovely woman. Imagine someone so young calling her child, she thought with weary amusement, then turned to smile at the girl who was to act as her maid. About her own height, but a bit plumper and with shiny red hair and freckles that would rival Keddy's, the girl smiled at her widely in return.

"Shall I help ye to undress, m'lady?" Glynis asked.

Eva almost demurred, as she wasn't really used to help. While it was true that Mavis had been pressed into acting as her lady's maid a time or two, it was mostly to fuss over Eva's hair. She generally dressed and undressed herself. However, Eva found that her energy appeared to have drained away and she was suddenly so exhausted that undressing seemed a terrible effort. The assistance would be welcome.

"Yes, please," Eva murmured as she approached the girl and the tub she stood beside.

"Where is she?"

Magaidh MacAdie glanced up as Connall crossed the great hall to the trestle table where she sat. "She's sleepin' o' course. The poor lass was exhausted after such a strenuous journey. She bathed, ate, and fell right to sleep." Her gaze slid to Ewan as he too sat down. "Could ye no have stopped fer at least four or five hours last night to give the girl a rest? Tis obvious she's no used to sech long journeys."

"I ordered him to ride straight through," Connall excused the man as they settled at the table. A servant immediately rushed forward with ale. Connall nodded his thanks, but didn't touch his drink.

"Well, I hope 'twas fer a good purpose. The lass has a sorry case o' saddle sores from the journey."

"Better saddle sores than dead," Connall said. "With the trouble we've been having of late, it seemed a sensible precaution."

Magaidh's mouth tightened at the reminder of the recent difficulties that had arisen around the MacNachtons and MacAdies. The rumors had started again, some of their people had been killed, and there had been two attempts on Connall's life, though they weren't sure if these attacks were connected to the rumors. Pushing these grim thoughts away, she merely said, "Well, I had Glynis put some salve on the sores. She'll recover soon enough."

Connall grunted at this news, then glanced at Ewan. "Did she whinge about being sore?"

The man shook his head. "Nay. Said nary a word o' complaint. No aboot the length of the journey or ought else."

Connall's gaze narrowed on the other man. Ewan was so obviously pleased to be able to offer this news, he was left to wonder what the man *wasn't* saying. "Were there any problems at all?"

The man shifted uncomfortably, leading Connall to believe he'd been right. There *was* something. "Ewan," he said in warning tones.

"No a problem really," the man finally said. "There was a tense bit though when the men thought her mad."

"What?" Magaidh looked shocked. "Well, 'tis nonsense. She's a perfectly lovely lass."

"Aye. She is. I mean she isna mad," Ewan said quickly. "It's jest she was talking to her horse fer a bit and the men mistook it fer her talking to hersel' and began to fret that she was—"

"Talking to her horse?" Connall interrupted.

"Er . . . Aye. It seems the mare isna used to long journeys outside o' Caxton, and she was soothing the beast. A lot," he added, feeling he should mention that. If there was something wrong with the lass, her husband should be prepared.

Connall considered this information, but merely nodded. It didn't seem a problem to him if the lass wanted to soothe her mare. He was rather fond of his own mount.

The three of them fell silent and Connall finally turned his attention to the drink the servant had set before him. The ale was tepid and bitter, just the way he liked it. An hour ago he wouldn't have enjoyed it nearly as much as he did now, though he'd had another thirst needing attention. One he fought as often as he could, but had to give in to eventually to live.

"Ye should've at least greeted the girl."

Connall glanced at his mother. She was giving him that reproving look he hated so much. It always managed to bring guilt to the fore in him, as it did now. "I thought she'd prefer to rest and recover from her journey first."

"Aye, but surely a hello wouldn't have harmed?"

Connall shrugged uncomfortably and concentrated on his drink. He hadn't intended avoiding his new bride in the way he had. It had been a spur of the moment decision. He'd come out of the keep on being told the men were back, expecting to greet her, but on arriving and finding her not in evidence—though he'd spied the skirt of her dress between the legs of his milling men—he'd been content to leave the meeting until later. Actually, he'd felt relief on avoiding the meeting as he'd walked away.

Connall was finding this business of marriage rather dismaying. He agreed with his cousin, Cathal, that it was necessary, but that didn't mean he had to like it. In truth, he had put the actual doing of the deed off these last months while Cathal had gone out and found himself a bride back in the spring. Connall supposed he had been waiting to see how that turned out before bothering about it himself. In the end, it had turned out surprisingly well. His cousin's bride, Bridget, suited Cathal perfectly and the pair were now enjoying wedded bliss. If Connall's own marriage went half as well, he'd be content.

That thought brought Eva Caxton to mind. Theirs was not a great love match, but he had met and liked the girl when he'd spoken to her, though not so much that he had decided to marry her then. In fact, when he had finally decided that it was time to stop putting off his duty and to get married, he had at first found himself stumped as to who to marry. He could hardly count on his Nightriders to stumble upon a lass in distress and carry her home to him to wed as had happened with Cathal and Bridget. As for contracting a marriage in the usual way, that had seemed an unlikely event for him to manage. His clan did not enjoy a good reputation just at present what with the rumors about their ancestry and such coming back into question. Connall had almost thought he'd set himself an impossible task, then he had recalled his enforced visit to court.

His presence had been demanded there to stamp out the rumors about him and his people. Now that the English had signed the treaty of Picquigny with France and were keeping up their truce with Scotland, it seemed that good King James had a desire to see peace in his own small part of the world. He'd demanded Connall and his cousin Cathal's presence at court to help silence the rumors around their clans. Cathal had managed to avoid the task, but Connall had made the journey . . . and a hellish one it had been too. It was while he was there that he had met and spoken to Eva Caxton. He had passed only a few moments in her company, but she had stuck in his mind, and Connall had asked about her, only to learn that her brother had brought her to court to try to find her a husband.

Normally, this would not have been a problem for such a lovely young girl, but the brother was said to be a greedy miser who hoarded the gold he'd been left by his wealthy parents and claimed poverty to all who would listen. He was trying to palm her off without a dower, and had been failing miserably at the task since everyone at court knew that his smoke screen about poverty was just so much nonsense.

Eva Caxton had left court the day before Connall had, and without a marriage offer. Deciding that if she were still available, she would do as well as anyone else, Connall had counted on her brother's greed to aid in the endeavor and had sent Ewan and five men with gold to barter for her. He had fully expected that—so long as she was still available— Ewan would be bringing him back a bride. And he had, of course, though Ewan had claimed it was a close thing. Jonathan Caxton had been all set to shuffle the girl off to an abbey the very day after Ewan and the men had arrived. Had Connall hesitated about the decision just one more day, she would have been beyond his reach and he would have been left to find another family desperate—or greedy—enough to sell him a daughter of the house.

Connall wasn't sure whether he should be glad the task was done or not. He supposed it at least meant one problem was taken care of. Now he just had to get the woman with child and—

"We should hold a proper wedding now she's here."

Connall's thoughts died abruptly at that suggestion from his mother. "What? Why? Ewan stood in fer me at the proxy wedding. Tis all legal. Or will be once we consummate it."

"Aye, but surely 'twouldn't hurt to hold a small ceremony here to make it all official—"

"The proxy wedding was official," Connall interrupted.

"Aye, but ye werenae there fer it."

"So?"

Magaidh sighed. "Do ye feel married, son?"

Connall paused to consider the matter. In truth, he didn't feel any different than he had the day before, or the day before that and he had to wonder with some irritation, just what being married was supposed to feel like.

"Ye see." Magaidh didn't bother to hide her satisfaction. "Ye doonae, do ye?"

Connall scowled, unwilling to admit anything of the sort. Another wedding was nothing but a waste to his mind, but his mother was determined to argue the case.

"It'd be better fer both o' ye. I doubt the proxy wedding was anything more than a couple o' words spoken by the priest and contracts signed." Magaidh raised an eyebrow at Ewan as she suggested that, satisfaction suffusing her face when he gave a brief nod of agreement. "I doubt Eva feels any more married than ye. And it will give our people the chance to see her and see that yer married as well."

Connall closed his mouth on the protest he had been about to launch as Magaidh's last words caught his attention. It wouldn't be a bad thing for their people to witness the event, and he really should be sure she was recognized by one and all as his bride . . . and under his protection.

"Ewan, we need a priest," he announced firmly.

"I shall see to it, m'laird." The man was on his feet at once and moving toward the door to the keep.

"Jest send someone fer him," Connall instructed. "Then rest. Ye've had a long journey."

"Aye, m'laird." The door closed behind him with a thud.

Three

Eva awoke at once. There was no slow stirring to wakefulness, no abrupt jerking awake, she simply rolled onto her back, opened her eyes and felt alert and awake. Pleasantly so. Remaining where she lay for a moment, she let her eyes drift around the large luxurious room where she had slept. It was much more welcoming than her own room had ever been.

But she supposed this was her room now. At least, she hoped so. It looked like it might belong to the laird of a wealthy clan. That thought reminded her that she was married now. It was an odd thought. Eva didn't feel married, though she wasn't sure what being married should feel like. She felt no different than she had every day of her life for some time now. Well, perhaps that wasn't true. She did feel a bit odd. She was in a strange place, with strange people around her. And now had a husband who would share her life and her bed.

That last thought made her glance abruptly to the right side of the bed. It was empty. For one moment she had considered that her husband may have joined her after she had fallen asleep. But it would appear not. Eva was mostly relieved about this, but felt a touch of concern too. Why hadn't her husband joined her last night in what was most likely his own bed? He hadn't bothered to greet her on her arrival yesterday either. This seemed odd to her.

Eva hadn't really contemplated the welcome she'd expected on arriving at MacAdie, but had she taken the time and trouble to, she certainly wouldn't have expected it to be what had happened. Her husband had neither greeted her on her arrival, nor even come to see her as she ate her meal after her bath. Now, it appeared, he hadn't joined her in his own bed . . . Unless he had and had already risen to greet the day.

That thought made her glance toward the fur covered window. How late in the morning was it? Perhaps she had slept through his arrival and leave taking. Perhaps he *had* slept here. Where else would he sleep?

Pushing the furs aside, Eva slid her feet to the floor, giving a delicate shudder at the cool straw underfoot. Despite it being summer, the night had been cool and even now there was still a nip to the morning air, but the furs piled on the bed had kept her warm and snug. Leaving them reluctantly behind, she scampered quickly to the window and drew the fur aside enough to see out into the bailey below. A wave of warm air struck her face and she saw that the sun was high in the sky. By her guess it must be midmorning and guilt nagged her at once. She'd slept quite late. This was hardly the way to impress her new husband.

Eva let the fur fall back into place, then just as quickly pulled it aside once more. It was warmer outside than it was in the room at the moment. The furs had kept the warmer air out this morning, just as effectively as they had kept the worst of the cold air out last night. Finding a bit of cloth lying on the stone ledge of the window, Eva tied the fur back, glanced briefly down into the busy bustling bailey again, then turned back to the now sunlit room.

She would dress and go below to break her fast and finally meet her husband, she decided, then immediately began to consider what to wear. Unfortunately, there wasn't a lot of choice in the matter; there was the faded blue gown she'd worn for the journey here, or the threadbare grey gown she'd brought in her satchel.

Eva grimaced to herself as she glanced around in search of her satchel. The grey gown would be wrinkled, but it would be fresh in comparison to the dust covered blue one. She was trying to recall where she had set her satchel on entering the room the night before when a soft tapping sounded at the door. Giving up on the bag for now, Eva scampered back to bed and climbed in, then dragged the furs up to her neck and held them there as she called, "Enter."

The door opened at once and the servant girl who had helped her with her bath the night before poked her head inside. Spotting her sitting up in bed, Glynis smiled widely. "Yer oop."

The redhead slid into the room and nearly danced to the bed, waving a bundle of rose colored cloth in hand. "Lady Magaidh said to bring this oop to ye."

"Oh," Eva breathed out the word as the girl shifted the material and held it up for her to see. It was a gown, and quite the finest one Eva had ever seen. Tossing the bedclothes aside again, she crawled to the edge of the bed and reached out to brush the tips of her fingers gently over the soft cloth. "It's lovely. Are you sure 'tis for me?"

"Aye." The maid looked as excited as if the gown were for herself. "Last night, I took yer two gowns below. I was plannin' to wash the one and hang the other to let the wrinkles out, but when Lady Magaidh saw them, she said 'They simply wouldna do.'" Glynis grinned. "And she fetched this one fer ye. She said 'twas more befitting the Lady MacAdie. And she said 'tis yours now. Ye'll look lovely in it, m'lady."

"Oh." Eva breathed again, then blinked her eyes in alarm. Tears had filled them at the kindness. Embarrassed, she dashed them quickly away, then scrambled off the bed to claim the gown. Glynis grinned as she held it against herself and turned in a circle. Eva thought it was the most beautiful gown she'd ever seen. Certainly it was the most beautiful gown she'd ever owned. "Is it really mine?"

"Aye. Lady Magaidh said so. And she said we'd be havin' to see to a whole new wardrobe fer ye. One that befits the bride of the MacAdie."

"For me?" Eva asked with amazement. A whole wardrobe. How many gowns was that? She'd never had more than two at a time, sometimes only the one.

"Come, m'lady. I'll fix yer hair and help ye to dress." Glynis beamed widely. "I'm to be yer lady's maid." Her smile faltered briefly and she added an uncertain, "If ye think I'll do, that is. Lady Magaidh will assign anoother girl if yer no pleased—"

"I'm well pleased with you as my maid, Glynis," she assured her quickly and was relieved when the other girl began to smile again, but she had meant what she'd said; Eva felt sure that the two of them would get on just fine. Glynis had been very sweet and kind with her last night as she'd helped Eva with her bath and preparing for bed. Eva was certain that she had made the right decision several minutes later when Glynis finished working on her hair and presented a small mirror for her to see how she looked. The young maid had worked miracles. The little redhead had managed to make Eva look beautiful and that was not a word she had ever thought she'd use to describe herself, but she felt beautiful at that moment as she peered at herself in the small mirror.

Glynis had collected every last strand of Eva's golden runaway tresses and put them up on top of her head, then dressed it with ribbons of matching rose that Magaidh had apparently sent with the gown. Eva felt like a princess.

"Tis all right, is it not, m'lady?"

Recognizing the anxiety in the girl's voice, Eva forced

herself to stop staring at her reflected image and turned to give the maid an impulsive hug.

"Tis more than all right, Glynis," she assured her as she stepped back. "You've worked miracles. Thank you."

Flushing with pleasure at the compliment, Glynis took the mirror Eva handed back. "Yer mair than welcome, m'lady. Tis jest glad I am that yer pleased."

"More than pleased," Eva assured her, standing and brushing her hands down the soft cloth of the gown she wore. "Do you think Cook could find me something to eat? I know 'tis late in the day, but—"

"Oh aye, Cook has a lovely repast all set fer ye," Glynis interrupted to assure her. "Lady Magaidh warned her as ye'd probably sleep late after yer long journey, so she served normal breakfast fer everyone else, and made a special one fer ye. I was jest coming to check on ye when Ewan informed her ye were up, so she's like to have it all ready fer ye by now."

"Ewan informed her?" Eva blinked in surprise. "How did he know I was up?"

"He saw ye in the window, m'lady," she explained, then seeing Eva's embarrassment, added a reassuring smile. "Ye should go below and see what Cook fixed fer ye ere it gets cold."

"Aye." Eva shrugged away her mild embarrassment at being spotted in the window in the borrowed nightdress and turned toward the door. It was doubtful the man had seen much but her small figure from wherever he'd been in the bailey when she peered out, she assured herself, then paused at the door when she realized that Glynis wasn't following her. "Are you not coming?"

The maid shook her head as she bent to pick up Eva's nightdress. "I'll jest be puttin' things away first, m'lady. Ye go on. If ye need me, just send one o' the maids to fetch me."

Eva hesitated, oddly reluctant to leave the girl's company behind. She had only known the maid a day, yet felt like she was the only friend she had in the world.

"Go on," the maid urged. "Ye have to eat. Cook will be sore if ye pass up her meal after she worked so hard at it and all."

"Aye." Eva forced herself to open the door and step out, then pulled the door reluctantly closed, wishing all the while that Glynis were coming with her. She felt oddly uncertain and small all of a sudden. The only other time Eva had felt this way was when she'd had to venture out alone at court in search of her brother. It was such a large castle, and full of so many strangers, all dressed in their finery and peering down their noses at her faded and outdated gowns with disdain. It was the only time in her life that Eva had found herself concerned with her appearance. Usually, she didn't mind that her gowns were worn and old and not at the height of fashion, but after two days of being sneered at, and laughed at behind hands, all she'd wanted was to go home where she was accepted as she was. Unable to do that, she'd instead borne the rude behavior when necessary, then run and hid herself away as often as she could get away with it.

Reminding herself that she was no longer wearing a threadbare, outdated gown and that she looked every bit the lady of the castle, Eva forced her shoulders straight and headed along the hall. She heard the murmur of voices rising from the great hall before she quite reached the stairs. It sounded like two people talking, a man and a woman. Eva forced herself to take a deep breath and continue. Finally, she would meet her husband, she told herself and wasn't surprised that her heart picked up speed and began to race a bit. The racing stopped the moment she started down the stairs and chanced a glance at the occupants of the room below and saw that it was Ewan and Magaidh seated at the trestle table, not a strange man who might be her husband.

Eva tried to ignore the relief that coursed through her, but her feet moved a little quicker down the stairs now that she knew the dreaded meeting wasn't at hand. Really, she reprimanded herself silently, she should look forward to meeting the man, not dread it so.

"Good morn—oh!" She paused and blinked at the woman seated with Ewan at the table. Eva had thought it was Magaidh, but while she had the same dark good looks and similar facial features, this woman was older, closer in age to Ewan, she thought.

"This is Ailie, m'lady," Ewan stood to introduce them, drawing Eva out of her startled silence.

"Short for Aileen," the woman added as she too now stood and moved around the table to offer Eva a welcoming hug. "Welcome to MacAdie."

Eva smiled as Aileen stepped back. "Thank you," she murmured, but her gaze moved questioningly to Ewan. She hadn't a clue who the woman was. She knew so little about her new home.

"Ailie's me wife," Ewan said with some pride, then added, "And yer husband's sister."

Eva's eyes shot back to the woman with surprise. Aileen MacAdie looked older than Magaidh yet she was Connall MacAdie's sister, while Magaidh had claimed to be his mother. Last night Eva had explained away the other woman's youthful appearance to herself by deciding that Magaidh must be a stepmother. That explanation, she realized now, would work just as well to explain the age difference between the two women. Magaidh was obviously stepmother to Aileen as well. Eva supposed that meant that her husband was probably of an age with Ewan and Aileen, older than herself by a good twenty years. Not what she had expected, but not so bad, she reassured herself. At least he was not in his dotage. And really, what had she expected? A handsome and wealthy young man willing to buy her to bride when he would be so much of a catch on the marriage market? No, of course not.

"Are ye feelin' recovered from the journey?" Ewan asked, and Eva suddenly realized they were all still standing while she had pondered the matter. She was being rude. Moving forward at once, she settled at the table even as Ailie and Ewan did and offered the couple a smile.

"Yes, thank you. Much recovered," she said with a wry smile, knowing that she had probably slept much longer than he. Eva doubted if he had gone to bed as early as herself yesterday and he obviously hadn't slept as late. "And you?"

"Aye." He glanced over his shoulder toward a door and opened his mouth, but before Ewan could call out whatever order he had planned to, the door opened and several servants bustled in. Relaxing, he turned back and grinned at her. "Cook's made something special to welcome ye to MacAdie and we've been waiting all morning to see what 'tis."

"Oh, I'm sorry to have made you wait," Eva murmured, watching with curiosity as the maids began to set platters on the table. Red hair seemed to be a common trait amongst the MacAdies. Several of the servants had the same carroty red hair and freckles as Glynis.

"Doona fret," Ailie laughed. "Ewan's teasing ye. We didna expect ye to rise even as early as ye have. The trip here must've been exhausting fer ye. I doubt that I could have managed it as well as Ewan claims ye did."

Eva smiled at that compliment, but her attention was quickly caught again by the food being laid out before them. The most wonderful smells were coming from the platters and Eva suddenly felt starved. Her stomach was reacting as if she hadn't eaten since leaving Caxton, yet Ewan had given her oatcakes on the journey and she had eaten a full repast the night before of cheese and bread and meat.

"Hmmm," Ewan murmured as the servants finally finished arranging the food and moved off. "I see bannocks and crowdie . . . and berries of course. Oh look, she made black buns and Atholl Brose too. Mmmm." He grinned at Eva. "And she made enough for us all."

"Course I did!"

That snapped comment made Eva glance over her shoulder at the robust woman now approaching the table.

"Think I didn't know you'd be sniffing around the table, Ewan MacAdie? Yer a man ruled by yer appetites like every MacAdie around and before ye." She sniffed at the man, then turned to Eva, her expression turning into a welcoming smile. "Hello, m'lady. I'm Effie, cook here and this is me welcome to MacAdie fer ye. I'm hoping ye live a long and happy life with us."

"Thank you, Effie." She smiled at the cook. "This all looks lovely."

The woman smiled and nodded and glanced over the table. "I usually serve jest the bannocks and crowdie—or some other cheese—to break fast, and fruit too if ye've a taste," the woman informed her.

Eva glanced at the dishes the woman had gestured to as she spoke. The bannocks were simple oatcakes, the crowdie appeared to be a white cheese rolled in oats. The fruit on the table was all berries: raspberries, strawberries, tayberries, and brambles.

"But this morning I made the black buns and Atholl Brose special fer ye, as Ewan pointed out," she added heavily, then explained, "The black bun is a rich fruit cake with raisins, currants, and fine-chopped peel and such in it. Atholl Brose is a lovely pudding of oatmeal, honey, cream, and whiskey. I hope ye'll be enjoying them both."

"I'm sure I will," Eva assured her and wasn't just being polite. Her mouth was watering from the smells around her. The black buns and pudding and indeed the bannocks were all obviously freshly made. She flushed with embarrassment as her stomach growled, but Effie merely laughed and began to dish food into the trencher before Eva.

"Here ye are then, lassie. No need to wait. Yer stomach's wantin' filling."

Eva could have hugged the woman when the cook piled more food on the trencher in front of her than she ever would have dared to put on it herself. Guilty as she had always been made to feel for being a burden to her brother, Eva had always ate sparingly, and had always felt hungry for it. But Effie had no such qualms to restrain her and heaped the food on until Eva wanted to moan with pleasure.

"There we are then, and I'll be expectin' ye tae eat all of that so's ye don't insult me cookin'. We need to put some meat on those fine bones of yers," she announced. "Now, I'm back to the kitchens. I've lots to do ere the nooning repast."

"Thank you," Eva called after her, then turned back to survey her trencher with anticipation. Where to start?

It was a question that repeated itself in her head some time later as Eva tried to decide what to do next. She had enjoyed a lovely discussion with Ailie and Ewan while eating the fine fare the cook, Effie, had presented for her. Eva had eaten every last bite of her meal, and was now almost sorry she had. Her stomach felt ready to explode. Reprimanding herself never to be so greedy again, she'd stayed at the table talking to Ailie and Ewan about desultory subjects until her discomfort eased.

Eva had learned that, not only did she now have Ailie and Ewan as her new brother and sister-in-law, she also had two nieces and a nephew. She had rather hoped that they would be sweet young children she could spoil and rock on her knee, but Ailie had quickly corrected her in that. The couple's children were grown, with the son the oldest, having seen twenty-five years. One of the daughters had a daughter of her own. That child was young enough to spoil and rock on her knee at least, Eva supposed, and readjusted her idea of the woman's age in her mind. She had thought Ewan had seen forty summers and Ailie must be close behind. Now she suspected they were a touch older than that and had just aged well. Either that or Ewan had married Ailie right out of the cradle. That made Eva wonder just how old her husband was. Was Ailie the older of the two? Or was her husband close to fifty summers?

It wasn't unusual for girls to be married to older men, and a husband twenty years the bride's senior could be common, but thirty years or more was a bit much. Unwilling to think about that, Eva had tried to steer the conversation toward her husband and where he might be, but Ailie and Ewan had seemed resistant to her attempts. All Ewan had said about her husband was that he was away for the day, but should return around supper. Despite that, Eva had found her eyes darting to the keep door every time it had opened to admit someone, some part of her hoping and at the same time dreading, that he would change his plans and suddenly appear to welcome her as his sister, his mother, and even his cook already had. But it never happened. It seemed her husband wasn't troubled about making her feel welcome.

Eva found that a bit alarming. His willingness to pay a dower to claim her was at odds with the way he was now seeming to ignore her very presence. She tried to reassure herself that he was the laird here, and therefore busy and she could hardly expect him to bring everything to a halt for her. But Eva still found herself a bit disappointed. She was also a bit concerned. Perhaps he had seen the party arrive and caught a glimpse of her where she had not been able to see anyone else. He could have been on the wall as they rode in and rushed down to greet them. If that were the case, perhaps he had been disappointed in her looks and suddenly sorry about the bargain he had made.

That was an alarming thought. While Eva had been a tad distressed by suddenly finding herself bought to bride and dragged off to the wilds of Scotland, now that she was here, it wasn't so bad. Everyone, bar her husband, had been very kind and welcoming and Eva was starting to see that life here might be pleasant, she could even be happy. Besides, being sent home in shame, rejected by the man who had saved her from the abbey, was a consequence too horrifying to contemplate.

It seemed to Eva that it was in her best interests to prove her worth to her husband. Certainly she wasn't the prettiest girl in England—or Scotland for that matter—so her value had to be proven in more concrete ways. She had to prove her usefulness, Eva had decided. The fact that proving her usefulness had never secured her spot at Caxton was not one she allowed herself to ponder. It was too disheartening. Instead, once Ailie had excused herself to go visit with her daughter, and Ewan had removed himself to oversee the keep as first while her husband was away, Eva had sat at the trestle table as the servants cleared things away and tried to think what she could do.

Inspiration had struck just as the last of the things were cleared away and Eva popped up from her seat with excitement. She needed to find Glynis; she would need help with this endeavor.

Connall found Ewan waiting for him when he stepped out of the secret room where he slept during the daylight hours. That in itself was a bad sign as Ewan would usually have been at the trestle table enjoying his supper at this hour. The fact that he wasn't suggested there was a problem.

"What's happened?" he asked abruptly as he let the stone door slide closed behind him. "Has there been another attack?"

"Nay," Ewan assured him quickly. "Nay, nothing so serious."

"Then why are ye here?"

"Weell, there is a matter I wished tae speak with ye aboot.

Just a small matter really," he added when Connall began to frown.

"A small matter that has ye waitin' at the passage fer me to rise?" he asked doubtfully.

"Weell." Ewan hesitated, then said, "Tis aboot yer wife."

Connall's eyebrows rose in surprise, then lowered with displeasure. "Has something happened to the lass?"

"Nay." Ewan frowned. "Nought has happened to her."

"Then what is it, mon?" Connall was becoming impatient.

"She . . . er . . . Tisn't what's happened to her, 'tis what she's done, Connall," he said finally.

"Well, spit it oot, maun. What has she done?"

Four

"She *what?*"

Ewan winced at that roar and all his own worry and anger at Eva's actions that day washed away under sudden pity for her. Connall wasn't happy and he knew from experience that the man could be unpleasant when angry. Where he had been outraged himself earlier and upset on Aileen's behalf, Ewan suddenly found himself trying to minimize the matter. "Weell noo, Connall, her intentions were good. She just didnae understand the damage she could do. Anywhere else, her efforts to brighten the great hall wouldnae ha'e been a problem."

Connall waved his excuses away. "Is Aileen all right?"

"Aye." Ewan shifted, some of his earlier upset returning at the reminder of how Aileen could have been harmed by Eva's efforts. "Aye. She saw what Eva was doing from the stairs and sent a servant to fetch me while she went back to our room."

"Hmm." Connall looked a little less upset, but was still displeased. "Where's me wife now?"

"She was sat at table still when I came tae meet ye," Ewan answered, following Connall as he headed for the stairs.

"If a servant fetched ye, why'd ye no tell her to put them back up?"

"I did try to tell her that removing the furs from the windows and arrow slits in the great hall wasn't a good idea, but she was sure ye'd be pleased, and insisted on yer seeing it first and making the final decision," he said with remembered vexation. Ewan wasn't used to such flouting of his authority. As first, he was in charge when Connall wasn't available and everyone listened to him. Except Eva, it would seem.

Connall grunted and started down the stairs, but Ewan paused at the top of them, suddenly reluctant to be a witness to the upbraiding his new mistress was about to get, and was now almost sorry that he hadn't found a milder way of telling Connall instead of blurting it all out in high dudgeon as he had. In excusing the lass' behavior to her husband he had managed to get past his own anger enough to see that she hadn't really done anything so awful. In any other keep, her attempts to brighten the great hall would have been perfectly normal and perhaps even appreciated. Here it was not, but they could hardly expect her to know that.

After a hesitation, Ewan turned toward the chamber he shared with his wife and went that way instead.

"Is Connall verra angry?" Aileen asked as he entered.

"I thought ye'd still be at table," Ewan muttered as he closed the door.

"I didn't wish to embarrass Eva further by witnessing her upset when Connall reacts to the great hall with anger rather than the pleasure she had hoped fer," Aileen said quietly. "She was only trying to make a place fer herself and fit in."

"Aye." Ewan sighed as he sank into the chair opposite hers by the fire. "I wish ye'd pointed that out to me before I went to speak to Connall."

Aileen smiled at her husband. "I knew ye'd see that fer yersel' eventually, but wouldnae listen while ye were in such a temper. There's no talking to ye when ye're in a temper, my love. Much like Connall."

Ewan scowled at the comment. He could agree that Connall had a temper, yet here was his wife claiming he had one too, and he supposed, if he were to be honest, he would admit that he did.

"I hope he isnae too hard on her."

"Aye," Ewan agreed, but knew that he had rather wound up the man with his own upset, greeting him with it the moment he arose as he had. Sighing, he heaved himself to his feet. "I'd best go be sure he doesnae overdo it."

Aileen smiled and stood to kiss him on the cheek. "Remind him she was only tryin' to find a way to please her new husband."

"Aye." Ewan brushed her cheek with the back of one hand, marveling that he loved her as much today, if not more, than he had when he'd tackled Connall and asked to have her for his wife thirty years ago, then he turned and left the room.

The great hall was nearly empty when Ewan started down the stairs. This was unusual, on a normal night the tables would still be filled with people talking loudly as they finished their meals. It seemed Aileen wasn't the only one who had made a discreet withdrawal, he thought as he spotted Eva's lone figure at the table. She appeared a very small and lonely figure to him. Connall was crossing the great hall and just approaching her now.

Ewan started down the stairs, only then noting the men standing by the fire watching their laird approach his new bride. It was Donaidh, Geordan, Domhall, Ragnall, and Keddy, all the men who had ridden with him to collect her, and he descended the stairs to join them. He would watch from there and intervene only if necessary.

* * *

Eva picked nervously at the joint of chicken in her trencher. She had worked hard this afternoon and was exhausted and should have been starving too, but found herself attacked by a case of nerves instead as her gaze slid unhappily around the empty tables. She was beginning to get the feeling that her brilliant plan of that morning wasn't perhaps as brilliant as she'd thought. The reaction to her removing the furs from the windows and arrow slits to allow some proper sunlight in to brighten the place had not gone over well with anyone so far. Not even Glynis, and Eva had rather counted on the maid's support and encouragement, but instead the girl had tried to dissuade her. Unfortunately, Eva could be bullish when she had an idea, and—positive that her husband would like and appreciate her efforts—she had insisted on marching ahead with her plans.

Grimacing, she tugged the sleeve of her gown up and turned her arm over to examine the bruised and swollen forearm. Eva supposed that—had Glynis been at least a little more encouraging—she would have attempted to enlist the aid of a couple of male servants to aid in the endeavor, but fearing more resistance, she'd opted to do the chore herself, and had nearly managed to kill herself in the bargain. She'd nearly tumbled from the small ancient and rickety balcony that ran the length of the row of arrow slits when Ewan had come stomping into the great hall demanding to know what in God's name she thought she was doing. She'd stopped her fall by catching her arm on the rail, but then had been so irritated at the unnecessary accident—the man hadn't needed to startle her so with his bellowing and stomping about— that she had refused to undo all the work she had done and had insisted on waiting for Connall's pronouncement on the matter.

Now she was beginning to wish she had simply put the furs back up and forgotten the entire thing. The reaction of every last servant and soldier in the castle had not been encouraging. They had filed in for their meal this evening, all going quiet as they had spied the last rays of sunlight stabbing through the now uncovered windows, then had sat whispering amongst themselves until the last rays had died. Moments later, they had risen as one and hurriedly filed out.

Now Eva sat alone at table, wondering if her husband would bother to make an appearance. The man had been absent all day, "about his business" as Ewan had claimed and had yet to show himself. Eva had hoped to have a word with Aileen before she saw Connall, or at least before Connall saw her changes. She had been hoping for a bit of encouragement she supposed, some reassurance that Connall would indeed approve of the changes and appreciate her efforts. Unfortunately, her new sister-in-law hadn't come down since that morning and Eva was starting to fear that wasn't a good sign at all.

"Wife."

If she was slow to respond to that address, it was quite simply because it took a moment for Eva's distracted mind to recognize that she was the one being addressed. Not that she'd forgotten that she was married now and had a husband, but she hadn't considered that this meant that she was now a wife.

"Wife."

Eva turned slowly, her eyes moving with trepidation to the speaker, then she blinked in surprise. She had worried about her husband; who he might be, what he might look like, how old he must be and so on, but the man standing before her was nothing like she'd expected. She'd decided after meeting Aileen that he must be older, at least having seen forty-five to fifty summers, and she had worried about other things, such as what if he was unattractive to her? What if he had gone to fat at his advanced age or had bushels of unattractive grey facial hair? But this man was nothing like she'd expected; his hair was a midnight black as Aileen's was and he had the same deep brown eyes, but there the similarities ended. This man was no more than twenty-five or thirty years old and he was strong and well built with a flat stomach and wide shoulders. There was another fact, however, that was more surprising to Eva.

"We have met, my lord," she blurted.

Connall MacAdie seemed to be thrown off track by her words, and the grim, stern set to his features faltered briefly. He hesitated, then nodded. "Aye. At court."

"You spoke to me in the gardens," Eva remembered, smiling at the memory. She had fled there after dinner to escape the whispers and laughter about her plain, outdated dress. This man—Connall MacAdie she realized now, though she hadn't known his name at the time—had come across her out there. "You were very kind to me."

Her words seemed to make the man uncomfortable, and Eva supposed that men—warriors like the MacAdie laird was reputed to be—were discomfited to admit to a softer side. After a hesitation, he settled on the trestle table bench beside her and seemed to pause to gather himself. Eva smiled at him brightly, relief and pleasure glowing on her face as she awaited whatever he was gathering himself to say. She was so glad—grateful even—that he was the man who had bartered for her. That fact was washing all her worries and fears away, for surely his kindness in the gardens was a sign that he would be equally kind in marriage. And he was handsome too. Eva was suddenly positive that she was the luckiest girl in the world at that moment.

"Ye—" he began, but paused as he glanced up and caught her expression. His gaze narrowed. "Why are ye lookin' at me like that?"

"Like what, my lord?" she asked with a beaming smile.

"Yer all smiling and happy looking."

"I *am* happy," she admitted. "I never knew your name you

see, we did not introduce ourselves in the gardens, so I had no idea that you were the MacAdie, the lord I was married to and I was ever so worried that we might not suit. But now I know 'tis you . . ." She smiled brilliantly. "I just know everything will be all right."

Connall looked taken aback at her words, and Eva knew she was embarrassing him, but just had to tell him, "I worried that you would be old or fat and I would not find you attractive, but you are ever so handsome. Any girl would be pleased to claim you as husband. And ere I got here I worried that you might be mean or bad tempered, but you were so kind in the gardens at court, distracting me from my worries and embarrassment . . . Well, I just know I needn't worry about your being cruel. My sweet mama in heaven must have sent you to me to save me from the abbey. I am ever so lucky."

Connall simply stared at her, a blank look on his face. Eva waited a moment, but when he continued to stare at her as if at a loss, she cleared her throat and glanced around in search of something to talk about until he regained himself. And of course, her gaze landed on the now-uncovered windows and arrow slits. "I hope you do not mind," she began tentatively, then paused to clear her throat before nervously admitting, "In fact, I was hoping you would be pleased, but I—Well, I am new here of course, and wanted to do something to please you, something to prove my value, perhaps and . . . Well, I noticed that it was so dark and dreary in here with all the windows and arrow slits covered, so I set about removing the furs to allow some sunlight in during the day. It is night now, so you cannot see, but it is ever so much brighter without them." Eva glanced at him, pleased to see that the blank expression was slipping from his face. She was a little less pleased, however, to notice the grimness that now descended in its place. Alarm coursed through her. "Do you not like it?"

"Hmm." He seemed to be battling within himself over something, then he cleared his throat. "Tis no that I doonae like it," he said slowly, though Eva was pretty sure that was an out-and-out lie since his expression rather said he didn't like it at all. "But the furs shall all have to be rehung tonight."

"You do not like it," she realized with disappointment. "I felt sure—Tis so much brighter with them down during the day."

"Do ye no think that had I wanted the furs down, I'd have ordered it done meself long ago?"

Eva blinked at that comment. In truth, that hadn't occurred to her, but it should have, she supposed. Her gaze slid to the windows again. Really, it was so much brighter without the furs during the day . . . which he hadn't seen, she reminded herself, and said, "Perhaps if you saw them during the daylight, tomorrow morn, mayhap? If you still did not like it then, I could—"

"I'll no see it," he said firmly. "The furs shall be returned at once."

"But—"

"And in future, ye'll check with meself or Ewan ere making any further changes." He stood abruptly then, signifying that the subject was now closed. "I've things to do and ye'll no doubt be abed ere I return, so I'll bid ye good night and wish ye good sleep."

Eva stared after him in amazement as Connall MacAdie marched to the keep doors and out. He hadn't even stopped to eat, and what had he meant that he would see her on the morrow? Was he not going to come to her bed to consummate their marriage that night? She had wondered if he had joined her in the chamber last night and she had merely slept through his arrival and departure, but now she realized that this was not the case. He had not slept alongside her, forgoing consummating the wedding to allow her some much needed rest after her long journey, he obviously had not joined her, and had no intention of doing so tonight either.

Eva was distracted from these distressing thoughts by the

arrival of Ewan and the other men who had brought her here. Connall's brother-in-law avoided her gaze as he settled on the trestle table bench at her side. The other men followed suit as they found their own places on either side of them, then there was much throat clearing and uncomfortable shifting as Donaidh, Keddy, Geordan, Domhall, and Ragnall avoided meeting her eyes as well.

"Was he verra upset?"

Eva glanced to her left as Keddy finally asked that question. The redhead was finally meeting her gaze, though Eva almost wished he hadn't. The pity in his eyes made her stiffen her spine and force a smile as her pride exerted itself.

"Nay, not very. At least he did not yell or anything, but he did not care for the change," she admitted and bit her lip to keep it from trembling in distress at this magnificent failure of her attempts to please her husband.

"Well, it's no that he didnae like it, lass. He didnae e'en see it if ye'll recall," Geordan pointed out judiciously.

"Aye," Keddy agreed. "And ne'er would neither."

Eva glanced at the redhead with a frown. "Why would he not see it? Perhaps he missed it today, but surely tomorrow or the next day he would be around long enough to enjoy—"

"Nay." Keddy shook his head. "Cannae stand the sun, can he? No without it makin' him sick. He'd ne'er see it."

"What?" Eva frowned at this news, then glanced at Ewan who was glaring furiously at the young man.

Sighing, her husband's first turned to her, cleared his throat, then said, "I should've explained this to ye when I approached ye about it earlier, but ye were rather busy and I was so upset I wasnae thinking straight. Aileen and Connall cannae stand the sun. Their skin is fragile and the sun damages it," he explained slowly, sounding rather labored in the endeavor.

"You mean they react to the sun?" Eva asked, trying to make sense of his words.

That suggestion seemed to make Ewan brighten. "Aye,

that's it. They've a sort of reaction to the sun. It makes them fair sick. Connall's is so bad he avoids it altogether, or the best he can, and Aileen . . . well," his expression softened. "She can take more sunlight, but no straight on and no fer too long."

"I see," Eva said slowly, thinking to herself that this was perhaps where some of the vile rumors about this family came from. If they could not go out in sunlight because of a negative reaction . . . This situation wasn't totally alien to Eva. There had been a girl in the village at Caxton who'd had a similar ailment, only she didn't get sick, but broke out in spots whenever she stayed out in the sun too long. If Connall's family suffered a similar ailment and because of this avoided the sun, well, that would explain why they were rarely seen in daylight. She shook her head to herself at this thought. People could be ever so cruel about things they didn't understand.

Eva grimaced as she realized the extent of the gaffe she had made. She'd thought to bring some cheer to the keep, but instead had threatened the health of its inhabitants, and most likely not just her husband and his sister. If this trait was common to their family . . . well, most clans were interrelated weren't they? Cousins and such?

Her gaze slid to Ewan. "You obviously have no negative reaction to the sun?"

"Nay," he admitted. "I'm originally of the MacDonald clan. I became a MacAdie when I married Aileen."

Eva nodded, then glanced at the other men in question.

"I'm a MacAdie," Donaidh announced. "I'm son to Aileen and Ewan, but the sun doesnae bother me."

"Then you are nephew to me!" Eva exclaimed, then frowned. "Why did no one tell me ere this?"

Ewan and Donaidh glanced at each other, then the father shrugged and said, "It's no important."

The son nodded, "Aye, and ye didnae ask, did ye?"

She clucked a sound of annoyance, then blinked at the realization that her new nephew was of an age with herself.

"I'm a MacAdie," Keddy said, distracting her from her thoughts. "But while I try to avoid the worst of the sun, it doesnae affect me like it does Connall and Aileen. I jest get more freckles." He grinned at her.

"Tis the same with me," Ragnall announced, flashing a freckled smile at her.

"Domhall and I are brothers; MacLarens by birth," Geordan informed her. "My ma moved us here when our da died and she married a MacAdie. We were jest wee lads then."

"I see," Eva said on a sigh, then glanced at Ewan again. "Is this why Aileen did not come down for supper?"

Ewan nodded solemnly.

"Oh dear," Eva sighed. "I am ever so sorry. You must apologize to her for me. I did not realize—I did not know or I never would have—" Pausing in her explanations, she stood abruptly. "Glynis!"

"What're ye doin', lass?" Ewan asked with a frown as he gained his feet beside her.

"I will rectify the matter at once," Eva announced firmly, then addressed the maid as she came running up, "Please fetch back the furs for the windows, Glynis. I must return them at once." She gave them all a reproving look as she added, "Had someone troubled themselves to tell me of this sun reaction business, I never would have removed them in the first place."

"We should've told ye," Keddy said sorrowfully as Glynis rushed to the corner where the furs were stacked.

"Aye," Ewan agreed. "That being the case, we'd be pleased to rehang the furs fer ye."

"Nay. I took them down and I shall put them back up," Eva said firmly, moving to meet Glynis halfway as the girl came rushing back. "And I shall apologize to Aileen myself as well." She shook her head as she took the furs. "As Connall said, had he wanted the furs down he would have ordered it done long ago. Obviously I do not yet know how things are done around here, but I should learn ere I start trying to change things."

"It'd be no trouble at all fer the men and meself to rehang the furs, Lady Eva." Ewan was following her, and his men following him, as she marched to the rickety wooden staircase that led up to the landing along the row of arrow slits.

"Nay. I can manage it," Eva assured him. "But, perhaps one of you would be good enough to take my husband a drink and some food. I fear he was so upset he left without eating." She frowned over that as she started up the stairs, craning her neck in an effort to see over the stack of furs, and taking wide steps in an effort to avoid stepping on her gown and tripping herself up. "On second thought, you no doubt have enough to do, and I should probably be the one to take the food to him, as it is my fault he was too distressed to eat. Perhaps that and an apology will help him regain his appetite."

"I'm really thinkin' ye should let one o' the men—" Eva heard Ewan begin his suggestion again, but it ended on a gasp of horror as she—despite her great care—stepped on the hem of her gown, tangled her feet in it and stumbled back down the half dozen stairs she had mounted. Her cry of alarm was echoed by Glynis and the men on the ground.

Five

"There!" Magaidh smiled at Eva as she pulled the linens and furs up to cover her in the bed. "Ye jest rest noo, lass. Ye'll feel better come the morn."

Eva sighed miserably. The woman had been incredibly kind. Indeed, they all had. Ewan had performed a quick examination of her right there at the bottom of the stairs she'd fallen down, with the men worriedly overlooking the enterprise. Once assured that she wasn't too horribly injured, he had carried her up the stairs with the men and Glynis trailing.

Magaidh had met them in the hall on her way down and changed direction, accompanying them to the room Eva had been given. After sending the men away to tend to the furs, the other woman had ordered Glynis off in search of a special salve for her bruises and some sort of herbal drink to soothe her, then had helped her to undress. Once Glynis had returned with the salve, Connall's stepmother had rubbed it gently into Eva's scrapes and bruises herself, before urging her to drink the not unpleasant potion she'd sent for. Now she had tucked her up in bed.

"Have you a bad reaction to sunlight as well?" Eva asked suddenly. She wasn't tired and really didn't wish to be alone.

Magaidh hesitated, then nodded.

Eva sighed unhappily. "I suppose that is why you haven't been downstairs all day either? Because I took the furs off the windows and let the sun in? I am sorry, Magaidh. I didn't realize."

"Tis all right, child. Ye couldnae ken."

"Nay, but I should have asked if there was a reason for the furs. I shall ask in future ere trying to change anything," she assured her.

"I'm sure ye shall." Magaidh smiled but Eva didn't feel any better.

"I've angered my husband."

"Nay. Well, mayhap a little, but he'll recover. He's a man, men doona like change. All of this is change fer him too," she pointed out.

Eva couldn't hide her disgruntled expression at those words, or repress the mutter, "Not much change, except that he is avoiding his own room now that I am in it."

Magaidh's eyebrows rose at her words, but a small smile lifted her lips at Eva's suddenly embarrassed expression. She supposed the herbs must be kicking in and loosening her tongue that she should have made such an embarrassing admission.

Magaidh settled on the edge of the bed. "I suppose, being a man, that me son has no bothered to explain about the wedding?"

Eva blinked at that question. "Wedding?"

"We thought 'twould be good fer ye to be married again, properly, now that ye're here and both together. It'll be a chance for the clan to witness the event and to meet ye."

"Oh." Biting her lip, Eva considered that this put a different picture on things. It was possible her husband would wait until after this second wedding to bed her, which was very thoughtful. But then she had known from their brief conversation in the gardens that he was kind. "That would be nice. And no, he had not mentioned it."

Magaidh made a tsking sound and brushed at the skirt of her gown. "Men can be such a trial at times, do ye no think?"

A giggle slipped from Eva's mouth at these words, though she couldn't for the life of her think why she found them funny. It must be the potion, she assured herself. She was absolutely positive it must be the potion that made her ask, "He is not sorry then that he chose to marry me?"

Magaidh smiled gently at her distressed words and brushed a strand of golden hair behind Eva's ear. "Nay. O' course not, lass. What is there fer him to be sorry fer? Ye're a lovely bride. And ye're already making an effort to fit in. Nay, I'm sure he's no sorry."

"Oh," Eva sighed. She was starting to feel a little sleepy now, but had questions to ask. Like what had happened to Connall and Aileen's mother? Or did they indeed have the same mother? Or was the age difference between them because they had different mothers? And how long had Magaidh been married to Connall's father, who must surely have been quite a lot older than she, but instead she asked, "When is this wedding to be?"

"Soon as the priest arrives. Connall sent a man to fetch him back and Effie is doing her best to prepare fer a large feast after the wedding. We're thinkin' to hold it on the chapel steps rather than inside so that all can witness it."

Eva nodded at this news, then frowned. "But Aileen and Connall and yourself and who knows how many others have those reactions to the sun. How—?"

"We'll hold it directly after sunset," Magaidh assured her. "By torchlight. It'll be lovely."

"Oh. Aye. Of course." Eva smiled slightly, her mind filling with imaginings of a bailey full of people, the soft light of torchlight and she and Connall and a priest . . .

"We'll have to sew a new dress fer ye. Something lovely.

I be thinkin' the priest won't be long in coming so we'd best set to work on it right away. Perhaps Aileen and yerself could pick out the cloth during the day tomorrow and then we can set to work tomorrow night."

"Tomorrow night. Will you not help choose the material?" Eva asked. She rather liked this woman.

"I'll not be available during the day."

"You won't?" Eva frowned.

"I often visit the MacNachtons," Magaidh said vaguely. "They're me clan ye understand."

"Aye," Eva said the word on a yawn. The herbal potion had definitely kicked in.

"There. Yer tired now. I should let ye rest." Magaidh stood and headed for the door. "Sleep well, wee Eva."

"She *what?*" Connall roared as he dismounted. He was just returning from a raid with some of the men, one of their special raids in search of sustenance. Connall avoided feasting on these raids as often as possible, but accompanied the men to be sure they returned alive and well. It was getting dangerous for them in the area and he insisted that they travel further afield in search of fresh victims. The only way to ensure that they did, and that none gave in to their hunger and stopped closer to home, was to accompany them himself.

The last thing he'd expected on returning was more trouble with his wife and the news that she had injured herself alarmed him more than he would have expected.

"She was trying to replace the furs to fix her mistake," Ewan was quick to explain. "But her hands were full of the furs, ye see, and she couldnae hold her skirts out o' the way, then her feet got tangled up in it and she tumbled down the stairs. It was only six steps," he added swiftly in an effort to reassure Connall. "She twisted an ankle and suffered a few more bruises, but is fine other than that."

"A few *more* bruises?" The MacAdie was scowling.

"Aye, well when she stumbled backward on the landing this afternoon, she scraped her arm up a bit and—"

"Why was this no' mentioned to me earlier?" Connall barked. "Ye didnae mention this when I woke this evening."

"I didna ken, did I?" Ewan excused himself. "I saw her stumble a bit, but she caught herself on the railing and assured me all was well, then when I was checking her for scrapes and bruises after 'her fall this night, I saw her arm and she told me that 'twas from earlier." He grimaced. "It looked fair sore. I'm surprised she wasn't complaining over it, and I'm thinkin' she'll be fair banged up on the morrow from this night's accident as well. She ga'e her ankle a fine wrenching in the fall, and scraped one leg badly too."

Connall scowled at this news. "Why did one of the men no replace the furs? What was she doing attemptin' it herself?"

"I did try to convince her to let the men do it, but she insisted that she'd taken them down and should be the one to put them back. She's English," he said with a shrug as if that explained all.

Shaking his head, Connall tossed the reins of his mount to one of the lads who had come running up from the stables, then marched past his first into the keep.

"She's sleeping," Magaidh announced as he marched past where she sat at the trestle table talking to Aileen.

Connall ignored this and marched upstairs. Asleep or not, he would see her and see how much damage she had taken. She was his wife. It was his place to look after her.

Glynis was seated by the dying fire in the room, watching over her lady as she sewed a small tear in a rose gown that lay across her lap. The maid glanced up with surprise at their entrance, relaxing when her master nodded that she should remain where she was and he crossed the room to stand by the bed.

"She's snoring."

Connall glanced around in surprise at that shocked hiss from Ewan. He hadn't realized the man had followed him, but he had, and his first wasn't the only one Connall saw as Donaidh, Geordan, Domhall, Ragnall, and Keddy spread out in the room. Magaidh and Aileen had also trailed them up and now tossed repressing glances at the men.

"The herbal potion I gave her is most likely to blame," Magaidh said firmly. "Twould put her in a deep sleep."

Connall grunted at this and turned to glance at his wife. She had faint bruising on one cheek and he frowned as he reached down to run a finger lightly over it.

"Her face slammed into the rail on the way down," Keddy whispered and shook his head. "But that ain't near as bad as her leg and ankle."

Connall immediately tugged the linens and furs gently aside to peer at her leg. She was wearing a white cotton sleeping gown and was sweet looking in slumber. He didn't have to lift the gown out of the way, it was twisted high around her thighs, almost indecently high, he decided and turned a scowl on the men gaping down at her. All but Keddy caught his look and immediately turned away, but it took an elbow in the ribs from Geordan to get Keddy's attention. Noting Connall's scowl, Keddy too dropped his gaze.

Relaxing a little, Connall turned back to his wee bride and frowned at the shape of her legs; the ankle of one was swollen and bruised, and the calf and upper leg of the other was scraped and bruised. Recalling Ewan's comment about her arm, he lifted his gaze to it now, noting the tender looking scrape and bruising there as well.

Easing the blankets carefully back into place, Connall turned and waited for the men and Magaidh to move out of the room ahead of him, then gestured Glynis out of the room as well and followed.

"She didna cry, ye say?" Connall asked with interest as he closed the door behind himself.

"She shed no a tear, m'laird," Ewan reaffirmed.

Connall glanced at his mother and the maid. "No even once the men were out of sight?"

"Nay," Magaidh assured him, the word reinforced by Glynis's, "Nay m'laird."

He merely nodded, but he was thinking most women would have wept copious tears and whinged unendingly. This was looking hopeful. Perhaps she would be a fine bride.

"She's no to carry anything while walking the stairs," he instructed them all, but was addressing the maid. "And should she wish to do anything strenuous or dangerous, ensure that one o' the men are called to do it fer her. She is lady here and shouldn't be performing physical labor."

"Aye, m'laird." Glynis bobbed.

Connall nodded, satisfied that he had handled the matter in the best possible way to ensure the woman wouldn't hurt herself again. His mistake had been in forgetting her background. Most ladies would never have considered removing or replacing furs themselves; they would have directed servants in the doing, but Eva came from Caxton, where she had been valued so little her brother had tried to palm her off without a dower. No doubt he had made her feel a burden in other ways. She was probably trying to make herself valuable, he considered and he wouldn't have that. As her husband it was his place to ensure that she understood her value. He'd begin to work on that on the morrow.

"I really doonae think the laird will be pleased with this, m'lady," Glynis protested for at least the hundredth time as she trailed Eva across the bailey.

"Nonsense, Glynis," she said firmly for at least the same number of times. "There is no reason at all that my husband, Connall," she tested the name on her tongue. "There is no reason that Connall should be upset by my tending to the injured and unwell. Ladies all over England perform this task. Tis much more acceptable than removing and rehanging furs," she assured the maid. Glynis had told her about Connall's edicts since her accident. Apparently he had informed her the night before that "his wife" was not to carry anything while ascending or descending stairs, then had approached her again this morning just ere sunrise to order her to keep Eva from doing anything that was not the expressed sphere of the lady of the manor to perform.

The maid had obviously taken these orders to heart. Glynis had recounted them to Eva the moment she'd arrived at her bedchamber to find her awake, and had repeated them every five minutes since then; while she had helped Eva to dress, then as she had taken her arm to assist her to limp below to the great hall, and even while Eva had sat to break her fast. It had gotten worse since Eva had announced her plans for the day, however, and the girl was growing positively strident now as they approached the stables.

Eva had come up with her plans for the day as she'd lain in bed enjoying that early morning, fuzzy, just-woken-up feeling.

Having decided that changing anything at MacAdie was not a good idea until she had a better understanding of her new home, Eva had learned her lesson. MacAdie keep was run just as its lord and master wished; there was nothing really for her to improve at the moment. She would have to find another way to prove her worth and that she could be an asset here.

After considering the tasks that were usually the province of the lady of the castle, Eva had decided that—for now at least—tending to the ill and showing her healing powers was her best bet. Certainly, the servants didn't need directing, and even had they, she hadn't a clue what she should be directing them to do. MacAdie keep had been running along well enough long before she showed up, so tending to the ailing it would be, Eva had decided.

Then, of course, she had moved to get out of bed and barely managed to bite back a startled cry when pain had shot through her. But Eva wasn't the sort to give in to aches and pains. Besides, she was hoping that the activity would distract her from the pain and perhaps loosen up those aches.

She had thought it was all a simple, perfectly sensible plan. Of course, that was before she had asked Glynis to take her around to anyone she knew was ailing, and the girl had said 'ailing?' in a blank voice, then shook her head. "We're a pretty healthy lot here, m'lady. In truth I cannae think o' anyone unwell at the moment."

Eva had not believed the redhead at first, but when Ewan had assured her it was so, she'd had no choice but to take it as truth, then she'd considered the matter and decided it was probably for the best anyway. She hadn't been allowed to bring any of her medicinals with her here, so had nothing to treat anyone with anyway, which had led to her new plan of what to do this day. She would visit the surrounding woods and clearings to see if she could find anything useful to treat the more common ailments such as an infection. Glynis hadn't liked this idea at all and had glanced around for support, but Ewan had left the table by then which Eva could only think was her good fortune. She was rather certain the first would have disliked the idea at least as much as Glynis, if not more and might have scotched the plan. As it was, however, with him gone, Glynis had been on her own and had tried to dissuade her by suggesting that a servant be sent to search the area for what she wanted. Eva had patiently pointed out that no one but she would know what she was looking for. Though Glynis had still protested, Eva had ignored her and gone about doing as she pleased with her usual stubbornness, sure she knew best.

"Still, m'lady. Perhaps ye should be askin' him ere ye—"

"Glynis," Eva interrupted patiently. "Do I take the time to ask my husband ere I do every little thing, I shall never get anything done. Besides, he never seems to be about to ask anything of," she pointed out and grimaced at the irritation in her own voice. She had seen little enough of her husband since arriving at MacAdie, and though she was trying not to let it bother her, it did seem to her that he was showing her less attention than she might expect from a new groom.

"But yer leg is paining ye," Glynis pointed out, apparently deciding an alternate argument was necessary. "Ye should be restin' it, m'lady, else it will surely swell more."

Eva made a face at that suggestion. The girl was absolutely right about that, of course. In fact, it felt as if her ankle swelled a little more with every step she took, but Eva was determined not to give in to it and continued grimly forward, much relieved to see that they had reached the stables. "I shall be able to rest my leg on horseback, Glynis."

"Oh," the girl drew the word out in a worried sound that made Eva roll her eyes. "I'm really thinkin' that the laird isnae gonna like this. He'll thrash me fer lettin' ye ride oot o' the keep alone, he will."

"I will not be alone, Glynis. I will have you with me," Eva pointed out.

"Aye, m'lady, but that's jest as guid as alone if yer attacked. At least let us ask one o' the men to accompany us?" she begged.

Eva felt guilt besiege her at the girl's panicked state. She herself knew that Connall would not be pleased about their riding out alone, but suspected that if she asked Ewan to send a man with them, he would put paid to the plan altogether. Assuring herself that all would be fine and the trip would be without incident, she said almost apologetically, "We are not going far, Glynis. I promise, I—Oh hello." Eva paused as her attention was turned by the sight of a beautiful dog lying near the entrance to the stables. "Who are you?"

"That's Angus's dog, m'lady," Glynis informed her unhappily. "He's paralyzed and no verra friendly."

"Poor thing," Eva cooed, smiling when the dog wagged his tail. "He looks friendly enough to me. He's just wanting some attention, poor creature."

"Nay, he—" Glynis broke off with a cry of alarm as Eva held a hand out for the dog to sniff and the tail wagging, calm looking animal suddenly turned into a snarling, snapping beast who decided to take a chunk out of that hand.

Connall spotted Ewan waiting for him the moment the stone door to the secret chamber started to slide open, and knew at once that this could not be a good thing. The man had been his first since the year after he had married Aileen some thirty years ago, and in all that time, Ewan had only been awaiting Connall's rising a handful of times. Now he was waiting for the second time in two days . . . in the two days since his new bride had arrived and Connall immediately began to see a pattern.

"What has she done?" he asked abruptly as the door slid closed behind him. "She hasnae taken the furs down again has she?"

"Nay."

To Connall's mind, Ewan was looking a little put upon and as if he was happy that his laird was awake to take over the responsibility of his wayward wife. "What then?"

His brother-in-law didn't bother to sugarcoat it, he just said, "She's been bitten."

"Bitten?" Connall echoed with amazement. "By what?"

"By Wolfy."

"What?" Connall exclaimed with disbelief. "Wolfy? The mutt from the stables? But he's paralyzed at the back end, he can't but drag himself around a bit and that not far."

"Aye. Weell, she decided to befriend him, didnae she?" Ewan said dryly, then shrugged and added, "He wasnae feelin' verra friendly."

"Dear God." Connall rubbed his forehead with exasperation. "How bad is it?"

Ewan wrinkled his nose. "It bled badly and looked a fair mess, but Aileen says there'll be no permanent damage."

Connall sighed his relief at this news, started to turn away, then paused to ask warily, "Is there anythin' else I should ken?"

"The priest has arrived," Ewan announced cheerfully and Connall felt some of the stiffness leave his shoulders. This was good news at least, he thought, turning to move toward the stairs now.

"Good, I might yet get the woman wedded and bedded and hopefully with child ere she gets hersel' killed," Connall muttered as he began to jog lightly down the stairs.

"She does appear to be prone to accidents." There was a touch of amusement in Ewan's voice as he followed on his heels.

Connall snorted at what to him seemed something of an understatement. "Tis obvious the lass cannae be left to her own devices. I want ye men to keep an eye on her when I'm no about."

"I suspected ye might," Ewan said dryly as they reached the great hall and started toward where Connall could see his wife seated at the trestle table. His footsteps slowed however as he overheard what the priest was saying. He was trying to scare her with the tales that had grown up around his people, Connall realized with disgust. The man was trying to convince her to flee the keep and escape to safety with him. He heard Ewan growl next to him in outrage at what the holy man was saying, but raised a hand to silence him. His own first instinct was to storm forward, drag the good priest up by his pious collar and toss him from the castle, but he wished to see how his wife handled the situation first. Then he would decide whether to let the man perform the ceremony before he tossed him out, or merely toss him out and fetch another priest.

Six

"Fie, Father!" Eva glared at Father MacLure, hardly able to believe what he had said. First he had spewed all the same nonsense tales that Mavis had told her back at Caxton, then he had suggested the two of them slip away to the stables and flee at the first opportunity. He was suggesting she flee from her husband and her home! She was in such a dudgeon that she added, "Shame on you for listening and *carrying* such tales, surely there are words against such behavior in the Bible?"

The priest flushed at her reproof and squirmed briefly, then straightened his shoulders and said, "Are ye sayin' then that the tales are no true?"

Eva was irritated by his persistence in the matter. "I was told the tales ere coming here, all that nonsense about the MacAdies being nightwalking, soulless blood feeders. Yet six of them rode for two days, in full sunlight to bring me here, as I am sure it was with you. Did you not travel during the day?"

"Aye, we traveled in daylight," the priest admitted. "But there was only one man sent to bring me back."

"Really? Only the one?" Eva asked with interest and had to smile. When she had complained to Ewan and the men that Connall had sent them to fetch her like a cow he wished to purchase, they had told her that the fact that he had sent six of them, as well as whom he had sent, showed her importance to him. They had said he would only send one man for a cow, and that the one man would not be any of them. Eva knew not who had brought the priest, but as Ewan, Donaidh, Ragnall, Domhall, Keddy, and Geordan had all been about the keep the last couple of days, she knew it was not one of them. It seemed the priest was not as important to Connall as she herself was. In fact, he apparently was no more important than a cow, she thought with amusement, but didn't think it was a good idea to share this news with the overblown man.

"Were they all MacAdies?" Father MacLure asked, drawing Eva's attention back from her thoughts.

She knew what he was getting at. Mavis had claimed that the MacAdies had non-vampires among them, servants who did their bidding, and after the kindnesses she had been shown by these people, she would not listen to this nonsense. "All who live within these walls are MacAdies, Father, including myself now," she said firmly, then added, "As for this nightwalker business, 'tis all nonsense based on the fact that Connall and his sister suffer a negative reaction to the sun. We had a girl like that in our village and it is grateful I am, that no one thought to claim her a soulless, nightwalking blood feeder."

"A reaction to the sun?" the priest asked.

"Aye."

"Hmm." He appeared to consider that, then asked, "But what o' the claim that they doonae age?"

Eva snorted. "Well that is certainly stuff and nonsense, just look at Aileen. Would you say she is not aging?"

The priest's gaze slid along the table to the older woman, still beautiful despite her age, but he shook his head. "Well, aye, *she* is, but 'tis said that Connall MacAdie has barely aged since reaching adulthood over thirty years ago."

Eva stared at him blankly. Connall had reached adulthood over thirty years ago? That would make him . . . fifty-five or sixty, depending on what the father considered adulthood and what "over thirty years ago" meant. Nay, that was impossible. There was no way that her Connall was fifty-five or sixty years old, Eva told herself, as an image of his handsome young face came to mind. Dark hair, deep brown eyes, healthy *young* skin. Nay, Connall had not reached adulthood thirty years ago . . . Perhaps his father had, but Connall would barely have been born. That thought made her pause and eased the panic that had been building inside her. Of course! A smile of relief curving her lips, she glanced at the priest and said, "Father, my brother's name is Jonathan."

Her comment obviously startled the man, and Father MacLure looked confused for a minute, then said, politely, "Well . . . That's a fine name."

"Aye," Eva agreed pleasantly. "And so was my father called Jonathan, my brother was named after him, you understand . . . As I am sure Connall was named after his own father," she added firmly. "There are simple explanations for everything. Tis just that—as you said yourself earlier—the MacAdies socialize so rarely with others—probably because of these ridiculous rumors—that it merely adds to the superstitious claims." Eva sighed over this, thinking with some vexation that she would have to change that, then added, "Besides, while I have been here only a short time, I have seen no sign of the vampirism that is claimed. And, really, would soulless nightwalkers send for you to perform a marriage that has already been performed once?" she asked. "It was my husband's idea to hold a second, proper wedding, not mine."

"Well . . ." Father MacLure hesitated. It seemed to her that he really didn't want to believe that these people were just that, people. It was almost as if the idea of their being monsters was too exciting a possibility to let go of. Eva was becoming terribly impatient with the man when his gaze drifted behind her and he suddenly froze.

Eva sighed inwardly. It didn't take a wizard to tell who was standing behind her, as the priest had suddenly gone as pale as death and was now rising slowly from the bench, either in polite greeting, or preparing to flee. Still, she glanced over her shoulder to see who it actually was.

Aye, it was her husband, and he had obviously overheard a good portion of their discussion, at least enough to make him look like thunder. Eva had never seen anyone look quite so cold and furious at the same time, and had to admit that he was really an intimidating sight. Were she the one he was glaring at, she might have been frightened. Fortunately, he was glaring at Father MacLure, not herself, and really, in her heart, she didn't blame him. It was rude to accept your host's hospitality, sit at his table, dine on his food and drink his wine, then attack him behind his back, and she supposed he deserved what he was getting. But at that moment, Connall MacAdie looked as if thrashing him would be his choice and Eva couldn't condone that while she had the wedding to attend to.

Nevertheless, her husband did not thrash the man or even verbally lash him as she half expected, but merely growled, "Sit."

Father MacLure sat at once, apparently intelligent enough not to answer the man just now. Eva felt herself begin to relax as her husband swung one leg over the bench between herself and the priest, forcing the priest to scoot away to make room for him. Ewan followed suit, forcing himself between Connall and the priest so that the holy man now sat far enough away that he could cause little trouble. Eva glanced at her husband sharply as he suddenly grasped her injured hand and began to unwrap her dressing.

"Tis fine, my lord," she assured him, though he hadn't asked how it was, and didn't bother to acknowledge her words either, she noted with irritation. Eva didn't trouble to explain that it was an animal bite; Ewan had no doubt already explained that. Her gaze moved over her husband's head to his first and she gave Ewan a reproving look for tattling on her so, but the man merely grinned back, unrepentant.

"Kill the dog," Connall snapped, drawing Eva's attention to the fact that her bandage was undone and the ragged wound revealed.

"Nay!" she cried as Ewan stood to do his laird's bidding. Her gaze shot back to her husband whose fingers had tightened as they clasped the wrist of her injured hand. "You cannot kill the dog, 'twas my fault. I tried to pet him."

"He is a danger. He could bite someone else."

"He is paralyzed in the back legs and a danger only to those foolish enough to approach him such as myself. Surely everyone here knows better than that? Please, my lord," she begged, her conscience grasped by the idea of the paralyzed beast being killed because of her own stupidity and stubbornness. After all, Glynis *had* told her the dog wasn't friendly.

"He is bad-tempered," Connall pointed out.

"Well, and I should be bad-tempered too were I paralyzed in the back . . . er . . . from the waist down," she substituted. "Please, my lord, 'twas my own fault and really 'tis not as bad as it looks. Aileen assured me there is no permanent damage," she said.

Connall stared at her for several minutes, his eyes locked on her face for so long she almost felt the need to squirm under his piercing gaze. But she did not drop her eyes. She needed to win this argument and save the dog, else suffer endless guilt because of its death. Her conscience could not bear it were the dog destroyed because of her thoughtlessness.

After what seemed a very long time, though it was probably only a matter of a moment or so, Connall released her gaze and began to rewrap her wound.

"Ewan."

"Aye?" The man waited, appearing as curious to know what Connall had decided as she was.

"The weddin' will be held on the steps in an hour. Make sure everyone knows and attends, and inform Cook I expect a proper feast afterward."

"Effie's been cooking since ye sent fer Father MacLure," Ewan informed him. "And I warned her the moment he arrived. Tis why supper has been put off, she was sure ye'd wish the wedding to take place at once with a feast to follow. The rest o' the clan knew ye'd wish it so too, and they're all jest waitin' to hear when the wedding'll be. I'll go tell them now to be ready in an hour."

Connall nodded and his first moved off to do his bidding, pausing briefly at his wife's side before leaving the keep. Finished with her bandages, her husband now stood. "Ye should prepare yersel'."

He was gone before Eva could offer her gratitude that he had spared the beast in the stables, and just as suddenly, Aileen was there, offering her a smile. "We should see ye dressed, lass."

"Oh." Eva stared at her with alarm. Magaidh had said something the night before about choosing cloth today to sew a gown for the wedding, but Aileen had been missing from the table when Eva had come down to breakfast and then after the incident in the stables, Eva had simply forgotten all about the dress. Not that it mattered, even had they chosen the cloth, they could not have sewn a gown in the hour before the wedding. She had nothing to wear.

"How fortunate I had several servants sewing today."

Eva glanced over her shoulder as Magaidh spoke those words. The woman was approaching, a wide smile on her face and a gown of a silky, deep green fabric in her arms.

"I ken I suggested choosing cloth today, but on going below after leavin' ye last night I learned that Connall expected the priest to arrive by supper this evening and I decided I'd best make some arrangements in case he should come. Should he not, ye could choose a different cloth and design if ye liked, but if he did, at least ye'd no be completely unprepared." She shifted the gown to hold it up before her. "I hope 'tis to yer liking. I thought that the green would bring out the green o' yer eyes."

"Tis lovely," Eva assured her, tears welling in her eyes at the woman's thoughtfulness. How could people be saying such vile things about these MacAdies? They were so kind to her. Her husband was arranging a second wedding to ensure she felt properly married. Magaidh had supplied her with a new wardrobe—Glynis had appeared with several more gowns that morn, including the dark blue one she now wore, claiming that Magaidh had sent them—and now, the woman had made sure she would have a special gown to wear for her wedding. Eva felt cared for for perhaps the first time in her life, at least, for the first time since her parents' deaths when she was young. It made her heart ache with something she could not describe. It was perhaps a bit of gratitude, but she was not sure what the rest of it was, but it hurt. In a good way, but it hurt just the same.

"Ah, lass," Magaidh said kindly, apparently understanding what she was feeling by the tears in her eyes. "We are treating ye only as ye deserve to be treated. Now come, we shall make ye ready."

"She looks beautiful."

Connall grunted at that comment from Ewan, but he couldn't take his eyes off the lass. His bride. Magaidh and Aileen had turned her into a fairy princess. The gown she wore was long and flowing and the color of the forest by daylight, something he had so rarely seen that it was as precious to him as gold was to misers. Rather than cover her long golden hair with a hat or veil, they had merely left it down, weaving flowers and ribbons into it so that it lay in long glossy waves that trailed over her shoulders and shone in the torchlight with fiery glints. She looked both young and beautiful.

Connall felt his chest expand with pride. He had chosen well.

Eva tried to maintain her smile and hide the nervousness she felt as she moved through the parting crowd to the church steps. The wedding had yet to actually begin, and was already different from the proxy wedding, which had been a rushed affair held in the Caxton chapel in broad daylight. Her brother had hustled her and the six Scots there the moment the last of the negotiations were made, introducing Ewan along the way as her husband's proxy. The priest had mumbled a few words with only her brother, Mavis, and the five Scots accompanying Ewan to witness it, and it had been done.

This time, Eva was bathed and perfumed and garbed in the finest dress she had ever seen, one she was sure surpassed even the fine fashions she had witnessed at court, then she was led down the stairs and across the bailey, walking a path made by the parting of the clan members and lit by the torches that many of them held. That torchlight added a moody and rather beautiful air to the event, perhaps it could even have been called romantic, and Eva was glad that her husband had thought to hold a proper wedding for her. She truly felt as if she were being married this time, where she hadn't at the first wedding. On top of that, her mind was not beset with chaos and confusion, thanks to the horror stories Mavis had told. They no longer loomed like a cloud in her mind, but were a dim memory, overlapped by the kindnesses these people had shown her; Glynis with her help and friendship, Effie with her warm welcome, Ewan and the men with their caring and concern both times she'd been injured, Aileen with her sweetness and aid, and Magaidh with her generosity and care. Even her husband had shown her kindness in allowing the dog to live because she asked it, as well as in what she supposed he considered to be a kindness in not bedding her, before this wedding. Aside from that, despite his constant absence, she had learned a lot about her husband these last few days. Eva had not asked questions about him, knowing that would make his people uncomfortable, but she had looked, listened, and learned a great deal despite that.

Connall MacAdie was a well-respected clan chief. He had earned his people's trust and was even liked by them. Eva had heard several examples of his fairness in judgment and skill in battle just by listening to those around her and it was becoming obvious that he was considered a fair and just man. He definitely wasn't feared as an abusive lord would be and Eva was relatively certain that he would be a good husband.

Aye, this wedding was much different from her first. This time Eva did not experience trepidation for the future. She was sure all would be well.

"All will be well."

It was only when Ewan leaned forward and murmured "What will be well?" that Connall realized that he had spoken the reassurance to himself aloud.

"Everything," he answered vaguely, ignoring the curious look his brother-in-law cast him.

"Should the MacNachton no be here?"

Connall sighed at this question, knowing it was one he couldn't ignore. "Aye. Mayhap, but I didna think o' that until I was dressing fer the weddin'," he admitted, then shrugged.

"But I hadnae really intended on this wedding originally; it was Magaidh who suggested it and I only agreed when she pointed out that it would allow all to know and recognize their lady."

"Hmm." Ewan nodded, then said, "'Tis a much nicer weddin' than the one in England."

Connall raised an eyebrow at this comment and the man shrugged.

"'Twas a rushed, businesslike affair. Caxton acted as if he feared I would change me mind on yer behalf and insisted on it being held at once. He rushed us oot to the chapel ere the ink had dried on the paper. It was rather unseemly to me and 'twas obvious Lady Eva was upset and embarrassed, but as ye'd said to get it done and get back quick as possible, I didnae argue." He shook his head at the memory. "I was dusty from travel, without e'en the opportunity to pat me plaid down, and she wore a faded grey gown she'd obviously donned that morn to work around the castle, but we stood before the priest as he mumbled a few incomprehensible words in Latin, then 'twas done." His gaze slid to Eva. "This should please her much more."

Connall followed his gaze to his wife. She looked lovely and—while she was not exactly smiling, there was a peaceful look on her face, an acceptance and perhaps even a quiet pleasure that suggested to him that perhaps Ewan was right and Eva was pleased. He hadn't considered whether or not she would be pleased when he'd agreed to his mother's suggestion, but was now glad if she was. Connall had spent little enough time with the woman up to now, but he was kept abreast of her daily activities and had listened carefully to what his people did and did not say when giving their reports. They all seemed to accept her with relative ease, no one saying anything to suggest otherwise. All were impressed with how she had handled herself so far, and even her effort with the furs was seen as merely a misguided attempt to make a place for herself. The only criticism anyone could find was that she seemed somewhat clumsy by nature, but even then they admired what they considered to be her courage and strength in the face of adversity. She wasn't what they considered to be the typical whingeing English-woman they had expected, and that seemed to impress them more than anything else.

Aye, all would be well . . . So long as she took the news he had to impart to her without horror or hysterics. Connall grimaced to himself at that thought. He would have to tell her of his origins eventually and wasn't looking forward to the task because he wasn't sure how she would take it, or even how he was to approach the subject. But she would have to be told. Connall felt sure it would be better to explain it himself in calm, reasonable tones than to have her find out on her own and perhaps flee in terror. He would give her a little more time to adjust before he did though, Connall decided and was relieved to have the excuse to put it off.

Eva finally reached the chapel steps and mounted them to join Connall, Ewan, and the priest. Connall gave her a slight nod, then made an effort at a smile, though he felt so tense—a sensation he wasn't at all used to—that he suspected it looked more like a grimace. Giving up on the effort, he urged her around on the top step so that they stood side by side, facing Father MacLure, then he gave a start of surprise when he felt Eva slip her small, uninjured hand into his and squeeze it gently. Connall immediately felt the tension slip from his shoulders at that trusting action. Aye, all would be well.

Eva was quite sure that the wedding at Caxton had not taken nearly as long as this one was and was positive it was because Father MacLure was overfond of the sound of his own voice. Unfortunately, the man did not have a very expressive speaking voice and his monotonous diatribe encouraged her mind to wander. Eva had caught herself wandering several times now and each time had forced her thoughts back to the ceremony and what he was saying, but eventually she gave in and let her thoughts drift. Her mind wandered first to wondering what Cook had managed to prepare for the feast that was to follow the ceremony. She knew that Effie had been working for days on the repast and had no doubt that she would have come up with something special. Whatever it was, there was no doubt it would be tasty, the woman had yet to serve anything that wasn't absolutely delicious.

From that subject, Eva's mind naturally wandered to what would follow the feast . . . the bedding. The very thought of it made her start to tense up again.

Despite the fact that her parents had both died when she was barely nine, and she'd had no mother to educate her in these matters, Eva was not ignorant on the subject of men and women. Mavis had seen to that. The girl spent most of her time working in the kitchens when not pressed into service as her lady's maid, so it was in the kitchen with the rest of the servants that she slept, though she occasionally had slept in the great hall if Cook was in a mood. Sleeping there with all the rest of the servants, Mavis had seen—and eagerly recounted to Eva—much of what went on between a man and woman—at least among the servant class.

The maid had described it as a sort of wrestling match that ended when the man took his pillock, "rather like a large boiled sausage," she had described it, and stuck it up between the woman's legs. Eva had never fancied the idea of having a boiled sausage shoved up between her legs and found her feet shifting together to press her thighs more tightly closed as she stood before the mumbling priest. Then her gaze dropped to the side of its own accord, to peer at the point where her husband's boiled sausage would be.

Although he normally wore his plaid, or had since she'd

arrived, today Connall had chosen to wear the outfit she had seen him in at court for their wedding; a fine dark blue doublet and white hose. Eva was flattered that he had troubled himself to dress up for the occasion, but it meant that his figure was now rather on view and her eyes widened in alarm at the size of the bulge visible beneath the hose. Mavis had said that the bigger the bulge, the bigger the boiled sausage, and her husband appeared quite huge to her. Not that she had ever before seen a man's sausage or troubled to notice the size of their bulge, but Connall's bulge looked rather large to her anxious eyes.

Eva squeezed her thighs a little tighter closed as she tried to imagine him wrestling her to the bed and assaulting her with his sausage.

"Eva?"

She jerked her gaze guiltily up to his eyes, thinking she had been caught rudely staring at his sausage, but the expectant expression on his face and the way he nodded toward the priest, who was also eyeing her expectantly, made her realize she had missed something.

"Do you?" Father MacLure prompted at last and Eva understood and stammered "I do." When the good father nodded and began to speak again, she couldn't stop her eyes from sliding down and to the side to look her husband over again.

As she stared at the bulge that she was almost positive was growing under her gaze, Eva briefly considered if it would not have been wiser to have said "nay" rather than "I do," then immediately began to remonstrate with herself. Did she wish to go to the abbey and be a nun? For that's what would have happened had she said nay to the vows. And really, everything else here was so nice and pleasant; she no longer left the table hungry because she ate as little as possible to keep from angering her brother, she no longer worked herself to the point of exhaustion in an effort to be as little of a burden as possible, and the people here were all so nice to her. Surely she could manage to forbear the sausage stuffing?

Eva grimaced at her own choice of words. Sausage stuffing? It made her sound like a fowl being prepared for supper.

"You may kiss the bride."

Eva glanced up with surprise at those words. Was the ceremony finally over? The priest's words and the fact that Connall was turning her toward him as his face lowered to hers, seemed a good indication that it was. Eva squeezed her eyes closed and waited for his kiss, wondering what it would be like, then opened them with surprise when his lips rubbed gently and sweetly over her own. She rather liked it . . . and found herself arching up on her tiptoe to press her own mouth more firmly against his, but he was already straightening again.

Embarrassed at her own response to her husband, Eva took a step back to put some space between them as the crowd in the bailey began to cheer. It was only as she set her foot down in midair that she recalled she was standing on stairs. In the next moment, she found herself tumbling down the church steps to the accompaniment of several alarmed and startled shouts and shrieks.

Seven

Eva put her sewing down with a little sigh, then raised her face to the sunlight and closed her eyes. It was very peaceful here in the gardens and she was glad Glynis had insisted that she come out and sit on a fur in the sun to sew. The maid had proven herself to be a treasure and without her cheerful chatter and care, Eva didn't think she could have maintained her wits this last week since the wedding.

A pained expression flickered across her face at the thought of her wedding day. The ceremony had been beautiful, and the feast splendid, Effie had—as expected—outdone herself. Unfortunately, Eva only knew this from what others had told her, she herself hadn't been in attendance at the wedding feast, she'd been unconscious in bed having several new scrapes and bruises—gained from her tumble down the chapel steps—tended to by Magaidh and Aileen.

Heaving a sigh, Eva opened her eyes again and glanced down at the dress that lay on her lap. Her gaze automatically moved from there to consider each of her injuries to date. Her hand was much healed from the dog bite and a scab was all that was left, so she'd taken the bandages off the day before yesterday to allow it to dry and heal. Her arms were a patchwork of varying shades of bruises, from a dull blue to yellow, though the scrapes there were healed. Her legs looked much the same, she knew, but at least her ankle, which she had wrenched again in the fall, was almost as good as new again, twingeing only when she forgot it and turned too quickly. Eva knew she'd been lucky that she hadn't broken anything in that fall, but the injuries she'd had were enough in her mind, as they had seen her wedding night put off yet again. To Eva, it was rather like putting off a tooth-pulling, the anticipation was an agony to suffer. She would rather have the deed done.

That would happen soon enough, she supposed. There had been no further accidents since the wedding to hamper her recovery, and physically she was almost back to normal. Otherwise, however, she was a mess. Eva felt as if she had ruined everything. Oh, everyone here was still as kind to her as could be, but they now treated her either like fragile glass . . . or an idiot. She was not allowed to lift anything above the weight of a thimble, and was not allowed to carry anything at all when she walked. These were her husband's orders. He had also ordered that two men were to accompany her at all times to ensure that the orders were carried out. Eva felt the usual indignation rise up in her at the thought that she had watchers . . . like the veriest of children who could not be trusted to play without setting themselves in danger's way.

Her resentful gaze shifted to her present watchers and away again; Donaidh and Geordan were relaxing against the garden wall, talking idly. They would remain there so long as she remained where she was sitting, but if Eva shifted the dress from her lap and start to rise, they would be on either side of her, taking an arm to help her up lest she stumble and fall and hurt herself again.

Aye, she was now the village idiot.

Her gaze slid back to the dress she had been working on.

A confection in blues, it was another of the new gowns for her fine new wardrobe. Magaidh and Connall had insisted she should have several, and half a dozen maids had been set to the task of creating them. Eva was helping, or supposed to be helping, by hemming the skirt of the gown across her lap, but she wasn't really in the mood for sewing this afternoon. Instead, she thought she might prefer a good cry, but of course, that was impossible with Donaidh and Geordan hovering nearby.

Eva heaved another sigh as her gaze wandered to the two men who were acting as her guards today. They would remain with her until the sun set and her husband arrived for his supper. She had learned a lot more about the workings of the castle during the past week. The men were not always discreet when she was about and she often overheard their conversations, enough to know that her husband was not off attending to business during the day as she had first been told, but that he was resting away from the sun. His sun reaction made it so that he avoided attending to clan business during the day and left that in Ewan's capable hands. Connall took over the chore from the moment the sun set until it rose again in the morning.

Eva had at first thought that Ewan must then have the heavier burden when it came to running the keep, but had since come to the conclusion that this was not so. It seemed Connall and his sister weren't the only MacAdies troubled with a negative reaction to the sun. By her estimate, at least half the people here were and they too rested during the day, coming out at night to accomplish what most would do during the day in any other castle, which meant MacAdie was as busy, if not busier at night than it was during the day.

Eva had also learned that her husband led raiding parties at night, though she had endeavored to ignore this information and had stopped listening to that particular conversation once she'd understood what the men were talking about. Such things as night raids on neighbors were frowned on by the English, though she knew 'twas common enough in Scotland. Not approving of her husband's activities, Eva simply didn't wish to know about them, so closed off her attention when the men spoke about such things, but she had learned enough to know that Connall was kept busy from dusk till dawn.

Well, not the entire time, she supposed. The men stopped watching her when Connall made his appearance, because he took over the task himself. The man who had been absent for the first several days after her arrival, had taken to spending time with Eva now that they were wed. He joined her to sit at the trestle table for supper, though he often got distracted with the reports the men were giving and didn't eat as much as she felt he should. Sometimes there was business that needed tending to right away; if it was something that took him out of the keep, he would set two men to guard her until he could return. If it was simply a meeting he needed to have, he would suggest she sit by the fire and he would join her there shortly. Either way, he always joined her for a couple of hours at night, often to play chess with her.

Eva had hoped to redeem herself with her abilities in chess. Her father had taught her the game when she was quite young and she had played it with her older sister, Lynette, until Lynny, who had been as dowerless as herself, had been sent off to the abbey. While she had not played in the two years since Lynette became a bride of God, Eva had managed to retain her skill and had even beaten her husband a time or two. However, while he claimed to be impressed by her intellect, nothing had seemed to change his mind about her ability to look after herself without guards to watch over her.

The sun went behind a cloud and Eva stirred where she sat. It was getting late, the sun was following its downward path and would set soon. She supposed she should go inside, put the dress away, and prepare for supper.

* * *

"If we're finished, I think I'll go to see my wife," Ewan announced.

Connall nodded and glanced toward the great hall fire as the other man stood and departed. Eva was curled up in a chair before the roaring blaze, sewing as she waited for him to finish his meeting with Ewan and join her as had become his habit since the wedding. Connall had found his gaze wandering to her several times as he had listened to Ewan's report and had noticed that Eva drew herself a little tighter into a ball each time the keep door opened. It was wet and blustery tonight, with a chill that he hadn't really noticed until he'd noted Eva's shrinking from it. He wasn't bothered much by cold, but it seemed as if his wife was.

Standing as she paused in her sewing to chafe some warmth into her arms, Connall moved to her chair and held out his hand. "Come, we'll play chess in our room tonight. Twill be warmer there by the fire without the breeze blowing in ever' few minutes."

Eva smiled her relief at his suggestion and took his hand to rise, commenting, "Tis growing cool at night."

"Aye. Summer is coming to a close, the nights grow longer, the days shorter, and the air chill," Connall said as he gestured one of the houseboys over to collect the chess game. He himself took the gown from her hands, freeing her to hold her skirt up as they mounted the stairs. He didn't miss the exasperated little sigh she gave at his thoughtfulness, but ignored it, knowing she was feeling that they all thought her incompetent. Connall didn't bother to explain that it was just a precaution until she was on her feet again and knew her new home well enough that—even should she be distracted—she would not thoughtlessly go tumbling down a set of stairs or bang into something. With a little time here, Eva would get to know everyone and all the nooks and crannies of the house so that she would be in less danger.

At least from common accidents, Connall thought, with a frown. There had been another attempt on his life the night before last. It was the third attempt in the last year since the trouble had started. Connall had been riding with the men on the way to a raid when an arrow had sailed through the darkness, narrowly missing him but hitting the man riding next to him. It had been a flesh wound in the arm and quickly healed, but the incident was bothersome for two reasons: One was that the attacker had made the attempt in the open, at night, when Connall was surrounded by his Nightriders who had, as one would expect, immediately spread out and begun to search the woods. The fellow had been extremely lucky and escaped capture. Extremely lucky, as most of the men with him had a nocturnal predator's night vision, which was what bothered Connall: If the attacker knew anything about them and had still attacked under such risky circumstances, then he was obviously growing desperate, and desperate men were unpredictable.

The other reason the incident worried Connall was that someone else had been injured. This time it had been just a flesh wound and had healed quickly as was the wont of their sort, but what if he had been riding with Eva? What if she had been the one to take the arrow meant for him? And what if it had struck her heart rather than her arm?

That didn't bear thinking about, Connall decided, and admitted to himself that he had become a tad attached to the woman in the last week or so. He found he enjoyed their evenings by the fire. Eva was intelligent and amusing and as charming as she was lovely, and the matter-of-fact way she spoke of what he considered to be an atrocious childhood after her parents' death, touched him in a way that the tale of her brother's cold and uncaring behavior would not have affected him had she told it with a self-pitying attitude. But that wasn't her attitude. Eva appeared to be philosophical about it, and accepted it as her lot in life, even considering herself lucky. It could have been worse, she said, with a simple shrug, and he could not but admire that . . . And admire her.

His gaze slid to her as she led the way up the hall to her chamber, and dropped down to her behind and the way the cloth of her gown covering it moved with each step. Connall had put off consummating the marriage after the injuries from her fall, but he was thinking that she appeared well healed now, well enough perhaps to become his wife in deed as well as law.

Glynis had already tended to the fire, Eva saw as they entered the room, and it had obviously been burning for a while, for the chamber was notably warmer than the great hall. The girl seemed always to be thinking ahead and looking after such details. It was wonderful having her assistance. Eva hadn't realized what she had been missing in not having a lady's maid all these years, but truly appreciated the many small things the girl did and made a mental note to thank her in the morning.

She found herself oddly nervous as she led the way to the chairs by the fire. Eva had played chess with her husband many times the last week, but this time somehow seemed different. For one thing, her chamber was much smaller than the great hall, and Eva was very aware that it was her sleeping chamber, as well as terribly conscious of the large bed at the other end of it, and the fact that they had yet to consummate the marriage. She knew that Connall had been considerate in letting her heal after her last accident on the steps after the wedding, but while she appreciated it, it left her in a constant state of anxiety as to exactly when he would decide she was healed enough to approach her. In truth, Eva had been growing increasingly anxious with each passing day, until tonight, the anxiety was like a band around her stomach, tightening with every step she took.

Oh, this is awful, she decided, and thought that perhaps she should turn and tell him to get the business over with. Stopping by the chairs, Eva turned to face him, opened her mouth to speak, then closed it abruptly as she caught sight of the houseboy carrying the chess game. She'd completely forgotten about the lad. Completely. Biting her lip, she dropped into the nearest chair and sat silent as one of the chests that held her new gowns was dragged between the two chairs and the game was set out on it.

Connall thanked the lad for his aid, then asked him to have Cook send someone up with wine for both of them.

Once the boy had left, Eva cleared her throat and eyed her husband. "My lord, I appreciate your kindness since arriving; first with holding a proper wedding once I arrived, then in . . . er . . . postponing the . . . er . . . consummation of the wedding until I had recovered," she stammered, aware that she was blushing furiously. She hadn't really considered how distressing this conversation would be before starting it, but now that she was well into it, there was nothing to do but finish it.

Clearing her throat, she straightened her shoulders and marshalled on, "But really, my lord, 'tis a nerve-wracking situation and I would . . . well . . . If we could get it over?"

Connall stared at her blankly, clearly taken completely by surprise at this outburst, then he frowned and echoed, "Get it over?"

"Aye . . . well . . ." She forced a smile and began wringing her hands together as she explained, "'Tis rather like knowing that someday soon, though you are not sure when exactly, you will have to approach the blacksmith about knocking a rotten tooth out."

"Knockin' a rotten tooth . . ." Connall was staring at her with disbelief, though she didn't understand why. Nor did she understand why, when he finally spoke, he sounded somewhat upset. "Me lady wife, I realize ye havenae—What on earth makes ye think—*'Knockin' out a rotten tooth'?'*"

Eva bit her lip, unsure what she should say to improve the situation. He seemed rather offended by the comparison. "Well, I have never—I mean, from what I have been told, it does not sound like something to look forward to, my lord."

"What ha'e ye been told?" He sounded as if he were forcing patience.

Eva considered whether she had the courage to repeat Mavis's description and was quite sure she didn't. It was one thing to be told that by another woman, it was quite another to repeat it to the man with the boiled sausage he intended to use on you. She shook her head helplessly, but Connall apparently wasn't in the mood to humor her.

"What'd that useless brother o' yers tell ye?"

"Oh, it was not Jonathan," she assured him quickly. "It was my maid, Mavis . . . Well, she was not truly my maid. She worked in the kitchens, but did occasionally act as lady's maid to me . . . Well, once or twice. She traveled to court with us because Jonathan said I needed a lady's maid there," Eva explained lamely, then fell silent, aware she'd been babbling.

"I see, and what did this Mavis tell ye aboot what goes on between a husband and wife?"

Connall was sounding a little less angry now, she noted with relief. Still, it was difficult to imagine telling him so she said instead, "Well she was describing what went on between the servants, not necessarily between husband and wife, if you see what I mean?"

"Stop stalling," he said quietly. "A wife shouldnae fear telling her husband ought."

Eva sighed at these words, it was becoming obvious that he wasn't going to let this pass and she was going to have to repeat what Mavis had said. She was beginning to wish that she had never opened her mouth, but had simply awaited his pleasure in silent suspense. Unfortunately, she hadn't done so. Deciding that there was nothing for it, she gathered her courage and blurted, "She said it appeared that the man and woman wrestled a bit and then he stuck his boiled sausage up between her legs."

Connall made an odd sound, somewhere between a cough and snort, then turned his head abruptly away so that she could not see his expression. Eva was not certain at first if he were angry or shocked, but then she noted the way his shoulders were shaking and suspected the man was actually laughing at her. Indignation quickly rose up in her, but before she could say anything, there was a knock at the door. Eva glared at her husband as he glanced around, then stood and headed for the door.

"Yer flouncin'!" Connall crowed with amusement. "Damn me, I'd ha'e sworn ye were no a flouncer, but yer flouncin'!"

Realizing that she was indeed flouncing, Eva tried to correct her step, but was simply too agitated to manage it. Giving up the attempt as she reached the door, Eva wrenched it open, then quickly replaced the scowl on her face with a forced smile when she spied a wide-eyed Glynis standing in the hall, bearing a tray with a bottle of wine and wineglasses on it.

"Thank you, Glynis." She reached to take the tray from her. "And thank you for lighting the fire."

"Oh but—" the maid tried to snatch the tray back, no doubt recalling her laird's order that his wife was to carry nothing, but Eva was in a sorry mood and stepped back out of reach, then pushed the door closed with her foot. She whirled back toward the room then and almost crashed the tray into her husband.

"I shall take that. No need to risk an accident," he said mildly as he relieved her of the tray and carried it to where the chess game was set up.

Eva no longer felt like playing chess, if she ever had, and she definitely did not feel like finally living up to her wifely duties, not that she ever had felt that either. All she really wanted at that point was to be left alone to lick her wounded pride, so, she stayed where she was by the door, glaring at her husband's back as he set the tray down and set about pouring wine for both of them. She continued to glare at him as Connall then lifted both glasses and carried them back to where she stood. An arched eyebrow was his only response to her irritated glare, then he handed her a glass, took a sip of his own and said, "Mavis got it wrong, lass."

Eva narrowed her eyes. "She did?"

"Aye. Drink yer wine."

Eva automatically took a sip, then asked, "What did she get wrong?"

"Well, there is much she left out, or perhaps was simply unable to see in a dark great hall at night with who knows how much distance between her and the people in question."

"What did she leave out?" Eva asked.

"Well, for one thing, she left out the kissing."

"Kissing?" Eva's interest was definitely engaged now. She still recalled that brief brush of lips after the ceremony and the way her mouth had tingled.

"Yes. Like our wedding kiss, only more."

"More?" she echoed with interest. "More what?"

"Drink yer wine," he instructed instead of answering.

Eva took an impatient gulp, then repeated, "More what?"

"Tis difficult to describe," he said, then raised one eyebrow again. "Perhaps I should show you?"

Eight

Eva stared at her husband uncertainly as she considered what to say to his question *"Perhaps I should show you?"* What she wanted to say was, Yes. Eva had enjoyed his kiss at the end of the wedding ceremony and would not mind experiencing that pleasure again. Then too, she really was curious about the "more." She gave the smallest of nods and raised her face to his, her eyes squeezing shut as she did. Almost immediately, she felt his lips move gently over hers as they had at the wedding, a soft, sweet caress of his mouth across the delicate skin of her own. Eva almost found herself sighing at the touch it was so pleasant. Then it changed a little, becoming a little firmer and she moved eagerly forward, happy for the increased pressure and the warmth it sent rushing through her. This time she couldn't hold back her sigh, and her lips parted slightly beneath his. Connall immediately tilted his head more to the side and opened his own mouth to catch the sigh, then she felt his tongue slip out of his mouth and into hers.

Eva's eyes popped open with surprise, then closed again. She had seen couples kissing like this before, servants she had come across unexpectedly at Caxton, catching them out in brief embraces. It had seemed an odd and hungry kiss, not really all that pleasant, but she found it was quite pleasant indeed, and it *was* a hungry kiss, or at least it made her hunger, though she wasn't quite sure for what.

Her mouth instinctively opened further under the onslaught and when Eva felt his tongue glide over her own, she heard a moan pierce the air around them and knew it came from herself, but didn't much mind. It didn't seem to bother Connall and so long as it didn't stop his kissing, Eva didn't care. She could be embarrassed later, but for now, she thought she could be quite happy to have him go on kissing her forever.

Several moments passed, or perhaps only one—she was having difficulty keeping hold of her thoughts, let alone time—then she heard the sound of splashing water. Eva wasn't sure where it was coming from until she felt Connall take the wine away from her, leaving that hand free. Her other though was caught up in the material of his plaid, clutching it as if it were her only hold on sanity in a world gone mad. Now she allowed the other to tangle itself there as well, so that she could hold him close to her lest he decide to end the kiss.

"There is more," Connall told her as he eased the kiss.

"More?" Eva echoed. She was vaguely disappointed as he retracted his tongue from her mouth, but was also distracted by the way his lips were nibbling along her chin toward her ear.

"Hmmm. Other kinds of kisses." He reached her ear and did things there that made her gasp in surprise and shift up onto the tips of her toes.

No one had ever—she hadn't even considered—dear God, had someone set her skirt on fire? It felt as though her lower regions were being consumed by heat . . . and she liked it, Eva decided, moaning and arching and tugging at the cloth of his plaid as his mouth moved on to her throat now, his tongue whipping her into a frenzy. Mavis had managed to leave this part out. And fie on the maid for doing so, she thought vaguely; Eva was quite sure this was the best bit of the whole thing.

The thud of the wineglasses hitting the floor made her start, but then Connall distracted her with his hands, catching them at her waist, then running them up her back and back down. He didn't stop at her waist this time, however, but continued down until he was cupping her buttocks. A shocking caress indeed, but she liked it. She liked the way he pressed his lower body into hers too, and the hardness that she felt.

Connall left one hand there, holding her firmly against him, then lifted his lips from the collarbone he had been teasing with his tongue, and covered her mouth with his own. This kiss was even more passionate and hungry than the other had been and Eva felt herself melt into him, as a warm liquid sensation pooled in her lower belly and slid down to where he moved against her. Dear God, the kissing was heavenly. It was amazing, exciting, overwhelming, and—where had the top of her gown gone, she wondered vaguely. Somehow it was now pooled around her waist, exposing her naked flesh to the room at large, not that Connall could see her, with his mouth on hers, she assured herself but—

"Oh," she murmured the word into his mouth and bucked against him in surprised reaction as one calloused hand cupped, then closed over one of her exposed breasts.

Connall caught the soft word in his mouth and filled hers more fully with his tongue. The action prevented any possibility of protest as he gently kneaded and squeezed the breast, then began to torment its nipple, catching it between thumb and forefinger and rolling it gently before lightly pinching it.

Eva had the wildest urge to push the man to the floor and rub her naked chest over him. Instead, she began to kiss him back in earnest, becoming a partner in the activity instead of a quiescent recipient. She thrust her tongue into his mouth, rubbing it across his, then withdrew it to suck on his tongue instead. Eva didn't know if she was doing this well, she was merely following instinct, but it felt so good she didn't much care, either.

The pressure of the bed against the back of her knees several minutes later was when Eva realized that Connall had been moving them both across the room to the bed. The feeling of fur against her backside was when she first noticed that her gown was no longer around her waist, but was gone altogether, as were her undergarments. She wasn't wearing anything at all, not a stitch, not—

"Oh." This time the sound came from much deeper in her throat, as Connall broke their kisses again and ducked his head straight down to claim the nipple he had been so effectively caressing. If she had thought his touch there exciting and stirring, his lips closing over the tender and already excited flesh was earth-shaking.

Eva tossed her head and arched against him, unashamedly rubbing her lower body against the hardness she could feel between his legs. His boiled sausage might not sound attractive, but it felt good pressing against her. At least with the plaid as a barrier it did, she thought, then she stiffened and let her eyes shoot open as she felt him slip one hand between their bodies and dip between her legs. The cool, calloused skin of his fingers smoothed lightly across her heated flesh and Eva reacted as if it were a brand, her entire body leaping in his arms, her legs closing instinctively to trap his hand even as she pushed herself against him.

She was of two minds at that point: She was so sensitive that the touch seemed almost unbearable, yet she didn't want to stop. Her body reacted to her confusion, squirming to get away from his touch one moment, then arching into it the next. Connall resolved the issue for her by trapping her legs with his own, then forcing them further apart and holding her in place as he touched her.

Eva tossed her head on the fur, small unintelligible mewls

coming from her throat, intermittently peppered with "Oh nos," which were immediately followed by "Yes, please." In truth, she didn't know what she wanted, whether it was for him to stop, not stop, or perhaps just for him to make the need go away and stop driving her mad with his caresses. Then he added a new touch to his repertoire and Eva felt something alien push into her, stretching her even as he continued to caress her. Eva groaned at the sensation, some part of her mind sensate enough to know that it wasn't his boiled sausage because she could feel that pressed against the top of one thigh. All she could think of was that it was a *finger* sliding in and out of her.

Eva went still for the briefest of moments as the very alien nature of the caress struck her, but he was still touching her where she was most sensitive and her body began to quiver in confusion and need, then move of its own accord into his touch. Eva began to moan again, the sound growing more intense with each stroke. Her body was now suffering a tightening sensation that became more intense by the moment and was concentrated where it was receiving his attentions.

Just when she felt sure she would shatter under the building pressure, the tension suddenly snapped, and Eva cried out and dug her nails into Connall's shoulders. Her body arched and bucked beneath the furor, then she cried out again as pain followed the pleasure, wiping out everything before it and shocking her into stillness. It was no longer his hand between her legs—he had replaced it with his boiled sausage.

"Tis the only time 'twill hurt." Connall panted those words near her ear and Eva finally realized his presence on top of her. Odd as it may be, for a moment she had been so startled by and concentrated on the pain that she had almost forgotten him altogether.

"Tis because yer pure."

Eva was still panting and out of breath, so merely nodded to let him know she had heard and understood him.

"The pain should go away soon. It doesnae last."

Eva nodded again. In truth the pain was already receding, leaving her body limp and pulsing beneath him in a rather pleasant way.

"Is it leaving?" Connall asked and Eva couldn't help but notice that he sounded desperately hopeful.

Eva nodded again.

"Och, thank the good Lord," he muttered against her forehead, then pressed a kiss there, before turning his lips to her mouth and kissing her there again as well.

Despite the shock she had just received, the passion she'd thought now dead, stirred lazily within her under his kiss. It stirred again when he eased his boiled sausage out of her, then just as slowly and gently eased it back in. Eva felt a sudden need to arch and stretch beneath him, then instinctively wrapped her legs around his hips and pulled him tighter against her when he next stroked back into her body. She wanted to hold him there and rub against him, but he wouldn't be held and withdrew yet again. This time, when he moved back, it was more a thrust than a slide, his body almost slamming into hers.

Eva gasped at the sensations that were shooting through her. The pain was not completely gone, there was a touch of tenderness, but the pleasure was returning and building back up to its earlier levels so quickly it was difficult to believe they had ever been sated the once. It was also overwhelming the minor discomfort that grew less with each passing moment. Eva scraped her nails up his back, clutching him close and moaning as he continued his actions and drove them both to the place where she had felt sure she would simply shatter and die the first time.

She was not alone when she reached it again, even as the tension snapped in her and her body began to quiver and shake beneath his. Eva heard Connall gasp something in

Gaelic in her ear, then thrust one final time before stiffening and crying out himself.

This time when she lay, limp and pulsing, Connall lay atop her, panting and limp as well. Whether he was having the same pulsing sensation as she was, she didn't know, and she was too exhausted to ask. So much so, that if it weren't for the fact that breathing became easier, she wouldn't have noticed when Connall moved off her to lay at her side. Eva stirred when he turned her in his arms and curved her into his body so that her bottom pressed against the shrinking sausage that had shown her so much pleasure. But when he then pulled the furs up to cover them both and just lay there with one arm curled around her, holding her against him, Eva allowed herself to drift off to sleep.

It was some time later when she awoke to slow caresses and sweet kisses and Connall proved to her that the pain really did occur only the first time. Then she slept again until he stirred her once more. This time the fact that he was dressed, made it obvious that he had left the room and was returning and she helped him to strip before he joined her.

It was near dawn when they collapsed exhausted, side by side, and dawn's grey light was creeping around the edge of the furs at the window. Eva was just drifting off to sleep when she felt Connall stir. At first, she simply thought he was shifting in the bed to a more comfortable position, and allowed herself to doze again, but the soft click of the door closing a moment later made her sit up in bed, suddenly wide awake.

Where the devil was he going? He had slept somewhere else since her arrival, just where exactly she wasn't sure, but surely he would sleep with her now that they had consummated the marriage? Wouldn't he?

After a hesitation, Eva got up, took the new dark blue robe that had been made for her and drew it on as she moved across the room. The flames had died in the fireplace long ago, her room was as dark as a tomb except for the stray of grey light which crept in around the furs at the window, but there wasn't enough light to be seen from the hall, she was sure. Eva didn't hesitate to ease the door open and peer out into the hall, blinking as the torchlight there assaulted her eyes. There were several torches to light the way, but only one at the top of the stairs was lit. However, it was enough light for her to make out the dark shape of her husband walking down the hall to the opposite end. The man hadn't even bothered to put on his plaid again, but strode down the hall naked as the day he was born, his pale skin gleaming in the torchlight.

She saw him stop at the end of the hall, touch two places, then the stone wall that faced the hall at that end of it suddenly slid open and Eva gasped as her husband stepped inside and it began to close again. She was about to call out and hurry after him when a dark shape suddenly separated itself from the top of the stairs and moved after her husband. Eva snapped her mouth closed and waited.

She had no idea who it was, but their stealthy movements didn't make her think that they belonged there. The figure moved to the far end of the hall and she saw him run his hands over the stones as if in search of the places her husband had pushed. Eva watched tensely until, after several moments of fruitless searching, the dark shape apparently gave up the search and began to move back up the hall. She immediately eased her chamber door closed to a sliver, lest she be seen, and simply watched the person, hoping that she'd be able to tell who it was when they passed the torchlight at the top of the stairs.

Eva was sorely disappointed when the figure passed through the light and she saw that he was wearing a dark hooded cape, the hood pulled so far forward that it shadowed his face. All she could see was the tip of his nose as he reached the stairs, then he turned and moved silently down them.

Eva slid from her room and crept to the top of the stairs to watch the figure disappear into the shadowed great hall below, then glanced up the hall to the wall through which her husband had disappeared. After the smallest of hesitations, she followed her husband and the stranger's path and moved to the wall to run her hands over it as had the man before her. She used her right hand to press the two stones she felt sure she had seen Connall touch with his right hand, but nothing happened. Eva pressed them again, a little harder. Still nothing. Irritated, she slapped the wall in front of her with her left hand, then gasped as the stone wall suddenly slid open.

After a hesitation, she pushed it further open and stared into gaping darkness. Eva couldn't see a thing and was filled with sudden trepidation, then she forced her shoulders up. A husband should sleep with his wife, and if he wouldn't, then a wife should sleep with her husband. At least that's how it seemed to her. After all, Aileen slept at night with her husband, spending the days locked inside because of her reaction to the sun, but awake so that she could be up while her husband was awake. Eva understood that Connall slept the day away, leaving Ewan to run the castle while he rested, then running it himself at night, but then, shouldn't she too keep the same hours? And shouldn't they sleep together?

Besides, she was terribly curious as to why the man slept in this dark hidden room. Ewan had said that his reaction to sunlight was worse than his sister's, so she could only presume that even the hint of light that crept around the furs was unbearable to him. That being the case, she could sleep in total darkness too.

Sleep in it, perhaps, she thought a moment later, but she couldn't seem to force herself to step into it. Grimacing, she hesitated, then hurried back up the hall, pausing at the top of the stairs to be sure no one was coming up them and might see the open door. The room she'd found was obviously a secret and she didn't wish to reveal it to anyone. Assured that the stairwell, like the hall, was presently empty, she hurried on to her room, paused to glance back once more, then rushed inside, snatched up the nearest candle and hurried back out, relieved to find the hall still empty.

Eva moved to the torch at the top of the stairs, lit her small candle by it, then sheltered it with one hand as she moved back to the entrance to the hidden room. Somehow, the tiny light from the candle seemed to make the darkness beyond the entrance even more frightening. Eva didn't hesitate however, but stepped through into the room beyond. Not a room, she realized, but a narrow hall that ran straightforward.

Grimacing, she hesitated, then glanced back along the proper upper hall, supposing she couldn't leave the entrance open like this, though she wished she could. Sighing with resignation, Eva eased the door closed, trying not to wince when she heard a click as it locked in place. She moved the candle over the stone panel, frowning when she didn't see a handle of any sort to unlock it. Eva supposed there was some secret to opening it from this side as well and almost panicked, but then recalled that her husband was in here with her somewhere and he could let her out if necessary.

If he was still in here.

She frowned at that sudden thought, but knew that it was at least possible that he had stepped out of the room while she had stepped into her own. Eva rolled her eyes at that thought. Surely he wouldn't have left the door open, were that the case? In fact, he should have been quite upset and rushing about with distress that someone had opened it, if he had found it open. Nay, he was here. Somewhere.

She turned back and tried to peer up the dark passage, but her small candlelight didn't seem to reach far at all and she couldn't even tell how far it went. Finally forcing herself to leave the door, Eva started forward, holding her candle out before her at full arm's length in an effort to see as far ahead as possible. It was a plain dark stone hall, no torches in sconces to see by, no rushes on the floor, and then suddenly she saw a door on her left. A plain wooden door with a handle. She peered at it uncertainly, then glanced along the continuing hall with a frown.

Eva supposed she had expected the hall to end at one room and not continue on. After a hesitation, she decided to continue along the hall, just to see what else there was to see, at least that's what she told herself. She wasn't willing to admit that she suddenly felt anxious about confronting her husband. Leaving the first door, Eva moved on, crossing another good distance before coming to the end of the hall and another door.

Oh, now here was a fine quandary. Which door should she try first? She could have spent a good deal of time debating that issue and avoiding the actual doing, but a sudden mumbling came to her softly through the door where she now stood. Eva stilled and leaned toward the door as the sound came again, a nonsensical sleepy mumble, but in it she was able to recognize her husband's voice.

Reaching for the handle, Eva opened the door and stepped inside, preparing to be berated should her husband be annoyed with her. There was no berating, however, only silence and darkness as thick as that in the hall.

Eva pursed her lips, then left the door open and eased further into the room until the edge of the candlelight touched the side of a bed, and began to move across it as she continued forward. When it fell on her husband's face, he scowled in his sleep and mumbled a complaint, then rolled onto his side away from the light.

Eva immediately pulled the candle back, lest she wake him. Letting him sleep seemed a smart thing at that point, men could be so grumpy on first waking. Moving back to the door, she eased it silently closed, then shielded the candle with her hand to prevent it reaching too far and accidentally waking her husband as she moved back to the bed.

Connall was sprawled on his side in the middle of the bed, leaving just a sliver of bed for her to claim should she wish to and Eva debated the matter. Turn and make her way back up that long dark hall to the door she didn't know how to open? Or crawl into that sliver of space and sleep with her husband where she belonged?

She'd stay, Eva decided and set the candle on the chest beside the bed. When she straightened, thoughtlessly removing the hand she had been shielding the light with, candlelight immediately splashed over Connall and he began to grumble in his sleep again. Eva instinctively bent to blow the candle out in response, then sighed as she was plunged into complete blackness.

Ah well, she didn't need light to undress and the bed was right beside her, she reassured herself, then tried not to imagine what kind of creepy crawlies might now be moving about in the darkness. Rats and spiders came to mind, but she forced them away. Still, her movements were perhaps a little quicker than necessary as she tugged her robe off and felt around for the linens and furs to crawl beneath them. Eva slowed to a more cautious speed once her feet were off the floor and safely tucked under the bedding, then eased herself down to lay on her side next to her husband on the sliver of bed he had left free.

Connall mumbled when she cuddled up against his back and slid one arm around his waist, but he didn't wake up. Eva wasn't really tired at this point and lay wide awake for a long time wishing there was firelight or candlelight to at least see something, even if it was only darker shadows in the darkness, but eventually, she drifted off to sleep.

Nine

Someone was blowing in his ear.

Connall lay still as sleep left him, unwilling to give away the fact that he was now awake. It was only a moment later that he realized that whoever it was wasn't blowing in his ear, but breathing in his ear, and the same someone was pressed up against his back with an arm around his waist, he realized.

Confusion assaulted him and for a moment Connall thought perhaps he hadn't left his bride's bed and come to his usual sleeping spot as he'd thought he had, perhaps he'd dreamt that, but then he realized that this room was too dark to be the chamber where his wife slept. He was definitely in his own room, the one he had occupied since childhood, but someone was with him.

His mother, sister, and Ewan were the only ones who knew about this room, but Connall seriously doubted any of them would be snuggled up against him like this. At least, he sincerely hoped not. The warm body curled around his own was having an effect on him that it would just be wrong to have for any of those three individuals.

"Eva?" he asked hopefully.

"Mmmm." The body behind him shifted and stretched,

then curled even closer, tops of thighs pressing against his arse and the backs of his legs.

Connall squeezed his eyes closed as the semi-erection he had awoken with sprang into a full one. Dear God, he hoped it was his wife, perhaps his mother or sister had informed her of his room as a surprise. Deciding it was time to find out, Connall eased closer to the edge of the bed and the candle he usually kept there. He managed to light it, then lifted it in the air and glanced over his shoulder, a small breath of relief slipping from his lips at the sight of his wife curled up behind him. Setting the candle back on the chest, Connall eased onto his back in the bed, then on his side facing her and reached out to run one finger lightly along her cheek. He was torn between waking her up to ask how she had got there, and waking her up by making love to her. The way she murmured sleepily and turned her face into his touch reminded him of her sweet responses to his lovemaking the night before and made up his mind. He would find out how she'd got there soon enough. First things first.

Eva moaned and shifted as she became conscious of the hands moving caressingly over her body.

"Connall," she murmured the name sleepily as her eyes swept open. Candlelight spilled across the bed, gleaming on his dark hair as he bent his head over her to capture one nipple in his warm wet mouth.

"Oh," Eva moaned and arched into the caress. It was a heavenly way to wake up, one she had awoken to the night before and would be pleased to awaken to again and again she decided as Connall slid a leg between both of hers, allowing it to rub against the center of her. She thought it was a terrible shame that girls were not told what to expect once they were married. Had she known that this had awaited her here in Scotland, she would have been urging the men to ride faster.

Connall's mouth left her breast and Eva moaned in disappointment, then gasped in surprise, her stomach muscles jumping as his lips trailed a path across it. He had said last night that there was more to kissing, but she had never expected all the places that could be kissed, or how delightful those kisses could be. Eva would never have imagined that her husband would wish to kiss her stomach, delve his tongue into her belly button, draw his tongue along her pelvic bone, or—

"Ah!" She gasped with surprise, her eyes flying open as he suddenly urged her thighs apart and lowered his head between them. Suddenly assaulted by modesty and not a little embarrassment, Eva tried to squeeze her legs closed, but he pushed them further open instead and seemed to settle into the endeavor of kissing her there. Dear God, and she had thought his earlier kisses exciting!

Eva squeezed her eyes closed and clutched at the bed linens to ground herself as she was assaulted by pleasure such as she had never experienced. Her body was suddenly moving of its own accord, shifting, stretching, arching, and even bucking beneath his ministrations and she was vaguely aware that she was gasping and moaning and making little mewling sounds. It wasn't long before she felt sure that if he didn't stop soon, she would surely die from the pleasure. Oddly enough, she thought she might very well die if he did stop as well. Then, suddenly she couldn't stand it anymore and wanted to feel him inside her as he had been last night. Without thinking, she caught at his hair, tugging at it, trying to urge him up to slide into her, but Connall ignored her actions and continued with what he was doing, driving her mad with his tongue as he lashed the very center of her.

"Oh, no, no, no, please," she moaned. Then her body suddenly went stiff and Eva nearly shot upward off the bed as he slid a finger into her as well and her body reacted like the string of a bow suddenly released as it jerked in spasm. She was trembling and shaking with release as he finally straightened and sat up on his knees between her legs. Eva sat up at once and threw her arms around him, burying her face in his chest. Her breath came in sobs as she clung to him and Connall ran a hand soothingly down her back before catching her under her bottom and lifting her into his lap, guiding himself into her as he did.

Eva moaned, her head dropping back as she felt him push into her body, the action sending her into confusion, the lassitude that had claimed her was leaving, replaced by a returning excitement. He truly would kill her, she thought vaguely as he urged her legs around his waist, caught her under the thighs and began to raise and lower her on top of him.

Eva managed to survive the encounter, barely. Long moments later as she lay in an exhausted heap on her husband's chest where she had ended up, she listened to his heart beat and smiled vaguely to herself. Nightwalking, soulless, bloodlusters? The man had a heartbeat and everyone knew that vampires had no life in them; it was said that was why they craved the lifeblood of the living.

"Eva?"

She lifted her head and turned it so that her chin rested on his chest as she peered at him in question. "Aye?"

"How is it ye came to be here?"

"Oh." She flushed guiltily, then cleared her throat and said evasively, "I am your wife. This is where I belong. Husbands and wives sleep together."

"Do they?" he asked with vague amusement.

"Aye," she answered, then added, "Well, my parents did."

"Hmmm." Lifting a hand, he toyed with a strand of hair and teased, "Tis probably why they had so many children."

Eva smiled slightly, but didn't comment on that. Her parents had had ten children in all; one had been born dead, one had died within days of birth, but eight had survived. Jonathan was the oldest, but there had been another male who survived into adulthood before being taken by an infection after being wounded in battle. Eva also had five older sisters, all surviving; three of them had been married ere her parents had died, Jonathan had managed to supply a small dower for another, but Lynette, the next oldest to Eva, had been forced to become a nun when it transpired that there was no dower for her and no one would have her without one, much as Eva had almost been forced to do. Eva had told Connall about her family and her life in general over the last week as they had played chess. It was only now that she realized he had told her very little in return. She hadn't even known where he slept.

"I can see why you like it in here," she said now, as the candle at the bedside sputtered, and a glance showed that it had burned down to a stub and was threatening to gutter out. That would leave them in total darkness again. "It was so quiet and dark, I slept like the dead."

Connall's lips quirked at her comment, but he merely pointed out, "Ye havenae told me hoo ye came to be here. Did someone tell ye aboot this room?"

"Nay," Eva bit her lip briefly before admitting, "I awoke as you left the room. I could not understand why you would leave me to sleep elsewhere after . . . Well, now that we are properly married. I got up and hurried to the door and saw you come through the entrance at the end of the hall."

"And ye figured oot hoo to open it by watching me?" he said.

"Aye. Well, partly. I saw the two stones you pressed with your right hand, but the one in the middle was just luck. When I pressed the first two and it didn't work, I got frustrated and thumped the wall; it was pure luck that I hit the right stone there. I was startled as could be when it suddenly opened." She lowered her head, and ran one finger nervously back and forth on his chest, then glanced up from under her eyebrows and asked a touch anxiously, "Are you angry with me?"

Connall shook his head. "Nay. I'd ha'e been tellin' ye aboot this room eventually, but 'tis obvious I'll ha'e to be mair careful in future. I didnae e'en think to look around as I went. Anyone might ha'e seen me."

His words reminded her of the man in the cape, and Eva said solemnly, "Someone did."

Connall's eyes narrowed and a frown knit his brow as Eva told him about the caped figure who had followed him up the hall and tried—but failed—to open the secret entrance. They were both silent for a moment when she finished, then Eva asked curiously, "Why do you sleep in here? Is it to avoid the sun?"

"Aye," he said gruffly, then eased her off his chest and swung his feet off the bed as he sat up. "The candle'll be goin' out soon, we'd best shift ourselves ere we're left in the dark."

"I brought a candle with me as well," Eva said as she tugged the sheets up to cover herself and sat up in bed.

Connall glanced at the candle, but didn't light it, instead he set to work on his plaid. Eva watched him silently, one hand absently pushing her hair away from her face. It felt like a rat's nest to her and she wondered what time it was and if she might have a bath.

"Up now," he ordered. "Yer best to eat, 'tis night and ye havena eaten since this hour yester eve."

Eva blinked in surprise at this news, finding it hard to believe that she had been abed for nearly twenty-four hours. Well, her bed and this bed. Though they hadn't done much sleeping in her bed as she recalled. Forcing herself to let go of the linen sheet, she leaned forward from the bed to snatch up her robe where she'd left it lying on the hard stone floor. Eva frowned over the fact that there were no rushes on this floor. It must be cold on his bare feet, she thought with concern. Then her gaze shifted around the room.

With the one sputtering candle, it was no easier to see than it had been the night before, but then it didn't look as if there was much to see anyway. The room was as barren and cold as her chamber at Caxton had been.

"I understand you sleeping here to avoid sunlight coming in," she murmured as her gaze slid along the wall. She didn't see any sign of a covered window, but that didn't mean there wasn't one, it was hard to tell in this light. "But why is the room kept secret?"

When Connall didn't answer right away, she asked, "It is secret, is it not? I should not tell anyone of it?"

That made him pause and glance at her. "Aye. Tis secret. Tell no one."

Eva nodded. "Why do you sleep in a secret room?"

Connall sighed, hands on his hips, and considered his wife. What to tell her? How much to say? Was she ready to hear the full truth? Or should he leave that for a little longer and stick to partial truths? It was early yet to tell her the full truth, he decided. Half truths would have to do for now. "Me mother had these rooms built when I was but a child. Twas to keep me safe from the sun, but 'twas also as a precaution."

"A precaution?" she queried as she tugged her robe on.

"Ye've heard the rumors about our clan," he said slowly. When she nodded, he continued, "Well, people tend to fear what they doonae understand, and usually they try to destroy what they fear. These rooms are a safeguard against sech a thing."

Eva nodded her understanding. "Do you think that man last night is someone who fears you?"

Connall hesitated, then simply said, "There have been three attempts on me life in the last little while."

He saw her eyes widen with dismay and quickly changed the subject. "Come. Ye should eat . . . and . . . er . . . have a bath," he added, a small smile curving his lips. Her hair was a riotous mass on her head and he was sure no amount of brushing would remove the tangles caused by their love making. She would have to wash her hair to get them out, Connall thought as he blew the bedside candle out, and took her hand in the darkness to lead the way to the door. The tangles came from her tendency to roll and rub her head from side to side on the bed as he pleasured her, he knew. In future, he might have to hold her head in place as he pleasured her to save her lovely hair.

"Connall?"

He paused at the door at that whisper. "Aye?"

"I cannot see a thing."

"I'll lead the way. Trust me," he said with a squeeze of her hand.

"I do," she murmured and fell silent, following obediently behind him as he led her up the long dark hall to the entrance to the secret section of castle, and he believed it to be true. She did trust him, with a purity and innocence that touched him. She trusted him to keep her safe and happy, and he would, he decided.

Recalling the incident with the arrow the other night, he found his hand tightening around his wife's wee hand. The very fact that he had married her, might place Eva in danger. He didn't like to think what might have happened had the caped figure spotted her watching him last night.

He pondered the situation as he showed her the secret to opening the door from the inside, having to show her by touch since it was black as pitch in there. She would need to know how to open it from both sides as he had decided she would be sleeping in there with him from now on. The incident with the intruder was troublesome. It meant that either someone had gained the castle, managing to slip past everyone here, or the person was one of his own people. He didn't want to believe it, but the second option seemed most likely. A member of his own clan might wish him dead. But either way, he intended on seeing his wife safe.

* * *

Connall tossed his reins to the stable boy, and headed for the castle, his heart sinking at the sight of Ewan waiting for him. The man looked sleepy and disheveled, as if he'd fallen asleep while waiting for him and been awoken with the news that he had returned. The fact that he was waiting was what worried Connall, his first only waited when there was something to report. The last two times it had been an accident his wife had suffered, Connall suspected this would be number three.

"Well?" he asked as he reached the other man. "What's she done now? Tripped, stumbled, scalded hersel'? What?"

"Nothing like that, Eva's fine," his brother-in-law assured him quickly and Connall felt himself relax, only to stiffen again when the man added, "I think. Tis what she's doin' I'm worryin' aboot. She slipped away from Keddy and Domhall and they couldnae find her, then I spied her, but she was too quick fer me. I wasnae sure she should be in there, but I couldnae get in to question her and I'm not sure what she's doin', but she was cartin' all that stuff about and Glynis says that half the things from her bedchamber are missing and I suspect she's taken them all in there with her. Then I worried that the men would see, so I relieved them and took to waiting fer her to come out meself, but I think she'd made anoother trip while I was talkin' to the men and she hasnae come out since, and I can't find yer mother to fetch her oot to ask her what she's aboot, so I thought I'd best stick around till ye returned and—"

"Ewan," Connall interrupted with amazement. "Yer babbling."

The older man looked alarmed at this pronouncement, then complained, "It's yer wife, Connall! She'll be the death o' me, I'm sure. Between the scares with her accidents and—sweet Jesus! Me heart stopped when she tripped up on the stairs in the keep, then again when she tumbled down the chapel steps, and then there's her shenanigans tonight. I'm sure I've aged ten years since she arrived and I'm an old man to begin with."

"All right, old friend," Connall put a soothing hand on the irate man's shoulder. "Breathe. Jest breathe and calm down, then tell me what the devil yer talking aboot."

Ewan sighed and closed his eyes briefly, when he opened them again he said simply, "Eva."

"Aye." Connall nodded encouragingly. "She slipped away from the men ye had watchin' her?"

"Aye."

"And they came to ye and so ye started to help them look fer her?"

"Aye." Ewan grimaced. "We looked everywhere. I was starting to think she'd either fallen down the well or been kidnapped, and wonderin' how the devil I was to tell ye that, when I decided to check her bedchamber one more time."

"And ye found her there, but she got away," Connall guessed, recalling the man babbling about her being too quick for him.

"Nay. I spied her walking past the top of the stairs as I went up them. She was bustling along with a great armful of stuff, and I jest knew she'd trip o'er her gown or something and there'd be hell to pay, so I hurried up the stairs, but by the time I got there the hall was empty, wasnae it? I checked the rooms, but they were empty too and the only thing I could think is that she'd gone into the passage to the night rooms."

"Ah." Connall nodded with understanding. The rest of what the man had said made sense now. Ewan suspected Eva was in the passage, but wasn't sure she should be, and while he was one of the few people who knew about it, even he didn't know how to open it, there had never been a need. Which is what he had meant by not being able to "get in to question her." Connall considered the rest of what he'd said.

His wife had been carting great loads of stuff and—according to Glynis—half the things from the bedchamber were missing.

A sigh from his first, made Connall glance his way to note his weary expression. It was well past the time the man would usually be in bed. It was only a couple of hours till dawn when he normally would be rising. Putting the matter of what his wife was up to to the side for a moment, Connall thumped one hand on his brother-in-law's shoulder. "Yer weary."

"I'm old," Ewan sighed.

"Nay, yer no an old man yet, friend," he assured him. "Yer just tired right now. Doonae fret aboot Eva, I'll tend to her. As fer Mother, she rode with us tonight, that's why ye couldnae find her," he explained. "But come and I'll show ye how to open the passage. Had I shown ye ere this, ye'd ha'e gone to bed long ago. Come."

Connall led the other man through the great hall and up the stairs to the end of the hall. He showed him twice how to open the passage, then had him practice it twice to be sure he had it before wishing him good night and watching him move off down the hall to the room he shared with Aileen. His sister's reaction to the sun was a lesser version of his own and she could sleep in a normal chamber so long as she kept furs up on the windows. He, however, like Magaidh, needed the secured dark of a windowless stone room. Not that he couldn't bear sunlight altogether, his reaction wasn't as bad as some of their people's, but it burned him and made him sick. It had made the trip to court almost unbearable.

A soft click from the other end of the dark hallway drew his attention from his thoughts and Connall peered up the dark expanse, but there was no one in the hall. Deciding it must have been Ewan going into his and Aileen's room, Connall turned back to the passage door and stepped through, then closed it behind him.

Ten

Connall found Eva in his night room, muttering to herself as she attempted to start a fire in the fireplace. Distracted as she was, she didn't hear him enter, and he took a moment to peer around the room before making his presence known. His gaze swept over the changes she'd made with amazement; two walls now sported huge tapestries he recognized from the other chamber, the bed was littered with cushions and furs, and there were also several more candles in here now, all of them lit at the moment. Eva had also brought the two chairs from the other room and set them before the fireplace with the chest from the other room between them—he couldn't imagine how she had dragged that here on her own without being discovered.

Shaking his head, he started forward, then glanced down with surprise as he stepped on rushes. These too must have come from the other chamber and he had to wonder what the other room must look like now with half its rushes and furnishings missing. About as strange as this room now appeared to him, he supposed and glanced around again.

It seemed his wife had moved in. Connall had never considered that she might when he'd arranged to marry her. His own parents had slept in separate rooms with his mother in her room here in the passage and his father in the chamber Eva had been occupying. Obviously they had spent some time together in either room or Aileen and himself would not have been born, but for as long as he could recall, the two had actually done the sleeping part separately. But then they had slept at different times as well. His father, being human, had slept at night as was the custom, while his mother—to avoid the sun—had slept in here during the day as he did himself.

Connall supposed he had expected things to go much the same for him. He would spend some time with his wife in the early evening after arising, then perhaps visit her room in the dark hours before dawn, then sleep in here during the day while she was up and about. It seemed that his wife had other plans.

He peered around the changes again and shook his head. Connall felt rather invaded. The room was cozy and inviting, nothing at all like the sterile room he had slept in for the last almost sixty years. He was suddenly feeling . . . well . . . married.

"Oh, God's toes, you are a stubborn, stupid blasted . . ."

Connall found himself smiling as Eva growled and slapped at the bit of wood she was trying to light, as if punishing it for being difficult and he thought with amusement that perhaps being married wouldn't be so bad. The woman had a tendency to make him smile, something he wasn't used to, but found he rather liked. He had found himself smiling often while playing chess with her at night, Eva was witty and amusing and . . . well . . . really rather adorable at the moment, disheveled from her work as she was.

Pushing the door closed, he crossed the room and dropped to his haunches beside her. "Givin' ye trouble is it, me lady wife?"

"Oh!" she exclaimed, dropping back onto her heels with surprise at what to her must seem a sudden appearance. "You are back."

"Aye," he agreed, smiling at her.

She smiled back, then her eyes widened in alarm and she began fussing with her clothes and pushing at her hair in an apparent effort to make herself more presentable. She gave up the attempt almost at once and sighed as she forlornly admitted, "I wanted to clean myself up some and make myself more presentable ere you returned."

"Ye look fine to me," he assured her as he took over the task of lighting the fire.

"And the room?" Eva asked hopefully as she watched him do in minutes what she had spent nearly an hour now trying to accomplish. He made it look so easy, she thought with vague irritation.

"The room." He sat back on his heels beside her and peered around. "Tis . . . well, it looks more comfortable," he said at last.

Eva pursed her lips, trying to decide if that meant he liked it or not, then gasped with surprise when he scooped her up in his arms and carried her to the bed.

"Tis time fer bed," he announced firmly.

"But I am not tired, my lord," Eva protested. "I napped this evening."

"Did you now?" He peered at her with surprise.

"Aye." She grimaced, embarrassed to admit it. "It took a long time for me to drop off to sleep when I came in here last night. In fact, I would not be surprised if I had lain awake most of the day and dropped off just shortly before you woke me again."

He arched an eyebrow as he paused at the side of the bed. "If ye were takin' a nap tonight, when did ye do all this?"

"Right after eating supper," she explained. "When you headed out with the men. It did not take long, the rooms aren't far apart and I really haven't done much, but it wearied me a bit and I fell asleep for a while." She grimaced, then admitted, "A long while. I only woke up just ere you arrived. The candle I had left lit was guttering, so I lit more and then tried to light the fire."

"Hmm. Then ye willnae be tired."

Eva gave a squeal of surprise as he dropped her on the bed.

"And 'tis good I came back early enough to take the time to tire ye oot," he announced, reaching for the buckle of his belt.

"Husband?" Eva ran her hand over the arm across her chest and tilted her head in an effort to see his face. He had made love to her with as much passion and vigor as she could have wished, then they had talked softly for a while, but he had grown silent these last few moments and Eva suspected he was asleep. She wished she could join him in that state, but despite the energetic session he had just treated her to, she wasn't tired. If anything, she felt rather invigorated.

Positive he slept, she lifted his arm and eased out from under him, moving slowly and cautiously in an effort not to wake him. Once out from under it, Eva set his arm on the bed and pulled her robe on. She wanted to go to the old chamber and order a bath, she should probably check in with Glynis as well, the girl might be wondering where she was and perhaps even be worried. But, while Eva wasn't sure what time it was, she didn't think it was much past dawn. The castle inhabitants who slept nights would be sitting down to break their fast, Glynis among them, and Effie would be busy as could be in the kitchens. She thought it might be best to wait a bit before bothering them with a request for a bath.

Eva glanced around the room, debating what to do until then and her gaze landed on the dark blue gown she'd been wearing that day. It was one of the new ones, though it hardly looked like it at the moment, dusty and wrinkled as it was from her first working, then sleeping in it earlier. There was also a tear in one of the sleeves. Eva had caught it on something while moving things about earlier, though she would be hard-pressed to say when it had occurred exactly. She had only noticed the tear on rising from her nap before Connall had returned to the room.

Fortunately, the tear was along a seam and would be easily repaired and that seemed the perfect chore to keep her busy until it would be more convenient for her to take her bath. Bending, she collected the gown and moved to the chairs by the fire, then lay the gown across one of the chairs, and paused to place a couple of logs on the fire, before turning back to remove the untouched chess game and wine from the chest. Once those were out of the way, Eva opened it to search out the needle and thread she had placed inside after hemming the last of the gowns that were being made for her.

She had the lid up and was on her knees with her head buried in the chest when Eva heard the chamber door open. Her first thought was that it would be Glynis, and that the girl must be done breaking her fast. Perhaps it was later than she had thought and she could eschew the sewing for now and go take a bath. Eva had started to straighten to see if she was right, when she recalled that she wasn't in her chamber anymore. She was in the secret chamber . . . and Glynis didn't know about this room.

Eva froze, the hairs on the back of her neck suddenly standing on end. According to Connall, the only people who knew about this room, besides himself, were his mother, sister, and Ewan. And herself now, of course. She couldn't imagine any of them just walking into the room without knocking. Moving cautiously, she eased back on her haunches behind the chest, knowing it hid her from view at least from the door. Unfortunately, it also blocked her view of all but the top of the door as it was slowly, stealthily she couldn't help thinking, eased closed.

She waited silently, holding her breath as she listened to see if someone had just looked into the room or actually entered. After a moment that seemed to last an eon, the stirring of the rushes told her that someone had entered. Now, she *had* to look.

Moving carefully, Eva eased up slightly until she could just see over the top of the chest, then quickly ducked back down. Dear Lord, it was the man in the cape, or at least it was a man in a cape, she couldn't be sure, of course, if it was the same man she had seen the other morning, but thought it was a good bet that it was. He had obviously succeeded at figuring out the secret to opening the door, she realized.

Eva's gaze slid anxiously to the bed and she willed Connall to wake up and deal with the situation, but, of course, he didn't. And really, even if he woke up now, he would surely be so sleep-befuddled that he might be slow to react to whatever the fellow had in mind and end up hurt . . . or dead. Connall had said that there had been three attempts on his life in recent times and Eva very much feared that this was going to be attempt number four, and she was the only person presently conscious and capable of dealing with the intruder.

Now, she just had to figure out how, Eva thought with vexation. And quickly. The man had started moving toward the bed, reaching beneath his cape as he went. She didn't doubt for a minute that he was reaching for a weapon and Eva now glanced around for the nearest possible weapon she might use.

The wine, the chess game, a needle and thread . . . One of the chairs? Nay, it was well built and sturdy and she didn't think she could raise it and run across the room carrying it. Her best asset at this point was the element of surprise, and stumbling clumsily across the room with a chair—

Eva's thoughts died as her eyes landed on the fire. The

fresh logs she had thrown on it were already alight and burning merrily, but she hadn't placed one of them very well and while one end was buried in the flames, the other was sticking out over the hearth. Eva did not even think, one moment she was staring at the log as the idea formed and in the next she was reaching out for the log and launching to her feet in one fluid movement.

Her timing was close, she saw as she turned toward the bed. The intruder had pulled a sword from his waist and was even now lifting it over his head in preparation for what appeared to be a straight downward hacking movement. It looked to her as if he intended to cut off Connall's head. Afraid he would bring it down before she could cross the room and stop him, Eva let loose a shriek as she charged forward, swinging the log.

It was a scream that woke Connall, an animal sound of fear and fury that startled him awake and sent his eyes flying open. The first thing he saw was the sword descending toward him and he instinctively raised an arm in self-defense and rolled to the side at the same time. Out of the corner of his eye he caught a glimpse of his attacker being attacked as Eva swung a burning log into his stomach. The action wasn't enough to stop the downward impetus of the sword, but did bring the man around slightly so that the weapon was jerked lower along Connall's body and turned at an angle. He felt the bite of the metal into his side as he finished the roll and tumbled from the bed.

Grunting at the pain singeing through him, Connall grabbed for the wound. He didn't need to feel the blood pouring over his fingers to know his wound was deep and bleeding copiously, the air was suddenly rich with the scent of his own blood. Connall cursed but had little time to worry about it other than that at the moment. The image of Eva's pale face as she had run forward to try to save him was etched in his mind and he was very aware that she was on the other side of the bed at that moment with the intruder. His little Eva, small, blonde, and English, was battling alone for both their lives. He had to help her.

Letting go of the wound, he grabbed the edge of the bed and dragged himself up into a sitting position. His eyes immediately moved to the spot where his wife and the intruder should have been battling, but the spot was empty. All he could see was the open door and the dark hallway beyond.

"Connall!" Eva was suddenly at his side. It seemed he hadn't seen her at first because she'd been moving around the bed to him. "You're bleeding."

"Tis fine. It isna verra deep," he lied as she pressed her free hand to it.

Her gaze met his, then slid to the burning log she still held. After the briefest of hesitations and a glance toward the door, Eva stood and managed to retrieve the sheet out of the tangle the bedclothes had become, then shoved it at him. "Hold this on it, tightly. I shall be right back."

Connall instinctively pressed the cloth to his side as he watched her hurry around the bed again, toward the door. Afraid she was going to go for help and worried that she might meet up with their intruder again if she did so, Connall opened his mouth to call out to her, then closed it again when—rather than run through it—she skidded to a halt at the door and slammed it shut. Still carrying the log, his wife then ran to the chairs and began to drag one across the floor, apparently to bar it lest the intruder return. He found a small smile curving his lips at this action. He had done well in choosing Eva to bride. She had the courage to risk herself to save him, and the sense to prepare against a possible second attack. She was a damned fine woman.

Only when she had the chair levered against the door to prevent it opening, did Eva give up her makeshift weapon.

Running to the fireplace, she tossed it back onto its brothers, then hurried back to his side.

"Let me see the wound," she insisted, dropping to her knees beside him. She was tugging at his hand even as she spoke the order and Connall was feeling weak enough that he let her do as she wished. The wound was terribly deep and his blood loss, plus the reparations his body was having to make, were weakening him.

"There's so much blood!"

He could hear the fear in her voice, but could do little to soothe her. Connall was suffering a good deal of fear at the moment as well, but not for himself. "Eva, ye ha'e to go."

"What?" She glanced up at his face with confusion. "Nay, Connall. I must stop the bleeding."

"Nay. Go!" He tried to push her away, but it was a rather weak push, one she simply rebounded from and ignored. Connall scowled. He didn't care for feeling weak like this. "Eva, I am orderin' ye to go."

"Well, you can order all you bloody like, my lord husband, but I will not leave your side until I get the bleeding stopped," she snapped and Connall gaped at her, unable to believe his sweet, witty, lovely little bride had spoken to him so. Were wives not supposed to obey their husbands? He was sure he recalled that in the wedding ceremony.

"Come, we must get you on the bed."

Eva was on her feet now and pulling at him, he realized, and bloody hell if she wasn't somehow managing to lever him upward. Deciding he might get rid of her quicker if he aided in this endeavor, Connall did his best to help get himself on the bed, but if he had hoped she might then run for help, he had been sadly mistaken.

Once she had him there, she did rush off, but only to collect several candles from around the room. She lit them at the fire, then set them on the bedside tables, putting more light on the situation, then bent to examine his wound. He saw the surprise that widened her eyes.

"Tis not as bad as it first appeared. Tis just a flesh wound," she informed him with some relief, then confusion crossed her brow. "But there was so much blood."

"Eva," Connall growled, fighting instincts that were quickly consuming him. The wound had been deep when she'd first looked and had been deeper still when it had first happened, but his body was healing itself; knitting together and repairing the damage. The bleeding would soon stop altogether, the wound would fully close, and within hours there wouldn't even be a scar to show for the blow. This was all thanks to his bloodline, his Pictish ancestry on his mother's side. It held many such wonderful gifts for its possessor; a prolonged life, resistance to illness and—handy as it was in this instance— quick healing. But these miraculous gifts came at a cost and he didn't want Eva to pay the price.

"Eva, ye ha'e to go *now!*"

"You must be a bleeder," she commented as if he hadn't spoken, not that he had spoken very vehemently, Connall needed to replenish himself, he needed blood, a need that was growing unbearably strong.

"Tis not very deep, but it still must be closed." Without waiting for his comment on this, she hurried away again and he watched helplessly as she ran to the chest by the fire and dug around inside. Eva was back within moments, bearing needle and thread, but when she bent to peer at his wound again, she paused, blinked, then leaned nearer for a closer look before muttering, "I would swear the wound has grown smaller still."

Shaking her head at the ridiculousness of that observation, she began to thread her needle.

"Do no' waste yer thread," Connall said wearily.

Eva glanced up, then grew still as she peered at his face. "You look different."

He said nothing, knowing that his face would appear leaner to her, his eyes perhaps taking on more of a yellow tinge in the brown depths.

"You are very pale, but . . ." She was obviously trying to puzzle it out, but didn't understand and was growing frightened and confused.

"Aye, nae doubt I am pale. I lost a fair amount o' blood," Connall said, wishing he could ease this for her.

"Aye." She nodded slowly and tried to smile, but was having difficulty with it and he knew she could see the hunger in him. "You need food and rest to rebuild it."

"I need blood."

Eva stared at him silently, then her eyes moved back to his wound as if drawn there by some unseen force. He could tell by her expression that it was continuing to heal, growing smaller by the moment.

"You heal much more quickly than we do," she said finally.

Her voice was bleak and Connall winced at the knowledge in it. We. She had finally admitted to what was staring her in the face; the supposed reaction to the sun, the rumors, his wound healing so quickly . . . The fact that Aileen aged had probably confused her, but she was seeing it now. *You heal more quickly than we.* We. He was not one of her kind, at least not wholly. He was different. Connall always had been, and should be used to it by now, but somehow it hurt hearing Eva say it.

Her face was expressionless when she turned it back to him to ask, "Are you soulless?"

Connall knew that she was making a decision in her mind, one vital to their future. He had feared this moment, but felt hope in the fact that she hadn't simply turned away in horror.

"Nay. I'm no a dead, soulless creature as the rumors proclaim," he answered solemnly. "I'm jest different."

"But you cannot go out in sunlight. That is true?" she queried.

"I can, but it makes me ill and increases me need fer blood."

Eva nodded slowly. "Do you kill those you . . . ?"

"Feed on," he supplied, then grimaced over the question before saying firmly, "There's no mair need to kill those we feed on than there is to kill the cow who supplies the milk."

For some reason that comment brought a wry smile to her lips, then she sighed and he thought he heard her mutter, "So I will be the cow after all."

Connall was puzzling over that comment, when she sank to sit on the side of the bed and extended her arm toward him. "Go ahead, my lord. Take what you need."

He stared at her helplessly. *Take what you need?* He needed her and he needed her blood, but he couldn't do it, not like this. Connall could imagine sinking his teeth into her wrist and her watching him, shuddering with distaste and thinking him an animal. He didn't want her to see him that way. He never wanted her to see him that way.

Taking her hand, he drew it to his lips and ran them lightly across the sensitive skin there even as he grit his teeth against the knowledge that the blood he so yearned for was pulsing below the thin surface of her flesh. Eva trembled under the caress and Connall felt relief that her knowledge did not now make him so repulsive to her that she could not bear or respond to his touch. He continued to move his lips along her arm, nibbling a trail to the crook of her arm, further relieved when Eva released a soft moan.

He lifted his head then and caught one hand behind her head to draw her down for a kiss. Eva came willingly, kissing him with the passion he was used to and Connall immediately began to tug at the neckline of her gown until one breast popped free and he could close his hand over it. Eva began to kiss him more frantically as he caressed her, pressing into his touch, and though he knew he was rushing it, Connall couldn't stop himself from finding the hem of her skirt and sliding his hand beneath, to run along the inside of her leg until he found the center of her.

Eva gasped into his mouth, caught at his hand to still it and tugged free of the kiss to protest, "But you are hurt."

"Aye, so ye'll ha'e to help me, love."

"Help?" She looked uncertain.

"Aye."

Eva had eased her hold on his hand without thinking and he took advantage of this and started to caress her again even as he claimed her mouth once more. Connall thrust his tongue into her mouth to prevent any further protest, even as he thrust a finger into her, and was pleased when she gasped and her body arched in response. His control slipping, Connall struggled with his instincts for another moment before breaking the kiss and letting his lips trail to her ear where he growled, "Take yer gown off."

Eva hesitated, then stood to do as he asked and Connall took that opportunity to sit up and ease his way further up the bed until he could sit with his back braced. His wound was completely healed now, with no sign that it had ever existed and he caught her staring at where it had been when he finished settling himself. Reaching out, he took her hand and tugged lightly, pulling her forward. "Come. Sit on me lap and kiss me again."

She surprised him by moving without hesitation, but he realized as she straddled him that she was trembling, her body already in a heightened state of excitement as was his own. It took only a moment for him to understand why, it was the blood rush after battle, some said it was a result of excess energy after a fight, others said it was a need to reaffirm life after a brush with death. Connall didn't care what it was, but it was powerful and would aid him here, eliminating the necessity to go slowly.

Eva was straddling him, but still upright on her knees and Connall took advantage of the position to reach between her legs and caress her again with one hand as he tugged her head down for a kiss with the other. Her passion grew quickly and his along with it, her little moans and mewls of pleasure stoking his own desires, but his were twofold and demanding and Connall soon could not wait any longer. Easing his hand from between her legs, he caught her hips and urged her down, groaning into her mouth as she closed over him like a warm, wet glove, squeezing his flesh and making it grow harder still.

Eva felt some of her anxiety slip away from her as her husband groaned into her mouth. This was all new to her and slightly uncomfortable in that she was the one in control and feared doing it wrong. That sound of pleasure from Connall, however, eased her fears somewhat and Eva began to emulate his movements when he was in control and quickly raised herself back up, easing herself almost off him before letting herself slide back down his length again. The action elicited another groan, encouraging her further, but soon her own pleasure made her forget any anxiety and she began to move in the way that felt most pleasurable to her, her breath beginning to come in pants as the now familiar tension began to build.

When Connall's hand slid between their bodies again to touch her, the tension increased tenfold and she began to move more urgently, then Connall broke their kiss, his mouth moving to her neck and nibbling a trail there. Eva let her head drop backward, her breath coming fast and hard. She was a hair's breadth away from finding that sweet release he always gave her and cried his name in a desperate plea, then her eyes shot open as she felt his teeth slide into her neck even as his body slammed into hers. There was the briefest second of pain from his bite, then pleasure exploded inside of her and Eva screamed his name as her body began to shudder and pulse with release.

Eleven

"The lass saved yer life," Magaidh said solemnly.

"Aye." Connall stared down into his ale as he considered that Eva had saved him twice; first by fending off the attacker, then by replenishing some of the blood he had lost. Had she not been there and offered herself up to him as she had, Connall wasn't at all sure he'd have survived until the sun had set and it was safe for him to seek out sustenance elsewhere.

Connall ran a hand through his hair with agitation. He had spent his whole life knowing he was stronger and faster than most of those around him, certainly stronger and faster than all mortals. In truth, he supposed he had always considered himself somewhat superior because of this, but last night he had been the weaker one, his life dependent on a mortal, and a female at that. It had been a humbling experience.

"She's lucky she wasnae injured," Aileen murmured, then frowned. "Eva *is* all right, is she no? She wasnae injured so that she hasnae come down yet?"

"Nay, she's fine," he said and hoped it was true. Connall hadn't intended to take much blood, just enough to see him through until night fell and he could head out on a hunt, but in the excitement of the moment, with the hunger roaring in his ears and his body buried deep in hers as ecstasy rolled over them both, he'd taken more than he'd intended. Connall had only stopped when she'd gone limp in his arms, and could still recall the pallor of her skin as he'd lifted his head to peer down at her. Eva had lain limp and pale in his arms, and so very still. Connall had felt a fear like he had never before known clutch at him. It was only then, as he'd cradled her in his arms and pressed her head to his chest that he'd realized how much he'd grown to care for the woman. She had been trying since arriving to make a place for herself at MacAdie, but somehow had crept into his heart and made a home for herself there as well. He loved Eva and that knowledge had kept him awake to watch over her until his physical state alone had forced him to sleep.

Connall had awoken at sunset to find her curled up against him. She'd still looked awfully pale to him, but not nearly as much as she had the night before, and when he'd brushed a hand lightly over her cheek and she had murmured his name sleepily, relief had flooded him along with the knowledge that she was recovering. He'd decided to leave her to rest for a bit while he tended to his need to feed, and had dressed and left the night room.

Aware that he was too weak to defend himself properly should he be attacked ere he could feed again, Connall had been relieved to find Ewan, Donaidh, Geordan, Keddy, Domhall, and Ragnall still seated at the trestle table in the great hall. As the six men he trusted most at MacAdie, he'd enlisted their company for the ride. By the time they had returned half an hour ago, he had recounted the full details of the attack from that morning.

Connall had gone upstairs to check on Eva the moment they had arrived. Finding her still sleeping, he'd decided he'd have to wake her soon and make her eat, rest was good for restoring her, but food was just as important. He'd come below to order Effie to prepare a meal for the lass, then had come to sit at the trestle table to wait for it to be ready and found Ewan telling the women about the intruder and the attack that morning.

"So, you think he must have returned again last night and figured out how to open the door?" Magaidh asked now, drawing Connall back to the conversation at hand.

"Aye. Or he may have been in the hall, or watching from one of the rooms while I showed Ewan how to open it," he murmured, recalling how he had heard the click of a door closing. At the time, he'd explained it away as it being Ewan, but Aileen and Ewan's room was at the far end of the hall and he thought now that this had sounded closer to hand and suspected it had been the intruder closing the door of whatever room he had been watching from. There were a couple of empty bedchambers at the moment, rooms he hoped to fill with their bairns.

"We shall have to put a guard on the chamber entrance," Magaidh murmured, looking troubled.

"Aye. I've already arranged it," Connall assured her, aware that she slept in the night rooms too and would worry about that as well. He had decided to put a guard on the chamber while out with the men. More than that, he had decided that there should be two guards with Eva at all times while she was up, then two on the chamber while they slept. He'd left it to Ewan to sort out who did what.

"M'laird?"

Connall glanced around to find Glynis standing at his shoulder, holding a tray with food, and stood abruptly to take it from her, then paused. Eva had given him a great gift that morning; she'd given him his life and he wished to give her something in return, but wasn't sure what she might like. She asked for nothing and accepted the smallest things as great gifts.

"Glynis?"

"Aye?" The maid glanced at him expectantly.

"I'm thinkin' to gi'e me wife something, a treat to please her. Do ye ken anything she might like?"

The maid looked doubtful for a moment and Connall felt disappointment claim him that she might have no more idea than himself, then she murmured, "The only thing she's ever mentioned to me that she might like, m'laird, is to see the water."

"The water?" Magaidh asked with interest and the girl nodded.

"Aye. She grew up on the ocean, and has said a time or two that she's missin' it, so I mentioned that we had a loch nearby and she said she'd like to see it someday."

"She mentioned that to me once as well," Aileen murmured. "Said her favorite thing in the world was to slip away and sneak a swim once in a while when chores were done, and she missed doin' that here."

Connall frowned at this news. "Is there nothin' else she's e'er mentioned, wantin' or likin'?"

"Nay, m'laird," Glynis said apologetically. "She's no the sort to ask fer things, I think."

Connall sighed at this comment, knowing it was true, then nodded and turned to carry the tray upstairs.

A gentle hand running over her shoulders brought Eva slowly awake to find herself lying on her stomach in bed. Moaning a protest at being awoken, she rolled slowly onto her back and blinked at her husband, wondering why she felt so tired. Her eyes felt gritty and her mind sluggish, she was unusually cold and felt weak too.

"How do ye feel?" Connall brushed the hair back from her face, his smile not hiding the concern in his eyes.

"Tired," Eva admitted, then realizing it sounded almost a

whine, grimaced at herself and forced a smile. "Could you not sleep?"

"Tis night," he informed her, then added, "I brought ye something tae eat. Ye need to rebuild yer strength."

He helped her to sit up in bed and Eva found her gaze shifting around the room. A fire was burning cheerfully in the hearth and every candle she had brought from the other chamber was now lit so that the room was as bright as daylight. Once he had her seated upright with cushions behind her to prop her up, Connall turned to the table to collect a tray he had set there. Eva's nose began to twitch as she finally noted the mouthwatering smells filling the room and was suddenly starving. She peered eagerly at the food as he set the tray on her lap, wine, bread and cheese and some sort of stew, chicken she thought, and she made a face as her stomach rumbled. Eva was hard-pressed not to attack the food she was so starved, and even after she had eaten every last crumb of food he had brought her, she seemed still to be hungry. That fact made her ponder when she had last eaten.

Eva recalled having supper the night before, then coming up to make this room more comfortable, then falling asleep for a bit. She had awoken from her nap shortly before Connall returned and they had . . . Oh, yes. She smiled faintly to herself as she recalled his efforts "to tire her out." Not that it had worked, he had fallen off to sleep at once and she had planned to sew—

Eva stiffened as the memories of the rest of the night spun into her head. The intruder . . . hitting him with the burning log . . . Connall's wound and the way it had healed.

"Dear Lord, you *are* a vampire," Eva gasped, then covered her mouth to keep the wayward thing from spouting any other unwanted revelations.

Connall stiffened, his eyes shooting to her face. He had the oddest expression on his face, she noted. He looked . . . scared? Nay, apprehensive was a better description, and Eva had to wonder why he was looking so apprehensive when he was the soulless—

Nay, not soulless, she reminded herself, recalling their conversation from the night before. He was not dead, nor soulless, he had assured her and he did not kill those he bit. Connall had described himself as just different and while Eva thought that was something of an understatement, she reassured herself with that information, now. He was just different, still her husband, the kind, sweet, gentle man who had treated her as if she had value, and shown her such consideration, as well as taught her passion. Nothing else had changed, she reminded herself as her head began to spin. He was the clan chief of the MacAdie, and her husband. And really, as flaws went, vampirism was much more pleasant to deal with than his being a wife beater or some such thing. Wasn't it?

"Dear Lord," Eva breathed, shaking her head at her own thoughts, then she glanced to Connall again. He was uncharacteristically silent, his attention focused on her with an intensity that made her nervous. Her husband hadn't said a word since she'd blurted that he was a vampire and it was making her uncomfortable enough to start searching her mind for a way to make him leave.

"If you have things to do, you need not trouble yourself to wait here for me to finish eating. I can manage well enough on my own," she murmured at last, though the food was all gone.

"Tis no trouble to be with ye," he said with a frown and there was sudden anger on his face. "Yer no a burden to me, Eva, ye ne'er ha'e been and ne'er will be. Dear God, ye saved me life this morn, woman, no once, but twice. Ha'e ye no realized yer worth yet?"

"I—" Eva shook her head helplessly, confused by the tears suddenly pooling in her eyes. His vehemence was as surprising to her as the words themselves. She *had* saved his life that morning. She'd driven the intruder off with the log, then . . . well all right, the feeding bit wasn't that impressive. Anyone would have done in that instance, but she *had* fended off the intruder.

"Ye've courage and beauty and intelligence and are a worthy wife. E'en a king would ha'e pride in claimin' ye to wife. I have felt nothing but pride in claimin' ye meself."

"Despite my bein' accident prone?" she teased with a wry twist of the lips.

"Yer accidents are a result o' tryin' too hard to earn a place here," he said quietly. "But 'tis only because you doonae realize ye already ha'e a place here. Yer the Lady MacAdie. My wife."

Eva swallowed, her gaze dropping from his at those words. They made her heart ache for some reason.

"Why do ye look away? Do ye hate me now?"

Eva glanced back up with surprise. "What?"

"Now that ye know what I am?" he explained. "Will ye be wantin' an annulment? Beggin' to be set free? Wid ye rather a mortal man to husband? Should I take ye back to Caxton?"

Eva stared at him in horror, fear clutching at her heart at the very idea of what he suggested. Leave here? Leave the only place that had felt like a true home since her parents died? Leave these people who had been so kind? Leave Magaidh and Aileen and Glynis, and Effie and Ewan and the men? The very idea was horrifying, but not as wrenching as the idea of leaving him. The hours of talk and games and passion she had shared with him whirled in her mind. Moments when he had held her and gentled the hair away from her face, just cradling her to him and making her feel as if she belonged right there, in his arms. To lose that, never to enjoy it again . . . The very thought made her heart ache and Eva suddenly realized that her feelings for her husband went beyond gratitude or caring, or even the dutiful love a wife was supposed to have for a husband, but then she had known that morning when his life was threatened, she admitted to herself. It was the only thing that had given her the courage to charge the intruder rather than cower where she hid, it was what had made her keep her head and try to tend to him when she had realized how badly he was wounded and needed her. It was the only thing that had kept her from panicking or dropping in a dead faint when she had finally admitted to herself what she had been refusing to recognize all along and acknowledged that her husband was indeed a vampire. Eva had come to love her husband, and that love would allow her to accept much about him . . . including his being a vampire.

"Nay," she said finally. "I would not have the marriage annulled. You are my husband."

Connall looked torn for a minute, then said, "Why will ye keep it so when ye ken what I am?"

"I . . ." She peered at him helplessly, not quite having the courage to reveal her feelings.

"If 'tis out of duty, I'll no ha'e it. I'll no ha'e ye stayin' with me out o' duty and silently hatin' me fer what I am."

"I do not hate you, I—" She stopped short, fear crowding around her, then Eva saw the look on his face, the hope there and the fear. It was the fear that did it for her. Eva had spent the better part of her life feeling unwanted, and she would never see anyone suffer that, she would not have Connall doubting, even for a moment, that he was wanted, cared for, loved. Drawing on some of the courage that had carried her through the attack that morning, she blurted, "I love you."

One moment she was sat in bed, facing him, and the next Eva was enveloped in his arms as he babbled the Gaelic at her between peppering her face with kisses. The assault stopped just as abruptly as it had started when Connall caught her face between his hands and stared at her intensely for several moments as if memorizing her features. Eva stared back, wondering what would come next.

"Do ye really love me, Eva?" he asked at last.

"Aye," she said solemnly. "I love you, Connall MacAdie. With all my heart."

"And I love you, Eva MacAdie," he said, his voice husky, and before Eva could quite react to that, he kissed her. This kiss was different from any that they had shared before, it was deep, with the current of passion in it, yet tender and gentle and slow with a caring that nearly made her weep. When he eased, then finally broke that kiss, he then pressed his lips to the tip of her nose, each eye, and finally her forehead. To Eva, it felt almost like a blessing given by the pope and in a way it was, Connall was blessing her with his love.

"Right!"

Eva blinked. Connall had suddenly released her and bounded to his feet. "Ye'd best get dressed, wife. We're goin' out," he said with a grin.

"Out?" Eva stared at him blankly, feeling as though she had lost the thread of what was happening somewhere. "Out where, my lord husband?"

"Tis a surprise." He strode around the bed toward the door. "Ye'd best dress. Tis a nice night, one o' the last warm ones I think ere summer turns to fall, but ye'll be ridin,' so dress appropriately. I'll send Glynis up tae help ye."

"Glynis?" Eva asked with surprise. "But I thought these rooms were secret. How—"

"They're a secret no more," he said with a shrug. "No sense in keepin' 'em secret from our allies, when the enemy already kens where they are."

"Oh," Eva breathed, then raised her eyebrows when on reaching the door to the room, her husband suddenly swung around and strode back. Reaching the edge of the bed, he caught her chin, tipped her face up and kissed her again, this kiss quickly passionate and just as quickly ended.

"I'll see ye soon," he murmured, smiling at her dazed expression, then he straightened to stride away again. This time when he reached the door, he did not pause again but actually left.

"Where are we going?" Eva asked.

"Ye'll see," was all Ewan said, but she could hear the amusement in his voice. She had asked where they were going at least ten times since leaving the keep.

Eva had gone down to the great hall after Glynis had helped her dress to find her husband absent and Ewan waiting for her, claiming he had instructions to take her to Connall. She hadn't hesitated to go with him, not even when she had stepped out of the keep to find two horses waiting for them, nor when he had led her out of the safety of the bailey, across the clearing that surrounded the castle wall, and into the deep, dark woods beyond.

Not that they seemed as dark as they first had, Eva supposed, her gaze moving over the trees they rode past. It had seemed terribly dark and rather spooky to her at first, but her eyes had quickly adjusted, and it no longer seemed quite so spooky. In fact, it was almost pretty with the moonlight dappling a leaf here and a trunk there.

Nay, she had not hesitated to go with him, but Eva had asked where they were going, and would continue to do so, she decided. Her curiosity was positively killing her. But before she could ask the question again, they had broken into a clearing.

"Oh," Eva murmured as they both slowed to a halt and she took in their surroundings. The clearing was on the edge of a lake that was calm and serene and glinted with the moonlight's reflection. "Tis lovely."

"Connall'll be glad ye think so." Ewan turned his horse back the way they'd come. "Tell him I'll return as he asked."

"Oh, but where is Connall?" Eva turned in her saddle to ask, but if the man heard her, he didn't answer.

"Here."

Eva jumped nervously in her saddle and swivelled quickly back to stare at the man now approaching from the water's edge.

"Did ye think he'd jest leave ye here on yer own?" he asked with amusement.

Eva smiled back a tad wryly and shook her head. Connall had set guards on her to keep her from any more accidents. No, she supposed she hadn't believed he would have Ewan leave her alone in a clearing in the middle of the woods. "Nay."

"Nay," he agreed, and reached up to lift her off her horse, then pressed a kiss on her as he set her on her feet. It was a long, slow kiss that left them both breathless and Connall leaned his forehead against hers for a minute to catch his breath when it ended, then murmured, "Hello."

"Hello," she answered, her own voice husky.

Connall smiled at her ready response, then kissed the tip of her nose and took her hand to lead her to the water's edge, saying, "Glynis said ye were pinin' fer yer ocean. We're a wee bit away from the ocean here, but I thought ye might like the loch."

"Oh." She peered at the water, and to his face in the moonlight, her heart melting. This trip was in the way of a gift to her, he was trying to make sure she was happy. "'Tis lovely, Connall. Thank you for bringing me here."

"Yer welcome." He squeezed her hand, then suggested, "We could take a swim if ye've a mind."

She grinned, more than tempted by the idea. The entire time that Glynis had been helping her dress, Eva had been fussing over the fact that she hadn't the time to bathe before going below because her husband was waiting for her. A swim in a moonlit lake with her husband sounded a lovely alternative. "Yes, please."

Connall chuckled at her expression and immediately began

to undress. Finding herself a tad shy about being nude here where anyone might see, Eva was slower to start, but once Connall went charging off to splash his way into the water, she quickly removed the rest of her clothes and hurried to follow, feeling better once she was immersed in water and therefore had regained some modesty.

"Shy with me, wife?" Connall teased, moving closer to her in the water.

Eva splashed at him and scoffed, "Nay, some of us just have a bit of common decency."

He chuckled in patent disbelief, then tilted his head and peered at her curiously. "Why ha'e ye no asked questions?"

"Questions?" she echoed.

"About the way I am, and hoo I came to be this way. And why Aileen isnae."

Eva was silent for a moment. Those questions and many more had been tangling their way through her mind ever since she'd learned he was indeed a vampire, but she hadn't known how to approach the subject, not that there had really been a chance to until now. But, since he had brought the matter up . . . "How did you come to be this way?"

"I was born this way," he answered promptly. "It comes from me mother's side. Magaidh is a MacNachton, we're Pictish from early times."

"And she is one too then?"

"Aye. She's a full-blood. I am only a half-blood. My father was mortal."

"And Aileen?"

"She's half-blood too, like me."

"How old are you?" Eva asked curiously. Father MacLure had said he had reached adulthood more than thirty years ago, but—

"Six years older than Aileen." Connall's answer brought her thoughts to an end and Eva stared at him. Dear God, he was old. He looked damned fine for someone of such an advanced age. And that meant that Magaidh was older still, she realized, thinking of the beautiful woman who looked more like Aileen's daughter than the other way around.

"If Aileen is a half-blood too, why does she look so much older than you?"

Connall grimaced. "We ha'e found it acts different in each o' us. Some age, some don't, some cannae stand sun, some can . . ." He shrugged. "None of us understands how it works, but we do ken that the more 'tis diluted, the weaker the effect and so Cathal decided we had to continue to weaken the blood."

"Because of the trouble?" Eva asked, knowing that Cathal was his cousin, the MacNachton.

"Aye."

"And so you married me," she said quietly.

"Aye, and 'twas the best demned decision I've made in me life," he said stoutly, moving closer in the water to take her in his arms.

"I am glad you did," Eva murmured, wrapping her arms around his shoulders as their bodies drifted together.

"So am I," he murmured, pressing a quick kiss to her lips that appeared as if it might turn into a long one, but Connall ended it abruptly and raised his head. "Someone's comin,' a lone rider."

"I do not hear anything." Eva glanced around with a frown.

"Our hearing is better," he said simply, taking her arm to usher her out of the water. "Ye doonae ha'e time to dress, jest grab yer gown and go behind that bush. There's an entrance to a cave there where ye can hide."

"But—"

"Go," Connall ordered, giving her a shove toward the bush he'd pointed to. "And doonae come out until I say so. No matter what. Do ye understand?"

"Aye, but—"

"No, buts. Go." He pressed another kiss to her forehead and shoved her toward the bush, then turned to collect his plaid and his sword.

Twelve

There was an entrance to a cave directly behind the large bush as Connall had said, but Eva had never cared much for dark places and couldn't bring herself to go in. Instead, she crouched behind the bush and struggled to turn her gown right side out again as she watched her husband in the clearing. In her rush to get undressed and into the safety of the water, she'd left the gown in a terrible tangle, half inside out and half not, and she was having trouble untangling it with her attention on her husband as Connall grabbed his plaid as if to don it, then suddenly tossed it aside and hurried to the horses instead. Grabbing Millie's reins, he led the mare quickly around the bush to Eva's side. She gave up on the dress and straightened at once.

"I told ye to get inside."

"Aye, but—"

"Take yer mount in there and wait."

Connall turned away the moment that order was given, not bothering to explain it. Eva supposed that if there was trouble, he wanted to be sure that whoever was coming didn't guess that someone else might be present, and Millie would have been a dead giveaway of that fact. Taking the mare's reins, Eva led the animal into the cave a short way, then quickly hurried back out to see that Connall now didn't have time to dress, and stood naked in the center of the clearing, with nothing but the sword in his hand. Despite his being naked, he was a fearsome sight standing tense, feet slightly apart, body half-crouched as if ready to spring into action. She thought he looked magnificent, like a wild animal, then she heard a horse ride into the clearing.

Eva couldn't see who it was at first, but knew from Connall's reaction that all would be well. Her husband relaxed at once and straightened, then smiled and lowered his sword as he started forward. "Ye could ha'e shouted a warning so I kenned it was you."

"Where's the fun in that? 'Sides, I didnae ken if ye were here or no. Ye might ha'e been elsewhere."

Eva relaxed and blew a breath of relief out at the sound of Donaidh's voice. Shaking her head, she began to concentrate on her gown again, managing to get it untangled and pull it over her head as the men talked.

"Nay. I'm here. What's happened?"

"Happened?" Donaidh echoed.

"Aye. Well, ye must ha'e come looking fer me fer a reason. Has somethin' happened at MacAdie?"

"Nay. I jest wanted to talk to ye aboot these attacks," Donaidh answered.

"Ah, weell, let me dress first."

Eva pulled her gown over her head, then began to tug it down as she glanced out into the clearing where Connall had turned to walk back to his plaid. She saw him bend to set his sword on the ground, then snatch his plaid up and straighten with it and had started to glance down to what she was doing again when he suddenly stiffened, his back arching and the plaid slipping from his hands as an arrow suddenly appeared in his back.

Eva was so stunned at the sudden appearance of that arrow, that she didn't even gasp in surprise, she simply stood there, her hands curling in the material of her skirt and gaped as her husband slowly turned to face where she presumed Donaidh sat astride his mount. The moment he did, another arrow slammed into his chest and Connall stumbled back several steps under the impact.

"If ye go fer the sword, I'll hit ye again, but I'd rather no jest yet."

Eva managed to shake off some of her shock as Donaidh's voice reached her and immediately began trying to think what to do. She had no weapon, she had only her horse, but she had to stop Donaidh. She needed a weapon, or a plan, or both and began to look at what she had available near to hand.

"Ye were the intruder."

Eva paused in her search to glance toward her husband, his voice had been a harsh gasp and she saw that his face was wreathed in pain. It would seem that vampires might be stronger and faster, but they still felt pain.

"Aye." She heard the creak of leather from the clearing and presumed Donaidh was dismounting.

"Why?"

"Why?" Donaidh echoed as he stepped into view, approaching where Connall stood, swaying on his feet, both arrows protruding from him like fence posts out of the ground. The younger man didn't looked particularly angry or in any way emotional at all, really. She found it appalling that someone who had just shot his uncle could look so unaffected. "I'd think that'd be obvious. I've spent my whole life as yer only heir."

"Ye want to be chieftain." Connall looked as if he'd been struck between the eyes by that realization.

"Aye, I want to lead the clan and always kenned I would

eventually, until ye decided to marry," he said with disgust. "And no jest that, but to marry with the express purpose o' havin' bairns. I coudnae ha'e that."

Connall stared at his nephew, perhaps it was the pain wracking his body, or the weakness brought on by the blood he was losing, but he was finding it difficult to follow the lad's logic. "Donaidh, I've lived sixty years and didnae plan to die any time soon, what difference would a bairn make? What difference does a bairn make when I wasnae like to die and leave the clan to either him or you?"

"Well, I wid ha'e seen to the dyin' part eventually, with or without a bairn," his nephew said with a shrug and Connall could hardly believe this was the boy he had rocked to sleep as a babe.

"What were ye waiting fer then?" he asked bitterly.

"Mother and Father to die. I thought it only fair to let ye live a normal length o' life, at least a mortal one. I've always been fond o' ye, Uncle Connall. I planned to wait until they'd reached the end of their lives, then yer life would ha'e been at an end as weell. I could be patient until then."

"Ah, such affection." Connall's mouth twisted bitterly. "So long as yer parents were alive, I was safe . . . until Cathal convinced me 'twas time to marry."

"Aye, ye came back to MacAdie and talked about it at supper, I sat there listenin' to ye sayin' ye were to marry a mortal, weaken the blood further, breed babies. Ye made it obvious 'twas all a load o' bother to ye, but ye felt ye should do it."

"Aye, 'twas a bother to me at the time," Connall agreed. He had found it bothersome then, but that had quickly changed once Eva was here. She'd crept into his heart, making him love her, and now he could think of nothing more blissful than a lifetime with her, but Donaidh had no intention of allowing that. "Twas a bother to me, but a threat to ye."

"Aye." Anger suffused his face briefly. "Ye put all me plans under threat with that decision, but I wasnae sure what to do. Twas possible ye'd breed a daywalker like me ma, one who would age and die like a mortal and perhaps I could wait that long, but then he might breed too and that one might breed another mortal who would die thirty to fifty years later and so on. It could be endless. Or ye might breed another who widnae age like us and then I'd be right back where I was."

"And ye couldnae allow that."

"Nay." He raised his sword and held it upright between them as he turned it this way and that, as if examining the blade's workmanship. "So I decided 'twas time to kill ye."

"Ye were clumsy enough about it," Connall said, his eyes fixed on the man's blade. He wished he could snatch it away from the little beggar and teach him a thing or two, but the boy wasn't close enough yet. He would have to wait for a more opportune moment and hoped he wasn't so weak by then from blood loss that he couldn't do what he had to, to survive. He also hoped that Eva stayed put where she was. If he failed to save himself, he'd not have her die with him. She may even now be carrying that bairn Donaidh so loathed the idea of. His bairn.

"Ye doonae think I was trying to kill ye with the arrows, do ye?" Donaidh scoffed. "I ken better than that; they wouldnae ha'e killed ye."

Connall's gaze slid from the sword to his nephew's face and he saw the amusement there. The brat knew he was hoping to take the sword and was amused. "Aye. Ye do."

He had been attacked three times besides that morning when Donaidh had apparently grown desperate enough to try a direct attack in his own room. But the first attack had been an arrow shot at him on the way to this very loch. He'd been hit in the chest then too. Fortunately, some of the men had been returning from MacNachton where he'd sent them with a message for Cathal. They'd come upon him directly after he took the arrow in the chest and had done a quick search while he removed the arrow, then on finding nothing, they'd ridden with him to hunt to replace the blood lost. An arrow had been used in the third attempt too, the night one of his men was hit in his place.

"My plan was to weaken ye with the arrow as I have this time," Donaidh explained. "Yer bein' immortal, I knew I'd most like ha'e to cut yer head off to kill ye, that meant hand-to-hand and face-to-face, but once ye knew 'twas me, I coudnae afford to fail. If I weakened ye first, fortune would be more like to favor me. But Sean and Rabbie showed up ere I could approach to finish ye off."

"Ah," Connall nodded wearily, then glanced at him with confusion. "But the second time I took the arrow, ye were ridin' with me."

"Aye." His nephew gave a laugh. "Twasn't me. Twas a local farmer out poachin' in the night. He hit ye by accident. I found him when ye had us spread out to search the area. The man was scared silly, he was. Thought sure he was a dead man, but I jest let him go and told him 'twould be our secret. I found it handy fer ye to think 'twas another attack, especially since I was riding with ye at the time so ye couldnae think 'twas me. I knew ye were thinkin' 'twas connected to the trouble we've had o' late, but I feared if ye ever considered another source was possible—as yer only heir—ye may turn yer suspicions toward me. I hoped that the happy accident would lead yer suspicions away if ye did."

"And the fire in the crofter's cottage?" Connall asked, that had been the second attempt, the one between the two arrow hits and just before the men had left to collect his bride.

"That was just chance. I saw ye riding, followed ye to the cottage and saw ye go in. I kenned Willie was no there, he'd gone to see his ailing sister at MacNachton. It seemed a chance to end it. I crept up to the door, saw ye had yer back to me, hit ye o'er the head with the hilt o' me sword, blocked the door and set the place afire. I didnae stick around to watch or I wouldnae ha'e been so shocked when Father came riding back with ye on his horse."

Ewan had come looking for him with a message from Magaidh. She had just returned from MacNachton and knew Willie was there, and that he had gone in search of the man. His first, Donaidh's father, had arrived to find the cottage on fire and risked himself to unblock the door as Connall had regained consciousness. His horse was missing by then, frightened by fire, as most horses were, and it had headed back to the keep. Connall had ridden back with Ewan on the older man's mount.

"Ye didnae try again after returning with Eva," Connall commented.

"I was bidin' me time, I kenned I mustn't miss on the next attempt, it had to be simple and needed to be well thought out, and, so long as ye werenae yet sleeping with yer wife, I had time."

Connall nodded. "Then I consummated the marriage."

"Aye." Donaidh grimaced. "Glynis came back with the news. She said her lady looked so upset when she took up the wine, that she feared the two of ye were fightin' so she stuck around to listen and be sure all was well. She's verra fond of our Eva is Glynis. She said that if ye were fightin' ere she arrived, it stopped with the arrival o' the wine and Eva was finally truly Lady MacAdie. I knew my time had run out."

"So ye waited for me to return to the chamber and tried to follow."

He looked irritated. "I felt sure I had seen which stones ye'd pressed. Course, I didnae see the stone in the middle that ye pressed with yer other hand . . . until ye showed Father."

Connall didn't comment on this verification that the click of a door closing had been someone else. He was more interested in other things. "What if Eva is already with child?"

"That would be a shame," Donaidh said with what seemed true regret. "I like Eva. She's a sweet lass; pretty and clever and funny and a soft bundle in a man's arms."

Connall felt his teeth grind together at this comment and Donaidh assured him. "She hasnae been unfaithful to ye, Uncle. I held her in my arms on the ride down the hill and into the bailey when we brought her back. She was soft and smelled sweet. I might marry her mesel'. Twould probably please the people, but only if she isnae carryin' yer bairn already."

"I would not marry you if you were the last man on earth, Donaidh MacAdie."

Donaidh turned a shocked face toward the bush Eva had just stepped around and Connall silently cursed his wife's blasted courage. The woman had just signed both their death warrants. He watched with a combination of pride, anger, and a sense of defeat as she marched forward, toward what he thought surely would be her death. But what a glorious sight she was, all fire and fury as she marched forward, fists on hips and spitting mad.

"You ought to be ashamed of yourself, the church says coveting your neighbor's wife is bad, coveting your uncle's wife can only be but worse. And murder is most definitely frowned on, you have heard the saying an eye for an eye." She had reached a stunned Donaidh by then, and when Eva suddenly punched her fist upward toward his face, Connall saw the branch she clutched and was now driving toward his eye. For one, heart stopping moment, he thought she would succeed to strike him, but at the last possible moment, Donaidh jerked his head to the side so that the branch merely grazed the side of his head. He grabbed her upper arm and used it to swing her around until he had her locked with her back to his chest, one arm held in his hand, the other barred by his own arm across it.

"Uncle!"

Connall had shaken off his shock at Eva's sudden appearance at the same moment as Donaidh had and immediately started forward to grab his sword. He even had his hand on it and was straightening again when Donaidh called out so harshly. Now he glanced up reluctantly, to see that Donaidh had the edge of his sword pressed across his wife's stomach.

"Put it down or I'll slice 'er in half."

Connall's gaze shifted to Eva and his heart wrenched at the apology there and wished he could offer an apology of his own. He never should have brought her here, not until he had sorted out the business of who was behind the attacks. This was all his fault. His hand tightened briefly around the sword, then he let it fall, hoping against hope that some miracle would save them, or at least save Eva.

Donaidh relaxed and glanced down at the petite blonde in his arms. "Aunt," he greeted her dryly. "I hadnae realized ye were here and, in truth, really wish ye werenae."

"And I really wish you were not," Eva snapped, her fingers tightening around the stakelike bit of branch she still held in her left hand. All she had been able to find in her bush were some stones and branches. With panic for her husband's well-being urging her to hurry, she'd used the stones to cut a bit of a point on two of the sturdier looking branches, taking them inside the cave to do so without making noise that might draw Donaidh's attention. Her efforts had been crude and hurried, but she had decided well enough would have to do and had marched out with her hands on hips to hide the fact that she carried a stake in each hand.

Eva hadn't really been sure what to do even as she charged out, but the eyes had seemed a natural target to her. These men were strong, but strength was of little use if you could not see your target. Unfortunately, these men were quick too and the first strike had failed, but now she clutched her fingers around the second stake in her hand and tried to decide what to do. It seemed she had little choice, however. With his arm around her chest as it was, her upper arm was trapped. Eva had movement only in her lower arm, and not enough to aim properly or put much strength behind the blow. She could only hope that what little damage she did would be enough to give Connall time to grab his sword again.

Taking a deep breath, she swung her hand out, then back down, sinking the stake into his upper thigh with some satisfaction. It didn't go in far by her estimation, but far enough to make the man roar in pain and release her. Eva started to stumble away from him, aware that Connall was going for his sword again as she had hoped, but was suddenly caught back by a grip in her hair, and jerked around.

"Bitch!" Donaidh roared, and raised his sword. He was going to cleave her right there, she realized and shot her hands out to claw at his face, hoping to get his eyes, but clawing at anything she could reach.

Donaidh immediately shoved her away and Eva's feet tangled in her gown and sent her stumbling to fall on her back before him. She pushed herself up onto her elbows in time to see him raise his sword again. He was going to kill her right there and then. A roar from Connall made her glance around to see that he had his sword in hand once more and was stumbling forward, but she knew he would never make it in time. Then a soft "Unhn" from Donaidh made her glance back to her would-be killer and she saw that he had paused, sword raised above his head, back arched, expression stunned.

Eva stared at him, waiting for him to bring his sword down and wondering why he already hadn't, then he slowly began to turn away from her. The first thing she saw was the wound in his back, then she spotted Ewan behind him, already swinging his bloodied sword at his son's throat.

Eva closed her eyes, unable to watch father killing son,

but opened them again at the soft thud of something heavy hitting the ground next to her, only to close them quickly again at the sight of Donaidh's decapitated body.

Arms scooping her off the ground made her open her eyes again, however, and she stared solemnly at the grief on Ewan's grim face as he carried her to where Connall's plaid still lay.

"I am sorry," she whispered, tears pooling in her eyes for his loss.

"Ye've nothing to apologize fer. I heard it all. I am the one sorry." He set her on the ground next to Connall's plaid, then turned as his laird joined them. The two men stared at each other silently, then Ewan grimaced. "Ye'd best get those out ere ye lose any more blood."

Connall grasped the arrow in his chest and pulled it free with one vicious tug and an accompanying roar of pain. Aye, they definitely felt pain, Eva decided with a wince of sympathy. He was unable to reach the arrow in his back, however, and Eva was grateful when Ewan did it for him. It would have been an unpleasant and difficult task for her to perform.

"What will ye tell Aileen?" Connall finally asked as he settled on the ground next to Eva to allow his wounds the chance to close.

"The truth." Ewan said simply. He looked old and tired and seemed to have aged twenty years in the past few moments.

"I should ha'e been the one to kill him," Connall fretted. "Ye should ha'e let me do it."

Ewan shook his head. "I brought him into the world, I failed him somehow so he turned out that way, 'twas only right I took his life back." He ran a hand wearily through his hair, and said, "I doonae ken where we went wrong. How he—"

"Ye didnae go wrong, Ewan. Ye and Aileen were the best o' parents," Connall interrupted, then added helplessly, "Mayhap he was jest a bad seed."

"Aye. Mayhap." Ewan was silent for a moment, then shook his head and turned away. "I'll take him home to Aileen."

He moved with the stooped shoulders of a beaten man as he walked to his son's side, then he forced his shoulders straight and bent to grab Donaidh by the arms and pull him into a sitting position. Connall was immediately on his feet, despite the fact that his wounds had not fully closed. He quickly joined his brother-in-law and his first and, between the two of them, they managed to shift the man to his horse and lay him over the mount's back.

"I should ha'e done it for him," Connall repeated a moment later as Eva stood to join him and they watched the other man ride away, leading the horse with his son's body behind him.

"You could not have, Connall," she said quietly. "He had to do it himself."

"A man shouldnae ha'e to kill his own son," he said grimly.

"Neither should an uncle have to kill his nephew, but Donaidh needed killing and forced it on the two of you."

"Aye, mayhap." Connall was silent for a minute, staring off into the trees where his brother-in-law had now disappeared from view, then he scowled at Eva. "Doonae think I've fergotten ye disobeyin' me and puttin' yersel' at risk in a misguided attempt to save me."

She blinked in surprise at the sudden turn his anger had taken, then felt some anger of her own coming up to meet it. "Well, 'doonae' *you* think I've 'fergotten' you dared to give me such an order and expected me to watch you die like some hapless good-for-nothing twit."

Connall's anger immediately gave way under amazement at her words. "Did you say doonae? Are ye makin fun o' me speech, wife?" he asked with dismay.

"Would I do that?" she drawled.

His amazement slowly transformed, his tension easing and a small smile claiming his lips for the briefest of moments, then Connall sobered and drew her into his arms with a sigh. "Only you could make me smile at a time like this, Eva. Yer a cheeky lass."

"And yer a stubborn ass," Eva said a tad irritably, not having quite given up her anger. "Ordering me to stand by helplessly and what? Watch ye die? Not in this lifetime, my lord. Or any other, I should hope. I am your wife, your partner, your mate. I shall guard your back, your front, and your top to bottom to the best of my sad abilities so long as there is air in my lungs and strength in my body. Do not ever expect me simply to—"

Connall brought her rant to an end, simply by closing his mouth over hers. He kissed her with all the passion and hunger he felt for her, then eased the kiss slowly before gently easing away to kiss first the tip of her nose, her closed eyelids, then her forehead. "I love ye, Eva MacAdie."

Eva sighed against his chin, kissed him there, then added solemnly, "And I love you Connall MacAdie. And I will do till the day I die."

His arms tighted around her briefly, then he released her and took her hand to lead her to his horse. "Hmmm, I've been wantin' to talk to ye about that."

"About the day I die?" she asked as he mounted his horse, then before he could answer, said, "What about my mare, Millie?" Eva had left her mount in the entrance to the cave when she'd entered the clearing.

"I'll send someone fer her." Connall lifted her up onto the horse before him and Eva smiled then closed her hands over his as he wrapped them around her waist and pulled her back against his chest.

"Now, as I was saying," he murmured, arranging the reins, then urging his mount forward. "I agree with the need to marry a mortal to weaken the blood we carry, but once the bairns are born . . ."

Eva rested in her husband's arms and listened to his plans for the future with interest and thought she could stay like this forever . . . and she just might.

Please turn the page for an exciting sneak peek of
Hannah Howell's

HIGHLAND CHAMPION,

available now!

Scotland, Spring 1475

What was an angel doing standing next to Brother Matthew? Liam thought as he peered through his lashes at the couple frowning down at him. And why could he not fully open his eyes? Then the pain hit and he groaned. Brother Matthew and the angel bent closer.

"Do ye think he will live?" asked Brother Matthew.

"Aye," replied the angel, "though I suspicion he will wish he hadnae for a wee while."

Strange that an angel should possess a voice that made a man think of firelit bedchambers, soft unclothed skin, and thick furs, Liam mused. He tried to lift his hand, but the pain of even the smallest movement proved too much to bear. He felt as if he had been trampled by a horse. Mayhap several horses. Very large horses.

"He is a bonnie lad," said the angel as she gently smoothed one small, soft hand over Liam's forehead.

"How can ye tell that he is bonnie? He looks as if someone staked him to the ground and rode over him with a herd of horses."

Brother Matthew and he had always thought alike in many ways, Liam recalled. He was one of the few men Liam had missed after leaving the monastery. He now missed the touch of the angel's soft hand. For the brief time it had brushed against his forehead, it had felt as if that light touch had smoothed away some of his pain.

"Aye, he does that," replied the angel. "And, yet, one can still see that he is tall, lean, and weel formed."

"Ye shouldnae be noticing such things!"

"Wheesht, Cousin, I am nay blind."

"Mayhap not, but 'tis still wrong. And, he isnae at his best now, ye ken."

"Och, nay, that is for certain. Howbeit, I am thinking that his best is verra good, aye? Mayhap as good as our cousin Payton, do ye think?"

Brother Matthew made a very scornful noise. "Better. Truth tell, 'tis why I ne'er believed he would stay with us."

Why should his appearance make someone think him a bad choice for the religious life? Liam did not think that was a particularly fair judgment, but could not seem to give voice to that opinion. Despite the pain he was in, his thoughts were clear enough. He just seemed to be unable to voice them, or make any movement to indicate that he heard these figures discussing him. Even though he could look at them through his lashes, his eyes were obviously not opening enough to let them know he was awake.

"Ye dinnae think he had a true calling?" asked the angel.

"Nay," Brother Matthew replied. "Oh, he liked the learning weel enough, was verra quick and bright, but we could only teach him so much here. We are but a small monastery, nay a rich one, and nay a great teaching place. I think, too, that he found this place too quiet, too peaceful. He missed his family. I have met his kinsmen and I can understand. A large, loud, somewhat, weel, untamed lot of men they are. The learning offered to him eased that restlessness in Liam for a while, but it wasnae enough in the end. The quiet routine, the sameness of the days began to wear upon his spirit, I think."

Liam was a little surprised at how well his old friend knew and understood him. He had been restless, still was in some ways. The quiet of the monastery, the rigid schedule of the monastic life had begun to press in upon him and feel more smothering than comforting. He *had* missed his family. For a moment he was actually glad that he seemed unable to speak for he feared he would be asking for them now like some forlorn child.

"Tis hard," said the angel. "I was most surprised that ye settled into the life so verra weel. But, ye have a true, deep calling, dinnae ye?"

"Aye, I do," Brother Matthew replied softly. "I did e'en as a child. But, ne'er think I dinnae miss all of ye, Keira. I did and do most painfully at times, but there is a brotherhood here, a family of sorts. Yet, I will probably visit again soon. I have begun to spend a great deal of time wondering how the bairns have grown, if everyone is still hale and strong, and many another such thing. Letters dinnae tell all."

"Nay, they dinnae." Keira sighed. "I have missed them all, too, and I have been gone for but a sixmonth."

Keira, Liam repeated the name in his mind. A fine name. He tried to move his arm despite the pain and felt a twinge of panic when it would not respond to his command. When he realized he was bound to the bed, his unease grew even stronger. Why would they do that to him? Why did they not wish him to move? Were his injuries so dire? Was he wrong to think he had been given aid? Had he actually been made a prisoner? Even as those questions spun through his mind, he fought past his pain enough to tug against his bonds. A groan escaped him as that pain quickly and fiercely swept through his body from head to toe. He stilled when a pair of small, soft hands touched him, one upon his forehead and one upon his chest.

"I think he begins to wake, Cousin," Keira said. "Hush, sir. Be at peace."

"Tied," Liam hissed the word out from between tightly gritted teeth, the pain caused by speaking that one small word telling him that his face had undoubtedly taken a severe beating. "Why?"

"To keep ye still, Liam," Brother Matthew replied. "Keira doesnae think anything is broken save for your right leg, but ye were thrashing about so much it worried us some."

"Aye," agreed Keira. "Ye were beat near to death, sir. Tis best if ye remain verra still so as not to add to your injuries or pain. Are ye in much pain?"

Liam muttered a fierce curse at what he considered a very stupid question. He heard Brother Matthew gasp in shock. To his surprise, he heard Keira laugh softly.

"Twas indeed a foolish question," she said, laughter still tinting her sultry voice. "Ye dinnae seem to have a spot upon ye that isnae brilliant with bruising. Aye, and your right leg was broken. Tis a verra clean break and I have set it. After three days there is still no sign of poison in the wound or in the blood, so it should heal verra weel."

"Liam, 'tis Brother Matthew. Keira and I have brought ye to the wee cottage at the edge of the monastery's lands. The brothers wouldnae allow her to tend to your wounds within the monastery, I fear." He sighed. "They werenae too happy with her presence e'en though she was weel hidden away in the guest quarters. Brother Paul was particularly agitated."

"Agitated?" muttered Keira. "Cousin Elspeth would say he—"

"Aye," Brother Matthew hastily interrupted, "I ken what our cousin Elspeth would say. I think she has lived too long amongst those unruly Armstrongs. She has gained far too free a tongue for a proper lady."

Keira made a rude noise. "My, but ye have become verra pious, Cousin."

"Of course I have. I am a monk. We are trained to be pious. Now, I can help ye give Liam some potion or change his bandages, if ye wish, but then I must return to the monastery."

"Ah, weel then, best see if he needs to relieve himself," Keira said. "I will just step outside so that ye can see to that. Now that he is waking, 'tis best, I think. I shall just run up to the monastery's garden and collect a few herbs. I shall be but a few moments."

"What do ye mean *now* that he is waking?" demanded Brother Matthew, but then he grunted with irritation when the only reply he got was the door closing behind Keira as she hurried away. "Wretched wee lass."

"Cousin?" Liam asked, realizing that not only was his throat injured, but his jaw and mouth as well.

"Cousin? Oh, aye, the lass is my cousin. One of a vast horde of cousins, if truth be told. A Murray, ye ken."

"Kirkcaldy?"

"'Tis what I am, aye. Her grandmother was one, too. Now, I do fear that nay matter how gentle I am, this is going to hurt."

It did. Liam was sure he screamed at one point, and that only increased his pain. He welcomed the blackness when it swept over him, as he suspected the continuously apologizing Brother Matthew did.

"Oh, dear, he looks a wee bit paler," Keira said as she set the herbs she had collected down on a table and moved to stand at the side of the small bed Liam was tied to.

"He still suffers a great deal of pain, and I fear I added to it," said Brother Matthew.

"Ye couldnae help it, Cousin. He is better, nay doubt about it, but such injuries will be slow to heal. There truly isnae a part of this mon that isnae hurt. Tis a true miracle that only his leg was broken."

"Are ye certain that he was only beaten? Or that he was e'en beaten at all?"

"Aye, Cousin, he *was* beaten. I have nay doubt about that, but he could have been tossed off that hill, too. Some of these injuries could be from the rocky slope his body would have fallen down and the equally rocky ground he landed on. I dinnae suppose he was able to tell ye what happened to him, was he?"

"Och, nay. Nay. He spoke but a word or two, then made a pitiful cry and has been like this e'er since." Brother Matthew shook his head. "I wish I could understand this. Who would do such a terrible thing to the mon? I ken I havenae seen that much of the mon o'er the years since he left here, but he really wasnae the sort of mon to make enemies. Certainly nay such vicious ones."

Keira idly tested the strength of the bonds that held Liam still upon the bed and carefully studied the man. "I suspect jealousy is a problem he must often deal with."

Brother Matthew frowned at his cousin. She seemed far too interested in Liam Cameron, revealing more than just a healer's interest in a patient. A healer surely did not need to touch her patient's hair as often as Keira did Liam's thick, dark copper hair. Liam was certainly not looking his best, might well have lost a little of his beauty due to this vicious beating, but there was clearly enough allure left in his battered body and face to draw Keira's interest.

He tried to see Keira as a woman grown, not simply as a cousin he had played with as a child. His eyes widened slightly as he began to see that his cousin was no teasing child now, but a very attractive woman. She was small and slight, yet womanly, for her breasts were well shaped and full and her hips were pleasingly curved. Her hair was a rich, shining black, and hung in a thick braid to well past her tiny waist. That hair made her fair skin look even purer, a soft milk white with the blush of good health. Keira's oval face held a delicate beauty, her nose being small and straight, a hint of strength revealed in her small chin, and her cheekbones being high and finely shaped. What caught everyone's interest was her eyes. Set beneath gently arced black brows, and trimmed with thick, long lashes, were a pair of deep green eyes. Those wide eyes bespoke innocence, but their depths held all the womanly mystery that could so intrigue a man. He was a little startled to realize that her mouth, slightly wide and full of lip, held the same contradictions. Her smile could be the epitome of sweet innocence, but Brother Matthew suddenly knew men of the world would quickly see the sensuality there as well. He suddenly feared it had been a serious error in judgment on his part to allow her to tend to a man like Liam Cameron.

"Ye have a rather fierce look upon your face, Cousin," Keira said as she moved to begin preparing more salve for Liam's injuries. "He willnae die, I promise ye. He will just be a verra long time in healing."

"I believe ye. Tis just that, weel, one thing Liam did find hard to abide about the monastic life was, weel, was . . ."

"No lasses to smile at." She grinned at the severe frown he gave her for it sat so ill upon his boyishly handsome face. "I think, just as with our cousin Payton, this mon has a way with the lasses. Aye, and he need do nay more than smile at them."

"I dinnae think he e'en needs to smile," grumbled Brother Matthew.

"Nay, probably not. Come, Cousin, dinnae look so troubled. He is no danger to me now, is he? Aye, and e'en when he is healed enough to smile again, he can only be a danger to me if I wish him to be. Ye cannae think that, with the kinsmen I have, I havenae been verra weel taught in the ways of men." She glanced toward Liam. "Is he a bad mon, then? A vile, heartless seducer of innocents?"

Brother Matthew sighed. "Nay, I would ne'er believe such a thing of him."

"Then there is naught to fret o'er, is there. Tis best if we worry o'er our many other troubles. They are of more importance than whether or nay I can resist the sweet smiles of a bonnie lad. I have been here nigh on two months now, Cousin. There has been nary a sign of my enemy so I think, soon, I must try to get home to Donncoill."

"I ken it. I am fair surprised none of your kinsmen have come round. Tis odd that they wouldnae start to wonder on how long ye have stayed at a monastery, or e'en why the monks would allow it."

"Tisnae so verra unusual for guests, male or female, to linger in the guest quarters, and I paid weel for the privilege."

She smiled and patted his arm when he flushed with embarrassment over that hard truth. "It has been worth it. I needed to hide and mend my wounds, needed to o'ercome my grief and fear, and needed to be certain that, when I did go home, I wasnae leading that murderous bastard Rauf to the gates of Donncoill."

"Your family would protect ye, Keira. They would feel it their duty, their right, and willnae be pleased that ye denied them."

Keira winced. "I ken it, but I will deal with it. I also had to decide what to do. Duncan pulled a vow from me and I had to think hard on how to fulfill it, and how much it might cost me to do so."

"I ken it willnae be easy. Rauf is cunning and vicious. Yet, ye swore to your husband ye would see to it that his people didnae suffer under Rauf's rule if he failed to win the battle that night. He failed. He died that night, Keira, so your vow is much akin to one made at a mon's deathbed. Ye have to do all ye can to fulfill it." He kissed her cheek and started for the door. "I will see ye in the morning. Sleep weel."

"Ye, too, Cousin."

The moment he was gone, Keira sighed and sat down in the little chair next to Liam Cameron's bed. Her cousin made it all sound so simple. She dearly wished it was. The vow she had made to her poor, ill-fated husband weighed heavily on her mind and heart. So did the fates of the people of Ardgleann. Duncan had cared deeply for his people, a mixed lot of gentle and somewhat odd souls. It distressed her to think of how they must be suffering under Rauf's rule. She prayed for them every night, but she could not fully dispel the guilt she felt over running away. Although some of what Duncan had asked of her did not seem right, the people of Ardgleann could no longer wait for her to debate the moral complexities of it all, however. It was time, far past time, to do something.

She idly bathed Liam with a soft cloth and cool water. He did not really have a fever, but it seemed to make him rest more quietly. He was a strong man and she felt certain he would continue to recover. When he would be able to tend to himself, she had better have decided what to do about Ardgleann and Rauf. Once she knew why Liam had been hurt and was certain that no enemy hunted him still, she would leave him in the care of the monks and face her own destiny.

Keira felt an immediate pang at the thought of leaving the man and almost laughed at the absurdity of it. He was a mass of bruises and had barely said three words in as many days. She supposed that she felt some odd bond with him because she had been the one to find him. In truth, she had been drawn to him by a strange blend of dreams and compulsion. It had been a little frightening for, although similar experiences had occurred in the past, she had never seen things so clearly or felt as strongly. Even now she could not shake the feeling that there was more to it all than helping him recover from his injuries.

"Foolishness," she muttered and shook her head as she patted him dry with a soft rag.

Perhaps she should send word to his people, she thought as she began to make a hearty broth to feed to him when he woke again. From what her cousin had told her, Sir Liam's kinsmen were more than capable of protecting him. Keira quickly discarded the idea for the same reason she had given her cousin when he had suggested sending for the Camerons. Sir Liam might not want that, might be reluctant to pull his family into whatever trouble he had gotten himself into. She could sympathize for, she, too, hesitated to involve her family in her own troubles.

That, too, was foolish, she suspected. She had done nothing wrong, had not caused the trouble or invited the danger. If one of her family was in such trouble, she would be ready and eager to ride to their side. Which is why they would hesitate to tell her about it, she suddenly thought and briefly grinned. It was instinctive to try to keep a loved one safe, she decided. When her family found out the truth, they would be angry, perhaps a little offended or hurt, but they would understand for they would know in their hearts that they would have done the very same thing.

And, she told herself as she sat down at the small table near the fire, if this man was as close to his family as her cousin implied, he would do the same. The last time she had seen her cousin Gillyanne, she had heard a few tales about the Camerons. Even though the tales had been told to amuse everyone, they had revealed that the Camerons were probably as close a family as her own. There was also Sir Liam's manly pride to consider. It would undoubtedly bristle at the implication that he could not take care of himself. No, Keira decided, it was not a good idea to send for his people without his permission.

After a meal of bread, cheese, and cold venison, Keira took a hasty bath. She then settled herself upon a pallet made up near the fire. Keira stared into the flames and waited for sleep to come. She hated this time of the night, hated the silence, hated the fact that sleep was so slow to come, leaving her alone in the silence with her memories. Try as she might, she could not shake free of the grip of those dark memories. She could only suppress them for a while.

Duncan had been a good man, passingly handsome, and gentle. She had not loved him and she still felt guilty about that, even though it was hardly her fault. At nearly two-and-twenty, however, she had decided she could wait no longer for some great, passionate love to stroll her way. She had wanted children and a home of her own. Although she loved her family deeply, she had begun to feel an increasing need to spread her wings, to walk her own path. Marriage did not usually free a woman, but all her instincts had told her that Duncan would never try to master her. He had wanted a true partner and, knowing how rare that was, she had accepted him when he had asked her to be his bride.

She could still recall the doubts of her family, especially those of her grandmother Lady Maldie and her cousin Gillyanne. Their special gifts had told them that she did not love the man she was about to marry. They had sensed her unease, one she could not explain even to herself. Keira was not sure it was a good thing that they had not pressed her on that, then roundly scolded herself. They had respected her choice, and it had been *her* choice.

Why she had felt uneasy from the moment she had accepted Duncan's proposal of marriage was still a puzzle to her. Keira had smothered that unease and married him. Within hours of marrying him, the first hint of trouble between them had begun and within days of reaching Ardgleann the trouble with Rauf had begun. She had thought that explained all those odd feelings she had suffered, the reluctance and the wariness, but now she was not so sure. Every instinct she had told her that the puzzle was not solved yet.

Just as she began to relax, welcoming the comfort of sleep, a harsh cry from Sir Liam startled her. Keira hurried to his side to find him straining against his bonds, muttering furious curses at enemies only he could see. She stroked his forehead and spoke softly to him, telling him over and over where he was, who cared for him now, and that he was safe. It surprised her a little when he quickly grew calm again.

"Jolene?" he whispered.

Keira wondered why hearing him speak another woman's name should irritate her as much as it did. "Nay, Keira," she said as she placed her hand over his to try to stop him from tugging against his bonds.

"Keira," he repeated and grasped her hand in his. "Aye. Keira. Black hair. Confused me. Thought I was home. At Dubheidland."

"Ah. She is your healer?" Keira tried to wriggle her hand free of his grasp, but he would not release her, so she sat down in the chair at his bedside.

"Sig'mor's wife. Lady of Dubheidland. Thought I was home."

"So ye said. I can give ye something to ease the pain, if ye wish it."

"Nay. Thought I was caught again."

She could see that it pained him to speak, but could not resist asking, "Do ye remember what happened to you?"

"Caught. Beaten. Thrown away. Ye found me?"

"Aye, me and my cousin Brother Matthew."

"Good. Safe here."

"Aye, ye will be." She tried yet again to wriggle her hand free of his, but failed.

"Stay." He heaved a sigh. "Please. Stay."

Keira inwardly cursed the weakness that caused her to heed that plea. She carefully shifted her seat closer to the bed so that she could sit more comfortably as she waited for him to release her hand. After a few moments of silence, she wondered if he had gone back to sleep, but his grip upon her hand remained firm. To her surprise, he began to stroke the back of her hand with his thumb. The warmth that gesture stirred within her was a little alarming, but she could not bring herself to stop him.

This was not good, Keira thought. The light brush of a man's thumb over her hand should not make her feel warm. True, it was a very nice hand, the fingers long and elegant, but it was too benign a caress to stir any interest. Or, it should be. She looked at his battered face and sighed. To all the troubles she already had, she realized she now had to add one more. A man she did not know, a man whose face was so bruised and swollen it would probably give a child the night terrors, could stir her blood with the simple stroke of his thumb.

Connect with Us

Visit us online at
KensingtonBooks.com
to read more from your favorite authors, see books
by series, view reading group guides, and more.

Join us on social media

for sneak peeks, chances to win books and prize packs,
and to share your thoughts with other readers.

facebook.com/kensingtonpublishing
twitter.com/kensingtonbooks

Tell us what you think!

To share your thoughts, submit a review,
or sign up for our eNewsletters, please visit:
KensingtonBooks.com/TellUs.